The Last
Citadel

By

K. M. Ashman

More Books by K. M. Ashman

The India Sommers Mysteries
The Dead Virgins
The Treasures of Suleiman
The Mummies of the Reich
The Tomb Builders

The Roman Chronicles
The Fall of Britannia
The Rise of Caratacus
The Wrath of Boudicca

The Medieval Sagas
Blood of the Cross
In Shadows of Kings
Sword of Liberty
Ring of Steel

Novels
Savage Eden
The Last Citadel
Vampire

The Blood of Kings
A Land Divided
A Wounded Realm

Audio books
Blood of the Cross
The Last Citadel
A Land Divided
A Wounded Realm

KMAshman.com

Chapter 1

The Citadel's arrogant walls thrust themselves free from the all-enveloping water, reaching hopelessly for the unattainable sky. No similar constructions of polished granite accompanied this lone intruder in the unbroken seascape. No tree or mountain interrupted the flowing curvature of the distant blue horizon and not even the occasional silhouette of a scavenging gull broke the monotony of the vista. It was alone. Sweltering in the haze as the belligerent sun resumed its never-ending quest to batter the solitary city, its isolated occupants and their age-old secrets into unlikely submission.

Laying in what little shade the castellated buttress afforded, the captain of the guard snored gently, his second chin giving his shaven head a natural pillow as he slept off the effects of his alcoholic lunch, the empty ale-skin matching the spreading sweat stains under his arms.

Kenzo wrinkled his nose in a vain attempt to rid it of Fatman's stench. He hated this shift and he had never seen the point to it. There had been no attack for years, not since the slaughter of the Artists had forced the eight-tower treaty over ten years ago. That had been a terrible time and it had taken an age before the people of the Baker-clan had been trusted again.

Anyway, Moon-day was almost upon them and no one in their right mind would risk alienating themselves so close to Moon-day. The water was already visibly lower and when the full moon appeared on the last night of the month, it would recede even further, unveiling a spider's web of weed-covered causeways, acting as arteries of humanity between the limbs of the eight towers and the pumping heart that was the Citadel.

'Moon-day in three days,' said Kenzo, loud enough for his colleague to hear, but quiet enough not to wake the snoring captain from his ale-induced nap.

'Don't remind me,' said Braille, the older soldier, without taking his eyes from the empty sea, 'I've drawn guard again and that's the second time this year.'

'Bad luck,' said Kenzo, 'how did that happen?'

'No luck about it,' he replied, 'I lost in cards to that cheating swine Ufox, he had three suns to my three moons. I know he cheated and if I ever prove it...' he left the sentence unfinished.

'Can I get you anything?' asked Kenzo.

'Yeah, the usual two skins of ale and a bunch of herb, and watch those cheating Brewers don't short measure you. Last time, the bottoms of the skins were weighed down with Narwl bones and I only had enough ale for three weeks.'

Kenzo smiled secretly. The rage of Braille when he found his skins were only half-full of ale was legendary in the barracks. If it wasn't for the

5

fact that the water had already risen again, Kenzo was sure Braille would have torn down the Brewer's tower stone by stone. The jeers from across the water that night hadn't helped and Kenzo suspected that the card game had indeed been fixed, if only to ensure Braille stayed in the Citadel and didn't start another tower-war single handedly.

Braille looked over with a knowing smile.

'I suppose you'll be sniffing around that girl again. What's her name, Lena?'

'Leona,' corrected Kenzo, 'and for your information, I won't be sniffing around her, I will be taking ale and cake with her and her father.'

'Meeting her father!' hooted Braille. 'Why are you doing that? Surely, you don't mean to take her as a bride?'

'I may, what's wrong with that?'

'She is an Artist, for Saint's sake. What sort of wife will she make? She won't be able to cook or mend and will probably swan around all day reciting poetry or painting pictures.'

'She is beautiful,' said Kenzo quietly.

'Forget beautiful,' replied Braille, 'she probably thinks a bed's for sleeping in. No, take my word for it, young man, rent a Courtesan for the day. By the time she's finished with you, you won't want to see a woman for the next five years.' He guffawed at his own joke causing the sweaty captain to stir in his sleep.

'No thanks,' replied Kenzo, 'I am happy to wait for Leona.' He didn't expand that he had once sampled the delights of a Courtesan, and despite her being very pretty, had found the whole experience a bit distasteful and lacking in emotion. On Moon-day, any man could negotiate with the Courtesans and obtain any amount of their time, from half hour to a full day depending on what he was able to barter. As he recalled, the price he had paid was a bit steep too, a necklace of Narwl teeth for a half hour in the back of a cart. Daylight robbery in his mind.

The two soldiers looked out over the sea once again. Kenzo was twenty-one years old and just starting his career in the Citadel guard. He stood six-feet tall and his blonde hair fell in waves to his shoulders. His uniform was immaculate and he took his position seriously.

Braille, on the other hand, was ten years older and more cynical with life in the service. His beer belly was testament to a more relaxed outlook on life and he had only joined up in a panicky attempt to avoid the Prison-tower.

The afternoon silence dragged on, broken only by the occasional snort of the sleeping captain and the scene looked the same as it had for hundreds of years. Below them, an expanse of gently rippling water extended half mile to their front, before being interrupted by the outer ring of towers erupting sharply from the sea and encircling the Citadel in a defensive ring.

There were eight outer towers in all, each mirroring those on the inner Citadel wall, and each separated by the same salty seawater. Beyond the towers, the water stretched uninterrupted as far as the eye could see; a view that had never been interrupted by sail or mast.

Kenzo often wondered what lay over the horizon. He obviously knew that it was the end of the world in all directions, but sometimes he just wondered if there were other Citadels, other towers or other people. Imagine not having to eat the same Narwl meat day after day, or having to compare family documents every time you met someone you found attractive, just to ensure the bloodlines were far enough apart. Imagine being able to see over the horizon, just a little bit, just enough to see the source of the smoke he was sure he saw when he was a little boy of ten years old. As he remembered how he was teased when he told his friends, his flight of fancy dipped slightly.

'Mist,' some had said.

'Fog,' said others.

'Madness,' whispered the majority, and even though deep inside, he was absolutely certain that it had been smoke, he soon agreed that he could have been mistaken. There was only one place for madmen in Bastion, and that was the Prison-tower.

Having not experienced any other civilization, the soldier's somewhat limited imagination returned to the known limits of his own world and the delights that lay therein. Directly opposite was the Baker-tower; the main source of the Citadel treats. Delicious gravy-filled pastries that oozed their contents to mat even the neatest beard, complemented by soft aromatic breads and everyone's favourites, the red sugar-shell sweets.

No one knew how all the fantastic treats were made or even kept fresh for Moon-day, and many had died trying to find out the secret, but such was the way of the towers. Most had their own secrets and guarded them fiercely. The Baker-clan baked, the Weavers produced clothes and rugs of unsurpassed quality, and everyone looked forward to the barrels of ale that rolled across the slippery causeway once a month from the Brewer-tower. Each trade had developed their own secret methods, and though there were poor attempts at copying the processes within the Citadel, the quality of goods that the tradesmen produced was unsurpassed.

Kenzo turned his gaze to the Hunter-tower. At least, this one broke his boredom and gave him something to look at. Throughout the day, he had once again watched in admiration as dozens of the Hunters had manned their small, Narwl-skin boats and ventured out into the sea to carry out their vital role in the upkeep of the city. Some carried finely woven nets, perfect for catching the many shoals of fish that congregated in the shallows. Others scavenged around the base of the Citadel, collecting shellfish, shrimp and seaweed, while the younger men rowed far out to the deeper parts and hunted the Narwl, the giant but harmless fish that provided the main food source of the population. Yet, it wasn't always calm, and Kenzo knew that the Narwl

Hunters were always at risk of attack from the Ranah, the large predatory fish which took Narwl or man indiscriminately.

If he stared really hard, Kenzo could even make out the soul-cord tying the young men together in pairs; the self-imposed tether that ensured that if one Hunter was taken by the Ranah, the other would fight tooth and nail to save him from the predatory beast. Though deaths of Hunters were rare, when they did happen, two families wore the veil of mourning in the Hunter-tower.

Narwl were slow and stupid creatures, and the waters surrounding the Citadel teemed with them. In particular, they basked near the towers when the sea temperatures were right, feeding on the rich human waste that spewed into the sea from the piped outlets piercing the granite walls. Hunters often went days without success, but when a Narwl was caught, teams of men and women alike, hauled the giant fish up the tower walls on long ropes. One Narwl, when properly processed could feed over a hundred people for a month, and its pliable bones could be used for everything from needles to spears.

'Day dreaming again?' barked the captain, making Kenzo almost jump out of his skin. The sweating officer had woken and crept up behind the unsuspecting soldier, taking great glee in the fright on the young man's face.

'No, Sir!' shouted Kenzo, jerking upright and glancing over at Braille. The older soldier was suddenly the epitome of the model soldier, standing to attention and peering out over the water as if his life depended on it.

'It's the Baker-tower you should be watching, boy, not those fish-smelling Hunters. They are too wrapped up in their own importance to present a danger to Bastion. No, you just keep your snot stained face pointed in the direction of those back stabbing Bakers.'

'Yes, Sir!' responded Kenzo, his six foot frame assuming the position again, staring resolutely at the distant Baker-tower.

'You make sure you do, boy,' he said. 'I'm going to the guardroom to do some paperwork. Call down if you need me.'

'Yes, Sir!' shouted Kenzo once more, knowing fully that the captain would be snoring his head off within half an hour. Fatman walked down the stairs and both soldiers visibly relaxed. The rest of the shift would be easy.

'Give him five minutes and we can get some shuteye,' said Braille, reaching inside his tunic to get a smoke.

'That's against regulations,' said Kenzo. 'If Fatman catches you, you'll be skinning up in the prison before the sun sets.'

'Prison holds no fear for me boy,' he bragged, concentrating on his cigarette. 'As long as there's ale and women, I'd survive!'

Kenzo considered Braille's statement, quickly coming to the conclusion that he was probably right. Braille was a survivor. He would fight

8

any man, charm any woman, drink ale until dawn and still turn up for shift on time, albeit worse for wear, and would probably thrive in the Prison-tower. Kenzo shuddered slightly. Not for him, he had heard too many horror stories of what went on behind those foreboding walls.

The Prison-tower was the place where all miscreants were sent, should they transgress the severe laws of the Citadel. Though it was indeed a prison, there were no cells or iron grilles holding back problematic prisoners. No curfews or routines were imposed to restrict their liberty and to all extents and purposes, it was just a normal tower with all the same day-to-day dramas that could be found in Bastion. Babies were born and grew old, then died within those walls without ever seeing beyond its boundaries and new blood was introduced to the populace with the regular introduction of Bastion's new offenders. Murderers and thieves, subversives and political activists all ended their eventful days at the Prison-tower. Child pickpockets often stared upwards at the imposing structure as they were herded across the causeway on Moon-day, unaware of the lifetime of boredom, violence and the never-ending hunger-filled days stretching before them. There was no remission in the Prison-tower. No parole or short sentences there. You were either sent to the Prison-tower, or you weren't. It was a one-way ticket.

'Braille!' said Kenzo, a few minutes later.

When he received only a snore in reply, he realized Braille was already practicing a skill only he could do. Despite still standing up, his arms were folded on the parapet and his head lay on his arms, fast asleep. Unless he became the subject of a close inspection, he seemed alert and on guard.

Kenzo smiled and returned his gaze to the waters directly below his position.

'Is it me?' he asked quietly to himself, so not to wake his friend, 'or does the water seem to be a bit lower than usual?'

Chapter 2

The council chamber at the top of the keep was filled with the trappings of unimaginable wealth, as befitted the most important room in the city. A polished wooden table dominated the circular space, surrounded with eight Narwl-bone chairs inlaid with panels of beautiful timber artistry and gleaming star stones.

The gems were named after the myriads of shooting stars that were seen on the clearest nights, but were in fact, nuggets of quartz polished smooth by the actions of the sea and were found in the stomachs of young Narwl, who often took in the seabed gravel to aid digestion.

Opposite the entrance, a beautiful carving dominated the far wall, a floor to ceiling frieze, sunk deep into the granite. The scene depicted the first ever meeting held in this very room, attended by the eight original councillors and chaired by the founder of the city, Arial the Six-fingered Saint.

In this isolated city, where the only wood known to the residents was the gnarled and twisted vines which matted the stones of every building, Mahogany was the rarest and most fascinating commodity of all. It was hard like rock, yet warm to the touch. It could be carved with a sharp knife, yet floated if you were unfortunate enough to drop it into water, but better than this, was the way it shone when polished. A single Mahogany coin could buy a week in the Pleasure-tower for the ugliest of men and if the populace ever knew the opulence of this room, there would be riots in the streets.

Directly in front of the frieze, a high backed Mahogany chair was occupied by a man of extreme age dressed in the neutral white of the Citadel. This was Helzac, the Chief-governor of the Citadel who would hold the post until his death, from either old age or murder, whichever came first. The towers took it in turn to supply the Chief-governor, and the next in line often became impatient to assume the powerful and coveted position.

Seven other chairs surrounded the table, six of which were occupied by old men draped in the colours of their respective towers, whilst the seventh hosted a woman of outstanding beauty. Though obviously of a similar age to the others, the wrinkle free skin and clear intelligent eyes framed by the flowing silver hair combined to give the woman an aura of wisdom and perpetual youth.

Razor, the Hunter-tower councillor was on his feet, banging his fist on the valuable table in his usual aggressive manner, much to the unease of the other elders.

'Let us not forget,' he shouted, 'if it was not for the bravery of my men every day, Bastion would starve within months.'

'This is not the issue,' responded Kelly of the Brewers, 'and well you know it. We are all aware of the central part your Hunters play in the well-being of this city, Razor, yet we cannot allow their posturing and bragging to continue. I'm warning you, it is all I can do to hold back my Brewers.'

'And I'm telling you…' shouted Razor, but before he could finish his sentence, an authoritative voice echoed around the chamber.

'Enough!' roared Helzac. 'You are behaving like commoners. Not one of us can afford a new Tower-war, so it falls on us all to control our own trades. It is a joint responsibility and I expect everyone here to take the necessary steps to control their own people. Now can we all be seated and discuss the next item on the agenda?' He looked around the council, his gaze daring anyone to contradict him. Helzac was getting old, but despite his age, he still had the stature of a young man and could still hold his own in conflict with anyone.

Razor decided against further argument and sat back down in his seat.

'Ok,' said Helzac. 'If there is nothing else, we can continue.'

He turned to the only person in the room not seated at the table. The clerk jerked slightly, realizing they were looking at him and stood up quickly, referring to the seaweed papyrus that was his record.

'Um, your Excellencies, the next thing on the agenda is the representation of Pelosus.'

The heads of the towers looked at each other in surprise.

'We weren't aware of this,' said Kelly. 'It was not on the circulated agenda.'

'It was a late representation,' said Helzac. 'He insists it won't wait, so we will humour him.'

The clerk opened the door and whispered to one of the ever present guards outside. A few minutes later, the shuffling figure of Pelosus entered the chamber carrying a bundle of scrolls, dropping some in his haste to enter the council's presence.

'Approach!' ordered Helzac.

Pelosus walked up to the table and looked nervously around the council, his gaze pausing briefly on the distinguished features of Petra from the Pleasure-tower, recalling his own memories from many years ago on his only visit to her domain. She had been a simple Courtesan then and though she probably had no recollection of him or indeed any individual, he certainly remembered her. It had been the most memorable week of his life and had taken almost a year to pay off the moneylender.

'State your case, Pelosus,' she said with a smile.

'Your Excellencies,' he began, 'I have some grave news about Moon-day, well not Moon-day itself, that will be fine, I mean the actual moon, well, what I mean is…'

'For Saint's sake, man!' shouted Razor, causing Pelosus to drop more scrolls in his nervousness.

'Pelosus!' interrupted Petra softly and with a warm smile. 'Gather your thoughts and start again. There is no rush, take your time.' She threw a guarded scowl at Razor.

Pelosus took a breath, placed the remaining scrolls on the table and started again.

'Your Excellencies, as you are aware, my role is to study the heavens. Over the last few months I have seen signs in the skies that have given me cause for concern.'

'Mumbo-jumbo,' snarled Razor.

'Perhaps,' said Pelosus ignoring the insult, 'but you should be aware of these things.'

'Continue,' said Petra.

'It has always been a well-known fact that the moon circles the earth,' he started, 'It is also known that the moon's orbit is elliptical and this is why it seems is so much closer for one day every month. It is on this day it is closest to the earth.'

'Pelosus,' said Petra, 'we appreciate your knowledge, but these facts are known to us and we are very busy people, please make your point.'

'Yes, of course, your Excellency, please accept my apologies, but I was not aware what depth of knowledge to expect.'

'We are educated people,' Razor sneered.

'Yes, of course you are.' He looked around and started again. 'For many years it has been known that the cycle of the moon is slowing. In itself, this has never been a problem, but recently there has been a marked increase in the speed of the change. Now unless I have totally misunderstood a lifetime of study and the knowledge of my predecessors, I would say that's impossible. For months we have worked tirelessly to calculate how the moon can actually slow down and always, we come to the same conclusion.'

'Which is?' asked Helzac.

'It can't. It goes against all the laws of physics.' Seeing Razor's frustrated gaze, Pelosus quickly continued.

'You see, though the moon is fifty times smaller than the earth, we do not exert enough gravitational pull on it to slow it down. However, it was obvious that something was definitely happening, then one night the answer came. It was simple in its obviousness, but astounding in its implications.'

The room was silent, waiting for the explanation.

'There is definitely gravitational interaction between the two bodies,' continued Pelosus, 'But if I am correct and all the calculations make sense, it is not the moon that influences us but the other way around. In effect, the Earth is the senior body and the moon our satellite. He looked around, surprised at their lack of excitement at this astounding knowledge.

'And how is it that hundreds of your predecessors have not noticed this before?' asked Petra.

'They did not have the readings we have. The moon has always been a constant and there has never been a benchmark. Now that the rate is slowing, we can compare hundreds of records and every formula we apply proves the fact that the moon does indeed orbit the earth.'

'Ok!' said Razor. 'So the moon orbits the earth. Thank you very much, you may leave.'

'Razor!' shouted Petra. 'Give the man a chance for Saint's sake.'

'Thank you, your Excellency,' continued Pelosus. 'The thing is, if this is proven and I believe it is, then the entire view of our world changes. Everything on our planet is governed by the actions of the moon. Ordinarily this would not matter and we would continue as we always have, but as the moon is slowing, then it has huge implications. The thing is, the speed of all the planets is controlled by the sun, around which we all orbit and its influence is a constant.'

'You said the moon's speed cannot change,' said Helzac

'It can't,' confirmed Pelosus. 'It just seems like it is because the moon is getting closer to the earth's surface.'

'What are the implications?' asked Helzac.

'It has long been known that the moon has an enormous gravitational pull. In the days before Moon-day each month, it is the gravity of the moon directly above that draws up the water vapour from the sea at an enormous rate, therefore lowering the sea levels and uncovering the causeways.'

'But the water always rises again,' said Helzac, intrigued.

'Let me explain,' said Pelosus. 'When the moon is at its greatest and the water rises, it forms great clouds of vapour at high levels. These clouds are drawn ever upwards by the moon's gravitational pull, but before they reach the upper atmosphere, the moon moves on and the clouds release their water to fall as rain back into the sea. This is why the sea rises again the day after Moon-day.'

'But it is well known the day after Moon-day is always sunny,' said Petra, 'it has never rained.'

'That is because the moon's gravitational pull drags the clouds along with it as it passes through our skies and the rain falls far beyond our horizons. We only see it as a great tide that raises the level of the sea again around the Citadel.'

'So what you are saying,' said Helzac, 'is that as the moon slows, the tides will also slow and the causeways will not be revealed as often.'

'It's actually the opposite, your Excellency,' replied Pelosus. 'The rate the moon is slowing indicates that it will remain at its fullest in our sky for many days.'

'And what does that mean for us?'

'It depends how long it takes to cross the sky,' replied Pelosus. 'During this time, it will draw all the water from beneath its presence at an enormous rate and the sea levels will drop to levels lower than they have ever done before.'

'But when the moon disappears over the horizon, surely the waters will return as they have done before.'

'Some will, but I calculate that month on month, due to the increased gravitational pull and the amount of time the moon will be in our sky, much of the water will escape directly into the atmosphere and will not return.' He paused, looking around the room. 'After a few months, the process will accelerate until eventually, the entire sea will evaporate!'

'What?' gasped Razor.

'The sea will disappear, your Excellency' he said again. He had the attention of the whole council now and they stared at him in horror as the implications sunk in.

'How quickly will the waters drop?' asked Kelly.

'Based on other evaporations, my calculations show that it could drop up to ten feet a day, but I cannot calculate how much will be released back to the sea between Moon-days.'

'How deep are the waters?' asked Petra.

'I don't know your Excellency, with respect; perhaps the Hunter-clan may be in a better position to answer this question.'

All eyes turned to Razor and he sat thinking for a while staring into space, recalling a time from long ago. Eventually he spoke, quietly and calmly.

'As a young man, I dived to hunt Narwl more times than I have hairs on my head,' he said. 'On one occasion, my partner was taken by a Ranah and we were dragged deeper than any man had ever been. Despite our best efforts, our spears could not kill the beast and the water was red from my partner's blood. I quickly ran out of air and was being dragged down to my death.'

'Yet you obviously survived,' said Helzac.

'I did, for before he died, my partner used the last of his strength to cut the Soul-rope and I was free to reach the surface. We do not do this as Hunters, for if one dies, both die. It is our code.'

The group were silent, sharing the pain that the usually aggressive Razor was obviously feeling.

'I was falling unconscious and my ears had burst under the pressure,' continued Razor, 'but before I passed out, I saw the Ranah diving even deeper, hundreds of feet below. If this sea has a bottom, it is too far for even us Hunters to reach.'

'So,' said Kelly, 'even if the sea level does drop, there will still be water to make ale.'

'It's not as simple as that,' said Pelosus, 'as the water evaporates, it will leave any heavy particles behind. Fish, crabs, weed or anything too heavy to evaporate will remain.'

'So food will not be a problem either?' suggested Kelly.

'Or indeed clothing,' said Rimmer the Weaver, who had been listening silently during the whole process. 'If we can access the weed, we can still make fabric.'

The different clan leaders all started to talk at once, all outlining the dangers or opportunities these phenomenon posed to their own towers. Pelosus looked around the arguing group in frustration.

'Your Excellencies,' he started, 'please, can I speak? Excellencies, there is more.'

The babble was getting out of hand and the noise was deafening as the arguments raged.

'Excellencies, please,' he tried again, until finally he could take no more and did something unthinkable. He banged his own commoner fist on the priceless wooden table.

'Salt!' he shouted loudly. 'Salt is the problem!'

The entire group fell instantly silent, not because of what he said, but because of the audacity of the man striking this priceless artefact.

'How dare you!' growled Razor.

'You must listen, your Excellencies,' said Pelosus, 'I had to get your attention.'

'Continue,' said Helzac, 'and it had better be worth the strike, Pelosus, or you will see out the rest of your days in the deepest cells of the prison.'

Pelosus gulped and continued.

'It is not just the case of the water receding. If this was so, then all we would have to do is walk down to reach it. No, like I said, the water actually evaporates leaving all particles behind, solids and dissolved.' He looked around at their blank faces. 'Don't you understand? It's the salt that's the problem. The salt will stay!'

'Explain!' demanded Helzac.

'The more water that evaporates the saltier the sea will become. Soon it will become too thick for the plankton that swarms in the waters. The knock on effect will be almost instant and the food chain will collapse. All life in the sea will die, including Ranah and Narwl.' He paused for effect. 'The food will run out long before the seawater disappears.'

Again, they stared at him in silence.

'You mean the entire city will eventually starve to death?' asked Rimmer.

'Eventually yes, though most will be dead long before the food runs out.'

'How?' snapped Razor.

15

'Thirst,' replied Pelosus, 'when the drinking water disappears.'

'What do you mean our drinking water?' asked Petra, her demeanour now serious. 'We don't drink from the sea; the wells are full of clear water. Surely we can cover them up to stop them from evaporating.'

Pelosus forced the sweet memories from his mind as he looked into her knowledgeable eyes.

'Our water is naturally taken from the sea, your Excellency, and is filtered through the well walls, removing the salt. We know not how deep the wells are, but if the sea falls lower than the wells, then our drinking water will also disappear.'

They all sat back in their ornamental chairs in disbelief.

'Is there anything we can do to stop it from happening?' asked Petra eventually.

Pelosus shook his head.

'And you are sure of your work?'

'Yes.'

Silence fell again until eventually Helzac spoke up.

'If what you're saying is true, though at the moment nothing you have said convinces me of this, it depends on how long the full moon takes to cross the sky, right?'

'This is correct,' Pelosus replied.

'And at the moment it takes one complete day.'

'It does.'

'Then tomorrow there should be no difference. The waters will ebb and flow as normal.'

'The change is slow, but is getting quicker.'

'How quick?'

'It is hard to give exact figures.'

'How quick Pelosus?' growled Razor. 'When will we see the effects?' This time he was not reined in by Petra.

'Again, it is difficult to be accurate.'

'When?' shouted Razor, thumping the table for the second time that night!

'Two months!' stuttered Pelosus. 'In two months the moon will remain in the sky for two days and the waters will drop to previously unknown levels. After that, they may not return at all.'

Helzac once again broke the long silence that followed.

'Thank you, Pelosus,' he said, 'this is indeed a concern, however, there is nothing we can do tonight. Clerk, the meeting will be recorded but not released to the archives and you will keep what you have heard here secret, or forfeit your liberty. Is that clear?'

The clerk nodded his head vigorously.

16

'Tomorrow is Moon-Day,' continued Helzac, 'and we all have business to attend. If Pelosus is correct, there will be nothing different tomorrow and we have to create an air of normality to avoid panic. We will reconvene the day after Moon-day and discuss in detail the issues we have heard tonight. Are we agreed?'

'Issues,' laughed Razor. 'The world is coming to an end and he calls them issues.'

'Are we agreed?' repeated Helzac raising his voice.

Every council member confirmed their attendance.

'Pelosus, you will come too. Bring whatever you may think worthwhile. We have need of your help.'

Pelosus nodded and the meeting broke up, each councillor deep in thought about the Stargazer's news. However, one man remained alone in the council chamber, lost in his own thoughts. As he often did, he had remained silent throughout the meeting, but his mind was on fire with the implications. He stood up from his chair, but instead of leaving the room, he walked slowly up to the image of the man depicted on the carved frieze. For a long time he stared up at the benign figure, seemingly bathed in the air of celestial peace that the figure exuded.

'Not this time,' he said to the frieze under his breath. 'You will not prevail. We will not allow it!' With that, he spun around and quickly strode out of the chamber, slamming the door behind him as he went.

Chapter 3

Dawn was breaking as the priest walked out of the giant double gates in the city wall and approached the statue of Arial. The crowd behind him waited patiently until a solitary bell echoed across the city, and as the eighth peal rang out, the priest raised his hands upwards to roar out the announcement that everyone was waiting for.

'Moon Day!' he shouted, and the eight gates around the city swung majestically open, signalling the start of the most important day of the month.

In front of each gate a long walkway edged with waist high walls linked the Citadel with the outlying towers, and as the water receded, it flowed from the causeways through built in weep holes and back into the sea a few feet below. Trapped red crabs scurried to reach the safety of the water before the children, who were always the first through the gates to collect the rare harvest, greedily gathered up the slower ones.

Exactly half an hour later, the bells rang out again, this time the signal for the corresponding doors in the outer towers to swing open and enable columns of carts to leave each tower and head for the Citadel.

The tradesmen's carts were piled high with the specialties that they each produced, while the Courtesan's wagons were layered with soft luxurious cushions and enclosed with beautifully embroidered canopies, essential for the privacy needed by those who hoped to do a brisk trade within.

However, the column that emerged from the Watcher's tower was different. Their carts were empty, except for a folded tarpaulin on each cart. While the other columns made their way directly to the keep to set up the market, the Watchers positioned their empty carts at each city gate, waiting for the customers that would surely come, as they always did.

Within Bastion the crowds parted as the soldiers cleared a way through the throng, pushing aside the chancers who had gathered long before dawn to ensure they got the sweetest fruits, the strongest ale and the prettiest women. The atmosphere was alive with anticipation and the excited shouts of child and adult alike, echoed through the streets of the city as the crowd jostled for position.

'Out of the way, coming through', ordered the soldiers.

'Two coins for a barrel of your finest,' shouted a man.

Though pretending indifference, the lead Brewer winked at the caller, accepting the offer and acknowledging the deal would be sealed at the marketplace.

'How much for a skin of ale, mister?' asked a dirty faced boy to a soldier.

'More than you can afford, urchin,' he replied, 'now on your way.'
He cuffed the beggar around the ear and continued his march forward.

All around the Citadel the scenes were the same, with crowds
pestering the tradesmen for early deals as they crossed the causeways, and
though it was against the law to trade until the market was set up and the
bells rang again, many secret deals were agreed on long before they entered
the city. Hardly anyone in Bastion would sleep for the next twenty-four hours
as they revelled in the tradition that was Moon-day, the one day in a month
when money was no object, laws were relaxed, and morals went out the
window.

At the centre of the city lay the keep, the huge stone building that
was home to the council and the priesthood. Within its circular walls, a paved
courtyard, the only public area of open space within Bastion, hosted the
monthly market of Moon-day. At the centre of the courtyard lay the most
important building in the Citadel, the tower of the Saints. Some of the floors
were given over to the Guild of Sciences, whilst others were occupied by the
shift of midwives, the women who delivered the city's babies. The midwives
were actually females from the Watcher-tower and spend a month at a time
in the city, before being relieved by a fresh shift every Moon-day.

The topmost floor was the council chamber, where decisions of life
and death were made every day. Anything of value was stored within this
tower and whilst it was well known that there was an entire floor given over
to the histories, rumours also abounded amongst the poor that whole rooms
there were crammed full of money and jewels.

Within an hour, the keep had become a hive of frenetic activity. The
crowd heaved and the air was alive with the sound of bartering. Tradesmen
held up their wares for examination and the more affluent of the city bid
against their neighbours for the range of desirable treats on offer.

One of the Brewers had managed to secure a prime spot in front of
the tower doors, but despite this, his sales were poor and he needed to try
something different. He looked around at the dozens of wine skins on the cart
and though they all contained the same wine, one skin was brightly coloured
and stood out from the rest. Not one to miss an opportunity, he grabbed the
skin and held it up high before the crowd.

'Ladies and gentlemen,' he announced, 'what I have here is one of
the most amazing beverages we have ever produced in all the years of our
tower. The flavour is of the rarest of apples and its smooth texture flows like
honey down parched throats. What is more, the strength is such that it will
only take three draughts to get you drunk, think of the money you will save.'

'We know you well, Marek,' shouted a voice. 'It's probably Narwl
piss flavoured with sugar-shell.'

19

The crowd burst out laughing, for Marek was the least trusted of the Brewers, and hands stayed just a little tighter on their purses when he led an auction. He feigned shock, but discreetly pushed a strong smelling skin of ale back under the cart covering with his foot. That one would have to wait.

'I am shocked and hurt, friend,' he shouted. 'More than a year ago, I almost bankrupted myself buying the sweetest fruits the farmers could produce, and following a long lost recipe, laboured for over a year distilling this nectar, especially for the more discerning palate.'

'Get to the point, Marek,' shouted another. 'How much are you trying to swindle for this toilet water this time?'

Marek changed tack knowing that he needed different bait.

'No matter, friend,' he said 'it is way out of range of any man here, perhaps we should move on to the ale, for even though it is of unapproachable quality, it is after all the drink of the masses and therefore more suitable for the more common palate.'

'Yeah, let's get to the serious stuff,' someone else shouted, raising another laugh from the crowd.

Marek placed the wine skin down and made a show of looking for a skin of ale.

'Wait!' shouted a voice.

Marek hid a secret smile, the bait had been taken and all he had to do now was play the catch. He stood up and looked at a finely dressed man in the centre of the rabble.

'Made from apples and brewed for a year, you say,' shouted the man. 'How much for the skin, Brewer?'

'Alas, Sir,' he responded, 'I can obviously see you are a man of great means, but I despair that even you cannot afford a liqueur such as this. I fear its destiny is to grace the tables of the council only.'

The man looked around the crowd, preening in his self-importance.

'Then you know not who I am, Sir,' he shouted back, ensuring his voice carried over the crowd, 'I am Fredrick and I am the best Cobbler in the Citadel.'

Marek withheld a gasp at his good fortune. He did indeed know of Fredrick. In fact, he made it his business to know of all the wealthy families in the Citadel and the Cobblers in particular were loaded! He also knew that Fredrick had inherited his father's wealth and was well into the process of blowing it on wine, gambling and Courtesans. If he played this right, he would surely start Moon-day with a bang.

'On the contrary, Sir,' he said with a low bow, 'I am aware of your pedigree and indeed your renowned skill, especially with the ladies may I add,' he laughed, playing to the arrogance of Fredrick who positively glowed in the praise.

'Indeed this is the case,' preened Fredrick. 'In fact, I am about to purchase a whole month in the Pleasure-tower this very day, and I seek a suitable present for the Governess herself.'

A quiet murmur rippled around the crowd. Surely the Governess would not entertain this drunken creep, though it had to be said, everyone had their price.

'The Governess herself?' gasped Marek, feigning astonishment. 'Well yes, my liqueur would certainly be a suitable gift. I am sure that her Excellency would reveal even the secrets of the inner sanctum to the bearer, but even so, I have spent over a year preparing this juice of the gods and I fear that even one so dignified as yourself, would struggle to meet the price. No, I think I will bestow it upon the council and earn my tower credits for many years to come. Now, moving on, let's sell some ale.'

Fredrick's face glowered with anger.

'You will wait, Sir, I have not finished. There is none in the council, or indeed the Brewer's-tower, whom I call superior and I am offended that you doubt my wealth. I am Fredrick of the Cobblers and I demand this liqueur. Now, name your price!'

The crowd fell silent as even those in front of the other stalls watched the haggling in anticipation, most knowing that there was only one likely winner in this contest of wiles.

'My apologies, Sir,' said Marek humbly, 'I did not mean to offend. I should have realized that an auspicious family such as yours, could easily afford the measly five crowns for a once in a lifetime experience such as this.'

The crowd gasped at the amount. It was almost a lifetime's wages for the average labourer and all eyes turned to Fredrick.

The Cobbler hid his own gasp, throwing a false smile around the market.

'And for how many skins?' he asked, clearing his throat first.

'It is unique, Sir,' replied Marek. 'That is the beauty of this entrancing draught, there is no other, nor will there ever be any other like it. In fact, so rare is it's bouquet and taste that only the most discerning palate will appreciate its matchless qualities.' Marek hid his smirk well. He knew he had him, all he had to do now was reel him in. 'But of course,' he continued, 'if it is too steep, I could drop the price slightly.'

Fredrick hesitated, looking around the crowd. The price was astronomical. Yet, he knew he could not back out of it without losing any respect he had left. Even the suggestion of a price drop, an ingenious ploy by Marek, was a veiled insult and he knew he could not accept the offer. No, he was cornered and there was only one way out.

'Five crowns, you say,' he shouted loudly, looking around, 'I spend more than that on toilet wipes. I shall take your wine, Sir, and use it to bathe the shimmering skin of the Governess before immersing myself in the untold pleasures that heavenly body can offer.' He took out his purse to retrieve the coins and made his way through the crowd to retrieve his purchase. He handed over the money and as he turned around, everyone burst into spontaneous clapping and cheering. Fredrick held up the wine skin in imagined triumph and in his arrogance, thought the cheering was aimed at him and not Marek

The Brewer secreted the coins quickly about his person, astonished at the stupidity of the man. At the end of the day, it was only wine and though it had indeed taken a year to brew, it was without any help from him. It had taken six months to gather enough rotten apple cores and as long again for them to ferment. In fact, he had only remembered to bring it today, because his wife had complained about the pungent stink emanating from the back of her cooking area. He turned back to the crowd holding up a fresh skin in each hand.

'Now,' he shouted, 'who's for some ale?'

Similar scenes were repeated throughout the day at all the other stalls, and as the day went on and the more succulent joints and sweeter cakes were bought by the wealthy, the poorer members of the populace emerged to purchase the more affordable goods on offer.

Kenzo had struck a good deal with one of the Brewers and had haggled with a Baker for a modest, yet pretty sweet-cake. He made his way to the gates for his guests to arrive, and as if he wasn't nervous enough, was dismayed to find that one of the guards on duty was Braille.

'Oh no,' groaned Kenzo, realizing his every move was going to be scrutinized by his big buffoon of a friend.

'Hello, Kenzo,' Braille smirked, 'have you come to meet daddy?'

'I'm begging you, Braille,' said Kenzo, 'please don't spoil this for me,'

'Me!' gasped Braille assuming a look of hurt. 'Would I do something like that to a friend?'

'Absolutely,' stated Kenzo staring into the grinning soldier's eyes. Braille stared back with a smirk on his face.

'Okay, how much?' sighed Kenzo, knowing how Braille worked.

'Ten cups of your ale skin tonight.'

'Five.'

'Seven.'

'Six.'

'Done!'

Braille clapped his hand over his own mouth, confirming his part of the deal.

'Silence, right?' questioned Kenzo.

'Absolutely,' mumbled Braille through his fingers, a wicked gleam in his eye.

'Okay,' said Kenzo, and went over to sit on the perimeter wall of the causeway to await the dreaded meeting with his girlfriend and her father.

A few yards away, a black cloaked Watcher stood by his empty cart, waiting for the trade that always came. Soon a group of sombre people appeared, carrying a heavy bundle between them. The leader carried a basket and opened the lid for the Watcher to examine. With a nod, the Watcher accepted the payment and the group placed both the basket and the wrapped corpse on the cart. The family gathered around, somewhat reluctant to leave their deceased relative to the custody of the city's appointed undertakers. The distraught older woman, being comforted by the younger adults, was obviously the spouse of the deceased and Kenzo averted his eyes from the heartbreak as the family paid their last respects.

Kenzo knew that this scene was being repeated around all the city, for this was how the city dealt with their dead and how the Watchers made their living. For a price that was negotiated according to the wealth of the family, the Watchers would take the corpse to their tower and after preparing them for the afterlife, commit their bodies to the sacred fires, allowing their souls to be freed to join Arial in the heavens.

Over the next half an hour, three other families brought their deceased to the Watcher's cart and the novelty soon wore off with Kenzo, as the sweet smell of death seeped through the shrouds. Finally, he stood up as he recognized Leona walking alongside her father and walked forward toward them, offering his hand in greeting.

'Hello, Sir,' he said formally, 'I'm very pleased to meet you.'

'Yes, quite,' came the reply, with no hand offered in return. 'Right, let's get this over with.'

Kenzo glanced at Leona.

'Would you like to sit?' he asked, indicating the blanket he had placed on the now dry causeway wall, 'I brought your favourite ale and some cake.'

The father's face lit up when he saw the ale-skin and ignoring the bone cups, pulled the stopper from the neck with his teeth and drank direct from the skin. Leona and Kenzo glanced at each other nervously as they waited for him to come up for air.

'Cake?' suggested Kenzo pointing at the treat nervously.

'Naah,' grunted the father, 'let's get on with it.'

'Get on with it, Sir?' asked Kenzo

'Yup, let's get on with the bartering, the dancing starts soon.'

'I don't understand, I thought we were here to get acquainted.'

'Acquainted, my arse, you want to bed my daughter, and I won't let that happen unless you marry her first, so how much can you afford?'

'I'm sorry, Sir, there seems to be a misunderstanding, I was only...'

'Only what?' interrupted the father impatiently. 'Do you want to marry her or not?'

'Well, yes of course!' answered Kenzo. 'But …'

'But nothing! How much money have you got?'

'Err, well I have some savings and I have a good job, I suppose I could amass perhaps half a crown if I see a lender.'

'Half a crown,' guffawed the father. 'Do you hear that, sweet Leona? He values you at a mere half a crown.'

'It's not like that!' said Kenzo sharply, his anger rising.

'Then, what is it like, soldier?' sneered the father.

'Of course Leona is worth more than that, there's not enough money in the Citadel to match your daughter's beauty, but I am a mere soldier and I cannot get my hands on much more.'

'Then this conversation is over. Leona, come, I have ale to drink and women to bed.'

They stood to leave, Leona glancing at Kenzo in confusion as they walked back in to the Citadel.

'Wait,' called Kenzo, 'I will pay a full crown for your daughter's hand.'

The father stopped and looked back.

'Make it two crowns, soldier, and you will get more than her hand.'

'I can't find two crowns,' said Kenzo quietly.

'Two crowns and we have a deal. That is my final word. Well?'

Kenzo looked at Leona and her father in turn, at a loss what to do.

'I thought so,' said the father, 'let's go.'

'Okay!' shouted Kenzo. 'I will find two crowns, even if I have to steal them.'

The father walked back, extending his arm as if to shake Kenzo's hand.

Kenzo held his hand out to shake on the deal and was surprised when the old man stretched past him to grasp the ale-skin.

'Two moons,' said the father, 'you have two moons or I sell her to the Courtesans.'

Without another word, he walked back into the Citadel and as he dragged his daughter with him, she glanced over her shoulder, a look of despair on her face, Kenzo staring helplessly after them until they disappeared. A few moments later, he relaxed his gaze and turning slightly, his eyes met those of Braille.

'That went well,' said Braille and immediately fell into fits of laughter.

'Arsehole!' snapped Kenzo, only succeeding in making the soldier laugh even more. He pushed past his so-called friend and stamped back into the city.

'You've forgotten your cake,' shouted Braille through his laughter.

'Shove it!' shouted Kenzo as he strode forward, gutted. He had forgotten the expensive treat, but stubborn enough not to lose more face by returning for it.

The market was obviously ending. Kenzo walked through the city streets and passed many traders returning to their respective towers. The ceremonial arrival of the tradesmen wasn't repeated as the carts rumbled their return journey over the now dry causeways. Their human pack animals were just keen to finish the job and return to Bastion soon as possible.

The courtyard had been cleared of people and the Artists had locked the gates in order to prepare for the nights celebrations. Crowds started to gather in front of the keep, many adorned in their finest attire in anticipation of the imminent celebrations, but kept away from the gates by a row of guards in ceremonial uniforms.

At last, a great cheer rose from the crowd signalling it was time, and as the gates swung open, the cordon of soldiers moved to one side to avoid being crushed in the stampede. Kenzo was carried along with the crowd and found himself back in the courtyard, though this time it looked completely different.

Though he had been here on many Moon-days, the initial sight always impressed Kenzo. The courtyard had been decorated with banners of extraordinary designs and colours so bright they hurt the eyes, hundreds of lanterns hung from the walls in readiness for the darker hours and tight- rope walkers exhibited their skills high above the heads of the revellers in the crowd.

Musicians started up a gloriously engaging tune as the throng poured into the arena and as Kenzo wandered through the crowd, careful not to knock down a stilt walker or spoil the skills of the occasional painted juggler, he wondered which of the painted faces hid the beautiful features of his girlfriend.

As the space filled, the music picked up and the masked young men and women of the Artists danced amongst the crowd pouring free ale into eagerly offered bone cups. Herb cigarettes were passed out and many a misguided individual genuinely believed that the flirtatious behaviour of the Artists was genuine, and surely tonight, they would get lucky. Gradually, as the atmosphere intensified and with the aid of drink and drugs, everyone present was lured in to the intoxicating embrace of the carnival.

Suddenly everything came to a dead stop. All music, dancing and acrobatics came to a halt, and the arena fell silent. A robed figure ascended the stairs to the central stand and addressed the crowd.

'Friends' he roared out, 'welcome to the Tower of the Saint. You have tasted the delights of what awaits you this night, but as we are all aware, you get nothing for nothing. The sellers are amongst you, and you have until the bell tolls at midnight to pay your way. Anyone unadorned by then will be ejected, and as we all know, after midnight is when the fun really starts, so, dig deep, pay the price and enjoy!'

Immediately the musicians struck up again and the celebrations restarted. Kenzo continued through the crowd looking for Leona, stopping to stare at the occasional dancer or seller trying to recognize her features. A seller approached, her beautiful face smiling warmly at him.

'Hello, Sir,' she said provocatively, 'I would hate for someone as strong and handsome as you to have to leave early. Surely you wish to stay, for I finish work at midnight and will need company.' She placed her hand on his chest and stared deep into his eyes.

Kenzo smiled condescendingly at the well-rehearsed speech. She would repeat this a hundred times this night, as would all her friends. Still, he would need to stay to find Leona, so he dug in his pocket to find a coin. The pretty girl smiled and produced a small pot of gold paint and a tiny brush, painting an intricate design on his cheek to indicate he had paid the price.

'Thank you, kind Sir,' she said, 'see you later,' and after flashing him a glowing smile, disappeared into the crowd to find her next customer.

The beat was growing stronger and the whole crowd seemed to pulse with the rhythm as the atmosphere intensified. The ale flowed freely as the night progressed and Kenzo took his fair share, knowing very well that as soon as the gates were locked, there would be a charge for everything.

He estimated he had an hour before the bell tolled and made his way to the outer gates to escape the madness for a while. He walked out onto the drawbridge with the laughter and music still ringing in his ears and sat on a carved stone bench overlooking the city to enjoy the relative peace and quiet. Unexpectedly, he heard a voice from the shadows, trying to get his attention.

'Soldier!'

He peered into the darkness.

'Who's there?' he asked.

'Come close,' the deep male voice said again, 'I have an offer you can't refuse.'

In a city of intrigue and assassins, Kenzo was hardly likely to step into the shadows at the behest of a strange voice.

'State your business,' said Kenzo carefully reaching for his dagger located in a scabbard hanging from his belt.

'You have need of money and I have need of your services,' said the voice, 'I wish to make an arrangement.'

'What sort of arrangement?' asked Kenzo, his eyes straining to make out the face beneath the hooded cape.

'Come close, I cannot allow myself to be seen.'

'Ok, but you must know I will defend myself if attacked.'

'Understood, though you have my word this will not happen.'

Kenzo walked slowly into the dark recesses of the alcove.

'What do you want?' he asked.

'This is half of what you need, I believe,' said the voice.

The hooded figure held out his hand, a full crown clutched between his scrawny fingers.

'Who are you?' asked Kenzo taking the crown slowly.

'My name is De-gill,' came the reply, 'and I am from Watcher-tower.'

'Why do you give me money, De-gill?' he asked. 'What do you expect of me?'

'Information.'

'Such as?'

'We seek a child, one of our own who has gone missing.'

'Where?'

'Somewhere in your city.'

'What do you want me to do?'

'We cannot walk this city as you do,' he said. 'You have many contacts and can access doors that are denied to others. If you find this child, the rewards will be great.'

'How great?'

'The first crown is yours to keep as a sign of goodwill. If you let me know where the child is, there will be another.'

Kenzo swallowed hard, it was exactly the amount he needed to marry Leona.

'Two crowns for just some information?'

'Yes, but there can be more.'

'How?'

'Bring me the child and you will be a rich man.'

'What do you mean?'

'Bring me his corpse and you get a further five crowns. Alive earns you ten. It is as simple as that.'

'Ten crowns,' gasped Kenzo, 'just to bring you a child.'

'Yes, but he is not just any child and may not come quietly.'

'And you are happy for me to kill him?'

'If necessary,' said the Watcher.

'What sort of people are you?' asked Kenzo, 'who would happily pay so much to kill one of your own children?'

'Are we so different to one who seeks to sell his own daughter as a whore?' asked De-gill

Kenzo recalled his conversation with Leona's father earlier that day.

'You overheard our conversation,' he said.

'We overhear many conversations.'

'Where can I find this child?' asked Kenzo.

'All we know is that he is in the city somewhere.'

'Wonderful!' said Kenzo sarcastically. 'And how exactly am I supposed to recognise this child?'

'That crown says you will find a way,' said De-gill. 'Ask discreet questions and search the dark places. He will not be easily missed for his body is misshapen.' De-gill paused. 'One more thing, soldier, we have to have him before the moon is next full.'

'And if I find him before then?'

'Keep him under lock and key at all times. I will look from the Watcher's-tower every night at midnight. If you have him, signal by waving a red light. I will arrange collection.'

'How will you manage that?' asked Kenzo, a confused look on his face. 'You will be half a mile away across the water?'

'That is not of your concern.'

'And if I can't find him?'

'That is not an option.'

'But even so, it's a big city, so if I cannot find him, do I keep the crown?'

The Watcher flashed the briefest of grim smiles.

'Trust me, soldier,' he said,' if we do not find this child by the next Moon-day, money will be the least of your problems. Do we have a deal?'

'We do,' said Kenzo finally and held out his hand to seal the agreement.

De-gill ignored the gesture and slunk back into the shadows.

'Do not fail me, soldier,' he said as he disappeared, 'your life may well depend on it.'

Kenzo shuddered involuntarily. He had never liked the Watchers for they were too close to the afterworld for his liking, and after looking around to see if anyone had witnessed the strange meeting, made his way back into the keep.

Chapter 4

Crispin sat hunched in a dark corner with his cape wrapped tightly around him against the cold. His long black hair was tucked into his cape and his arthritic hands clenched a knife in anticipation of an attack at any minute. He had seen a Watcher pass this alleyway only a few minutes earlier and he knew it was only a matter of time until they found him.

Crispin contemplated his situation as he waited to die, for that was what was going to happen, he was sure of it. Oh yes, he would fight the best he could, but ultimately they would overpower him, they always did.

'Why?' he asked himself, what had he done so badly in his previous life that made him pay so dearly in this one? He knew he looked different to everyone else, he had a hunched back, arthritic hands and a gaunt face that hinted at malnutrition. Perhaps that was why they made him sleep in a cold stone cell?

The problem wasn't even due to the fact that he was only allowed out for an hour each night under armed guard, when the sky was at its darkest. No, that he could deal with, it was all worth it, for the one day a month when he was not allowed out of his cell, when there were extra guards outside the doors and the shutters were closed tightly over his window to block out the moonlight. Those twelve glorious, sleepless hours, where if he dragged his bed under the window and stretched upward on the tips of his arthritic feet, he could just about see out of a gap in the shutters. For it was that one glorious, soul cleansing night that he longed for with all his heart. That sweet starlit night when the refreshing moonlight washed over him like a flood, nourishing him in a way that the gruel he was fed never could.

Crispin had no idea why they were so afraid of him. He knew he was different, but that wasn't his fault. He had never met his parents and had been told they were dead. He accepted his lot and was happy to plod along between moons but recently something was changing. His body was aching, the guards seemed to have increased and the medicals were happening more often.

Ah yes, the medicals, where he was tied to a table and drugged with a bitter liquid before they probed, prodded, cut and sewed his scarred body before he passed out, only to wake again the following morning, bandaged and groggy.

However, all that was in the past. A few nights ago, everything changed when his door opened and a man he had never met entered his cell to give him a brief, but clear set of instructions.

'Listen to me and don't interrupt,' the visitor had said. 'You have to get out of this cell and go to the Citadel. I am here to help.'

Crispin was astonished. Escape his cell, the only place he had ever lived?

29

'But why?' he asked, 'how?'

'An hour before dawn on Moon-day, your door will be left unlocked. Make your way out to the courtyard and hide yourself beneath the shrouds on the last cart. Use only this cart, for it will be pulled by a friend and will take you to Bastion. When you reach the place, seek me out.'

'But what about the guards?'

'There will be no guards.'

'Why are you doing this?' asked Crispin.

'Because you are growing stronger and they cannot allow you to live. If you stay here, you will die.'

'Wait, where shall I find you? What is your name?'

'I cannot share my name in case you are caught,' came the quiet reply, 'but find the brotherhood and you will find me.' He paused before adding, 'stay alive, Crispin, your time has come, there will never be another chance like this.' He turned suddenly and left the cell, locking the door behind him.

Crispin stayed at the door listening to the receding footsteps. Minutes later, as he heard fresh guards come on duty, the deformed boy hurried back to his cot, breathless as the implications of the conversation sank in.

Crispin pulled his cloak tighter around him. That was two nights ago and this morning he carried out his instructions. As promised, his door had been unlocked and he had stepped over the sleeping bodies of the guards and empty wine skins, hinting at the drugged contents within. He had found the row of carts in the pre-dawn darkness and hid under a shroud on the rear cart. Soon after dawn, he heard the murmur of voices and then the creaking of the giant gates as the procession of undertakers made their way to join the celebrations in Bastion. Crispin lay terrified under the shroud, hardly daring to breathe.

The cart-master entered the city with the rest of his colleagues and soon branched off in a different direction to make his way to the pre-designated area he had occupied for many years. He wandered through the city, bypassing the market place until finally he reached his destination, stopping the cart before throwing back the shroud hiding Crispin.

'Go!' said the cart-master abruptly.

Crispin had a million questions to ask, but the scowl on the man's face warned otherwise.

'Where?' he asked.

The man shrugged his shoulders, replaced the tarpaulin and picked up the handles of the cart once more.

'Not my problem,' he said, 'my work is finished, now go!'

As the scowl-faced man pulled his cart away, Crispin scuttled into the welcoming shadows of Bastion. It had all been so easy, too easy!

Chapter 5

Pelosus gazed through his telescope before returning to his calculations yet again. Since he was a boy, he had studied the ways of the universe and apart from the breath-taking effects of Moon-day, they seldom changed. He knew the names of thousands of the brightest stars in the sky, could tell you what time the sun would rise and set every day of the next hundred years, and even predict the weather to a certain extent, depending on the brightness of the giant moon through the haze.

His predecessors had charted the cosmos many lifetimes ago and his room was filled with hundreds of detailed scrolls, ranging from star charts to the history of the people.

'Hmm, interesting,' he said to himself, crouching over his desk in his workroom, moving the plankton-orb closer to get better light. Below, the noise of the celebrations were certainly something he could do without but nonetheless, he worked on at his calculations, driven along by the tide of formulae that were now all beginning to make sense.

'What's so interesting, Pelosus?' interrupted an unexpected voice, causing him to jump.

The scientist spun around and was shocked to see the woman of his dreams standing before him.

'Your Excellency,' he stammered, 'I wasn't expecting you!'

'I thought it would be a nice surprise,' said Petra, Governess of the Courtesans.

Pelosus stared at her in awe. Her voice was as soft as a feather and smooth as honey; he wallowed in her gentle tones.

Slowly she walked toward him with a beautiful smile and lifted her hand to his face. Before he could realize what her intention was, she extended a finger and gently pushed up his lower jaw. The Stargazer gathered his wits and dragged himself back to reality.

'Right, yes of course,' he said, 'how may I help you?'

'Well, to start with,' she said, 'I require a seat and a glass of wine.'

'Um, I have ale,' he said before adding quickly, 'but it is a very good quality, I had it bought for me this very morning in the market.'

'Ale will be fine,' she said, her beguiling smile bathing him in its gentle warmth.

Pelosus pulled up two chairs and swept some scrolls to one side with his forearm. After pouring two glasses of ale, they sat down together by his worktable.

'Well, this is an honour, your Excellency,' he started.

The Governess of the Courtesans interrupted him.

'Are we alone, Pelosus?' she asked.

'Yes, though the clerk will be here soon with the evening meal.'

'Good, then we can talk freely. First of all, when we are alone you may call me Petra. Is that okay with you?'

Pelosus took a swig of ale, his eyes never leaving hers, lost in the deep gaze that pierced his very heart.

'Yes your Exc…I mean, Petra,' he replied, 'if that is what you desire.'

'It is,' she said, 'I want to become your friend, Pelosus, I want to be able to trust you and for you to trust me. From now on, what passes between us must remain our secret, do you think we can achieve that?'

'Of course!' said Pelosus vigorously nodding his head.

'Good, then let's get down to business.' She paused for a few moments, gathering her thoughts before looking up at him with a worried look in her eyes. 'The news you shared last night in the council,' she said, 'how certain are you that this will come to pass?'

'As certain as I can be,' he replied. 'In fact, if anything, my estimations are a bit on the conservative side. I checked the water level this morning and it is already lower than I expected.'

'Yes, I noticed this as well,' she said. 'Assuming everything you say is correct and the sea level drops; it will have devastating effects on everyone in Bastion, do you agree?'

'Yes, as I said at the council; thirst and hunger are inevitable, it is just the timescales that are an unknown quantity.'

'Is there anything we can do to stop this?'

'Your Exc… Petra,' he said with a hint of frustration in his voice, 'I answered these questions last night at the council. We cannot alter the orbit of the moon or its effects. There is nothing we can do.'

'Well, we'll come to that in a moment,' she said, 'but I just wanted to make sure we had no other option.'

'Than what?' asked the Stargazer.

'All in good time,' answered Petra, 'first we need to discuss anarchy.'

'Anarchy?'

'Yes, anarchy, you know what that means don't you?'

'Of course, but…'

'Pelosus, you may be right with your calculations but I believe many in this city will die long before the water runs out. When the danger becomes apparent, the wealthy will buy up all the food and water possible. Even though they will be only delaying the inevitable. As the poor start to die, they will turn on the wealthy and take what they need, killing if necessary in desperation to survive, it is human nature.'

Pelosus nodded, slowly following her logic.

'But the soldiers, won't they put down the riots?'

'In the beginning, yes,' she agreed, 'eventually, though, their weapons will become a means to obtain what they too desire. Society will collapse and the people will turn their gaze outwards, toward the towers.'

'But you are safe there,' he said, 'there is good distance of water between…' He left his sentence unfinished as the realization hit him. If the water level was low and the causeways uncovered, any mob would have total access to the towers.

'It would only be a matter of time before they broke down the gates,' said Petra, 'and my girls within would be at the mercy of the crowd.'

'But it isn't your fault,' said Pelosus, 'the moon, the water, it's a natural phenomenon.'

'You and I know this,' said Petra, 'but, do you think anyone will listen to reason? No, our lives will be worthless. The men will heap their frustration on my girls and kill them indiscriminately when they have finished.'

'You deal in lust,' said Pelosus. 'That's your trade.'

'We deal in pleasure, love and feeling, Pelosus,' she replied, 'it is different.'

Petra paused as she delicately sipped her ale.

'Pelosus,' she continued eventually, 'do you recall the beautiful time we shared, all those years ago?'

Once again his jaw dropped. After twenty years, she actually remembered him.

'I thought you didn't recall,' he mumbled, 'there must have been so many!'

'There were,' she said, 'but you were different. As I recall, you were a young apprentice and spent an entire week at my side.' She touched his face gently. 'Do you remember?'

'Every moment,' he said hoarsely.

'Me also,' said Petra, staring gently into the Stargazer's eyes, 'the thing is, Pelosus, I can't let my girls suffer the consequences of something that is not their fault, so if and when this catastrophe comes to fall, I want to be elsewhere.'

'Elsewhere!' he said simply, 'there is no elsewhere.'

She removed her hand and sat back to take another drink, staring at him in silence.

'There is no elsewhere!' he said again slowly, doubt creeping into his voice, 'is there?'

Petra stood up and walked around the room, her fingers playing along the scrolls sticking out of their slots in the walls.

'Pelosus,' she said eventually, 'what I am about to share with you has caused the deaths of many men. You must share this with no one. Yet, I want you to devote all your time on it from now on. Is this clear?'

Pelosus was intrigued. What was the information that was held dearer than any man's life? Quickly, he made a decision. He was a man of knowledge and always hungered for more. He needed to know this information, whatever the price.

'Yes, of course,' he said eventually, 'you have my word.'

'You may give me your word, Pelosus,' she said gently, 'but if you betray me, I will also have your life. Is that understood?'

'Absolutely!'

She continued her meander around the workroom walls before eventually continuing.

'Have you read all these scrolls, Pelosus?' she asked.

'Many times.'

'And you have an understanding of them all?'

'There are some charts that I don't understand, but apart from those few, I believe I do.'

'And what have you learned in all your years working in this tiny room?'

'The makeup of the heavens, the way of the weather, the history of Bastion.'

'The history of Bastion,' she said interrupting him, 'and what exactly have you learned about the history of Bastion?'

'You know the histories, Petra' he said, 'the scrolls are full of them.'

'Humour me!' she said.

'The histories tell us that our ancestors arrived here on the back of the great Narwl many thousands of years ago, and were saved from death when Arial made this city rise from beneath the sea.'

'Do you believe the histories, Pelosus?' asked Petra.

'Not to do so would be blasphemy punishable by death,' said Pelosus, fearing a trick question.

'Clever answer,' said Petra, 'neither a yes nor a no, but I understand your reluctance to speak freely. Let me phrase it differently. Forget what you have been taught, what do you know, as a scientific fact?'

'I know our planet is water covered and that we live and die by the actions of the sea,' said Pelosus, 'but the sources of information are so limited, it is difficult to prove any other theories, no matter how strange.'

As he talked, he watched Petra slowly retrieve something from within her clothing and place it on the table before him.

'Okay, Pelosus,' she said, 'please forgive me toying with your loyalties. I do not mean to cause conflict between your religion and your science, but there are things here we must discuss. You talk about sources of information and indeed, they are few and far between but let's start at the beginning. Forget everything you know or think you know and start again. What do you make of this?'

Pelosus looked down at the fabric she had laid on the table and for the third time that evening, his lower jaw opened in amazement. This time, neither he nor Petra made any attempt to close it.

Chapter 6

The sprawling rabbit warren of bustling streets and intriguing alleyways making up the city of Bastion, took every inch of available space between the central keep and outer city walls. High above the cobblestones, narrow arched bridges and entangled vines joined buildings at every level to provide a three dimensional aspect to the floor plan of the poor metropolis below.

Taverns and bordellos hid behind dirty doorways, conducting their illicit but thriving businesses which had been the mainstay of humanity since time began. Families forged close bonds with their neighbours, forming strong social circles who watched out for each other and jealously nurtured their individual identities. Food was shared; quarrels with rivals supported and each clan ensured that their own members were looked after.

Such were the inner streets of Bastion. A place where the strong survived and the weak perished. A claustrophobic warren of danger, where dark places and hidden alleyways provided sanctuary for the unsavoury and shelter for the secretive. It was dark, it smelled and it was scary, but it was a fantastic place for hide and seek!

Amber sat in almost complete darkness with her back against the cold, stone wall, slowly chewing the hard crust she had been hoarding under her thin wrap since morning. She was in her best hiding place and had never been caught here by the throng of kids currently scouring the Citadel for her. She looked up at the light leaking down through the metal grid an arm's length above her head, listening to the distant sounds of busy feet and occasional shouts of frustrated children seeking the un-findable.

The long abandoned sewage shaft lay forgotten at the end of a dead end lane, dry and surprisingly smell free. Nobody else knew about this hiding place except her cousin but he had long ago grown too old and boring to play hide and seek, so this place was hers alone.

Amber finished her crust and looked at the stone slab covering the tunnel opposite her in the gloom. Her cousin had placed the slab there many years ago to stop the smell from the live sewers below reaching the hiding place, and had filled the gap around the slab with mud, forming an airtight seal.

The children of the Citadel loved Moon-night as though they were forbidden to join the celebrations in the keep; they had their own traditions to follow. Amber was older than all the rest and though her body was changing, she still took part in the traditional games. After dark, they dressed up in masks and costumes and roamed the streets in their respective gangs, looking to terrorize their rivals from different areas of the city. It was a mark of great honour to leave abusive graffiti in opposing areas and the adults would wander the streets the following day, pointing out with pride whenever they saw a familiar logo in a different neighbourhood.

But it wasn't all fun. If you were separated from your friends, it could be a scary and lonely journey back to your own neighbourhood. Friends you played with for the rest of the month, quite happily became your deadliest enemies on Moon-night and captured stragglers often received a severe beating by their rivals.

That was the best part of it, as far as Amber was concerned and she seldom joined her friends running around the alleyways shouting and laughing, much preferring to work alone. No one knew these streets like Amber and she would carefully plan her route in the weeks preceding Moon-night, and when the occasion finally arrived, she would patiently stalk the back lanes in silence, taking her time until she reached the deepest recesses of the rival gang's areas.

This was such a night. Amber had managed to get deep into the Cobbler's quarter and was hidden down a side street in one of her favourite hiding places. There was more activity than usual tonight, with more groups of adults wandering the city. Nothing like this had happened before as far as she could recall and it was a bit frustrating as she had a particularly abusive flag she wanted to hang from the biggest Cobbler shop in Bastion.

When the activity died down, Amber lifted the grille of the disused drain and crawled out into the darkness. Slowly she crept down the lane with her back against a wall and had gone about halfway before a running cloaked figure came hurtling into the alleyway, knocking her off her feet. She lashed out, ready to give as good as she got and as her assailant fell sideways, she pounced on his prone body, drawing her fist back to punch her rival again.

The punch was never delivered and she froze mid-assault, holding her breath in fear as her intended victim held a knife up against her throat.

Amber's body was rigid. This was all wrong. Yes, a beating was a likely outcome of being caught, everyone accepted that but a knife was something totally different. She threw herself backwards against the wall and stared in astonishment as she watched the knife wielder sit up and assume a similar position against the opposite wall.

'What are you doing?' she gasped, 'why have you got a knife?'

An hour after the gates of the keep were locked, Kenzo finally found Leona, or rather, she found him.

'Where have you been?' he asked after she rushed into his arms.

'I had to finish my shift,' she said 'and get changed out of my costume.'

I looked everywhere for you tonight,' he said, 'I couldn't see you anywhere.'

'Well I saw you,' she laughed, 'several times.'

37

'I scoured the grounds,' he said exasperated, 'but gave up. Where were you?'

'Aha,' she said, entwining her hands with his as she stared up into his eyes. 'Therein lays the problem. You may have scoured the ground but did you scour the air?'

Her eyes lifted upward toward the trapeze artists, carrying out death defying tricks above the very drunk crowd.

'Oh no, don't tell me you do that,' he said.

'Why, is that a problem?'

'No,' he said, 'well, actually, yes, 'it's far too dangerous.'

'Oh Kenzo,' she laughed, 'don't be so silly. Trapeze Artists are trained since they start to walk and spend more time in the air than on the ground. Anyway, enough about work, come on I have finished for the night, let's dance.'

She dragged him deeper into the noisy throng that competed with the musicians for volume, whirling him round in circles and laughing aloud at the freedom that Moon-night brought. Gradually, Kenzo was caught up in the atmosphere and eventually all thoughts of trapeze artists, dark clad strangers and hunchback children were forgotten as he enjoyed the infectious company of the woman he loved.

Chapter 7

The first thing that struck Pelosus was the material from which the fabric was made. The only fabric he had ever encountered was mostly woven from weed fronds, or the rarer were actual pieces of Narwl skin, stretched, dried and beaten until soft, but this was so much more delicate. The document was woven from a fibre finer than any he had ever seen and edged on three sides with beautiful embroidery. It was delicate beyond comprehension and shone with the lustre of the brightest star on the darkest night.

'What is it?' he asked in awe.

'The fabric is called silk,' she said, 'and it is said it is secreted from the glands of an insect.'

'An insect? Surely not, I am a man of science and I would know of such an insect. The only ones around here are the spiders and the flies that plague our summers.'

Petra smiled.

'Pelosus,' she said sympathetically, 'you are indeed a man of science and you are very good at what you do, but you are limited in your knowledge.'

'What do you mean?'

'Over the years, have you ever thought that there may be more?'

'I have often become frustrated at gaps in the science, but I have scoured the library and these are the only scrolls we have.'

'No, Pelosus, these are the only scrolls you have access to.'

'There are more?'

'Perhaps.'

'Where?'

'All in good time, but for now, you must understand that there is more to this world than you or I understand. This silk,' she said handling the beautiful cloth, 'is indeed woven from the secretions of an insect, but none that you or I have ever seen. It was made many hundreds of miles from here in another place.'

'That can't be right,' said Pelosus, 'there is no other place.'

'That is what we have always believed,' said Petra, 'but there have always been rumours of another place, far beyond the horizon.'

'Where?' asked Pelosus.

'No-one knows exactly, but that is why I am here Pelosus, I want you to find out.'

'But how?'

Petra returned to the silk handkerchief.

'All we know is that many years ago, one of our previous Governesses, Sallette, accepted a commission from the Watcher's councillor and went to their tower for a month. Normally, we do not visit other towers,

39

for we can't guarantee the safety of our girls, but this was different. Times were hard and the Watcher offered her a price that was too good to turn down, so despite her better instincts, Sallette crossed the causeway on Moon-day and entered the tower with him.'

'And your people let her go?'

'Nothing they could do or say would change her mind. Our people were starving and the price offered was too great. She insisted, but they were so scared that she would be harmed, she finally agreed to signal every night from their tower walls, just to let them know she was safe.'

'And did she?'

'For ten days the signal came. Then suddenly it stopped and they feared the worst, but though frantic with worry, there was nothing they could do until the waters receded. When Moon-day finally came, they hardly waited for the waters to fall before they were up to their waists banging on their gate, demanding to see her.'

'Had she been killed?' asked Pelosus engrossed in the story.

'Oh no, Pelosus,' said Petra. 'She had suffered a fate far worse than that, she had fallen in love.'

'Fallen in love?' asked Pelosus. 'What's so bad about that?'

'Think about it, Pelosus,' she said, 'this was the chief Courtesan, the one who by tradition sets the standards for all others in our tower. Falling in love was strictly forbidden. Our business, no, our very existence revolves around physical relationships with as many men, or indeed women as possible. If we fall in love with one person, it is all over. How could we share ourselves with another if we are in love with only one?'

'What did she do?' asked Pelosus.

'She stayed in the tower,' said Petra, 'though not before coming to the gate to say her goodbyes. It was very hard and everyone wept hard for the loss of their sister.'

'It makes you wonder if the price was worth paying,' said Pelosus gently.

'Well that's the thing,' she said, 'we never did get paid, well, not what we were expecting anyway.'

'What did you get?'

'Well, when she was hugging her sisters to say goodbye, she wiped one of their tears away with this handkerchief.'

'And?'

'Before she re-entered the tower, she insisted the girl keep the handkerchief as a memento, but not before whispering a secret that has been passed down from her to me over many generations.'

'Which is?'

'She said, Guard this well, it is worth more than all the riches in Bastion. One day, it could save our sisters lives.'

Pelosus picked up the beautiful fabric. The entire surface was a pale blue, though covered with hundreds of darker tiny spots barely visible to the human eye. Around three of the edges a representation of a rambling vine, twisted over and over on itself as it bordered the silk, but apart from that, the fabric lacked any message he could see.

'What is so important?' he asked eventually, turning it over repeatedly in his hands. 'It is a beautiful substance no doubt, but if it is indeed proof of another place, I can't see how it can help.'

'Look again, Pelosus, though Sallette decided to stay with the Watchers, it would seem that during the month she was there, she became aware of a great secret, something of such importance that she had to encrypt and hide a clue, hoping that one day, someone would decipher it. We believe the handkerchief contains a message.'

He examined the silk again and in particular, the flowered vine that decorated the border. Though they were of a kind that he had never seen before and more colourful than the weeds that covered the stonewalls of Bastion, he had once glimpsed the courtyard behind the Farmer's tower gates and had seen a profusion of greenery and colours, so was aware that many such plants existed.

'What is it you want me to do?' he asked.

'Do whatever it is you do, Stargazer,' she said, 'study the silk, compare it to your records, trawl your knowledge and give us the meaning.'

He took a deep breath and returned his gaze to the handkerchief.

'I'll try, Petra,' he said 'but it's not something I am familiar with.'

A loud knock made them spin around to face the door.

'It's the clerk,' he said. 'He has brought the evening meal. Would you like to stay and share it with us? It will be humble, but the clerk is an excellent cook.'

Petra stood up to leave.

'I don't think so,' she smiled, 'I will leave you to your supper.'

She stood at the door as if waiting for something.

'Oh,' said Pelosus coming to his senses and rushing past her to open the door, 'please forgive me, I forget my manners.' He fiddled with the door handle before retrieving his keys from within his tunic.

Petra placed her hand on his arm.

'I cannot over emphasize the importance of this, Pelosus,' she said. 'Please give it your utmost attention.'

'I will try my best, Petra,' he said staring into her eyes.

'I'm sure you will,' she said gently, the warmth returning to her voice. 'Especially when you consider the reward you will receive.'

'Reward,' he said, 'what reward?'

'Me!' she said quietly and opening the door, she walked out of his chambers.

41

Chapter 8

Amber and the knife-wielding stranger stared at each other in the darkness.

'Who are you?' she asked, 'I don't recognize your face.'

'Why do you want to know?' the boy responded, 'did they send you?'

'Who?'

'The Watchers, if they did, I warn you I will not be taken back. I will die first.'

'What are you talking about?' asked Amber.

'You're not a Watcher?'

'No, I am not.'

'Are you from the Brotherhood?'

'I have no idea what you are talking about,' said Amber.

They stared at each other in silence before Amber took a deep breath and spoke again.

'Right,' she said, 'this is getting us nowhere, let's start again, though do you think you could lose the knife?'

Crispin hesitated a few moments but placed the knife down on the floor, though as Amber noticed, still well within reach.

'Okay,' she said, 'my name is Amber and I am from the Red-door gang. What gang are you from?'

'Gang? I know nothing about gangs,' he answered. 'My name is Crispin and I am from the Watcher's tower.'

Amber's eyes widened. A Watcher! She had only seen Watchers as they wheeled their macabre cargo back to their tower on Moon-day.

'What are you doing here?' she asked.

He stared back in silence.

'Crispin, are you okay?' she asked.

Slowly his shoulders started to shake and within a few seconds, his body followed suit. Amber looked on alarmed, thinking he was about to have a fit but within seconds she realized he was sobbing; his head held in his hands and unable even to speak.

Amber was shocked. She had never seen a boy cry, it just wasn't done. She hesitated for a moment before crawling across the divide to sit alongside him. Hesitantly, she placed her arm around his shoulders and jumped nervously when he fell into her lap, his whole body shuddering violently in time with his sobs.

'There, there,' she said awkwardly and started to stroke his hair as she had seen some of the older women do, though truth be told, not quite as rough as Amber's well-meant but robust technique, 'everything will be alright.'

Ten minutes later, the two new companions sat next to each other in awkward silence.

'I'm sorry about that,' said Crispin quietly.

'That's okay,' she answered, 'why are you so upset, Crispin?'

'The Watchers,' he said, 'they are looking for me and if they find me they will take me back to be killed.'

'Why?' she asked. 'What have you done?'

'Nothing,' he blurted, 'I have been locked in a cell all my life, but now they want to kill me.'

'How do you know?'

Crispin quickly recalled his meeting with the man from the Brotherhood and how he had come to be in this place.

'So what are you going to do now?' she asked.

'I don't know, I suppose I have to try to find this Brotherhood but I don't know where to start.'

'Well, you can't do anything tonight,' she said. 'There are all sorts of groups out there looking for someone to beat up. It is Moon-night after all.'

Crispin looked up at her before lifting his gaze to the heavens, his whole demeanour changing.

'Is that what you call it?' he whispered. 'Moon-night. It's such a beautiful name.'

'Steady on, Crispin,' laughed Amber, 'you're beginning to get creepy now. Right, let's start making plans. First, we have to hide you and you have come to the right person. Not only do I know every hiding place in Bastion, but you are less than a few yards from one of my best places, follow me.' She stood up and made her way back up the lane, closely followed by Crispin. Within a few minutes, they both sat at the bottom of the disused sewage pit.

'You will be safe here,' she said. 'If they look into the lane, they will see its empty and won't come up this far.'

She looked at his scared face, hanging on her every word.

'When was the last time you ate, Crispin?' she asked.

'Yesterday.'

She searched her wrap for her last crust and gave it to him, watching with interest as he silently savoured every small piece.

'It tastes nice,' he said. 'What is it?'

'Surely you've tasted bread before,' she said.

He shook his head.

'Is there more?' he asked hopefully.

'No, but I will go and get some. I won't be back until dawn, so you stay here and I will return as soon as possible.'

He nodded and watched as she climbed out of the pit and replaced the grille.

43

'Don't forget,' she said from above, 'stay here. Nowhere in the city is safe for you tonight. I will return in the morning.'

'Okay,' he answered hoarsely from below.

'Right, I'll see you soon,' she said and disappeared from view. Not that he noticed her leave, he was too engrossed by the sight of the giant moon being unveiled from behind its curtain of clouds far above. Amber hurried down the lane. If she was quick, she still had enough time to hang her abusive flag from the pole of the Cobbler's shop before dawn.

Back in the quiet lane, Crispin's deformed hands were visible on the bars of the sewer grille, as he gazed longingly up toward the night sky. A long, quiet moan whispered from the darkness.

'Moon-night,' he sighed to no one, 'such a beautiful name.'

Chapter 9

Amber arrived back in her house just before dawn. She smiled to herself and wished she could see the faces of the Cobblers when they saw the flag she had hung from one of their balconies. Usually she would be out and about at first light with all her friends, walking the city to see their achievements and of course, ripping down any that had been left in their own quarter, but today was different. Today, she had more important things to do.

Hurriedly, she raided the food box for whatever she could find. There was never much there usually, but today was the day after Moon-day and her uncle would have bought whatever he could afford in the market.

She opened the lid, pleased to see that it had indeed been stocked. She had to be quick as her uncle would be back from the keep soon and she didn't want to be caught. Her uncle was a kindly man, but like everyone else in the city had a taste for ale. She moved two skins aside and rummaged beneath. She wouldn't take the Narwl steaks, for there was only one for each week until next Moon-day. They would be missed and anyway, it was their weekly treat when her, her uncle and cousin Kenzo, all sat down and ate together.

She paused for a second, realising that what she was doing was wrong. Food was hard enough to come by at the best of times and the thought of stealing from her own family to feed a stranger felt uncomfortable to say the least. Not that she had a problem with stealing food, she was quite good at it on market day but stealing from your own family was wrong!

Suddenly her face lit up with an idea. She was allowed breakfast, so if she just took that and gave it to Crispin; then everything balanced up. Quickly she searched for the large bag of dried Narwl biscuits she knew would be there and took the two that would have been hers anyway. She heard a noise and spun around guiltily to see Kenzo entering the house, looking a bit worse for wear.

'Hangover?' she asked.

'It's not a hangover,' he replied,' I just have a bit of a headache. It's all that music.'

'Nothing to do with the ale then?' she said with a smile.

Kenzo was very fond of his cousin having grown up alongside her since her parents died when she was a baby.

'I only had a few,' he said. 'It must have been off. I'm going to bed.'

Amber's mind raced as she spotted an opportunity.

'Aren't you having breakfast?' she asked. 'The Narwl biscuits are lovely and fresh this morning.'

Kenzo groaned. The thought of eating chopped Narwl offal, dried and baked into palm-sized biscuits made his stomach lurch.

'I don't think so,' he answered.

'Why not?' she continued, 'they are still warm... and moist... and aromatic.'

'Oh God,' he said putting his hand over his mouth, 'I feel sick.'

'You must have a bug,' she said sweetly, receiving a scowl in return. 'Well if you don't want them, can I have them? I was up all night in the Cobbler's quarter and I'm starving.'

'Whatever,' he said and made his way to his bunk behind the curtain. Amber heard her cousin collapse onto his cot.

'Kenzo,' she said as soon as he had settled.

'Go away,' he mumbled.

'Can I ask you a question?'

'What?'

'Have you ever heard of something called the Brotherhood?'

'No,' he said, 'now leave me alone.'

Amber quickly retrieved her cousin's two biscuits and made her way out of the house and back toward the Cobbler's quarter, eating a biscuit as she went.

The silent lanes of the night before were busier now, as the previous night's revellers staggered back to their respective homes. Amber nodded at occasional familiar faces as she passed, making a mental note of who looked like what and who was with whom. Everyone knew everyone in Bastion and the city thrived on gossip. She worked her way against the human flow of traffic and soon entered the Cobbler's quarter, waiting for quite a while before the street was clear enough for her to enter the lane. Finally, the people cleared and Amber ran quickly up to the drain cover.

'Crispin?' she called quietly, 'are you awake?'

Receiving no answer, she peered down into the darkness, trying to spot his sleeping form.

'Crispin!' she called again, 'are you there?' As her eyes became accustomed to the darkness, her heart sank as she realized that the sewer was empty. Crispin had gone!

She spent the morning wandering around all the hidden alleyways in the vicinity, looking for any sign of the frightened boy, eating a second biscuit as she went. Now Moon-night was over, there was no problem mingling with the locals and life continued as normal. A familiar face appeared around a corner and called her name.

'Amber!'

She paused, and groaned quietly as she recognised one of the Cobblers. She didn't like Flip. He was sneaky, nasty and a bully.

'Hello, Flip,' she said.

'What are you doing up here so early?' he asked, looking around, 'and where are your ugly friends?'

She smiled at him.

'Oh you know me, Flip,' she said, 'I like to work alone.'

'No luck last night?' he asked with a smirk.

'I wouldn't be so sure,' she smirked back, 'I'd take a look above your shop if I was you.'

Flip's smirk changed and was replaced by a scowl.

'So what do you want up here?' he asked.

'Nothing from you, Flip,' she said, 'I'm just looking for a friend.'

'I've seen none of your smelly group around here,' he said, 'perhaps they've gone down to the gates to see the water.'

'Why would they want to do that?' she asked.

'Oh, you haven't heard? The water is still low and in fact, it's getting lower.'

'What do you mean getting lower?' she asked.

'Getting lower,' he repeated sarcastically, 'I can't make it any clearer than that, the water level has dropped lower than it has ever done in the past.'

'Perhaps it is just late,' she said

'Maybe,' he said, 'but the thing is, it is so low at the moment, you can see right to the bottom and there is something underneath.'

'Something underneath?' she asked, 'what do you mean?'

'Oh for Saint's sake,' he said, 'stop asking stupid questions and come and see for yourself.'

Amber thought for a moment. She was having no luck finding Crispin, but the thought of spending any time with Flip did not appeal. Still, she was intrigued.

'Okay,' she said, 'let's go.'

They went toward the outer city wall, joining others that were heading in the same direction, most the worse for wear, it had to be said, but all eager to see this strange phenomena. As they neared the gate, the crowd got thicker and soon they had to weave their way between the throng, jostling for position. Eventually, they were through the gate and were astonished to see the causeway crammed with people. And not just this causeway, the two others they could see were similarly crowded.

The crowd hummed with noise as the conversation passed back and fore.

'What is it?' asked a voice.

'Hell,' someone answered.

Amber was fascinated and renewed her efforts to get through the crowd to reach the edge of the causeway. Finally, after crawling through some legs she hauled herself up the perimeter wall and leaning her arms on the edge, looked over to see what everyone was staring at.

At first, she struggled to make anything out in the water as the occasional breeze made the surface ripple, but as the wind died and the surface stilled, her eyes widened in amazement. Not only was the water more than thirty feet below, but visible just beneath the surface was the outline of the top of a building, and not just one building, she realized, but many streets of buildings disappearing into the distance.

Amber found herself wondering who used to live there. In all the stories she had ever heard and in all the weekly lessons she had ever had when she was younger, no one had ever mentioned another level of the city. They had always been taught that the Citadel was all there was and their ancestors had reached there on the back of the great Narwl.

There was no one, or indeed, anywhere else in their history. That was what they had always been taught and the tutors should know, after all they knew everything. Unless of course, they had lied!

Chapter 10

Pelosus woke up on his cot in the corner of his room, his consciousness fighting against his body's need to stay asleep.

'What time is it?' he asked groggily.

'It's almost midday,' answered the clerk, pouring cold water into a washing bowl. 'You must have worked late last night.'

'Yes, quite,' answered Pelosus, his memories coming flooding back. 'After you left I had a lot of work to do.'

'Aaah, preparing for tonight's meeting of the council, I suppose?' answered the clerk over his shoulder

Pelosus stared at the clerk's back. He had forgotten about the meeting.

'Yes, that's right,' he said, 'though what they expect of me I don't know.'

'Well, first thing,' said the clerk, turning around with a plate of Narwl biscuits and warm wine, 'is I suggest you get yourself down to the gates of the city and see the water.'

'Why?'

'The level has dropped dramatically, and what's more, it has revealed another city under the surface.'

'Another city?' gasped Pelosus, 'I never knew.'

'Me neither,' said the clerk, 'it's not in any of the archives.'

Pelosus took a bite of a biscuit, his brow furrowing in thought.

'Why not?' he asked. 'Why would it not be in the archives, I mean, the records go right back to the start of the city, right?'

'As far back as the arrival of the great Narwl,' answered the clerk, 'though the details of that event are conveniently missing.'

'Mmm,' mouthed Pelosus through a mouthful of biscuit, 'not surprising though, there's not many who believe that fairy tale, but surely something as important as the building of our city would be documented.'

'I suppose they were too busy,' said the clerk.

'Possibly, anyway, pass me my robe, I need to see this.' He dressed quickly and munching the last of his late breakfast, made his way out of the keep and into the streets.

Within fifteen minutes, Pelosus stood on one of the eight causeways, absolutely amazed at the sight before him. The water was far lower than he had predicted and lay more than thirty feet below. More amazingly, the water had dropped so far that the stone routes that had always been referred to as causeways, had been revealed as an age-old misconception. They weren't causeways at all, they were arched bridges!

49

Pelosus looked down at the submerged city, visualizing how impressive these bridges would have looked to the people down below as they looked upwards, heaven knows how long ago.

It was interesting to see the reaction of the other Citadel inhabitants as they too saw the scene for the first time, wondering who or what lived there. The more imaginative, favoured a strange theory involving a species of fish people who had built the submerged city around Bastion without them knowing, while others got an attack of religion and prayed to the Six-fingered Saint for protection.

Overall and totally unexpected was an overwhelming feeling of vertigo. All their lives, the inhabitants of Bastion knew only the limited constraints of the granite city and on the one day a month that they got to see outside of the walls, even though the waters had fallen, it stay lay all around them like a protective blanket. Now that perception had been stripped away, not only was the water level thirty-foot lower, but the submerged city street lay far below that.

The concept was entirely alien to everyone and most, having taken a look, quickly made their way back within the familiar walls which had enveloped them like a giant pair of protective arms all their lives.

Pelosus stared downward in fascination. Below him lay row upon row of stone buildings, shimmering in the rippling water. The streets stretched as far as he could see, from the Citadel walls right across to the outer towers. Dark shapes swam lazily between the buildings, their streamlined bodies cutting easily through the water with a gentle flick of their tails. This was no surprise, as it had long been known that the water between the city and the towers were breeding grounds for Narwl, and it was forbidden for any hunting to take place within the outer walls.

He made copious notes, absorbing as much information as he could and was so engrossed was his scientific mind, that he all but forgot the seriousness of the implications. Soon he realized that all the people had gone back to their safe and boring lives inside the Citadel. All except one, a young girl whom he had seen skulking around the market occasionally on Moon-day. The two of them exchanged smiles.

'Hello,' said Amber.

He offered a tight-lipped smile as a response and continued his work. Amber sat on the wall, her legs hanging over the void.

'Fascinating, isn't it?' she said

'Yes, I suppose it is, really'.

'Is it right about the fish people?' she asked. 'I heard they've got bodies like us and a massive tail like a Narwl.'

'No,' he said, 'there are no such things as Fish-people.'

'Might be?' she said, a doubting look in her eye.

He put his pad down on the perimeter wall.

'Look at those buildings,' he said 'they were built by people like us.'

'How do you know?'

'If you look carefully, you can see windows and doors and that building there,' he said pointing to one with a flat roof, 'has a stairway on the outside, probably so that somebody could climb onto the roof to take in the sun. Now, why would Fish-people need stairs?'

Amber looked at the city with fresh interest in her eyes.

'I knew that,' she lied.

Pelosus smiled and silence reigned again.

'I wonder what happened to them,' said Amber eventually.

'I assume that the water must have been much lower a long time ago,' answered Pelosus, 'and when it rose, they either came into the city or drowned.'

Amber jumped off the wall onto the bridge, leaning over to look at the city beneath the crystal clear water once more.

'I think they drowned,' she said.

'Why do you think that?' answered the scientist.

'They must have,' she said, 'there's no way up. Anyway, I've got to go, goodbye.'

'Goodbye,' said Pelosus and stared at the scene below once again. The girl was right. No sign of a staircase was on the outer wall of the Citadel, or indeed any opening that might lead through the wall to an inner staircase. That was very strange and though he obviously couldn't see all the way around the Citadel walls, the absence of access left him with a feeling of unease. For the rest of the afternoon, Pelosus walked around all eight bridges, taking notes describing the scene below. But one thing overall became apparent as the day closed, from his high viewpoint, there seemed to be no entrance from the city below into the Citadel. The people who had once lived around the base of Bastion's perimeter walls would have been trapped between the city and the outer wall. There was no way in or out!

Amber resumed her search for Crispin, spending the rest of the afternoon checking every hiding place she could think of without any luck. Finally, she returned to the disused sewage pit where she had last seen him and climbed down to see if he had left any clues.

She sat with her back against the wall, thinking the problem through. She had questioned everyone she could and checked everywhere. If he was wandering around the city, she would have known, for quite apart from his appearance, the state he was in meant that he wouldn't have got a block away without someone seeing him and word spreading. As she wondered if the Watchers had found him and taken him back, her nose crinkled at the faint smell of sewage from the live sewers below.

She stared at the old pipe where it left the shaft. How could she smell sewage? The tunnel was sealed.

Amber jumped up and walked over to the slab covering the disused sewer. The seal was broken and it was apparent that the slab had just been leaned back in place. She realised that the reason she hadn't been able to find Crispin was that he had never left the shaft at all; he had simply crawled through the tunnel and into the sewer system.

She sat back against the wall and stared at the tunnel entrance in the gloom, contemplating whether to follow him or not. She had crawled down there once a few years ago and though the smell was bearable after a while, the tunnel branched off in different directions and before long she had become lost, terrified that she would die down there and no one would ever know. Kenzo had finally came in and found her, but for a long time she hadn't returned to the pit. She certainly didn't want to go back in there now, but if Crispin had gone that way, perhaps he was lost too. Perhaps he was as scared as she had been and was just as desperate for someone to find him.

She made her decision and knowing she would need a light, made her way back to her uncle's house, hoping he had remembered to charge them for the night. Many a time he had forgotten and they would have to retire to their respective beds early due to the blanketing darkness that filled the Citadel. It wasn't as if it was difficult. All he had to do was soak the coral orbs in a pail of fresh seawater for an hour. Though, she wasn't aware of how the biology worked, she did know that when the orb was removed from the water, the tiny plankton on the ball died off and their rapidly decomposing bodies rotted, and they gave off a powerful green glow that lasted over eight hours.

Within an hour, she was back in the shaft with a plankton lamp, some food and her knife. Without any further hesitation, Amber entered the sewers to search for Crispin.

Chapter 11

Pelosus entered the council chamber for the second time in two days and stood awkwardly waiting to be noticed. The clerk ushered him to a small chair that had been placed at the table especially for him, nothing as grand as the council member's chairs admittedly, but a chair all the same. They were all there, all the ruling trades from the outside towers, the most powerful people of the entire Citadel. These were the people who made the laws and it was by the whim of these individuals how the population lived and died. Pelosus sat quietly, listening to the conversation being led by Helzac.

'But are your divers able to reach them?' he was asking.

'No problem,' answered Razor. 'We can stay down for about three minutes at a time.'

'Good, send down those who can be trusted to keep their mouths shut. We don't want any rumours spreading discontent within the city.'

'Why so secretive?' asked Kelly, 'It's only a couple of flooded buildings. What is there to be worried about?'

'We have no idea what we can expect,' answered Helzac, 'the less the people know at the moment, the better.' He looked across at Pelosus. 'You are late!' he snapped.

'My apologies, your Excellency,' answered the stargazer.

'No matter,' interrupted Petra, 'you are here now.'

'Do you have any update?' asked Razor.

'Apart from the fact that it is happening faster than I calculated, there is no further information,' he answered.

'So, you maintain that the sea will fall even further?'

'Yes, but as the moon moves on, the rate will slow,' he answered.

'How is the water and food situation?' asked Kelly.

'The wells are lower, though there is still plenty of water,' answered Pelosus. 'The food stores are half full and yesterday's market was as good as ever, though I understand that the towers can only sustain one more market before the lack of resources takes its toll.'

'Do you have any recommendations?' asked Helzac.

'Well, first of all, I think that we should tell the population what to expect,' he started.

'No!' snapped Helzac cutting him short.

'But if they know' continued Pelosus, 'they can take steps to minimize the effect. They can make catchments to store the rain and evaporation hoods to catch the moist air as it rises to the heavens, all sorts of things to help.'

'We cannot tell the people they are going to die,' said Helzac, 'there will be riots in the streets.'

'We need not go into detail,' said Petra, 'but if we don't do something, it will get worse much quicker. Surely we should use every resource at our disposal to ease the situation until such time we have an answer.'

Heated conversation broke out around the table until Helzac called for silence once more.

'Okay,' he said, 'from tomorrow we will make it illegal to waste water with immediate effect. Everyone will store as much as they can from the rains.'

'What about food?' asked Kelly.

'There are still plenty of Narwl,' said Razor, 'so we are okay at the moment, but if the water drops much further, we won't be able to reach them.'

'How long can we last with what we have?' asked Helzac.

'One month, perhaps two if we impose rationing.'

'Do it,' said Helzac.

'What about us?' asked Rimmer the Weaver. 'We do not produce food, so my tradesmen are at risk. Clothing and shoes will be the last thing people want when they are starving.'

'I've thought about this,' interrupted Pelosus, 'in the circumstances, we will need buckets for the people to store the water and catchments for the rain.'

'Catchments?' asked Petra.

'Large sheets of waterproof material that can be draped between walls. The evaporated water will hit the catchments early in the mornings and condense on the cool fabric. The run off can then be collected in buckets. There are huge amounts of weed available at the moment due to the low water level and if we can harvest this quickly, the Weavers can use their skills to make everything we need.'

'And who will pay for this?' asked Rimmer.

'Now is not the time to think of wealth,' said Razor.

'I think not of wealth,' snapped Rimmer, 'whilst we weave to save the people, we still have to eat. How will this be done?'

For the next hour the councillors did what they did best, they haggled and made deals between themselves and by the end of the meeting, agreements had been made between all the towers as to how they each would survive. An agreement that was actually quite good when it came to looking after the tradesmen but it seemed to Pelosus that the commoners of the Citadel were quite far down the list. As the meeting ended, Helzac summed up the arrangements.

'Okay, the Brewers, Bakers, Farmers and Hunters will increase production to full capacity. The Weavers will produce the goods we need and receive five percent of all food production from the other trades. Petra, you will ensure the particular skills of your ladies are available to the rest of us in return for another five percent.'

Petra nodded. It was the best she could have hoped for. She was painfully aware that her tower had the least practical commodity to offer and when a trade was perceived as weak, there were always others in the city waiting to take over their tower. As long as she had the protection of the others, they were safe, for now!

'We agree that the occupants of the Prison-tower will go on to minimum rations with immediate effect,' continued Helzac, 'and when the time comes, their share will be the first to stop. Obviously, this excludes the ruling council and their families who will move to the safety of the keep. Pelosus will make suitable arrangements. That just leaves the Watchers.' He turned to the ever-quiet councillor from the Watcher's-tower. 'What do you offer, De-gill?'

'I think you know what we offer, Helzac,' he said quietly. 'I would imagine our services will be in demand more than ever. We will continue to remove the dead, for the same deal as the others.'

No one liked De-gill or his colleagues but they were all painfully aware of the important services they provided.

Helzac glanced around the others and seeing no dissenting faces, confirmed the arrangement.

'Agreed,' he said. 'Pelosus, you will oversee the rationing. In addition, mobilize the guard and cancel all leave. They will report to you in the first instance and you in turn will report to me. I think that we may have need of their services before this is over.'

The formal part of the meeting ended and the clerk arranged for refreshments to be brought. Warm wine was served along with cakes from the Bakers and small groups formed to discuss the seriousness of the situation in hushed tones. Pelosus sat alongside the clerk, not sure whether to leave or not but sat up with renewed interest as Petra approached.

'Would you excuse us?' she asked the clerk politely.

The clerk smiled and left them alone.

'Hello, Pelosus,' she said sweetly.

Once again the Stargazer was overwhelmed by his emotions. It was less than twelve hours since he last spoke to her and yet her beauty still entranced him. Not trusting himself to speak, he simply smiled an acknowledgement to her presence.

'You seem to be acquiring some merit within the council,' she said, 'what with overseeing the evacuation of the Prison-tower elite, organizing the rationing and commanding the army, you will be a very busy man over the next few weeks.'

'It would seem so,' he agreed, finally finding his voice.

'I hope you will find time to continue with our little arrangement,' she said, flashing one of her glorious smiles.

'Absolutely, Petra,' he said, 'I will engage the clerk to help with all the other tasks. He is very efficient but our agreement will remain my sole responsibility.'

'Good,' she said, 'one more thing, Pelosus,' she leaned forward to whisper in his ear, 'in company, you address me as Excellency. Petra will be reserved for our more, shall we say, intimate meetings.'

He nodded grimly, regretting the schoolboy error.

'I will be in touch,' she said and walked away to join a different group. The clerk returned to join Pelosus bringing two cups of wine.

'What did she want that was so private?' he asked.

'Oh, just some questions on the fairness of the rationing,' lied Pelosus. 'Are you sure this is okay?' he asked, indicating the cup of wine.

'No-one said we couldn't,' said the clerk, 'and anyway, it is usually after the meetings that most of the detail is thrashed out.'

'Oh,' said Pelosus. Despite sharing a set of rooms with the clerk for the last year and a half, they did not spend much time together as their duties were vastly different. The clerk's role was to record the diaries and minutes of Citadel life while the Stargazer's job was purely as a scientific researcher and advisor to the council.

They both sipped their wine, watching the councillors as they mingled, aloof in their self-importance and Pelosus took the opportunity to study the Mahogany panel at the far end of the room in more detail.

'What do you think he would make of all this?' asked the clerk.

'Who?'

'Him, the glorious founder of this city of ours,' answered the clerk, indicating the carving of Arial.

'You think he actually existed?' asked Pelosus.

'Why, don't you?'

'I don't know what to believe anymore,' said Pelosus, 'everything is changing so quickly.'

'Oh he existed alright,' said the Clerk. 'Everywhere you go in the city there are pictures of the Saint, even engraved into the walls. He was a definite person, though details of his life are not well documented in the archives.'

'It seems that much of what we believe is not in the archives,' said Pelosus.' It makes you wonder what else isn't recorded.' They both sipped their wine as they looked up at the priceless carving.

'Pelosus,' called Helzac, 'I am sure you are enjoying my wine, but you have work to do. I suggest you retire to your rooms and make a start.'

Pelosus sunk the last of the quality wine and made his way to the exit door.

'If you will excuse me, your Excellencies?' he said and left the room to retire to his quarters.

56

Chapter 12

Kenzo woke from his much needed sleep feeling much better. The last of the hangover had gone and he was ravenous. He went to the food box, careful not to wake his father, who had taken to his own cot sometime after Kenzo.

'He must have had a successful night with the ladies,' thought Kenzo smiling.

Taking a slice of thick bread, he spread it with a generous layer of crab meat and rammed far too much in his mouth, struggling to chew on the huge mouthful as he poured a jug of cold water into a bowl for his wash. The day was half-gone and he only had one day left of his leave. He thought of the time he had spent with Leona the night before, smiling at the fantastic memories. He couldn't wait till tonight when they had arranged to meet again, without the knowledge of her father of course, but that just added to the magic.

He pulled himself back to reality. Tonight would come soon enough but this afternoon would be spent looking for the mysterious child he had been told about the previous day. He took the coin from his pocket and looked at it for a long time, wondering what it was that was so special about this kid that warranted such a high payment.

Kenzo placed the coin at the very bottom of the food box, tucked away in the corner knowing it would be safe there. Grabbing a second slice of bread as he passed, he left the block and headed into the city, soon becoming aware of the weird state of the waters outside the city walls as he made his way through the crowds. He allowed himself a few minutes to see the phenomena before continuing on his quest. Obtaining the money to buy Leona from her father was far more important than some freak of nature.

He walked around Bastion talking to all the dross and wasters of the city. The guard also acted as the city's police force and over the last year, Kenzo had come to know most of the miscreants and drunkards personally. Despite Fatman's instructions, Kenzo had always been fair and in return had built up a network of reliable informants, but no one had even heard of the child, yet alone seen him. Finally, he sat outside an illegal hooch joint sharing a glass of the fierce drink with an old friend of his father who had fallen on hard times.

'Who is this kid?' the old man asked.

'Oh, just someone I promised to find for a friend,' replied Kenzo, 'you know how it is, ran away from home or something.'

'Is there some sort of reward for finding him?' asked the old man.

'Why do you ask that?' asked Kenzo, suddenly defensive.

'Well, you're not the only one to ask about him today,' he said.

'Who else is asking?'

'You don't know?'

'Tell me.'

'What's it worth?'

'Oh come on, Jed, for old time's sake.'

'Old time's sake doesn't fill my belly, Kenzo,' he said.

'I'll buy you another drink.'

'Two!' answered Jed.

'Okay two. Now, who else is seeking the child?'

The old man smiled.

'Your cousin!' he said.

'Amber?' asked Kenzo incredulously.

'Amber!' confirmed Jed. 'She was here only this afternoon.'

'Why was she looking for him?'

'Who knows?'

There was a pause before Kenzo continued.

'Where did she go?'

'Three drinks?' asked Jed hopefully.

'You're pushing your luck now,' laughed Kenzo. 'Okay, three drinks and that's your lot. Now, where did she go?'

'She didn't say, though I do know she was last seen in the Cobbler's quarter!' said Jed and called the bar owner to refill his glass.

Kenzo thanked the man and left the tavern to make his way to the Cobbler's quarter, his mind now suddenly focused on the task in hand. If the Watchers wanted this child so badly, and were willing to have him killed in the process, he could be dangerous. In fact, the Watcher named De-gill had specifically warned Kenzo that the boy wouldn't come quietly.

Kenzo realised that this adventure had now taken a sinister twist and the fact that Amber was involved made it all the worse. He broke into a trot, thoughts of weddings and money discarded. Foremost in his mind, was finding Amber, the rest could wait.

Kenzo reached the Cobblers quarter and started asking around. There was no need to be circumspect this time as he was simply asking about his cousin. Amber was well known in Bastion, especially by the kids, so that was where he concentrated his efforts. Within ten minutes, he started to obtain information.

'Yes, Amber was here,' was the usual reply and 'no I don't know where she is now.'

'Why, is she in trouble?' asked a particularly dislikeable boy when questioned.

'No, nothing like that,' said Kenzo, 'have you seen her?'

'Not since we saw the water together,' said Flip. 'I didn't stay long, but she did.'

'Who was she with?' asked Kenzo carefully, not wishing to give too much away about the boy from the Watcher-tower.

'No-one, but when I left she was talking to an old man. Perhaps he murdered her!' he said his eyes widening.

'What old man?'

'Dunno his name, but he had some posh robes on.'

'What did he look like?'

'White scruffy hair and long white beard,' said Flip shrugging his shoulders. 'Like I said, long white robes. Worth a coin or two if you ask me.'

'Anything else?'

'Well, he didn't stop scribbling on his pad as I recall.'

'Thanks!' said Kenzo and tossed him a sugar-shell sweet he had been saving for later. He needed to find that man and with that description, it shouldn't be too difficult. He retraced his steps to the tavern once again to speak to Jed and found the old man slumped against the wall snoring gently in the late afternoon light, an overturned beaker at his side.

'Jed, wake up,' he said shaking him gently, already regretting buying the old man the extra drinks, 'it's me, Kenzo, I need your help.' The old man opened his eyes and struggled to focus on Kenzo's face.

'Hello, Kenzo,' he slurred. 'Haven't seen you for ages. Wanna buy me a drink?'

'I don't think so,' said Kenzo, 'you've had quite enough. Listen, I need your help.' He passed on the description he had received from Flip.

'What's it worth?' asked Jed hopefully, repeating the mantra he used dozens of times every day.

'Jed, Amber could be in trouble,' he said, 'I need your help.' He looked at the old man's unfocussed eyes. 'Jed, come on,' he said urgently, 'she could be hurt.'

'It sounds like the star man,' answered the drunk eventually, 'try him.'

'Star man, who's the star man?'

'Works in the keep, looks at the stars. Easy job, if you ask me, I could do that.'

'Thanks, Jed,' said Kenzo. He called the owner over from the tavern and gave him a small coin. 'Give him a cot to sleep it off,' he said, 'and when he wakes, give him a meal.'

'Won't get much for this,' muttered the landlord.

Kenzo grabbed the landlord by the scruff.

'You and I both know that is plenty,' he snarled, 'now put him to bed and make sure his belly is full when he wakes. I am back on duty tomorrow and feel the need to inspect the taverns around here for licenses. Do I make myself clear?'

'You're a guard?' asked the landlord nervously

'Yup and this is my very close friend,' he said.

The landlord thought furiously, the last thing he wanted was to upset a guard, it wasn't the threat of inspections that worried him, he could always bribe his way out of that, but the possibility of boycott was a real concern. The guards were his best customers.

'Leave it to me,' he said and bent over to pick up the snoring figure of Jed. 'Come on, old man, I think you and I are about to become bosom buddies.' He looked up at Kenzo who gave him an acknowledging nod before turning to leave the alleyway once again

----

Chapter 13

The pipes of smaller live sewers piercing the walls on either side soon joined Amber's dry tunnel, and though there was little evidence of their disgusting purpose due to the heavy rains that flushed them every night, she still crinkled her nose at the stench. She picked her way along the drier pathway at the side of the main channel following it downstream and within a few minutes, came to a junction with another sewer tunnel that she remembered from the last time she was here. On that occasion, she had gone downstream and got horribly lost. She shuddered at the memory, so when the light from her lamp picked out Crispin's muddy footprints leading upstream, she was more than a little relieved.

She followed the channel up as far as she could, until the footprints stopped and was surprised to see a small, perfectly formed archway at head height, obviously the way that Crispin had gone.

She pulled herself up and crawled through the archway, coming out onto a ledge high above yet another tunnel.

'No, not a tunnel,' she thought, 'this was a passageway!'

Gone was the stinking channel of filth and the slimy walls of the sewers, growing with heaven knows what. This was a perfectly formed and carefully constructed passage disappearing left and right into the darkness. Amber was excited, a secret passageway beneath the city: her secret passageway that no one else knew about.

She dropped to the floor below and stood quietly in the darkness listening for any sound. The smell of filth had been replaced by something else, something familiar and though it obviously wasn't as bad as the sewage, it was still quite pungent and unpleasant.

Amber found a slight imprint of dried mud on the stone floor from Crispin's shoe, and made her way down the sloping passage eventually reaching a crossroads. Up until now, she had simple choices to make, with just a simple left or right turn as she went along. This time she had a choice of three different directions, left, right, or straight on.

She lowered the plankton orb to illuminate the floor, hoping to reveal any sign of the fleeing boy but the damp stone meant there was no sign of any prints. After a few moments consideration, she marked the tunnel she had come from with her knife and walked straight across to the opening opposite her.

Within minutes, Amber stopped in awe as she entered a large chamber. A huge pit seemed to drop away at her feet while above her, the shaft continued up into the darkness. A ledge ran all around the circular room with dozens of passages leading off, each identical to the other, and Amber knew there was a severe risk of getting lost. The new smell was very strong in the chamber and peering downwards into the pit, she confirmed what her nose already told her, brine.

The plankton orb reflected off the seawater just a few feet below, but as the ledge she was on was still soaking wet, Amber realised that a few hours earlier, the water level must have been much higher. She turned around and placed her hand high on the wall and sure enough, it was covered with still damp seaweed, confirming the water had even been higher than the doorways around the shaft.

She held her lamp up to shine the light around the rest of the chamber, trying to see if there were any clues to which way the boy had gone, but seeing none, she decided to use a process of elimination. She would start with the first tunnel to her left and if she had no luck there, would continue around the chamber in sequence until she found him.

Decision made, she carefully marked the entrance from which she came and walked into the first corridor, holding her lamp before her.

The going was much more comfortable now as the passages were larger than the sewers she had used earlier. Every so often, she passed smaller arched openings in the walls on either side, and though each entrance also had a small alcove carved into the rock alongside, each containing a few candles and a tinderbox, she resisted the temptation to explore.

Amber hurried on but was getting concerned. Not only was she far away from familiar territory, there was the possibility of bumping into someone in the gloom. Anyone could be waiting around any corner, alerted by the glow of her lamp, or the fall of her foot. If they, whoever they were, were willing to kill Crispin, she was sure they would have no problem making it two victims. Murder was common in the pressure pot that was Bastion.

Finally, she stopped and considered the situation carefully. She had enough excitement for now and her mind was spinning with information overload. She needed to get back to take all this in and though she had no idea how much time had passed, she felt tired and hungry. Crispin would have to wait; she needed help and would return to the city to tell Kenzo everything. He would know what to do.

She stood up and retraced her steps, finally returning to the chamber containing the seawater shaft. She found the mark she had left on the wall but as she re-entered the familiar tunnel, she froze mid stride, hearing a noise ahead of her.

She listened carefully, afraid to move. She heard it again, a cough ahead in the darkness between her and the ledge that led to the relative safety of the sewers. Slowly, she covered the plankton lamp with her robe, conscious that it would give her away, not knowing what to do. She started retracing her steps, walking backwards in the darkness away from the noise.

For the first time in her life, Amber was really scared! She decided to run, to seek somewhere to hide in these vast Catacombs. All thoughts of intrigue and adventure were forgotten with the realization that her life was at risk, but before she could even turn, the option was snatched from her. A clawed hand closed over her mouth from behind and an unseen assailant clamped her arms to her sides. Amber's eyes bulged with terror and her body became rigid, her brain unable to comprehend what was happening in the darkness, and though she knew she had to fight, the vice like grip around her body and mouth meant that she put up a rather feeble resistance as her captor dragged her deeper into the unknown depths of the Catacombs.

Chapter 14

Kenzo made his way to the keep to seek out the star man, hoping that he may have an idea where his cousin was. Though he knew the gates would be closed to the general populace, he also knew access and egress was allowed to those who lived inside, the artists. He was due to meet Leona at the ninth hour and she would come out of a smaller side door to meet him. Kenzo nursed a hope that perhaps he could sneak inside to find the old guy, or failing that, he would ask Leona to speak to him on his behalf. He sat on the bench outside the keep waiting for his would-be fiancé, looking down at the sprawl of Bastion below him. One by one the windows with no shutters glowed as the occupants lit their rooms against the oncoming night.

You could tell the ones who had a bit of money, they were the windows with white light, the kind given off by Narwl-fat candles that could be bought from the candle makers in the city. They would buy the fat from the Hunters on market day and form it into candles using dried weed wicks purchased from the Weavers. But they didn't last long and you obviously had to buy new ones on a regular basis.

The plankton orbs on the other hand, could be used over and over again. All you had to do was suspend the porous ball in a bucket of seawater for an hour and it would exude its dim green glow for most of the night. Most blocks had orbs and though the light was vastly inferior to the candles, once they had been bought from the Hunters who harvested them from the submerged rocks that supported the city walls, they lasted a lifetime, often passed down from generation to generation.

He watched the sky darken. He often sat up here, enjoying the evening breeze and staring down at the city. In a world with enormous encircling walls, any view at all was precious, and this one was one of the few available. The city became quieter as it settled down for the night, for though some men frequented the taverns and bordellos, very few of the populace ventured out at night, and gradually, silence fell over the Citadel.

A disturbance became apparent at the bottom of the slope and Kenzo recognized the figure of Braille and another soldier as they walked up the hill toward him. He looked at the insignia on Braille's upper arm and groaned. He wore a bright red armband, the insignia of guard supervisor and had a stupid grin on his face.

'Hello, mere mortal,' said Braille as he neared Kenzo, 'I've been looking for you everywhere. Get your shit together; you're wanted back at the barracks.'

'I'm on leave,' objected Kenzo, 'I still have a day left.'

'You must be blind as well as stupid, boy,' gloated his friend, as he thrust his arm forward in case Kenzo had missed the symbol of his new role, 'I am now your official superior, which means when I say shit, you crouch and strain, savvy?'

Kenzo groaned. Braille would be unbearable now. He was promoted often due to the other soldiers fear of him, but it never lasted long. He soon became bored and the rank was usually stripped from him after a few days, due to some fight or sexual indiscretion, but until that happened this time, Kenzo's life would be made hell by his friend.

'All leave is cancelled according to his holiness, the fat one,' continued Braille, 'there's some sort of emergency on and it seems we may be needed to crack a few skulls tomorrow.' The grin erupting on his face indicated the joy that thought gave him.

'Can't you just give me a few hours?' asked Kenzo, 'I'm meeting Leona in ten minutes.'

'No can do, matey,' said Braille. 'You are the last one and if you don't come back with me, I'll be in deeper shit than I normally am, and that's deep! Of course, I could always introduce you to Brenda,' he smiled sweetly.

Kenzo scowled.

'You wouldn't,' he said, his eyes narrowing in disbelief. Brenda was Braille's favourite cosh and had broken more heads in its career than Kenzo had eaten Narwl steak.

'Try me,' Braille grinned.

'Oh come on, Braille' pleaded Kenzo, 'you're supposed to be my friend.'

'What's the point?' asked, Braille, 'we both know you're not going to get any action with her until you're married.'

Kenzo was tempted to tell Braille about Amber and the strange boy, but decided against it.

'Ok,' he said eventually, 'give me a minute to leave a message at the gate for Leona.'

'One minute,' agreed Braille, 'or Mrs Cosh will be saying hello to Mr Skull.'

Kenzo threw Braille a false grin, which was returned sweetly by the giant oaf, and ran across the bridge to leave a message with one of the duty guards at the gate. When he returned, Kenzo was dismayed to see the other soldier doing press ups at Braille's feet.

'What's going on?' he asked.

Braille smiled his stupid smile at Kenzo.

'Got to keep up standards,' he said, 'lots of responsibility when you're an officer.'

'You're not an officer,' said Kenzo slowly, 'you're a squad leader, that's one coin a month more than a soldier, with temporary authority as required.'

'Whatever you say,' grinned Braille, 'but it's one coin more than you, shit for brains, now,' he tapped his cosh lightly on Kenzo's head, 'assume the position and give me ten.'

'What?'

'Failing to obey a command, soldier?' That's a further twenty,' boomed Braille.

'Braille,' shouted Kenzo, 'you can't do this.'

'Insubordination,' he tutted, raising his eyebrows in mock surprise, 'that's another thirty, boy.'

Kenzo, shook his head in disbelief and dropped to his knees, giving his friend one more stare of disgust before starting his press ups.

'That's right, mere mortal,' boomed Braille, 'shout em out, soldier! One, two, three...'

The quiet of the night was shattered by voices of the three soldiers echoing around the city walls as they counted the press ups, though soon only two could be heard as Braille was never quite sure after thirteen, so he sat back on the bench to have a smoke.

'It was hard work being an officer,' he thought.

All the way back to the barracks, Braille rubbed in the fact that he was now Kenzo's superior and expected to be treated as such.

'You're not an officer,' snarled Kenzo for what seemed like the hundredth time. The novelty had worn off and Braille was now getting on his nerves. Much more of this and perhaps he would take his chances and knock him out. He stared at the back of his friend's seemingly neck-less head joining the massively wide shoulders and thought of the money he had earned betting on the results of Braille's many bare-knuckled fights around the city.

'Perhaps not,' he thought, 'but if this continues, I'll certainly give him a piece of my mind!'

His brow frowned, realizing the absurdity of that last thought and just silently trotted behind this brute of a man. Loved by women, feared by men, there was no knowing what breath-taking feat of stupidity was looming in this giant's mind next. He was annoying, frustrating, a bloody pain, and the best friend anyone could ask for. Kenzo stopped suddenly, running in to Braille's stationary form.

'What?' he asked realizing his friend was waiting for an answer.

'I said,' repeated Braille, 'do you think us officers get an extra ale ration?'

Kenzo groaned again.

'For Saint's sake, Braille,' he shouted, 'you're not an officer.'

It was no good, Braille had already continued his trot down the cobbled street, extolling the virtues of the officer class to the other soldier forced to listen to him as he ran at his side. Kenzo followed them with a deep sigh. It was going to be a long night!

The following morning saw the full guard formed up for the first time in years. There were five hundred men in total, grouped into squads of

66

ten. Two paces in front of each squad was the squad commander and Kenzo was frustrated to see that he was in Braille's squad again. Standing up on the steps of the barracks facing the guard, were two men, Fatman and an old guy he hadn't seen before, dressed in a white gown, with white hair and … a long white beard.

'It can't be,' thought Kenzo to himself, 'I'm not that lucky!'

Fatman called them to attention.

'Okay, scum,' he shouted, 'pin back your lugholes and listen to what this man has to say. He is very important.' He stood to one side, allowing Pelosus to step forward to speak.

'Soldiers of the Citadel,' Pelosus started formally, 'I am here on the direct orders of the Governor and have assumed his authority over the guard. Over the next few weeks, there may be situations arising in Bastion that will need your, shall we say, particular skills.' Nervous laughter rippled around the ranks. 'For reasons that will soon become apparent,' he continued, 'food and indeed water is likely to become harder to find in Bastion and the council has decided to introduce rationing. It is highly likely that during this time, there may be disorder in the populace as some try to obtain more than their fair share. This will not be allowed to happen. *You* will not allow this to happen, so, at this very moment, scrolls are being put up around the city declaring martial law.'

'What's martial law?' whispered Kenzo.

'Permission to crack skulls,' whispered Braille over his shoulder.

'With immediate effect,' continued Pelosus, 'all leave is cancelled. The four quarters of the city will each have six squads, rotating in twelve-hour shifts. Three squads will work the quarter, while the other will be on standby in the barracks in case back up is required. It will be your responsibility to keep the peace using whatever means necessary.'

Kenzo looked at the back of Braille's head. He could almost feel the man grinning.

'During this time,' continued the old man 'you may be asked to do certain things that you may not be comfortable with. Some things may even horrify you. However, in recognition of this, there will be certain rewards.'

The soldiers were transfixed.

'First of all, there will be no rationing in the barracks. Three square meals a day will be provided and in addition, there will be one free ale skin provided, per week, per man.'

The soldiers voiced their approval at the unexpected bonus.

'Secondly, your wages will be doubled with immediate effect, the extra to be paid on the conclusion of the crisis.'

More nods of approval.

'Finally,' said Pelosus, 'each man will be allowed one hour a month with a Courtesan of their choice at no cost!'

This time a massive cheer resounded off the walls and the soldiers started talking loudly amongst themselves, not quite believing their luck.

'*Quiiieeeettt!*' shouted Fatman, but it was quite a while before the men gradually fell silent again.

'Alright,' said the white haired man, 'most of the squads will be stationed in the barracks and will take care of the city, two however, will be stationed in the keep, providing a rotating guard on the gates. What you do in the barracks, stays in the barracks but as the city council are situated in the keep, a certain level of decorum is required. No drinking, fighting or fornication will be allowed and for this reason, we ask for two squads to volunteer for this duty.'

In contrast to the noise of a minute ago, the silence was absolute. No one wanted the keep duty. Life as a soldier in Bastion was ninety-nine percent boredom and this was an opportunity not only to exercise their authority but to reap unheard of rewards as well. No, everyone wanted the city job, everybody that is, except one.

Kenzo's mind was racing. They were being offered a chance, not only to work in the keep but to be stationed there as well. It was the answer to his prayers, not only would he be nearer to the strange man who was last to see his cousin, but he would be living almost within Leona's home. He couldn't believe it.

'Braille!' he hissed.

The large squad commander had developed an unhealthy interest in Fatman's shoes, desperate not to make eye contact with the captain or the Stargazer.

'Braille,' hissed Kenzo again.

'What?' he whispered back over his shoulder.

'Volunteer for the keep,' said Kenzo

'Are you off your head?' answered Braille, 'not in a million years, my friend, now shut up and keep still.'

'We will take the keep, Sir,' shouted one squad leader from further down the line. Everyone looked unbelievingly at the man concerned. Peron was famous for leading a healthy life, not partaking of ale or women, as when he died he wanted to enter the kingdom of the Saint as pure as possible. His squad erupted in rage at his actions but Fatman quickly shouted them down.

'Well done,' shouted Pelosus, 'we need one more squad.'

'Braille,' whispered Kenzo frantically, 'please, do this for me.'

'Shut your mouth, private,' came the hissed response, 'I'm not missing this for anyone. It's going to be one big party for…'

He never finished his sentence as he flew forward, sprawling in the dirt of the parade ground, his arse stinging from the almighty kick from the sole of Kenzo's boot. He sat up spitting dirt, wondering what had happened.

'Well done that man!' shouted Fatman. 'We have our two squads.' Everyone else cheered loudly, not only because that they had avoided the graveyard shift but also at the irony that the biggest boozer, hardest fighter and most relentless womanizer of them all, was going to miss the once in a lifetime event that would have put his best skills to use.

Braille didn't hear the cheers; all he could do was stare up from the dirt, oblivious to the hilarity bouncing off the barracks walls. Hilarity that was not evident on the terrified face of Kenzo as he stared wide eyed back at the squad leader, not only horrified at the audacity of what he had just done, but aware that as Braille slowly drew his finger across his throat, that he was in deep, deep shit.

Kenzo stood on guard at the gates of the keep, ironically, in exactly the same place where he had given his note to one of the other soldiers two days earlier. He looked up at the sun to check the time. A few more minutes and his shift would be over and he could try to make contact with Leona.

His tongue played along his still swollen upper lip. It wasn't hurting any more, and the loosened tooth seemed to have settled down. If it wasn't for his broken nose and blackened eyes, no one would have guessed at the severe retribution administered by Braille in the barracks last night. It could have been worse and only the frantic promise of a free skin of ale every month for the rest of his life had persuaded Braille that it was not in his interests to beat Kenzo to a pulp. It wasn't the beating that annoyed Kenzo, it was a price worth paying, but the fact that he had seen Fatman lurking in the shadows enjoying the spectacle, made it a whole lot worse.

Still, what was done was done and he was actually inside the keep. His double shift would finish soon and he could start making enquiries. Ufox approached to relieve Kenzo.

'Time's up, Kenzo,' he said, 'Braille's finally allowing you a break.'

Kenzo grimaced back, fingering the new lump on the bridge of his nose.

'Not the first break,' he said sarcastically.

'Well, you can't say you didn't ask for it,' he said. 'What were you thinking?'

'I have my reasons,' said Kenzo.

'Would this reason live in the keep and have long black hair?' asked Ufox.

'She's part of it,' said Kenzo, 'but at the moment, I'm more worried about my cousin, Amber.'

'Amber?' answered Ufox, 'I know her, pretty thing, gonna be a stunner in a year or two. What about her?'

'Missing,' said Kenzo, 'and the only clue I have is right here in the Keep.'

'Have you reported it to Fatman?'

'I tried, but he only laughed in my face. Said we're in a middle of a crisis and he's got no time to waste resources on a missing kid.'

'It figures,' said Ufox, as the midnight bell rang out from the keep, 'anyway, time is up, go and get some sleep. Oh, and try to keep out of Braille's way. He may be your mate, but he's still sulking.'

'Thanks for the tip,' said Kenzo, and he went through the door into the keep.

There had been no interaction with the Artists since the soldiers had arrived and both groups kept out of each other's way. The Artists went about their normal business and there was a constant stream of traffic to and from the central well, as they drew water to store in whatever containers they could. The announcements about rationing had been made the previous day and though there had been initial unrest with the crowd, it was soon calmed down when the troublemakers were singled out for what Fatman called 'special' attention. Since then, the city had been fairly quiet. There was plenty of food in storage and though the sea had risen somewhat, it had still not reached the level it had been just before Moon-day. Soon, the feeling in the populace was that perhaps the council had been wrong and all this would soon blow over.

Kenzo walked toward the hall they had been allocated within the keep walls. He was exhausted and the beating had taken it out of him yesterday and he had just done a twenty four hour shift. He was almost asleep on his feet and pausing only to get a bowl of stew from the pot as he passed, he walked slowly to the bed space he had been given. Luckily, the snoring echoing around the room told Kenzo that Braille was fast asleep, so at least he didn't have to listen to him whingeing again. He sat on his bed, his back against the wall, planning what he would do next. First, he would eat, as he was starving. Next, he would have half an hour's sleep, that's all, half hour was all he needed, then he would find Leona. She could take him to the old man, and then he would find Amber. Yes, that's what he would do, but first…but first…

Braille sat up suddenly, wondering what had woken him. He looked across at the slumped figure of Kenzo on his cot, steam still rising from the stew on the floor where it had spilled from the dropped bowl. He rose from his own bed and walked across to Kenzo's comatose figure, reaching down to grab the boy by his shoulders.

'Braille, enough,' said a voice from the shadows, 'don't hurt him anymore!'

The giant man looked into the darkness briefly before laying the boy gently down on his cot and covering him with a blanket.

'Hurt him?' he said quietly. 'What do you take me for? He's my mate!'

70

Chapter 15

Pelosus stared at the silk handkerchief left by Petra for what seemed like the thousandth time that night. Since the declaration of martial law, he had been run off his feet and the only time he could give to it was during the night. He looked up, disturbed at the sound behind him and spun around to see the clerk with a cup of warm wine and a couple of Narwl biscuits.

'Ready for a break?' asked the clerk.

The Stargazer took a deep sigh and leant back in his chair.

'Go on then,' he said yawning, 'I'm getting nowhere here.' Despite his examinations, he was still none the wiser. There was certainly no message that he could see anywhere on the silk. He had held it up to the light, searched for hidden text amongst the embroidery and even applied certain chemicals known to reveal invisible ink, but all to no avail.

'That's pretty,' said the clerk sitting down, 'what is it?'

'Oh this,' he said, 'just a handkerchief.'

'It's beautiful,' said the clerk.

'Yes it is,' murmured Pelosus quietly.

'Where did you get it from?' asked the clerk, picking up the delicate silk to examine it closely.

'Oh, I bought it from the market,' Pelosus lied, 'those Brewers would sell their parents if they thought they could make a profit.' They both laughed. The avarice of the Brewers was famous throughout the city.

'Why are you working so late?' asked the clerk, 'you hardly sleep at all these days.'

'It's this business about the moon,' said Pelosus. 'It weighs heavily on my mind. I have to believe there is a way out of this and if there is, I have to find it as soon as possible.' They passed a few minutes in small talk as they enjoyed the break.

'Oh well,' said Pelosus, 'I have to get back to work.' They stood up and the clerk passed the handkerchief back to the Stargazer.

'Don't lose that,' he said, 'it may be valuable one day.'

'I doubt it,' said Pelosus. 'Do you think the Brewers would let something valuable go?'

'Perhaps not,' said the clerk, 'but that's not Brewer in origin, 'It's from the Watchers tower.'

Pelosus stopped and stared at him.

'What makes you think that?' he asked.

'The flowers around the edge,' replied the clerk, 'they are Poison-orange and that plant is only found in the Watchers-tower.'

'Of course,' said Pelosus, 'I should have recognized them.'

'Easy mistake to make,' said the clerk, 'the vine is all wrong. Poison orange doesn't have any thorns and certainly doesn't twist as much as that. Anyway, I'm going to bed. See you in the morning.'

71

'Good night,' said Pelosus watching the clerk retire. As soon as the door closed, he spread out the handkerchief quickly, studying the decoration in detail. Now it had been pointed out, the vine did indeed seem odd, twisting and turning back on itself, repeatedly. He picked up a thin piece of blank parchment and placing it over the silk, started to trace the route of the vine with a charcoal scribe. The line flowed and looped as he reproduced the embroidery with his pencil, and where it disappeared behind the flowers, he joined the line to the next probable resumption of the vine.

Pelosus grew excited as the loops and curls of the duplicate began to form identifiable letters on his parchment. Within minutes, he looked down at the document, eyes wide with astonishment at what he saw. Encircling the page, written in beautiful handwriting was a simple sentence, and though on the handkerchief it was not visible, on the parchment it was crystal clear.

'Beware the Brotherhood'

Pelosus read the script over and over again, wondering about its meeting.

'Brotherhood', he thought, 'I'm sure I've heard that name before. Despite wracking his brain, he could not recall where he had seen or heard the word recently and it niggled away at him for a long time. Despite this, Pelosus was beside himself with excitement. If nothing else, this message, alongside the beautiful fabric called silk, proved that Petra's information was of value. She had said that the handkerchief held a message and if she was right about that, she may just be right about the other place. This avenue of investigation was worth pursuing.

For the next hour or so, Pelosus pored over the message, wracking his brains about what the cryptic message might mean, but he was out of his depth. Eventually he retired to his cot exhausted. He had succeeded in finding the message but had no idea what it meant. As he dozed off, his mind returned to the word.

'Brotherhood,' he thought, 'Brotherhood.' Where have I…?'

Suddenly, he sat bolt upright and jumped out of bed. He ripped off the bed covers, and threw the mattress across the room, before tipping his cot up on its side.

There it was, very faint but still visible in one of the wooden slats of his bed. Using a fine pointed blade of some kind, one of his predecessors had inscribed six ominous words.

'Beware the Brotherhood of the Sark!'

Pelosus stared at the ancient message over and over again. What did it mean? Who were the Sark? Why did one of his predecessors go to so much trouble to leave this message, yet hide it so well? The questions came thick and fast and he had no answers. Slowly, he reassembled his bed and lay down exhausted. He needed more information and had an idea where he could get it. Before he fell into a restless sleep, he had decided on a course of action that could put his very life in danger.

Pelosus was waiting for the clerk when his breakfast arrived the following morning, causing a raised eyebrow of surprise from the clerk.

'Surely you haven't been up all night?'

'No, I managed a few hours' sleep,' he replied.

'Good, the way you're going you will die of exhaustion way before the food or water runs out.'

'Can you spare a few minutes?' asked Pelosus suddenly.

The clerk looked worriedly at him.

'Are you okay, Pelosus?' he asked.

'Yes, sit down,' he said, 'I wish to talk with you.'

The clerk did as instructed.

'Please, help yourself,' said Pelosus indicating the brew the clerk had brought in. He joined him at the table accepting his own cup of brew.

'How can I help?' asked the clerk.

Pelosus took a deep breath.

'It's like this,' he said and proceeded to tell the clerk everything he had learned so far. The clerk sat back, listening in astonishment and waiting in silence for Pelosus to finish.

'Well?' he said, when he had finished, 'what do you think?'

The clerk stared at him for a long time in silence.

'Why are you telling me this?' he asked eventually, 'if Petra warned you to keep silent on forfeit of your life, why entrust me with this information.'

'I need help,' admitted Pelosus, 'I can't do this on my own. Yes, I have knowledge of the heavens but in this case, I don't think it will help. I need someone who is familiar with the ways of the Citadel and the machinations of the ruling trades. I also need someone whose knowledge is a match for, and if possible, exceeds my own. You are that man. You are familiar with the council as you take the minutes of every meeting and have full access to the library. If anyone has access to more information than I, it is you.'

'What do you expect of me?'

'Just your help, to decipher the mystery and in return, I will ensure your safety is protected when this entire sorry episode comes to its climax. Hopefully, we can find this other place she speaks of and you and I will join the ruling elite in safety.'

'You do realise I should report this indiscretion to Petra,' pointed out the clerk, 'you could be executed. Why do you take this risk with me when I have known you only two years?'

'I am a good judge of character,' answered Pelosus, 'and know an honest man when I see one. After all, you wouldn't be in the position you are now without the complete trust of the council and even if you do report me, by my calculations, we will all be dead within two months anyway. Perhaps an assassin's blade between my ribs may be preferable to death from thirst.'

'I will not betray you,' said the clerk eventually, 'I will help. Perhaps together we can resolve this problem and aid everyone in the city, not just the trades.'

Pelosus nodded in agreement.

'I have to speak to the soldiers first thing, but come to my rooms at nine bells, we will start work then.'

The clerk nodded and stood to leave.

'Oh, by the way,' said Pelosus, 'I have worked with you for almost two years and I still don't know your name. I can't keep calling you clerk.'

The clerk smiled.

'No, if we are to work together, perhaps it would be better to get to know each other better. Please, call me by my first name.'

'Which is?' asked Pelosus.

'Petit,' said the clerk, 'my name is Petit.'

'Nice to meet you Petit,' laughed Pelosus as he shook his hand, 'it would seem our future is entwined.'

'It would seem so.' answered the clerk aloud, then silently to himself as he left the room, 'more than you could possibly imagine.'

Chapter 16

Amber woke up and opened her eyes. It was as dark with her eyes open as it had been with them shut and she lay shivering on the damp floor, not knowing how long she had been there. Her memory came back slowly, recalling the frantic struggle as her captor had carried her further into the subterranean depths beneath the Citadel. Slowly she got to her knees and crawled forward, one hand held out in front of her, immediately touching the clammy surface of a stone wall. She turned around and sat with her back to the wall, staring into the claustrophobic nothingness.

The blackness was overwhelming and she had no idea of space. She could be in a room a mile square or four foot square, there was no way of telling. Amber brought her knees up to her chin, embracing them with her arms and closed her eyes in fear. At least the darkness of her eyelids held no surprises. A few seconds later, or was it hours, she couldn't tell, a faint noise in the distance sprung her eyes open in fear. She scanned the area to her front, refocusing on something that had caught her eye. Two tiny pinpricks of light had been lit miles in the distance, solid, un-flickering white stars in the blackness of a starless sky. She focused on the lights intently; it was the only release from the suffocating black blanket.

A minute later, the lights went out, reigniting half a second later. She stared, not sure if she had imagined it or not. About thirty seconds later, it happened again, the lights going out and reigniting half a second later. Over and over the sequence repeated. White lights burning for thirty seconds, then they would go out, then half a second relight again, until eventually Amber could judge within half a second, when they would extinguish. She stared for an eternity, the flashing pinpricks of light consuming her very existence, over and over again. What was their meaning, was it some sort of signal? Their regular pattern reminded her of something, something familiar, and something comforting.

Then it came to her, yes, the colour was all wrong but with a stretch of her imagination, she could almost imagine they were eyes. That was it; the pattern of the lights reminded her of someone blinking in the darkness. Not two lights miles away, but a few feet away, blinking in the darkness. Blinking…eyes in the darkness…a few feet away!

Amber's scream resounded around the subterranean room and out into the maze of passages that riddled the bedrock beneath the city.

For the second time in a matter of hours, Amber emerged from unconsciousness, this time from the faint that had overcome her in her terror. She stayed curled in a foetal position on the floor, hardly breathing in her fear. She lay for an age, her back toward the eyes, afraid to turn, afraid even to imagine who or what was there. Eventually, the dampness of the floor forced her to move and with a rush, she sat up against the wall, staring at the place where the eyes were a few minutes ago. They were still there.

'Who are you?' she whispered coarsely, her dry throat making the words unintelligible. She cleared her throat. 'Who are you?' she asked again, this time much clearer. The pinpricks of white moved slightly in unison as the creature in the dark moved its head slightly to look directly at her.

'Who am I?' asked a deep strange voice, 'I wish I knew, Amber of the Red-door gang!'

Amber jumped slightly at the answer, but strangely comforted at the fact that this creature at least had a voice. At least it was human.

'You know my name?' she asked.

'Of course, you told me your name yourself, less than a day ago.'

'Crispin!' she gasped, 'is it you?'

'It is,' he said.

'I've been looking everywhere for you,' she said, 'but your voice, your eyes, they've changed. What's happened to you?'

'I don't know, Amber of the Red-door gang,' he said, 'I am weak and I am in pain. Carrying you here used the last of my strength, but you are safe now, the danger has passed.'

'What danger?'

'The Watchers, they were following you in the tunnels. They had set a trap for me near the sewer, but you were walking into it. I couldn't let that happen, so I grabbed you and brought you here.'

'But why didn't you say something? Why did you hold my mouth shut?'

'I could not risk you calling out,' said the strange voice, 'there are Watchers everywhere.'

'What happened to my head?' she asked feeling the lump once again.

'I dropped you,' said Crispin, 'my strength has gone.'

She watched the pinpricks extinguish, this time for several seconds and she realized he had shut his eyes.

'Are you all right, Crispin?' she asked eventually.

The lights lit up again.

'In truth?' he said weakly, 'no, Amber of the Red-door gang, I am not alright. I think I am dying.'

This was too much for Amber. She was holed up in a black hole heaven knows how far underground with a dying boy. All the fun and adventure had fled long ago. This was serious and she needed help. She crawled across the room to the invisible boy.

'Crispin,' she said, 'you need help; tell me how to get out of here and I'll bring my cousin. He will know what to do.'

There was silence for a few moments.

'It's too dangerous,' said the voice eventually.

'We have no choice, Crispin and now I know what I am up against, I will be more careful. I can look after myself.'

'You are the only person ever to offer me kindness, Amber of the Red-door gang,' he said, 'it is too late for me. I don't want you to get hurt.'

'Look,' snapped Amber, 'first of all, stop saying Red-door gang. My name is just Amber and I'm doing this whether you like it or not, now if you know the way out of here, just tell me, otherwise I could take twice as long.'

'Okay,' he said eventually, 'the entrance lies to your right. I can't give you directions because I don't know where we are myself. Take this,' he added.

Amber felt something hit her on the foot and felt around with her hands until she found the object Crispin had thrown. She picked it up, recognizing her pocketknife.

'Thanks,' she said, 'how did you get it?'

'I took it off you when you were asleep. Couldn't risk you waking up and doing something stupid.'

'Okay,' said Amber, 'try to get some sleep. I will be back as soon as I can, and this time with help, don't go anywhere.'

'I am going nowhere,' he said.

'Okay, where did you say the doorway was?'

'To your right.'

'How do you know which way I am facing?'

'I can see you.'

'In this darkness?'

'Darkness?' he said. 'To me it is lighter than the brightest day. Good luck, Amber of the Red-door gang, be safe.'

Amber shuddered involuntarily but didn't answer as she crawled out of the side room and into the unfamiliar tunnel.

Chapter 17

Kenzo woke up to the sight of Braille's stupid grin looking down at him.

'Wake up, sweet-cheeks,' boomed Braille.

'How long have I been sleeping?' asked Kenzo, yawning.

'Eight Hours,' grinned Braille. 'Snoring like Fatman after a skin of ale. Would have slept longer too if I let you, but you've got a visitor.'

'A visitor? Who?'

'Oh, no one special, about seventeen, long black hair, pretty face. Look, if you're not interested, can me and the boys have a crack coz...'

Before he could finish, Kenzo had jumped up and grabbed his tunic.

'Leona,' he shouted and ran out of the block.

'Guess you are interested after all,' said Braille quietly

'Four hours!' he shouted. 'Make sure you're back for your shift or I'll nail your arse to that bloody bell.'

'I'll be back!' shouted Kenzo over his shoulder.

Kenzo ran out of the room and across the courtyard to where Leona was sitting on the edge of the well. He stumbled to a halt just before her.

'Oh Kenzo,' she said, 'what happened to you?'

Kenzo felt his nose gingerly.

'Oh, just a barracks room brawl,' he lied, 'no damage done, how are you?'

'Me? Oh I'm fine, though father is not happy that the guards are stationed in the keep.'

'Not happy that I'm in the keep, more likely.'

'Well, that too,' she chuckled. 'Anyway, I made some enquiries, and found out that your squad was here. Isn't that lucky?'

'Lucky, yes,' said Kenzo, running his tongue over his swollen lip. 'Look, I've got four hours off, do you want to do something?'

'Like what?'

'I don't know; go for a walk or something.'

'Yes, sounds nice, but before we do, can you do something for me?'

'Anything!'

'Can you take a wash? I'm sorry Kenzo but you stink.'

'Wash? Yes of course, stay there,' he said and ran back to the billet, emerging fifteen minutes later, shaved and washed, his hair tied back and glistening in the sun.

'Ready,' he said. 'Where do you want to go?'

'I know,' she said, 'let's go down to the causeways, there's something going on down there.'

'Ok,' he replied, 'but there's something I want to ask you.'

'Let's go,' she smiled and took his arm. 'We can talk as we go.'

They left the keep and walked down through the city to the nearest gate. A crowd had gathered on the causeway to the Hunters-tower watching with interest what was going on below.

'What's happening?' asked Kenzo to no one in particular.

'The Hunters are exploring the city under the water,' someone replied, 'they are bringing up all sorts of things.'

Sure enough, a row of Hunters dressed only in their loin cloths were sitting along the edge watching their colleagues below. For those used to hunting Narwl, a simple descent to explore the sunken buildings was easy as they could stay down for several minutes at a time. Kenzo recognized one of the Hunters and approached him to see if he could find out more.

'Hi there,' he said casually. The Hunter acknowledged his greeting. 'I'm Kenzo,' he continued, 'we've met before, I believe.'

The Hunter frowned.

'Don't think so,' he said.

'You were a bit worse for wear. I think it was a few moons ago, my friend arrested you for fighting with the Bakers.'

'Ah yes, I remember,' said the Hunter, 'you're the one who let me go.'

'That's right,' said Kenzo, 'no harm done as I recall.' Kenzo had a policy of fairness and was often repaid with trust in this city of suspicion. They both turned their attention back to the divers in the water.

'Been down yet?' asked Kenzo casually.

'Yup, quite amazing really,' he said, 'it's a city just like that inside the Citadel. Must have been heavily populated too, there are hundreds of houses down there.'

'Looking for anything special?' asked Leona, 'I heard a rumour that fish people live there.'

The Hunter laughed.

'No,' he said, 'we are the nearest thing to fish people you'll find in these waters,' he paused, 'but between me and you, there is treasure down there.'

'Treasure?' asked Leona, fascinated, 'what have you found?'

'All sorts of things,' he said, 'but one in particular is priceless.'

'What is it?' she asked excitedly.

'Hang on,' he said 'we're about to haul it up.'

For the next ten minutes, Kenzo and Leona waited patiently as the Hunters became preoccupied with what was happening below the waterline. Divers changed places and they overheard snippets of the conversations between the Hunters as they went about their task. There was great excitement as a Hunter surfaced.

'Get ready,' he called, 'we've got it loose and it will be up any second now.'

The crowd leaned over the wall, impatient to see what they had found. Suddenly, something shot out of the water like a leaping Narwl, splashing back down to lie floating on the surface.

'Wood?' someone asked.

Kenzo agreed, but not just any wood, even with the film of algae over its surface they could see it was Mahogany and therefore worth a fortune. The swimming Hunters guided the wood to the bridge and their colleagues soon pulled it up onto the stones. The crowd gathered around to see the valuable artefact.

'What is it?' someone asked.

'I think it's a sign,' said one of the Hunters.

'Surely not,' said another, 'a sign made from solid Mahogany, what a waste.'

'What does it say?' asked Leona leaning forward for a better view.

'I can't see,' said Kenzo, 'hang on, they're cleaning it up.' He watched fascinated as the algae was scraped off by the Hunters to reveal the wood underneath. Leona's excitement waned as she watched Kenzo's face change. The excited smile had gone, replaced with a frown as the words were revealed.

'Kenzo, what's the matter?' she asked.

'That sign,' he said, 'I recognize the words. I've heard them recently.' All of a sudden, his eyes opened wide as his brain recalled the memory. 'Amber!' he whispered.

'What, Kenzo you're frightening me, what's the matter?'

'Those words carved on the wood,' he said, 'they're the last words Amber said to me before she disappeared. Come on, we have to go. I've wasted too much time already.'

'What do you mean?' she asked, the concern clear on her face. 'Kenzo, where are we going?'

'We've got to find an old man,' he said, 'and I've not got much time.'

'Okay,' she said and looked back to see what had caused this sudden change of mood in the young man.

'The Brotherhood of the Sark,' she read slowly, 'what does it mean?'

'Maybe nothing,' he said, 'maybe everything. Come on.' He took her hand and led her back up to the keep. He needed to find the white haired man.

On the way back, Kenzo told Leona everything he knew.

'I have to find this man,' said Kenzo, 'do you know him?'

'But why?' she asked, 'all you know is that she talked to him. What do you think he can tell you?'

'I don't know,' he said, 'all I know is he is the last person to speak to her that I know of. Perhaps she told him where she was going. Please, Leona, you have to help me, I know he lives in the keep; you must know him.'

'You don't know what you ask, Kenzo,' she said nervously, 'the man you seek has the ear of the council and they prohibit us giving any information about them to anybody. If they found out I took you to one of their own, they would throw me and my family out of the keep.'

Kenzo looked at her, realizing that an exiled artist would not last long in the city without the support of their trade.

'That won't happen,' he said, 'I won't let it. I don't want to be taken to his chambers, I just want to ask him some questions and I can do that in the open, all I need is his permission to approach. Please, Leona,' he said sensing her hesitation, 'I have nowhere else to turn.'

'I doubt he will talk with you,' she said, 'but he will talk with me. I will ask your questions.'

'Talk to you,' he said, 'but how?'

'The man you seek is called Pelosus, he is the Stargazer and I...' she looked down in embarrassment.

'What,' asked Kenzo lifting her chin, 'Leona, what is it?'

'I clean his rooms,' she said suddenly.

'You clean his rooms,' he said blankly.

'Yes, I know it's not very glamorous, Kenzo,' she said hurriedly, 'but we all have to live and I have my father to support and I...'

'You are a cleaner!'

'I can walk the tightrope,' she said, 'but I get afraid and one day...'

'Leona,' he said over her nervous chatter.

'I would have told you before, but I thought if you knew I was a cleaner you may not like me anymore and ...'

'Leona,' he said more forcibly, 'stop talking for a moment.'

She fell quiet and looked at the floor. Kenzo lifted her chin again and kissed her gently on the lips.

'I would love you if you were the most destitute beggar in Bastion,' he said, 'and anyway, I have a feeling that when I find Amber, she will know where to find this boy and when I find him, we will be rich beyond our wildest dreams. In fact, we will be able to hire our own cleaner.'

'You don't mind?' she asked nervously.

'Of course I don't mind, you silly thing.'

'Oh, Kenzo,' she sighed, 'I'm so relieved, I knew it was only a matter of time until you found out and I have been trying to think of a way of telling you. The quicker we can marry the better as far as I am concerned.'

'Artist, gymnast, cleaner, it makes no difference to me, Leona,' he said, 'it's you I have fallen in love with, not your occupation.'

She held him tightly in silence.

81

'Though after we are married,' he continued after some thought, 'I don't suppose you could get one of those sexy gymnast outfits could you?' The gentle kick he received in the ankle was worth it to see her smile again. 'Anyway,' he said holding her to his chest and looking over her head into the distance, 'first of all, we have to find Amber and to do that we need to speak to your Stargazer friend.'

'Leave it to me,' she murmured, 'I'll do it tonight.'

'Beware the Brotherhood,' quoted Pelosus, 'what does it mean?' Pelosus and the clerk had spent hours in the archives searching for the meaning to the phrase Pelosus had discovered on the handkerchief without success. 'I give up,' said Pelosus sitting back and rubbing his eyes, 'absolutely nothing here gives any indication that there may be another place outside of Bastion. It just seems to be a random religious sentence.'

'Yet it must mean something,' said the clerk, 'why hide it otherwise?'

'I don't know,' said Pelosus, 'perhaps we've missed something on the silk.'

'Could have, I suppose, we are getting nowhere here, let's have another look at the handkerchief.'

They both stood up and left the archives to go to Pelosus's chambers at the top of the keep but as they approached, Pelosus stopped short, his keys in his hand.

'What's the matter?' asked the clerk.

'The door is open,' said Pelosus, 'and I know I locked it.'

'Are you sure?'

'In the circumstances,' he said, 'I made doubly sure.'

'Do you think there is anyone in there?'

'There's only one way to find out,' said Pelosus and pushed the door wide open with his foot.

Leona spun around at the sound of the door crashing open and stared at the Stargazer and the clerk standing in the middle of the room.

'Leona!' shouted Pelosus, 'what are you doing here?'

'I'm sorry, Sir,' she said, 'I did knock but there wasn't any answer so I used my keys, I was going to leave you a note.'

'A note?' he asked, 'why would you leave me a note? What is so important that you came up here to ask me a question at this hour?'

She looked at him and the clerk.

'Come on, girl,' said Pelosus, 'spit it out.'

'Well, it's my fiancé, Sir,' she said, 'his cousin is missing and he thinks you may be able to help him find her.'

'Me, find a missing girl,' he said, 'how in heaven can I help to find a missing girl?'

'It would seem that you were talking to her a few days ago' she said, 'down at the causeway, the day after Moon-day. Amber, her name was.'

'Amber,' he said. 'No I don't recall an Amber, oh, hang on, there was that urchin from the market, she didn't say her name but a very astute young lady as I recall. Would that be her?'

'That's her,' said Leona, 'she went missing straight after and Kenzo, that's my boyfriend, hoped you may know where she went.'

'No, I'm sorry, Leona,' he said, 'I have no idea where she may have gone. She didn't say anything. Tell your boyfriend I can't help him, though if I hear anything I will let you know. Now, if you don't mind, we have work to do.'

'Thank you, Sir,' she said, 'and I'm sorry for the intrusion.'

'Think nothing of it,' he said, 'now if you don't mind….' he stood to one side opening the way to the door, his meaning plain.

'Good night, Sirs,' said Leona, and brushed passed the two men to hurry out.

Pelosus turned to find a candle, pulling up short as he heard the cleaner's voice again.

'One more thing, Sir,' she said from the doorway.

'What is it Leona?' he said over his shoulder, 'can't you see we are extremely busy?'

'Sorry,' she said, 'I just wondered, do the words, "Brotherhood of the Sark," mean anything to you?'

Kenzo leaned against the gate and pulled the collar of his tunic up around the neck in an attempt to keep out the night chill. He had been here for an hour and would be for the next eleven with only an hour's break for food. At least he felt a lot better than he had last night; it seemed that Braille had forgiven him, to an extent.

He heard a noise from the other side of the gate. It wasn't guarded on that side, people wanted to get in, not out! The gate opened and he turned to see what lunatic wanted to leave the safety of the keep at this hour. The last person he expected was Fatman. He sprang to attention.

'Well, well, well,' said Fatman, 'what have you been up to now, gutter trash?'

'Sorry, Sir?' queried Kenzo.

'You and trouble,' said Fatman, 'seem to be best of friends these days.'

'Sorry, Sir, I don't understand,' said Kenzo.

Fatman pushed his face tight against Kenzo's face, his stinking breath forcing Kenzo back slightly.

'Look, shit head,' snarled Fatman, 'it pisses me off when I am woken at this time of night with orders to come and get you. It pisses me off even more when I am told that I have to leave my warm bed and an even warmer

83

woman to come and get you, personally.' His voice was rising in decibels as he forced his face into Kenzo's, the corresponding volume of spittle rising accordingly.

'And when I ask the reason why,' he continued, 'and am told it is none of my business and you are not to be punished, well, I'm about as pissed off as a man can get in one lifetime. Now do you understand?' he screamed, the spittle soaking Kenzo's face.

'I understand you are pissed off, Sir,' ventured Kenzo.

'That's right, boy,' he hissed, 'in the world of the pissed off, I am the pissed off king and you can bet your pretty arse that I am going to make you pay for this.'

'For what, Sir?' asked Kenzo, 'I don't know what it is that I am supposed to have done?'

'Done?' he answered sarcastically, 'you haven't done anything, your holy presence is required by some shit sucker in the council chambers, and you have to be there five minutes ago. Now shift your lazy arse back to barracks, someone is waiting for you there. You haven't heard the last of this.'

'Yes, Sir,' shouted Kenzo, and ducked through the door, passing the relief guard on the other side.

'Sorry Ufox,' he said, 'this has got nothing to do with me.'

'Whatever,' Ufox answered with an air of resignation, 'we're getting used to it now.'

'Sorry,' grinned Kenzo again, 'I'll pay you back.'

'That's right,' said Ufox returning the false smile, 'you will.'

Kenzo ran across the courtyard to the barracks where he saw a shadow in the gloom waiting for him.

'Kenzo,' said Leona, 'is that you?'

'Leona!' he replied, 'what's going on? I am supposed to meet someone here. Apparently I am wanted by the council.'

'It's me you're supposed to meet, silly,' she said, 'and it's not the council that wants you, it's the Stargazer.'

Kenzo's eyes widened.

'You spoke to him,' he said, 'did you ask him about Amber?'

'I said I would, didn't I?' she said with a smug smile.

'Well,' he said impatiently, 'what did he say, does he know where Amber is?'

'I don't think so,' she said. 'He admitted to talking to her but was adamant she didn't say where she was going.'

Kenzo's face dropped.

'If he doesn't know, then I don't know where else to look.'

'Anyway,' she said pulling his arm, 'come on, I've got to take you back to speak to him, and we're already late.'

'Hang on,' he said, holding back, 'if he doesn't know anything about Amber, why does he want to speak to me?'

'I don't know,' said Leona, 'but when I mentioned the Brotherhood of the Sark, he suddenly seemed very interested. I think he wants to ask you about them.'

'All I know about them is that Amber mentioned their name, whoever they are, and that the Hunters found a sign in the submerged city with their name on it, that's it!'

'Well, it seems that he thinks you may know more and wants to speak to you. Come on, we'd better not keep him waiting.' Leona led him across the open space and toward the restricted area of the keep reserved for the council and their servants. They climbed the winding staircase to the top floor and knocked on the ornate door.

'Come in,' came a voice and Leona led Kenzo through into the Stargazer's chambers. Pelosus and the clerk were sat at a round table facing the door, two empty chairs faced them and the clerk invited them to sit. They sat down and the clerk poured them a glass of wine each.

'You are Kenzo, I understand,' started Pelosus.

'I am, Sir,' answered the soldier.

'And you have been seeking information about your cousin?'

'Yes, Sir, she has been missing for a couple of days.'

'People often go missing in Bastion, Kenzo,' he said, 'why do you think I can help you with this one?'

'Amber is very street wise, Sir,' he answered, 'she knows every nook and cranny of the city, and is friends with every rogue, in every back street. Of all people, Amber is a true child of Bastion and knows her way around. She would not put herself in a situation she could not handle. She is a born survivor.'

'Quite,' said Pelosus, 'but you yourself admitted that she bothers with rogues, perhaps she went too far and suffered the consequences.'

'Perhaps so, Sir, but I know Amber and she can look after herself. I believe she is still alive.'

They all sat quiet for a moment.

'This is all very well,' said Pelosus, 'but it doesn't change the fact that I don't know where she is. I will of course make enquiries and rest assured I will let you know if I find anything, but until then, I can't help you, however, there is a small matter in which you can help me. It would seem that you may have certain information about a little known Brotherhood within the city and I would like you to furnish me with what you know.'

'I know very little, Sir,' said Kenzo dejected, 'it's just what my cousin said a few days ago. If I was not so hung over, she may be here now.'

'What exactly did she say?' asked the clerk.

'Nothing really, she was just keen to know what I knew about something called the Brotherhood.'

'Which is?'

'Nothing.'

'Yet it would seem that she knows something otherwise she wouldn't have asked.'

'It would seem that way,' he answered.

'Is there anything else, Kenzo?' asked Pelosus, 'anything at all that you are aware of that may shed light on this Sark business.'

Kenzo thought furiously, he couldn't quite put his finger on it, but there was a link here, something that he needed to cling on to. The Brotherhood of the Sark seemed to be the common thread that linked them all and while the Stargazer thought there was more information to be had, the longer Amber stayed in the equation. He decided to take a risk.

'There is one more thing,' he said, 'I don't know if it will help, but I am aware that she was seeking a boy and he has links with this Brotherhood.'

'What boy?'

'I don't know, but I am aware he has a deformity and is in the city somewhere.'

'And how do you know this?'

'She told me,' he lied, careful not to reveal his own interests in the boy or the conversation he had had with the Watcher. Again, there was silence while everyone digested the information.

Eventually Pelosus spoke again.

'Look, Kenzo,' he said, 'there is much we don't understand here, but it would seem that we both seek similar things. This boy has links with the Brotherhood of the Sark and it is entirely feasible that your cousin has found him. Therefore, it is in all our interests to find them both, so I have a proposition for you. You will join us in the search for the boy and your cousin. We will use the substantial resources available to us to seek the possible whereabouts of both, while you will be our foot soldiers on the ground. We would have, shall we say, some difficulty navigating the city without arousing suspicion, whilst you two have been brought up in Bastion and can mingle unnoticed with the lowest of the low. No offence intended, of course.'

'None taken,' said Kenzo.

'Some taken,' murmured Leona under her breath.

'What about my duties?' asked Kenzo, kicking her leg under the table.

'Leave that to me,' said Pelosus. 'You will be given indefinite leave with immediate effect. This will take precedence over all other tasks and you will deviate for no one and report directly to me. Is that understood?'

'Fine with me,' said Kenzo, 'where do you want me to start?'

'Get back out into the streets and start asking questions,' said Pelosus. 'Leave no stone unturned. Use your contacts. Be nice, bribe them if necessary, but worm your way in to the underclass of the city. Someone, somewhere, must know where they are.'

'And you?' asked Kenzo.

'While you explore the underbelly of the population, we will arrange the breaking of heads. This city is not very big and between us, I reckon we should have an answer before nightfall tomorrow. Are we agreed?'

'Agreed!' said Kenzo. At last, something positive was being done and with the weight of the council behind him, it was only a matter of time before he found Amber.

'One more thing,' said Petit, 'let's keep the Brotherhood of the Sark to ourselves for the moment. All we need to share is that we seek a missing boy and a girl. No need to stir up a hornet's nest.'

Kenzo agreed.

'When do we start?' he asked.

'No time like the present,' said Pelosus, 'you have until morning before I mobilize the guard. Anything else?'

'Nope,' said Kenzo, 'thank you.'

'Don't thank me,' said Pelosus, 'just bring me this boy.'

Kenzo and Leona left the chambers and made their way to the keep gates.

'Hadn't you better tell your father?' asked Kenzo as they ran across the courtyard.

'Forget him,' answered Leona, 'he's blind drunk and won't even notice I have gone until he wakes tomorrow midday when his belly needs filling. By then, we may well be back, let's worry about him then.'

'Okay,' said Kenzo, and they made their way out of the gates and across the bridge to the city, Kenzo throwing Ufox an apologetic smile as he passed.

'Enjoy yourselves,' shouted Ufox sarcastically to their departing backs, 'don't worry about me, I'll be right here if you need me.'

The couple glanced guiltily at each other and disappeared into the back streets of Bastion, leaving the derisive taunts far behind.

For the rest of the night and most of the next day, they sought out all the contacts that Kenzo had made throughout his short career, asking questions as to whether anyone had seen Amber. Once again he was unsuccessful so he turned his attention to the children. Kenzo spotted the sly looking boy who had helped him a few days earlier and approached him again.

'Are you sure you don't know anywhere she could have gone?' he asked, 'or anywhere she may have been recently. Please think, perhaps this will help.' He held out a small coin in his hand, but closed it quickly when Flip tried to grab it. 'Information first,' said Kenzo.

'Look, all I know is the night before was Moon-night, and she must have had a good hiding place, coz she hung a disgusting flag on our shop and when I catch her I'm gonna break her nose.'

Kenzo smiled gently. Good old Amber, she hadn't forgotten everything they had learned all those years ago. Between them, they had ruled Bastion on Moon-night, popping up from all sorts of hiding places.

'That's it,' he said suddenly, 'why didn't I think of it before? Here,' he said, giving the coin to Flip, 'you've been a great help.'

Flip frowned, not quite sure what he had done, but pleased he had got a coin out of it.

'Come on,' said Kenzo pulling Leona's hand, 'I think I know where she is,' and dragged her down the road. Ten minutes later, the young soldier and his girlfriend stood at the bottom of a disused sewer pit, looking at the open end of the pipe used a few days earlier by Amber and Crispin.

'I should have known,' said Kenzo. 'She went down there a few years ago and got lost. Luckily I found her, but I wouldn't have thought she would go there again.'

'It stinks,' said Leona.

'Don't worry,' he said. 'It's not used anymore; the smell is from live sewers further down.'

'Still stinks,' she said quietly.

'Come on,' said Kenzo crouching to enter the large pipe, 'let's go.'

'You have got to be joking,' she said. 'Surely, you don't intend going through there.'

'We have to,' he said, 'we're running out of time.' He stood up. 'Leona, what's the matter?' he asked seeing her shaking.

'I'm sorry, Kenzo,' she said, 'it's just that I'm afraid of small spaces, I don't know why, but they terrify me, I can't go down there. Please, don't make me.'

'Hey,' he said embracing her, 'no problem. You go back to the keep, I'll do this alone.'

'Are you sure?' she asked.

'Positive.'

'Thank you,' she said, 'I'll do that but promise me you'll be careful.'

'Careful is my middle name,' he replied, 'now go, and please hurry.' He lifted her out of the sewer pit and watched as she dragged the grille back over the shaft entrance.

'Be careful,' she said again and blew him a kiss before disappearing from view.

Kenzo wasted no more time and entered the sewer system to find his cousin.

Amber lay curled on the floor in a dark tunnel totally lost. Her knees hurt from falling over more than once and she was soaked through after falling into a shallow pool in the middle of the floor, losing her knife in the process. Eventually, weak from exhaustion and hunger she had sat down to rest. The Catacombs under the city were a maze of tunnels; intertwined at all levels. She closed her eyes for a few moments, just to rest them from the constant strain of trying to see in the dark but before she knew it, Amber had fallen into a deep sleep.

Not far away, Crispin was entering his own trance like state, though nothing like that of Amber's. His back was aching more than ever and his clothes were irritating his skin. Using what strength he had left, he ripped off his clothing and threw them into the darkness, welcoming the relief the cool damp air brought to his burning skin.

Still it itched and burned and Crispin clawed frantically at his own flesh, tearing the skin with his uncut nails in a vain effort to gain relief. He started salivating, spitting out copious strings of saliva and mucus. His neck ached and muscles below his jaw started to contract and expand in involuntary spasms, as he produced more and more secretions from glands at the back of his mouth. Repeatedly, he spat out the gelatinous substance, struggling to keep up with this unwelcome production from within his own body.

Gradually, he realized that where it fell on his skin, the relief was instant. He raised his hands to his mouth in the darkness, pulling out length after length of tacky excretions and pulled them down to stick to his burning skin. The quicker he pulled, the more he produced and his hands worked frantically as he stretched it out over his body, cooling the fiery skin and easing the pain with its anaesthetic properties. Where some of the more violently ejected secretions had hit the wall or ceiling, it stuck instantly and swelled in structure, absorbing the moisture from the damp air of the subterranean room. Soon huge sheets of gelatinous spittle hung from all the walls and ceiling and though the strands were relieving, Crispin finally realized the implications if he became stuck. He struggled frantically to escape its cloying grip, only succeeding in entangling himself even more in its all-enveloping embrace. Soon his body was shrouded with the strange wrappings and though his hands fell limp as he descended into unconsciousness, his mouth kept ejecting the sticky web like substance out onto the floor. His body jerked and convulsed within the cocoon and the covering grew in thickness as layer stuck to layer, building a thick wall encompassing his human flesh.

Eventually the small room was silent as the thrashing stopped. The floor was covered in a thick layer and in places; it hung from the walls as if made by thousands of spiders over hundreds of years.

The stillness of the room was disturbed by the slightest of movement coming from the otherwise still cocoon hanging from the walls. The rhythmic rise and fall betrayed the moving chest of the entrapped boy, as his lungs struggled vainly to draw in oxygen, but eventually they gave up the effort, but just before they stopped completely, a further miniscule flicker indicated the last spark of life.

The one eyelid still visible fluttered open as his brain struggled to comprehend the enormity of the situation. Despite using the very last vestiges of will and strength, the scream of terror that emanated from the boy's throat was weak to the point of inaudibility, and as the eyelid slowly closed for the last time, the room fell to an all-encompassing silence.

The luminescence of the cocoon slowly died as if accompanying the boy on his final journey, and gradually, the sticky blanket thickened and hardened in the darkness until the room was totally filled with the rock hard excretion that entombed Crispin's body.

The lower Catacombs returned to the state of stillness that it had enjoyed for hundreds of years, but if it had listened carefully, every couple of minutes or so, it may have picked up the faintest of sounds as the entombed boy's heart still beat, slowly, faintly, rhythmically, with purpose and intent!

Chapter 18

Amber licked her cracked lips with her swollen tongue, realizing she was thirsty and was surprised to feel cool water dabbed gently onto her mouth. Her tongue automatically sought out more of the liquid as she struggled to come around and she heard a faint unfamiliar female voice in the distance.

'Not too much,' said the voice, 'a little bit at a time.'

Suddenly her eyes flew open, and she gasped in pain at the sunlight streaming through the open shutters. She turned her head into the soft pillow to avoid the pain.

'It's okay,' said the female quickly, 'you're safe now, Amber, take your time.'

Amber opened her eyes slowly allowing them to become accustomed to the light.

'Where am I?' she asked.

'You're in the keep,' said the female voice, 'Kenzo brought you; he found you in the tunnels.'

'Tunnels,' said Amber slowly, yes there was something about the tunnels, something important. She turned onto her back and looked into the face of a pretty young woman.

'Hello, Amber,' said the woman 'my name is Leona and I've been looking after you for the past few days.'

'Can I have a drink?' asked Amber hoarsely.

'Of course you can,' she said and poured a beaker of water from a jug before placing it on the bedside table. She helped the girl up to a sitting position and plumped the cushions behind her back. She passed Amber the drink and waited patiently as the girl drank the cool water quickly before asking for another. When she had drunk the second, Amber looked around the unfamiliar room. It was prettily decorated and it obviously belonged to a female.

'Is this room yours?' she asked.

'Yes,' smiled Leona. 'It's not much, but it's clean and I thought you would be better off here than in those male dominated rooms you share with Kenzo and your uncle.'

'It's pretty,' said Amber forcing a smile. 'How long have I been here?'

'Two days and one night,' answered Leona. 'We thought you were dead when Kenzo brought you out and you've been asleep ever since. Oh look at me, I am completely forgetting my manners, you must be starving. Do you want something to eat?'

Amber nodded and watched Leona ladle a bowl of soup from a pot on the hearth.

'It's only Narwl broth,' she said returning to the bed, 'but it is quite nice. I made it myself.' She spooned some of the juice gently between Amber's swollen lips and as the young girl's taste buds came back to life, she leaned forward in anticipation.

'Slowly,' said Leona. 'You haven't eaten for heaven knows how long and your stomach may not take it. We wouldn't want you to be sick now, would we?'

'Where's Kenzo?' asked Amber.

'He had to go and see someone. He won't be long.'

Amber suddenly grabbed Leona's wrist, stopping the next broth laden spoon from reaching her mouth.

'What about Crispin?' she asked, her eyes open wide with fear.

Leona's brow furrowed.

'Crispin?' she said, 'I'm sorry, I don't understand.'

'Crispin, the boy in the tunnels with me, where is he?'

'Oh Amber,' said Leona with concern, 'Kenzo only brought you out. There was no one else.'

'But he is there,' cried Amber, 'he is hurt and I promised I would bring help, we have to go back.' She tried to get out of bed, but was held down by Leona.

'Amber!' she said, 'Amber wait, listen to me.'

Amber stopped struggling for a second, looking earnestly into Leona's eyes.

'When Kenzo found you,' she said, 'you were unconscious in a corridor that led away from a sea-filled chamber.'

'Yes,' said Amber, 'that's where Crispin is, in a side room down that tunnel. We have to go and help him.'

'Amber,' said Leona, 'we can't, the tunnels are full of seawater.'

'What do you mean full of water? I walked through it, there was no water.'

'The sea levels have risen again, Amber,' said Leona, 'it would seem that you were only able to walk through them because the sea was low at the time. I don't know how, but now it has risen again, and they have filled with water. When Kenzo found you, it was only feet away from where you lay. A few hours later, and you would have been trapped down there, or worse.'

'But, Crispin,' interrupted Amber.

'There's nothing we can do for him,' said Leona quietly, 'it is too late. If he is still there, then …' She left the sentence unfinished as Amber burst into tears, holding her tightly as she sobbed into her shoulder.

'Oh, Amber,' said Leona, 'I am so, so sorry'

Back in the keep, Pelosus and the clerk sat quietly listening to Kenzo as he told them about Amber.

'So, you found your cousin,' said the clerk, 'what about the boy?'

'There was no sign of the boy,' said Kenzo, 'she was unconscious in one of the sewers. It would seem she had just got lost on one of her stupid adventures.' He didn't expand on the details of the flooded tunnels as he still hoped that he could find the boy's body when the waters next receded. There was still the reward to claim after all and De-gill had said, dead or alive.

'Okay,' said Pelosus, 'I'm glad your cousin is safe. As soon as she is well enough, bring her to us. I would like to meet her, she sounds like a colourful character. Thank you, Kenzo, you are excused of duties to nurse your cousin and as a thank you for your help, you will return to duty on Moon-day next.'

'Thank you, Sir,' said Kenzo and left the room. 'Another two weeks off,' he thought, 'Fatman would be really pissed off.'

After Kenzo had left, Pelosus turned to Petit.

'Do you believe him?' he asked.

'Not at all,' he replied, 'you?'

'No, he is hiding something, but it is pointless putting him under pressure. I think our best chance to find what this Sark business is all about is to nurture our relationship with the girl. I'm not sure where this is leading, but there are far too many loose ends here. In the meantime, we still have the silk to decipher.' They sat for a while, drinking wine, taking it in turns to examine the handkerchief.

'It is quite beautiful,' said Petit, turning it over and over in his hands.

'Unlike anything I have ever seen before,' agreed Pelosus, 'and though it is an exciting thought to think it came from somewhere else, the concept is quite hard to grasp.'

'Pelosus,' said the clerk slowly, 'I think we have got too close to this and need to take a step back.'

'What do you mean?' asked the Stargazer.

'We are getting nowhere with this silk, and I think that we need to start afresh. Re-examine the facts to see if we have missed something.'

Pelosus stared at him, waiting for the explanation that would surely follow.

'Look,' he continued, 'we have no idea where this silk leads, but we do know where it came from.'

'Do we?' asked Pelosus.

'From Petra, I think that she may have more knowledge about this than she's letting on.'

'Perhaps she does, but there's not much we can do about it. We can hardly ask her what else is she hiding and besides, she's not here.'

The clerk stared at him, his brows rising as a thought came to him.

'But she was,' he said slowly, 'she was here, in this very room talking to you.'

'So what?' asked Pelosus.

93

'Think back' said the clerk, 'when she left, I was outside in the hall with your supper. I had to knock on the door because I had forgotten my keys.' He looked at the Stargazer's blank face. 'For Saint's sake, Pelosus,' he said, 'think about it. You were on your own in your chambers and yet suddenly she was behind you. What is she, some kind of spirit?'

'Don't be disrespectful,' warned Pelosus, 'she is as human as you and me.'

'You think so?' asked the clerk, 'the door was locked, Pelosus, and I know of no human that can walk through a locked door!'

Pelosus stared at him, his eyes wide with understanding.

'You're right,' he said eventually, 'I had locked the door when I took my bath and I didn't bother unlocking it as I knew you had your own keys.'

'And you are certain she was nowhere inside.'

'Absolutely, my chambers were empty.'

'And there is no other door?'

'I've lived in these chambers since my predecessor died over twenty years ago,' responded Pelosus, 'there is no other door.'

'There has to be,' said the clerk, 'unless the Governess can walk through stone, somewhere in these rooms there is another entrance and we are going to find it.'

'Why?' asked Pelosus. 'What good will it do, even if there is another door and any of the council chose to use it, who am I to argue? The council do as they please.'

'Think about it, Pelosus, didn't the Governess hint there may be other scrolls? You are as high as you can get short of being a council member and yet even you are denied sight of them. Imagine what they could contain, histories that we can only guess at, blueprints of the Citadel since it was built, artwork, poetry, who knows? There may even be the answer to your problem.'

'I doubt it,' said Pelosus, 'why involve me if they already have the answers?'

'They may be the ruling classes, Pelosus,' said the Clerk, 'but that doesn't make them any more intelligent than any of us. The Governess had the handkerchief for heaven knows how long without discovering the message, yet you found it in a matter of hours. They have had a life of pampering and luxury and the only time they exercise their brain is when choosing what to have for their evening meal. No, the Governess needs you and if she has access to more information, then you should be able to see it. For Saint's sake, Pelosus, you have been tasked with saving the city. Surely, that overrides any misguided loyalty.'

'You don't understand,' said Pelosus, 'Petra and I, we go back a long way and if I keep to my side of the bargain, there may be a chance that we can get together again.'

94

'She is a Courtesan, Pelosus,' snapped the clerk, 'she says that sort of thing to dozens of people every day. It's her job.'

'But she remembered me after all this time; she recalled the time we spent together.'

'Wake up, Pelosus!' said the clerk his voice rising, 'she probably didn't remember you at all. All she had to do is check her records. The Pleasure-tower keeps meticulous accounts recording the customers, just like all the others. She already knew your name and it's a safe bet that at one time or another, most men in the city have visited the Pleasure-tower. All she had to do is check the accounts and there would be a record there.'

'The accounts!' said Pelosus numbly.

'Yes the accounts, you are no more to her than a ledger entry. I'm sorry, Pelosus but you have to focus here. The prize is life for all in the Citadel, not an impossible relationship with the Governess of the Courtesans.' He placed his hand gently on the old man's shoulder. 'Now, let's look for this door.'

Many of the walls within Pelosus's chambers were clad in beautiful carved panels and they concentrated their efforts there, seeking any sign of a loose panel or hidden doorway that may conceal an entrance. They even removed the scrolls from their alcoves to search behind them, all to no effect. When they finished examining the walls, they turned their attention to the floor, searching for a trapdoor in the flagstones, again with no luck.

'Told you,' said Pelosus, 'no other entrance.'

'Let's think about this,' replied the clerk, 'where were you when you became aware of her presence?'

'Sitting in this chair,' he replied.

'Right, you were sitting there, so we can be pretty certain she didn't appear from anywhere in front of you, you would have seen her, right?'

'Correct!' said Pelosus.

'Therefore she must have come from this quarter of the room, somewhere near the door.'

'Perhaps she's got her own key.'

'I don't think so, for the simple reason you would have heard the door opening.'

'Fair point.'

'So we can assume the entrance is in this area,' he said throwing his arms wide, indicating the wall containing the door.

'We've already checked,' said Pelosus with a sigh.

'Well, we will check again,' he answered before they both resumed the examination, this time in minute detail, the clerk on his hands and knees checking out every crack or mark on the floor. Suddenly he called out.

'Pelosus, come here,' he said, 'Look at this.' He pointed at mark on the floor, curving about two foot into the room.

'What made this mark?'

'It's just where the bottom of the door rubs on the floor when it's opened.'

'It can't be,' said the clerk.

'Why not?'

'It's too far out; it is at least two inches past where the arc of the door edge would swing.'

Pelosus opened the door to check and sure enough, the mark on the floor was two inches further in to the room. He took a pencil from the table and continued the fragment of the circle toward the doorway, careful to keep the arc as true as possible. When the arc had been drawn to its natural conclusion, it met up with the inside of the doorframe where it met the wall.

The clerk laid his head on the floor examining the bottom of the doorframe.

'It's not bedded in,' he said. 'There is a tiny gap. I think this frame was meant to move.'

'That doesn't make sense,' said Pelosus. 'Why would the frame move? You wouldn't gain anything.' They opened and closed the door a few times, but the frame remained solid in place. Opening the door again, they examined the passage leading through the wall from the corridor to the doorway. Like all other doorways, the walls were over four foot thick and built from solid granite blocks. Again, the clerk tried to move the frame without any success before Pelosus, who had been watching in silence, spoke up.

'Shut the door,' he said.

'What?'

'Come back in here and shut the door,' he said again.

The clerk did as he was bid, and they both stood looking at the inside of the solid door. The clerk thumped the palm of his hand against the door in frustration. 'I know it's here.' he shouted, 'but where?' He turned around, surprised to see Pelosus standing with a smirk on his face.

'What are you smiling about?' he asked before adding, 'you've worked it out haven't you?'

Pelosus nodded.

'You were right,' he said, 'in fact we were both right. There is only one door, yet there are two doors.'

'I don't understand,' said the clerk.

'I believe the frame does indeed swing into the room, though as yet, I can't see the purpose,' continued the Stargazer, 'all we need to do is unlock it.'

'How?'

'With your key.'

'Enough,' said the clerk, 'you are teasing me now, please explain.'

'It's simple,' said Pelosus, 'the door is locked, but we have the key. In fact, we both have keys. We've always had the keys.'

'I only have the key for my own room and for that lock there,' answered the clerk.

'The one lock has a dual purpose,' said Pelosus, 'if I am right, the door contains one bolt that locks the door to the frame, and another bolt that locks the frame to the wall. It is this bolt we need to disengage.'

'With you so far,' said the clerk.

'If I am correct,' said Pelosus, 'we have to first lock the door into the frame, and then unlock the frame from the wall.'

'What good will that do?' asked the clerk, 'it will still open into the same corridor.'

'I don't know,' said Pelosus 'but there is one way to find out.' He walked to the door and placed the large mortice key in the lock, turning it securely into the locked position. He looked at the clerk. 'Here goes,' he said and pushed the key further into the door with a resounding clunk! The clerk's eyes widened in surprise, he hadn't thought of that!

'Let's try again,' said Pelosus, and turned the key the opposite direction. Surprisingly it turned easily and it was with some satisfaction that he heard the faint sound of internal mechanisms falling into place. 'Try it,' he said.

The clerk needed no more invitation and pulled gingerly on the handle of what should have been a securely locked door. Not only did the door respond easily to his pull, but the frame came as well, the whole assembly swinging smoothly and silently inward, released from its usual fixing to the solid stone reveal.

The two men stared unbelievingly at the sight before them. It was obvious now, that the door frame was also attached to the bottom half of the panelling which covered the wall adjacent to the doorway, and as the whole thing swung inward, the lower panel also swung in, revealing a waist high opening carefully formed in the substructure.

'Ingenious,' gasped the clerk.

'I don't believe it,' said Pelosus. 'All this time, and we never knew.'

'Why should we?' asked the clerk, 'our lot is to work and to serve. Who knows what untold secrets are known by the council?'

'Where do you think it leads?'

'I have no idea,' he said, 'but, we are wasting our time standing here, bring some candles.'

'Wait,' said the Stargazer, 'let's not be hasty. Petra or anyone else could be in the tunnel or around any corner and despite what we believe; the council still has the power of life or death.'

'What are you saying?'

'At the moment, we have the advantage here, we are aware of the tunnel, though not where it leads. Let's not lose that in some rash action

97

within the first few minutes. We should consider carefully the most opportune moment, when any council member are unlikely to be in this passage.'

'Actually I agree,' said the clerk, 'and I know just the time.'

'When?'

'After the next council meeting. They usually stay long after the proceedings have drawn to a close, sharing the best that each of their towers can produce. The best wines, the sweetest cakes, the choicest cuts of Narwl steak, all are reserved for the council.'

'What about Petra?' asked Pelosus already dreading the answer.

'Let's just say, she arranges the entertainment.'

'I don't believe you.'

'Believe what you want, I have seen it with my own eyes. They summoned me once in the middle of the night to answer some outrageous wager that was going on. I am no prude Pelosus, but what I saw in that chamber that night made me blush. Anyway, the fact is that they often stay in the chamber until dawn the following day. If the meeting finishes at ten bells, that gives us at least eight hours to investigate the tunnel. What do you say?'

'Agreed,' said Pelosus, 'though I still think you are wrong about Petra. She is far too classy for that.'

The clerk's eyes rose to the ceiling in mock frustration.

'You are obsessed man,' he said. 'Now, let's close this door before someone comes along.'

Though Amber hadn't realized it, she had spent several days in the tunnels and had been close to death through thirst and hunger. Over the next two days, she spent most of the time in Leona's room as the young woman nursed her back to health. One morning, Kenzo came back from visiting his father and was pleased to see Amber up, dressed and drinking warm brew with Leona.

'How are you feeling?' he asked as he walked into the room.

'Great,' she said, 'much stronger.'

'We've been for a walk this morning,' said Leona, 'twice around the keep.'

'Twice round the keep,' said Kenzo feigning astonishment, 'that must have taken hours.'

'Ok, funny guy,' said Amber, 'don't get smart. Do you want a beaker of brew?'

'I'll do it,' he said.

'No, please,' she said, 'I want to,' and stood to put the pot back on the fire.

Kenzo and Leona exchanged glances. Except for when she had first awoken, Amber had not mentioned her experience in the tunnels at all and they were getting worried. It was not healthy to keep it all boxed up inside.

Amber made three fresh beakers of brew and they all sat on Leona's bed sipping the warm liquid. Leona's father had moved into a lady friend's rooms for a few days, his journey eased by a few coins and a visit from Pelosus's representative.

'Should be able to go back home tomorrow,' said Kenzo.

'She can stay as long as she likes,' said Leona. 'I am quite comfortable in father's bed for the time being.'

'No, it's okay,' said Amber, 'it will be good to see the rest of the gang again.'

Silence fell again.

'Amber?' ventured Kenzo 'There's something we need to talk about and it may be a bit difficult for you.'

She put her beaker down.

'I'd rather not talk about it,' she said.

Kenzo took her hand.

'I know it is difficult,' he said, 'but I need your help. All I want to do is ask you some questions. If it gets too hard we'll stop but, it's just that Leona and I want to get married and the only way we can afford it,' he paused and looked at Leona before continuing, 'the only way we can afford it is to find the body of your friend.'

'Who, Crispin?'

'Yes,' he said. 'There is a reward for finding him and if we can return his body then we will get five crowns. That's enough to get married, buy a small place and set us all up in business.'

'You want to sell his body,' she said incredulously.

'No, it's not like that; our aim, my aim,' he said, correcting himself, 'was always to find him alive, but you always came first. When I found you, I had no idea he was anywhere near. Even if I did, it was probably too late.'

'Why can't we just leave him in peace?' she asked.

'Because there are others that are seeking him too,' he said. 'Nobody but us three knows he is dead, so the search goes on, but whatever happens, he will not be allowed to rest.'

Leona interrupted.

'From what I can gather, Amber,' she said, 'you are the only one who showed him friendship. I'm sure that given the choice he would rather you profit from this than anybody else.'

'I am not going to lie to you, Amber,' said Kenzo, 'the money will be very welcome. But I am also intrigued as to why there is such a price on his head. Why was he so special that the Watchers and the council are so keen to find him?'

'I don't know,' said Amber, 'I just know that he was different.'

'These are strange times, Amber,' said Kenzo, 'there's martial law in Bastion; the reduction in the water level has revealed a second city we never knew of and now the death of this strange boy. Somehow I think they are all linked and if the council and Watchers are so interested in Crispin, then I believe he may be the key. Perhaps if we find Crispin, even though it is too late for him, he may still be able to give us a clue as to what is going on.'

'But how?' asked Amber, 'even if I knew how to find that horrible place again, you said it was under water. How could you get to him?'

'Well, I have made some enquiries,' he said, 'and if I am correct, the water will soon fall again. When it does, the water in the tunnels will also recede and we should be able to find his body.'

'When?' asked Amber.

'Moon-day,' answered Leona, 'in two days' time.'

Amber sipped her brew again and thought for a few minutes before replying.

'I can't tell you where he is,' she said eventually, 'it is too difficult to explain, but I can show you.'

The statement sank in slowly.

'I can't take you back in there, Amber,' he said, 'it is too dangerous.'

'You have no choice.' she said, 'I am the only one who knows where he is.'

'But you were lost for days, why do you think you can find your way back.'

'I got confused on the way out, I was panicking, but when Crispin first carried me into the tunnels…'

Leona interrupted.

'Crispin carried you in to the tunnels?'

'Yes, I'll explain later, but anyway, when he carried me in, I made a mental note of the twists and turns. I think I should be able to remember where he took me.'

They fell silent one more time.

'I don't think you have a choice, Kenzo,' said Leona eventually. 'There's no way you will find him in that maze. At least, Amber can take you to the approximate area, and then you will have a chance.'

Kenzo stared at Amber.

'Okay,' he said, 'we'll do it, but this time we will go prepared.'

Out in the city, the talk was of the forthcoming Moon-day. Though there had been rationing, it was not as bad as the people had feared and since the water had risen again, the feeling was that the worse was over and preparations were afoot for the monthly festival. Amber, Leona and Kenzo made what preparations they could for their journey into the catacombs, packing a rucksack with anything they may need. Skins of fresh water, a ball of string and a first aid kit in case of injuries, joined dried Narwl biscuits in the pack. Kenzo packed a thin blanket, explaining that if they found Crispin, they would wrap his body in the blanket to bring him back.

'If his body has been underwater all this time, how will we be able to prove it is him?' asked Leona when Amber was out of earshot.

'The boy we seek has a hunchback,' replied Kenzo, 'I know of no other child in Bastion with such a deformity. If we find his body, I am confident the Watchers will meet their side of the bargain.'

Finally, the preparations were complete and all they had to do was wait.

Moon-day market went ahead as normal, though the atmosphere was distinctly more subdued than usual. Having had a taste of rationing, it seemed that everyone in the city had the same idea and tried to buy quantity rather than quality. The cheaper cuts of meat and the carts of biscuits were quickly cleared, while the more expensive wines and even some of the ales sold slowly. The Bakers in particular, struggled to sell their wares, with the luxuries they excelled in, virtually untouched on their carts as people planned their spending carefully.

Amber and Leona rose late on Moon-day and sat by the window watching the gymnasts and acrobats of the artists going half-heartedly through routines that would now, not be used. For the first time in living memory, the council had cancelled the carnival. Even after the dark days, when the rape of two teenage artists by a gang of drunken bakers started the three-day tower war, the carnivals continued. It was the one regular release from pressure that the populace enjoyed and the decision had not gone down well in the city. Finally, Kenzo appeared from the barracks and entered the room.

'Well,' he said, 'we have waited long enough. Shall we go and find out?' The three left the keep and walked down to the gates to see if the water had receded, only to find them shut and guarded by two soldiers.

'What's happening?' asked Kenzo as he approached, 'why are the gates shut?'

'Fatman's orders,' said the soldier, 'nobody allowed outside the city.'

'But why, we only want to see the submerged buildings,' said Kenzo. 'Surely there's no harm in that.'

'Submerged buildings?' laughed the guard. 'You guys in the keep are really out of the loop aren't you? It's not submerged anymore, Kenzo, the water covering the buildings has gone.'

'Gone, 'he replied, 'what do you mean, gone?'

'Disappeared completely. Apart from a few pools, the buildings below the causeways are dry, and have been since this morning.'

'How far has it fallen?' asked Kenzo, 'I mean, outside the towers, has all the water gone?'

'Oh no, the sea is still there, but much lower than last month. The word is that the Hunters can only just about reach the sea to hunt the Narwl.'

'Can we have a look?' asked Kenzo, 'after all, I am a guard.'

The soldier considered carefully before answering.

'Fatman said nothing about soldiers,' he said, 'you can go, but they,' he indicated Leona and Amber, 'will have to stay here.'

'Ok,' said Kenzo, he turned to the girls. 'Wait here, I won't be long.' They nodded their agreement and sat on a nearby bench to wait.

The duty guard opened the gates quickly.

'Don't be long,' he said, 'you're not exactly Fatman's flavour of the month at the moment.'

'Two minutes,' said Kenzo, and he slipped through the narrow aperture. He walked to the edge of the causeway walls and caught his breath at the sight before him. The first reaction was vertigo and his hands grasped the walls quickly seeking extra purchase. The city below was now unveiled in all its glory, a complicated metropolis of buildings of all shapes and sizes, disappearing into the distance as they followed the walls around the curvature of the city perimeter.

Kenzo was fascinated. It was everything a city should be, there were streets and alleyways, small houses and tall multi-floor buildings. Yes, they were the worse for wear and for the most part covered with rapidly drying seaweed, but their purpose was obvious. Sometime in the long forgotten past, people just like him must have occupied this place. If the council had known about this, they had certainly kept it quiet.

Like Amber before him, he noticed that there was no obvious way up from the city floor, and stranger than that, he noticed there seemed to be no gates leading through the outer wall.

Soon he heard a hiss from the city gates.

'Kenzo,' said the guard, 'come on, we are due to be relieved soon, I don't want Fatman finding out.' Kenzo reluctantly returned into the city perimeter.

'Have you seen it?' he asked the soldier.

'Yes, creepy innit? Makes you wonder where they've all gone.'

'Came up here, I assume,' said Kenzo.

'Doubt it,' said the soldier, 'too many.'

Kenzo stared at him. He was right. There were far more buildings between the encircling walls than there were in the upper city. If every one of them had been populated, there must have been thousands living down there. Whatever had happened in the past, one thing was certain. If the rising waters had forced them out, there would not have been enough room in the Citadel for everyone. Either they had drowned where they lived, or they had gone, elsewhere!

Chapter 19

Kenzo stood in the dark alleyway, holding Leona's hands in his.

'If we are not back tomorrow by ten bells, go to Pelosus,' he said.

'We've been over this a hundred times already,' said Leona.

'I know, I'm not worried about me, but Amber doesn't deserve to be in this position again. Promise me.'

'Don't worry,' she said, 'I promise, now go, the quicker you go, the quicker you'll be back.'

Kenzo kissed her tenderly.

'Come on you two,' called a voice from below, 'there'll be time for that later, let's go.'

Kenzo smiled and let Leona go before lowering himself down into the sewer shaft to join Amber. Leona dragged the grid over and blew Kenzo a last kiss before watching them both disappear into the sewer pipe. She waited a minute, before returning to the keep, unaware that all the time, another set of eyes was watching her.

Ten minutes later, Amber and Kenzo stood in the seawater shaft listening for any sound of movement in the darkness. Kenzo retrieved the ball of string from the pack and wedged one end into a crack in the wall before leading the way into the first tunnel. Within minutes, they came across the first junction.

'Right, this is where I found you,' whispered Kenzo, 'slumped against this wall.'

'It seems I was almost out,' said Amber, 'a few more minutes and I would have been at the shaft.'

'Doesn't matter,' said Kenzo, 'no harm done, now where do we go from here.'

Amber took a deep breath and closed her eyes.

'I remember we took two left turns, then a right and walked a long way up hill,' she said before opening her eyes again.

'First left? Second left?' he asked, 'how far along? Do you remember?'

'I don't know,' she replied, 'all I know is we turned left twice and then right. It was pitch black.'

'Of course it was,' said Kenzo, 'we'll just have to check them all, let's go,' and holding the lamp before him, walked deeper into the blackness. Sure enough, they soon came across a left turn and didn't hesitate to follow the tunnel.

'Oh well,' said Kenzo when they reached a dead end, 'it would have been too good to be true to get it right first time, let's go back.' They retraced their steps winding the string up as they went. Over the next hour or so, they checked numerous options until finally Amber stopped.

103

'Kenzo,' she said, 'this is it.'

'You think so?'

'I know it is.'

'How can you be so sure?'

'Look,' she said, and pointed to the floor. In front of her was a dip filled with seawater approximately four foot across. 'That's the pool I fell in.'

'Why do you think that is the same one?'

Amber bent over and picked up an old knife from the side of the pool.

'This is mine,' she said simply.

They continued slowly up the slope.

'Stop!' said Kenzo suddenly.

'What's the matter?'

'Amber, look around you,' he said, 'the walls and the floor, they are bone dry. We must be higher than the water level reached.'

'So?'

'You don't understand,' he said, 'if the water did not reach this high, then it means that Crispin wouldn't have drowned.'

'You mean he could be alive?' she gasped, 'quick, we have to find him.'

'Amber,' said Kenzo grabbing her arm, stopping her running past him, 'wait, it's been over four weeks. There's no chance he would have lasted this long.'

'You mean he would have been trapped in here until he died of thirst?'

'Probably,' he said quietly.

'Oh, Kenzo,' she cried, 'I promised him I would return. He must have waited and waited for me and I let him down.'

'It wasn't your fault, Amber,' he said, 'you weren't to know and besides, the water had risen. You couldn't have come back even if you were able to. You can't blame yourself.'

'But I promised,' shouted Amber, 'I let him down, Kenzo, I let Crispin down!'

Not much further into the Catacombs, the tiniest of movement flickered in the darkness, disturbed by the sound of crying in the distance. The white pinprick dilated as the strange consciousness took in its surroundings, its eyes focusing in the pitch-blackness of the room. Its memory of the time before was vague and its comprehension of the future was even vaguer but the one thing it was sure of, was it was getting stronger. It could feel every wave of blood as it pulsed through its veins and the contractions of powerful muscles as they twitched beneath his skin.

Something was happening but he was not sure what. Something was calling; he had a need to stretch, to extend his body, to escape from the binds that restricted his being. But there was time, he was patient, he could wait.

Amber and Kenzo continued into the tunnel with trepidation, afraid at what horror may await them in the semi darkness.

'What's that smell?' gasped Amber, 'oh my God, do you think it's Crispin?'

'I have often smelled death,' said Kenzo, 'and this isn't it.' They carried on, eventually coming across an open door and looked inside. The room was essentially empty except for pools of a white milky substance. Kenzo wrinkled his nose, the smell was obviously stronger in here and he suspected the pools were the source.

'What is it?' asked Amber.

Crispin touched the substance with his boot.

'Don't know,' he said, 'but it's very sticky.' They left the room and continued up the tunnel but within minutes, reached another dead end.

'It can't be,' said Amber, 'I'm sure this is the right tunnel, my knife was in the water.'

'There are no other rooms,' said Kenzo, 'unless you were in the room with the sticky stuff.'

'No, it was empty.'

'How do you know, you said it was dark?'

'It was, but if that stuff was in there, I would have known.'

'Perhaps it happened later, after you left.'

'Only one way to find out,' she said and they retraced their steps back to the room, staring into the eerie space. Kenzo held up the plankton lamp.

'Don't know what that stuff is,' he said, 'but the boy is not here, he must have left after you went to get help and got lost in the tunnels.'

'The poor thing,' said Amber, 'he must have been terrified.'

'Come on,' said Kenzo, 'no point in hanging around here.' But before he could turn away, he was catapulted forward into the room by Amber's falling body and they both fell onto the floor landing just short of one of the strange pools.

'Amber,' shouted Kenzo, 'what do you think you are doing?'

'It wasn't me,' shouted Amber getting to her feet, 'someone pushed me!'

Kenzo looked up at the doorway, seeing an outline in the darkness, the silhouette just visible in the faint light of the fading plankton ball.

'What do you think you're doing?' he shouted, 'who are you?'

'Crispin is that you?' shouted Amber, 'we have come to help you.'

The stranger remained silent, though the room suddenly reverberated as the ancient door was slammed into place. Kenzo rushed to the doorway but was dismayed as he recognised the sound of a heavy bolt being dragged into place. They were locked in.

'What are you doing?' shouted Kenzo, banging his fists on the door, 'let us out.'

'Let you out?' came a muffled voice from the other side of the door, 'oh I don't think so. We have waited far too long for this.'

'What do you mean?' asked Kenzo, 'open this door at once.'

'A birth,' said the voice in awe, 'no, not a birth, more of a reawakening, a religious experience, if you like and you two have a pivotal role to play.'

'You are making no sense,' shouted Kenzo, 'what the Saint is going on?'

The voice laughed out loud.

'Oh, how ironic; even in your futile attempts at enlightenment you take his name in vain.'

'What are you on about?' shouted Kenzo, banging the door again, 'who are you?'

'My name is irrelevant,' said the voice, 'for there are many such as me within the Brotherhood.'

'The Brotherhood? You mean the Brotherhood of the Sark?'

'I see our name precedes us,' said the voice.

'And this Crispin,' said Kenzo, 'does he belong to this Brotherhood as well?'

'Belong to the Brotherhood, oh that's rich. No, Kenzo, Crispin doesn't belong to the Brotherhood of the Sark, he is the Sark!'

'What exactly is a Sark?' asked Amber quietly.

'You will find out soon enough,' said the voice.

'But why do you need us?' asked Amber nervously, almost afraid to hear the answer.

'It is a fair question,' answered the voice, 'but trust me, young girl, you really don't want to know the answer. Now, if you have quite finished, I have to make the arrangements for his arrival.'

'Wait,' shouted Kenzo, 'you can't leave us like this.' The footsteps receded into the distance and within seconds, the room fell into silence again. They stared at each other in the gloom.

'What are we to do?' gasped Amber.

'I don't know,' said Kenzo and held up the lantern to inspect the room. 'There doesn't seem to be any other way out.' He held up the light to inspect the ceiling but it was far too high and the dim green light didn't reach that far.

'Well, I'm not going to just sit here and wait,' snapped Amber and she started banging on the door. 'Help,' she shouted at the top of her voice, 'somebody help!'

'Amber, what's the point?' asked Kenzo. 'There's no one down here. Nobody can hear you.'

'Then what do you suggest,' shouted Amber, 'we just wait here to die?'

'Don't forget, when we don't turn up, Leona will know something is wrong and will tell the Stargazer. He will organise a rescue party.'

'Can we wait that long?'

'I guess we have to,' said Kenzo, 'what choice do we have?' They both looked around to examine their surroundings. Several pools of the white sticky substance were evident around the room, glowing slightly in the darkness.

'What is that stuff?' asked Amber.

'I don't know,' answered Kenzo, 'I've never seen anything like it before.'

'It stinks!' said Amber and sat down to sulk.

As Kenzo sat beside her, far above them, something peered down through the darkness. The Sark watched the two humans with curiosity, fighting the instincts that came naturally. The male seemed strong and would no doubt, put up an interesting, yet ultimately futile defence while the weaker of the two, the female was fascinating. There was something about her, something familiar from deep in his memory. His eyes closed again to rest. His body was changing fast and though he needed constant nutrition, he had only just fed and needed to digest his last kill. The humans could wait. He would rest as his form neared perfection and when he woke again, he would feed.

Chapter 20

Pelosus and Petit sat once more in the Stargazer's chambers, sharing breakfast.

'You are dressed in rugged attire this morning,' said Petit, 'is there a reason?'

'There is, I have been tasked to descend to the lower city and undertake a survey before the waters rise again.'

'Can I come?' asked the clerk.

'I don't think so,' said Pelosus, 'Helzac instructed me to do this on my own. He wants no other eyes recording whatever is down there.'

'Shame!' said the clerk, 'it sounds fascinating.'

'At any other time I would agree,' said Pelosus, 'but considering our lives may depend on my other work, this is something I could do without. You stay here and scour the histories for any clue to that message. If I start straight away I should be back by dark and we can explore that passage.'

'Will do,' said the clerk and busied himself tidying up the room as Pelosus got ready.

Half-hour later, Pelosus walked out through one of the gates onto a causeway and was surprised to see Helzac and a soldier waiting for him.

'You are late!' snapped Helzac.

'Sorry, your Excellency,' he said, realising no excuse would be accepted.

'I will deal with you later,' said the Governor, 'in the meantime; this man will be your assistant.'

Pelosus stared at the grinning soldier in concern.

'Are you sure, Sir?' began Pelosus, 'surely I should take a man of science.'

'Nonsense,' said Helzac, 'you are the man of science; this soldier will be your muscle.'

Pelosus approached Helzac and whispered in his ear.

'Sir, I know this man, he is stationed in the keep and is nothing more than an ignorant oaf.'

'I am aware of his limitations,' said Helzac, 'that is precisely why I picked him, I want someone who's limits of aspiration lie with wine and women, not personal gain or political ambition. Who knows what secrets lie down there?'

Pelosus groaned and turned back to the soldier.

'So be it,' he sighed, 'where are the ladders?'

'Got no ladders, doctor,' said Braille, 'we are using this.' He held up a large wicker basket secured to the end of a rope.

'You have got to be kidding,' gasped Pelosus and turned to Helzac, 'surely there is a better way than this.'

'Braille will lower you down and climb down the rope after you,' said Helzac. 'It is better this way, the less people who know, the better.'

'What exactly am I looking for?' asked Pelosus.

'Information!' said Helzac, 'anything that may shed any light on the situation.'

'But why the secrecy?'

'Do not take me for a fool, Pelosus,' growled the Governor, 'despite the agreements of the council, I am aware that all seek to secure their own futures and there are plots within plots already underway. I wouldn't be surprised if you have already been approached by one or more towers.'

Pelosus stayed tight-lipped.

'Thought so,' said Helzac 'but it matters not. I am the Governor and am not burdened by the needs of others. All I want is a way out of here and down there may lay the answer. Report back to me and if you are successful you will be rewarded beyond your wildest dreams.'

'What about the soldier?' asked Pelosus.

'He is expendable,' said the Governor, 'when his job is done, he will be taken care of. Report back to me at last light.' He turned to re-enter the Citadel and the giant gates clanged shut behind him.

Pelosus walked over to the soldier and stared at the coiled rope.

'Is it strong enough?' he asked.

'Climb in, doctor,' shouted Braille, his stupid grin on his face, 'we'll soon find out!'

'I am not a doctor,' said Pelosus as he climbed in the basket.

'Look like a doctor to me,' said Braille and climbed up on the parapet, 'climb in then.'

Pelosus closed his eyes in fear, mumbling prayers to every deity he could think of before crouching as low in the basket as he could.

'Right then, here goes,' said Braille and hoisted the basket over the edge to lower it slowly down to the houses below, his muscled arms bulging under the strain. To Pelosus's surprise, the journey was smooth and uneventful and a few moments after he had clambered out of the basket, Braille came down the rope hand over hand until both men stood on the muddy floor of the long deserted city.

'Spooky!' said Braille looking around at the facades of long empty streets.

'Right,' said Pelosus, 'let's get started, look for any building that looks important.'

'Like a brothel?' queried Braille.

'No, not a brothel,' groaned Pelosus, 'something that may have artefacts that may give us an idea of the history of this place.'

The two men walked along the main street, poking their heads into any buildings showing promise. Every one stank of the sea and echoed with the sound of hundreds of crabs scurrying out of their way. Anything of interest was picked up and put into the large shoulder bags Pelosus had provided for exactly this purpose. Suddenly, the soldier's voice boomed out from another doorway.

'Doctor,' he called, 'quick, come here, I have something.'

Pelosus ran across the street and into a house where he heard the soldier cursing at something in the gloom.

'What is it?' he shouted.

'Hang on, I've got it,' answered Braille and backed out of an inner room dragging something with him.

Pelosus stared in fascination until Braille pulled his prize into the light and turned around with a triumphant smile on his face. Pelosus stared in disbelief.

'What in heaven?' he started.

'It's a Narwl!' proclaimed Braille, stating the obvious, 'a young'un admittedly, but still a Narwl. Got itself caught in a lower room out the back.'

Pelosus looked at the soldier in astonishment.

'I don't believe, you,' he gasped, 'we are looking for a way to save the lives of an entire city and you come back with a fish! What is wrong with you?' he shouted, 'are you stupid?'

Braille pulled his knife from his waistband, causing Pelosus's face to drop.

'Not as stupid as you may think, doctor,' said Braille, 'I may be a bit slow, but even I know something is going on and soon it could be every man for himself. Now I am what you call, one of life's survivors and if I am going to stand a chance of surviving this little crisis, then I am going to need money and plenty of it.'

Pelosus gulped and took a step backward.

'I don't have any money,' he stammered, his eyes never leaving the knife, 'not here anyway, but back in the city...'

'Don't you worry yourself, doctor,' said Braille, 'I am about to get all the money I will ever need,' and without another word, plunged his knife into the belly of the flapping Narwl.

Pelosus stared in disgust as the giant fish thrashed in pain and watched in horror as the soldier ripped open its belly to expose its second stomach. Soon the thrashing stopped and Braille's head and shoulders disappeared into the body of the fish. After a few moments, he re-emerged gasping for air clutching something in his bloody hands. He wiped it furiously on his leggings and held it up to the light.

'Told you doc,' he said, 'richer than a councillor's tart.'

Pelosus stared at the Star-stone in the soldier's hands. It was worth a fortune and no doubt would make this buffoon's life much easier in the last few months of his life.

'What do you think, Doc, after this is over, how about me and you take a trip to the Pleasure-tower and blow this little lot.'

'That's very kind, Braille,' he said slowly, 'but let's concentrate on the task in hand, shall we?'

'Suit yourself,' said Braille and walked out of the building to continue the search. After several more false hopes, Braille's voice boomed out again, echoing down the empty streets.

'Doc, over here, I think I've got something.'

'Oh for heaven's sake,' mumbled Pelosus under his breath, 'what this time, a dead crab, a broken cup, a shiny bloody stone?' He turned the corner and almost walked into Braille, stood in the middle of the street.

'What do you think, Doc?' he asked. 'Is this, the sort of thing you are looking for?'

Pelosus followed Braille's gaze upward and his mouth fell open in amazement. In front of them was the most ornate stone façade he had ever seen and though it was almost entirely covered with seaweed, he could see it was engraved with all sorts of detailed carvings from cherubs to flying angels. The whole façade was carved into the very walls of the Citadel itself and stretched over twenty foot high. The entrance was located half way up its face and accessed by a sweeping set of curved steps leading from the street.

It was obviously a place of worship and was the grandest building Pelosus had ever seen, either down here or in the Citadel. However, more than this, there was one thing that made Pelosus's heart race in excitement. It was no ornate statue or glistening jewel that caught his breath, but four words carved into the stone above the doorway. Brotherhood of the Sark!

Pelosus and Braille made their way up the curved steps to the entrance and stood before the gaping hole that formed the doorway. Drapes of red and green seaweed fell in swathes covering most of the entrance, but beyond they could see a passageway disappearing into the darkness. After a moment's pause, Pelosus retrieved a plankton lamp from his bag and pushed past the stinking growth to walk into the darkness beyond.

Though it was very dark, the plankton lamp gave off enough of a glow to light their way and they walked for a long time in silence. After about ten minutes, they finally emerged into an enormous cavern carved out of the natural rock, careful not to slip on the weed-covered floor.

'What is this place?' asked Braille in awe, his voice echoing around the massive chamber.

'Don't know,' said Pelosus. 'Any fixtures that may have been here have long ago rotted away. It seems like it is some sort of gathering place to me.'

'Why do you say that?' asked Braille.

Pelosus indicated the many rows of tiered steps at the base of the walls surrounding the entire room.

'Those seem to be some sort of viewing arrangement,' said Pelosus, 'each row of people would be higher than the row in front, so they could see over their heads to whatever ceremony was happening down here in the centre.'

'What sort of ceremony?' asked Braille.

'I'm not sure,' said Pelosus, 'it's so dark in here, it's hard to make sense of the layout. If there was more light, it may be easier.'

Braille retrieved a candle from his own pouch and lit it from his tinderbox before holding it up in the air. The room was now lighter but apart from more seaweed, there was not much more to see. Pelosus walked toward the centre of the room where the pile of weed seemed to be much thicker and pulled fruitlessly at the entangled mass.

'What is it, doc?' asked Braille.

'Don't know,' said Pelosus, 'but there seems to be something under here, give me a hand.'

'Nah, it stinks,' said Braille in disgust.

By now, Pelosus was beginning to realise what made Braille tick so he tried a different path.

'Might be worth something,' he said at Braille's departing back.

The soldier stopped, and looked over his shoulder.

'What do you mean?' he asked.

'This is obviously some kind of public meeting place,' answered Pelosus, 'whatever is under this stuff may be valuable to the council. I am sure they would be very grateful if we returned with some information that shed some light on this whole mad situation.'

'How grateful?' asked Braille.

'Free ale for a month,' suggested Pelosus.

'Two months would be more grateful,' said Braille, always on the lookout for a better deal.

'Two months,' agreed Pelosus, and within a few minutes the two men had uncovered a round stone approximately four feet high and twelve feet in diameter. They stared at the slab before Braille spoke again.

'Waste of bloody time, that was,' he said, 'there's nothing there but a bit of rock.'

'Hmm,' said Pelosus, 'it would seem this pedestal is the focal point. Whatever this room was for, everybody's attention would be on this piece of stone. Help me up; I'll see if I can get a different perspective.'

Pelosus climbed up on to the centre of the circular plinth and turned slowly, taking in the room from the higher angle.

'See anything, doc?' asked Braille.

'Not really,' said Pelosus, 'though I would imagine that some sort of ritual may have been carried out up here.'

'Sexual rituals?' suggested Braille, more in hope than expectation.

'Possibly,' said Pelosus, 'but I'm not sure. It all seems a bit sparse to be honest and the viewing platforms a bit organised. Ritualistic rape or murder would normally be in more intimate circumstances. The arrangement of the viewing platforms suggest that as many people as possible would cram into this room to see something special. Look over there; there are four entrances in all, each leading from opposite sides of the city. I can imagine hundreds of people streaming in from each tunnel to take their place on the viewing tiers to watch whatever it was that went on in here.'

'Doc,' said Braille looking up at him.

'What?' replied Pelosus, and glanced down at the soldier only to see that Braille was staring up past him at the ceiling above.

'Look up there,' said Braille.

Pelosus looked upwards and at first, couldn't see anything in the darker recesses of the domed roof, but after a few seconds, made out a much darker circle in the apex of the ceiling.

'What is it?' asked Braille.

'Looks like a hole,' said Pelosus, 'disappearing up into the belly of the Citadel.'

'Like a chimney perhaps?' asked Braille.

'Too big,' said Pelosus, 'it's about the same size of this slab, in fact, I would say exactly the same size. Anyway, time is getting on, perhaps we should be getting back.'

They walked back through the tunnel, eventually emerging back out into the open air. As they exited the tunnel mouth, Pelosus hit his head on something solid hanging down from the top of the entrance hidden in the weed.

'Shit!' he cursed, nursing the bleeding wound, 'what was that?'

Braille reached up and pulled away the sheets of weed revealing two pointed stones sticking down into the entrance.

'Must have slid down,' he said.

Pelosus stepped back toward the top of the entrance steps and stared at the opening.

'No,' he said quietly, 'I don't think they did. Pull away the rest of the weed.'

Braille reached up and tore away swathes of growth from above the tunnel mouth, finally stepping over the pile on the floor to re-join Pelosus a few yards away.

'By the Saints,' whispered Pelosus.

Braille turned around and stared up at the focus of the Stargazer's attention. The removal of the weed had revealed a carved face in the granite wall staring out over the city below.

It was longer than a normal human's head was, and seemed to be either the representation of a skull or a head with very thin skin covering the bone. The eyes were small alcoves carved into the rock and were obviously intended to hold large candles for further effect. The nose was thin and slightly hooked, but the scariest part by far, was the mouth. The tunnel naturally mimicked a set of gaping jaws and hanging from the top edge was an uneven row of sharp, predatory teeth.

The overall image was horrifying and Pelosus realised that when seen from the streets below, the effect must have been terrifying. His mind strayed to the thoughts of the populace who must have climbed these stairs to enter through the gaping jaws of this monster to take part in whatever horrors must have taken place in the cavern. A shudder rippled down his spine and realising it was getting dark, he turned to address Braille.

'Come on,' he said, 'let's get out of here.'

Chapter 21

Amber stared dismally into the darkness, the floor of the room just visible in the green light of the orb. Kenzo sat beside her, his head back and eyes shut as they waited for something to happen. They had been there for hours and had given up shouting ages ago.

To pass the time, Amber had watched intrigued as tiny insects waded into the strange white substance, seemingly attracted by its luminescence and she was quite surprised at how many must have been hidden in the shadows.

Even more fascinating was the fate of the insects and at first she was appalled, but soon become accustomed to their writhes of agony as the acidic fluid ate into the softer parts of their bodies. Soon, even the shells were dissolved and within minutes there was nothing left of the ill-fated creatures. The silence was absolute so when she heard a tiny sound from above, she nudged Kenzo nervously.

'What is it?' he asked.

'I heard something,' she said, 'up there.'

Kenzo peered upwards, holding the orb as high as he could but could see nothing due to the high ceilings.

'Do you have a candle in that pack?' he asked.

'I think Leona packed the whole kitchen,' said Amber, rummaging through the pack. She lit a candle and passed it to Kenzo.

He held it up and peered into the darkness again, struggling to see anything in the gloom.

'It's too dark,' he said, 'I can't see anything.'

'Kenzo look,' whispered Amber suddenly, her voice filled with fear, 'over there in the corner.'

High in the darker part of the void, a pair of piercing white eyes peered out of the blackness, reflecting the candle light.

'What the Saint is that?' gasped Kenzo.

'I don't know,' said Amber, 'and I don't want to find out.' She ran to the door and started banging again, screaming for help through the locked door.

'Amber, stop it!' shouted Kenzo, 'you're not helping.'

She stopped and returned to his side, staring up into the darkness.

High above, the Sark watched the humans closely. He had slept well and hungered for meat. White venom dripped from his mouth, the glands full to bursting with the juices necessary to soften its prey before he could tear living flesh from bone. He wasn't sure why he had waited so long, but would delay no longer. He needed to feed and his prey lay below him.

'It's moving!' screamed Amber and they watched in horror as the dark shape crawled slowly down the wall. 'Oh my God, Kenzo, do something.'

They both retreated and Amber hammered as hard as she could against the ancient door, screaming for help. Kenzo could just about make out the shape in the candle light and at first thought it was a giant spider, but though the body shape was indistinct, soon made out it had two legs and two arms just like them, though how it managed to cling so securely to the vertical stone wall, he had no idea. The creature dropped the last few feet, landing nimbly on all fours and his head shot up to stare at its prey with its glowing white eyes. Slowly it stood up straight and scanned the room from this new angle, checking for any unseen threats.

The soldier stared in horror. The creature was definitely human shaped, though much taller and thinner than anybody he had ever seen.

'Stay back,' shouted Kenzo holding up the candle and withdrew his knife from his belt to defend himself. The creature instantly recognised the weapon and snarled as it crouched lower, one clawed hand resting lightly on the floor, baring two rows of pointed teeth in challenge to this puny human.

Kenzo was terrified and he knew that his knife would be useless against this predator. The beast's eyes suddenly changed colour, burning a fiery red as he recoiled his muscular body to power the launch that would carry him to his prey, but a second before he leapt, a calming voice sounded across the room, causing it to hesitate.

'Crispin,' whispered Amber, her voice shaking, 'is that you?'

The creature's head spun to face her, his eyes burning like coals from hell.

'Crispin,' she whispered again, 'I know it's you. It's me, Amber. You remember me don't you? I helped you escape from those men a long time ago.' She stepped a pace forward, toward the beast. 'You wouldn't hurt me would you?' she asked, tears flowing down her face, 'I helped you, once.'

'Amber what are you doing?' hissed Kenzo.

She held up her hand to shut him up.

'Remember, Crispin?' she continued, 'we were friends.'

The Sark's instincts were in turmoil, the feeding urge was strong but there was something else, a memory struggling to reach the surface. Something was telling him not to attack but the need to feed was intense.

Amber took another step closer.

'Oh, Crispin,' she said gently, 'what has happened to you?'

A silence fell in the room except for the raspy breathing of the Sark. Indistinct whispers seemed to echo off the walls as if they could hear his thoughts, though never making out any recognisable words. For an age, nothing happened and the Sark settled down onto its haunches, struggling with the internal turmoil. Suddenly a strange voice called out from the corridor outside.

'Hello,' it said, 'is there anyone in there?'

'Open the door!' screamed Kenzo suddenly, making Amber jump, 'for Saint's sake open the door!' He heard the sound of the bolt shooting back and pushed the door open into the corridor. 'Come on!' he screamed and dragged Amber through the doorway.

The Sark's eyes flamed crimson red once more and he launched across the room, its clawed feet and hands held forward in a predatory grasp, ready to tear its prey apart. He slammed into the door, forcing it partway into the corridor before the combined weight of three bodies pushed it back.

'Lock it!' shouted Kenzo and with a bit of effort, Amber forced the bolt into its receiver.

An unearthly howl echoed through the tunnels as the Sark vented its rage on the door and Amber turned around to identify their rescuer.

'Flip,' she gasped, 'I don't know why you are here, but I have never been so glad to see anyone in my whole life.'

'I knew you were up to something,' said Flip, 'and followed you into the lane. It took ages to find your tunnel and when I did, I got lost for a while but then found your string. After that, it was simple.'

'Just as well you did,' said Amber, 'god knows what that thing would have done to us otherwise.'

'What is it?' asked Flip.

'I don't know,' said Amber, 'but I think it used to be someone called Crispin.'

'The boy you were looking for?' asked Flip in astonishment.

'It seems so,' interjected Kenzo. 'Come on, we have to get out of here quickly. I don't think that door will hold him for long. We have to let Pelosus know what is happening here.'

'Why?' asked Amber.

'Are you kidding?' gasped Kenzo, 'you saw that thing. If he gets out, heaven knows what will happen. No, we need to tell Pelosus so he can mobilise the guard to come down here and deal with it.'

'But it used to be a scared little boy,' said Amber, 'perhaps it is just some sort of illness that can be cured.'

'I'm with him,' said Flip, 'what that thing needs is a sword between its ribs.'

The door suddenly shuddered from a blow on the other side and the three jumped in fright, staring in horror as it splintered before them.

'Run,' screamed Amber.

Behind them, an enormous crash told them the door had given way and an unearthly howl echoed down the passage.

'Quick,' screamed Flip, 'he's coming.' They ran as fast as they could in the dark, with only Flip's plankton ball to light their way. Within seconds, they came to one of the junctions and Amber stopped, breathing heavily.

'What are you waiting for?' shouted Flip, 'that thing is gaining on us.'

'It's no good,' said Amber, 'it's too far back to the sewers; we have to hide, come on, this way.'

'Wait,' said Kenzo, 'that way is deeper into the catacombs, we will get lost.'

'Perhaps,' said Amber, 'but don't forget, if this thing used to be Crispin, then he hasn't been here before either, and this place may be just as confusing to him.'

'We could be going into a dead end,' said Kenzo.

'I don't think so,' said Amber, 'when I was lost down here, I wandered through hundreds of passages. It may be a maze but if we continue in that direction, we will definitely be caught.'

They all looked at each other for a few seconds before a noise from behind them made their minds up for them.

'She's right,' said Kenzo, 'we have no choice.' They ducked into the side tunnel and crept slowly away from the main passageway. Kenzo held up his hand and they all stopped, holding their breath as they pressed their backs against the wall, looking back the way they had come.

'Hide the light,' hissed Kenzo and Flip hid the plankton ball under his jerkin, plunging the tunnel into absolute darkness. Within seconds, the tall and strange silhouette of the creature stalked past the entrance to the side tunnel and even though it was completely dark, for a second, it seemed the space was even darker. As the steps receded, they breathed a quiet sigh of relief and turned to descend deeper into the catacombs.

For hours, they wandered the tunnels, finding nothing but dead ends and false entrances before finally sitting down for a rest against the corridor wall.

'That thing could be around any corner,' said Flip 'and we would never know.'

'That thing has a name,' said Amber, 'he is Crispin.'

'Amber, surely you don't hold any feelings for him,' asked Kenzo. 'Can't you see the danger?'

'Yes, but back in his cell he recognised me. Just for a second or two, he knew who I was and seemed calm. Perhaps I can talk to him, reach the person he once was.'

'I don't think that is going to work,' said Kenzo, 'any resemblance to the boy he once was has long gone and that beast is all that remains. No, we will take our chances in the tunnels and alert the guard as soon as we can. They can come down here and deal with it.'

'Right, enough talk,' said Kenzo, 'we have to keep moving, come on.' He reached down and grabbed Amber's hand, pulling her to her feet.

'I'm hungry,' said Flip as he followed behind them.

'You're not helping, Flip,' said Amber who had been aware of her own grumbling stomach for a long time.

For another couple of hours they wandered through the darkness until finally Flip stopped.

'I can't go on,' he cried, 'I'm hungry and tired.'

'Flip, we can't stay here,' said Amber, 'we have to keep going.'

'Why not?' whined Flip, 'we can call out for help, someone may hear us.'

'Crispin may hear us,' said Kenzo.

'I don't care,' said Flip, 'even if he does come, Amber can speak to him. He'll probably remember her and show us the way out.'

'Are you willing to take that risk?' asked Kenzo.

'I don't care anymore,' said Flip and slid down the wall to sit on the floor.

'Flip,' said Amber, 'You...'

'Quiet,' hissed Kenzo.

Amber turned to face him.

'What's the matter?' she whispered, 'is it Crispin?'

'I don't know,' answered Kenzo. 'Listen, can you here it?'

They all fell silent again and strained to hear what had attracted Kenzo's attention.

'I hear it too,' said Amber eventually, 'it sounds like, like water.'

They listened for a few more minutes, all agreeing that it sounded like running water. Finally, Flip broke the silence and jumped up in shock.

'Aaarrgh,' he shouted, 'I'm wet.'

'What do you mean?' asked Amber.

'The floor, it's covered with water.'

Kenzo held the failing Plankton lamp down and gasped as he saw trickles of water creeping along the floor of the tunnel. He reached down and scooped up a few drops in his palm, holding it to his mouth to taste it.

'Oh my god,' he said as he spat it back out, 'this is not good.'

'What's the matter?' asked Amber, 'Kenzo, tell me.'

'It's salt water,' said Kenzo, 'the tide must be rising again.'

'So what?' asked Flip.

'We have been travelling downwards for a while,' said Kenzo, 'and I reckon we are far lower than the normal level of the sea. If I am right, these tunnels are soon going to be flooded.'

The water was coming faster now and started to lap around the tops of their shoes.

'We can't stay here,' said Kenzo, 'we have to run.'

'But where?' shouted Amber.

'I don't know,' answered Kenzo, 'anywhere away from the water, now run.'

Within minutes, the water was pouring through the tunnel behind them and it was soon up to their knees and rising.

'Keep going,' shouted Kenzo from behind, all attempts of silence now irrelevant.

'Which way?' screamed Amber as she reached a junction.

'This way,' shouted Flip, 'it goes up hill.'

They ran up the slope and around a corner into an empty room.

'It's a dead end,' shouted Flip, 'go back.'

They quickly retraced their steps but came to a sudden stop as Kenzo blocked their way.

'Kenzo, move,' screamed Amber.

'I can't,' shouted Kenzo, 'there's nowhere else to go.'

Amber looked past her cousin and was horrified to see torrents of water now pouring down all tunnels.

'We're trapped,' cried Flip, 'we're all gonna drown.'

As the water level rose, they walked backwards, the water lapping at their feet. Within minutes, they were back in the room with the water rising around their knees. Amber grabbed Kenzo's arm in terror.

'Kenzo, what are we going to do?' she cried.

'Kick off your shoes,' shouted Kenzo, 'and your cloaks. Quickly, strip down to your underclothes.'

'Why?' shouted Amber struggling to make herself heard over the foaming water.

'We need to swim,' shouted Kenzo, 'and our clothes will weigh us down.'

'Swim where?' replied Amber, 'we will never hold our breath long enough to get out of here.'

'We don't have to,' shouted Kenzo, 'all we need to do is stay afloat, look up there.'

They all looked upwards and saw that rather than have a ceiling, the room stretched up into the darkness.

'This isn't a room,' shouted Kenzo, 'it's a shaft. If we can stay afloat, there may be other tunnels higher up. We can do this, Amber. Remember all those summer Moon-days we used to spend diving off the causeways and swimming between the towers?'

'But what if it is closed off?' shouted Amber.

'What option do we have?' shouted Kenzo, the water now up to his chest.

'I can't swim,' shouted Flip, 'I'm gonna drown.'

'You won't drown, Flip,' shouted Kenzo, 'all you have to do is tread water and even you can do that. Just lose your clothing and start kicking your legs. Watch me and do as I do.'

'Don't worry, Flip,' shouted Amber, 'we'll help you.'

Within minutes, they were floating, their feet kicking frantically to keep their heads above the water as it rose slowly up the shaft.

'Keep it up,' shouted Kenzo, 'you're doing fine.'

Chapter 22

Braille and Pelosus parted ways as they re-entered the keep, with Braille returning to the temporary Barracks while Pelosus made his way to his room to freshen up before reporting to Helzac. Within the hour, he was knocking on the Governor's door.

'Come in,' came the response and Pelosus entered Helzac's apartment for the first time.

Across the room, the Governor was looking out of the window toward the ring of outer towers in the distance. He glanced over as Pelosus entered.

'Stargazer,' he said, 'you have returned at last, and with good news, I hope.'

'Mixed news, Sire,' said Pelosus, 'yet fascinating all the same.'

'I will be the judge of that,' said Helzac. 'Sit down and tell me everything.'

They both took seats at the central table, facing each other across the polished Mahogany surface.

'First of all,' said Pelosus, 'our understanding of the second city seems to be correct. There is overwhelming evidence that a complete stand-alone civilisation existed down there, heaven knows how long ago.'

'People like us?'

'It would seem so. The dwellings are the same as ours and most contain the remains of all the same sorts of things you can find in any house today in the streets of Bastion.'

'Like what?'

'Furniture, platters, cutlery, that sort of thing. In one house, I even saw the remains of a child's cot and various playthings, so it is obvious that these people were family oriented. There are alehouses, market streets and even areas that seem to have been given over to the growing of plants. Everything you would expect to see in a thriving city.'

'But?'

'But that's where it gets confusing,' said Pelosus, 'we searched all day yet there was no sign of any exit through the outer wall to the sea or any method of accessing the main Citadel. These people were entirely confined between the two outer walls with no way of getting out. Whatever it was they did, they were entirely self- sufficient.'

'That's impossible,' said Helzac.

'You would think so,' said Pelosus, 'but I found these.' He opened his side bag and pulled out a range of items, placing them on the table before him.

'Bones?' said Helzac.

'Jaw bones,' confirmed Pelosus, 'but the like of which we have never seen before.' He picked up the largest and held it up. 'This is the lower jaw bone of a large animal,' said Pelosus 'but not a Narwl or a Ranah, look at the teeth. The beasts of the sea that feed our people have either no teeth, or the pointed incisors of the predator. These are flat and ground down through wear.'

'And?'

'Teeth get worn through constant grinding of food,' said Pelosus. 'Our old people display similar symptoms after chewing their food for a lifetime. The teeth of this jawbone suggest this animal was not of the sea, but of the land.'

'Preposterous,' said Helzac, 'there is not such a beast in existence nor has there ever been.'

'I know it is difficult to conceive,' said Pelosus, 'but all the evidence is there. The back of the jawbone is constructed to hold powerful muscle, the front teeth are arranged for gripping and pulling rather than tearing of flesh, and the rear teeth are obviously worn through grinding foliage of some sort. I think this animal was a grazer of plants and was farmed by the people of the second city.'

'You must be mistaken,' said Helzac, 'we would know of such things.'

'With respect, Governor,' said Pelosus, 'we didn't even know of the city, let alone how they lived. Yet as you say, the idea is indeed preposterous, so I sought further evidence and I found these.' He reached in his bag and pulled out six food platters.

'Platters of Mahogany,' said Helzac, in awe, 'these people must have been very rich or very stupid.'

'On the contrary,' said Pelosus, 'it would seem that Mahogany was quite a common commodity. Almost all of the platters I saw are Mahogany as well as furniture, carvings and ornaments. In fact, there is very little made of Narwl bone in the entire place.'

'Amazing,' said Helzac, 'we should arrange an expedition immediately to collect all this wealth.'

'Sire?'

'We can't leave all this down there,' said Helzac, 'we should collect as much as we can while the waters are low. If there is as much as you say, we will have to start immediately. You will make the arrangements.'

'Turn them over,' said Pelosus quietly.

'Sorry?'

'Sire, turn the platters over,' repeated Pelosus.

Helzac reached out and did as instructed, his eyes locked on those of Pelosus in annoyance at the Stargazer's tone of voice. He finally looked down, and his gaze stayed there for several seconds, before reaching out to turn the second platter, closely followed by the other four in quick succession. Finally, he looked up at Pelosus, his manner completely different. Each platter had a carving on the base and though the water had

122

worn away much of the surface, enough detail was still visible to make out the outline.

'What are they?' he asked.

Pelosus took a deep breath and blurted out the statement he knew was going to cause him trouble.

'Land animals,' he said, 'the likes of which, we never knew existed.'

Helzac was pacing back and fore across the room, muttering to himself as Pelosus waited patiently. He was staring at the carvings again, fascinated by their form for the hundredth time when Helzac joined him at the table.

'You are sure of this?' asked Helzac picking up one of the platters again.

'Yes, Sire,' said Pelosus. 'If you look carefully you can just about make out their form.' He picked up one of the plates and pointed out the outline.

'This one in particular is very interesting as it has a carving of a man alongside, so we can see the relative size.'

'It has four legs,' said Helzac in awe, 'and look at the head, it's almost twice the size of a man's and elongated. And the body, it is almost the length of a young Narwl.'

'It is rather large,' agreed Pelosus, 'but what is more interesting is the fact that the man in the carving is leading the animal by some sort of tether. They seem to be domesticated.'

'Is such a thing possible?' asked Helzac. 'Could we tame the beasts of the sea to come when called? The people would never go hungry again if so.'

'I don't know about that,' said Pelosus, 'but these pictures present more questions than answers.'

'And do you have a theory?'

'I do,' said Pelosus, 'though it is very controversial and may cost me my head.'

'We are alone,' said Helzac, 'and I give you my word that your views will remain private, no matter how strange.'

Pelosus considered carefully. Though Helzac was a brute of a man, he was known as fair and a man of honour. If he gave his word, then he meant it.

'Okay, Sire,' said Pelosus, 'I will tell you, but they are only theories at this point.'

'Continue,' said Helzac.

'Well, first of all, these platters seem to be a set and deliberately portray six different animals, ranging from the large one you have in front of you, right down to a small version that stands no higher a man's shin. The very fact that they are inscribed onto platters says to me that these were food animals. Along with the evidence of the jawbones and the large open spaces between the houses, I have concluded that they were indeed farmed for their meat and grazed on some sort of plant life grown purposely for their fodder.'

'Seems like an expensive hobby,' said Helzac. 'Grow valuable food just to give it to something else that then becomes food anyway. Why not simply eat the crops?'

'Who knows?' asked Pelosus, 'it may be the output of the meat was greater than a few bushels of plant life, it may be the taste or texture; we may never know, but suffice to say there is evidence that supports this theory.'

'Okay, we will go with this,' said Helzac.

'The problem is,' continued Pelosus, 'I can't see how they could have evolved thus in the confines of the city. Life takes tens of thousands of years to evolve, yet these platters depict at least six different species right here within the Citadel.'

'That's easy,' said Helzac, 'they could have come here like us, on the back of the great Narwl.'

Pelosus stared at the Governor in silence, wondering how far he could take this conversation without raising the man's ire.

'You do not talk, Pelosus,' said Helzac quietly, 'have your theories come to an end or have I said something that causes you concern?'

'Sire, what I am about to say is controversial and has cost many people their lives throughout history.'

'You are talking about the blasphemies?' suggested Helzac.

'I am,' said Pelosus.

Helzac considered for a moment before sitting back and folding his arms across his huge chest.

'Okay, Pelosus,' he said, 'we have come this far, we may as well get this all out in the open. Tell me everything you know, everything you have heard and everything you surmise.'

'Sire, as you are aware, our scrolls tell us that tens of thousands of years ago our ancestors roamed the ocean on the back of the great Narwl, the biggest beast ever to exist. Eventually, after a heartfelt prayer from the priests at the time, Arial, the Six-fingered Saint, descended from heaven and caused the Citadel to arise from the waters, giving us a permanent and bountiful home. However, within the underbelly of Bastion's population there have always been stories about an alternative existence. One where animals such as those depicted on the platters ran free in never ending spaces where a man can walk for days without sight of stone walls. Of places where wood grows straight out of the ground as weed grows from the seabed, and of fresh water flowing freely along the ground where any man can drink without paying the tally.'

'Fairy tales for lulling children to sleep,' said Helzac.

'Perhaps, but what if they are not? What if they are based in truth? Oh, I'm not saying that water can run freely or wood can grow uninhibited from the ground. Of course, that is preposterous, but what if the stories have a grain of truth in them? What if there are other places beyond the horizon that our ancestors once knew?'

'You are talking about land,' said Helzac, in a matter of fact tone.

'Yes, land,' said Pelosus, keen to explore his theories further now he had the ear of the most powerful man he knew.

'No such place,' said Helzac.

'You don't know that,' said Pelosus, 'after all, tear down this Citadel and cast the stones into the sea and would we not be standing on exactly that, a piece of land?'

'But why would we need land without walls?' asked Helzac. 'They protect us from the rain and the wind. They keep the warmth of our fires inside in the winter and provide shade in the summer. Without the Citadel, we would not survive.'

'I agree,' said Pelosus, 'but what is to say there are no other Citadels across the world, far from ours, yet sitting on larger pieces of land. It doesn't mean that the histories are wrong, the Great Narwl may indeed have carried us here and Arial may indeed have made the Citadel. Heaven knows that it is beyond the skills and knowledge of our people so I have no argument there, but the appearance of these,' he indicated the platters, 'makes me question my own deepest and most emotional beliefs. These animals cannot have developed here. It is as simple as that. Either they were brought here by the divine or were carried here on some sort of craft from elsewhere.'

'Craft? What do you mean, craft?'

'Boats like the Hunter's Narwl-boats only much, much bigger.'

'You are really stretching my imagination now,' said Helzac, 'I have seen no such craft and besides, even if such a thing was possible to construct, it would sink from its own weight. Narwl bone is too heavy.'

'Not if it was made of wood,' said Pelosus.

'Wood is too flimsy and absorbs water,' answered Helzac.

'Mahogany doesn't.'

Helzac stared at the Stargazer in contempt.

'Let me get this clear,' said Helzac, 'you are suggesting that our ancestors made floating craft out of one of the most precious materials known to man and pushed them out onto the sea to sail them over the end of the world. Not only this, but they had to find a place where water runs freely, food animals are there for the taking and wood sprouts straight from the ground. However, when they have found this paradise, they didn't stay there, they would capture various beasts and, after loading them onto these crafts and bringing them back to the Citadel, give them our crops and ultimately kill them for meat. Is that what you are saying?'

Pelosus squirmed uncomfortably in his seat.

'Put like that, it does sound a bit far-fetched,' he said, 'but it's the only way I can link these artefacts together. If I had more time, I could examine the city more but the waters are already creeping back. Next month they will be drier for longer, but time is running out. The further the sea levels fall, the harder to survive it will be, yet there is a lifetime of study waiting beneath the arched bridges.'

Helzac stood up and wandered around the room once more. Pelosus watched him walk, wondering if he had said too much. Stories such as these had raised their heads on several occasions in the Citadel's history and many a cult had been viciously exterminated for daring to blaspheme. There was even an occasion thousands of years ago, where the armies of the Citadel had wiped out the population of a whole tower when their leader claimed that Arial was a figment of the people's imagination, and that they all descended from small people covered with hair from lands across the seas.

The slaughter had been devastating and anyone with the remotest link to the tower of the scholars, as it had been known, was ruthlessly wiped out. Apparently, the flames from the bonfire of scrolls reached far into the sky for two days and nights and though Pelosus would never admit it, he often thought he would give one of his arms to have read that information.

But that was in the past and the population now followed the one true faith, the gospel of Arial, the Six-fingered Saint. Finally, Helzac broke the silence.

'Come here,' he said and Pelosus joined him in front of a particularly beautiful picture hanging on the wall.

'What do you think?' asked Helzac.

Pelosus looked at the picture. It depicted a scenario often seen from the Citadel walls. In the foreground, the Hunter's tower was silhouetted against the red setting sun and bodies could be seen diving gracefully into the water below on their daily search for Narwl. All around the Tower, dead Narwl could be seen being towed back to shore by their small boats and two huge beasts could be seen being hauled up the Tower walls.

Though the scene was obviously the subject of artistic license, it evoked the whole essence of sustainable life in the Citadel. Without the Hunters and the bounty of the sea, they would all starve.

'Beautiful,' said Pelosus, 'and obviously very old. Is it yours?'

'Not personally,' said Helzac, 'it is a fixture of this room and has been handed down through the centuries by each Citadel Governor.'

'It is very nice,' said Pelosus, wondering where this was leading.

'Nice?' said Helzac. 'Yes I suppose it is, in a way. Very comforting to know that even thousands of years ago, the way of life that we are all so familiar with existed in much the same way as it does now.'

'Though I think Razor would raise an eyebrow as to the success of the hunt,' laughed Pelosus, indicating the sheer quantity of Narwl in the picture.

'Yes, quite,' answered Helzac, 'though another word to describe this picture is disturbing.'

'Really?' asked Pelosus, looking at the picture once again, 'I don't see how, it is very comforting, actually.'

'Look again, Pelosus,' said Helzac. 'The activity draws your eye to the central scene, does it not? The beautiful sunset, the athleticism of the Hunters, the gracefulness of the Narwl and the success of the hunt, all designed to draw the viewer's attention. Most people look at a picture for a few moments, taking in the subject before resuming whatever other activity they had been engaged in. Very few actually take time to study pictures any more, as very few have the time, I however, do have the time and I love art. Look elsewhere within the picture, Pelosus and don't allow your mind to be lured by the central images. What else do you see?'

Pelosus stared at the picture once more.

'Not much, really,' said the Stargazer, 'the open waters of the sea, the curvature of the horizon, some passing clouds.'

'And within the clouds?'

Pelosus screwed up his eyes and moved closer to the picture.

'Nothing,' he said, 'unless you mean those tiny marks dotted everywhere.'

Feeling a tap on his shoulder, he turned to see Helzac holding a magnifying glass.

'Look again,' said the Governor.

Pelosus took the magnifying glass and focussed in on the marks on the clouds. Silence fell immediately and he moved from mark to mark, not believing his eyes.

'By the Saints,' he whispered, 'I don't understand. This cannot be, how on earth…?'

'So, Stargazer,' said Helzac eventually, 'you have come in here with your strange tales, hoping to enthral me with weird beasts and far off lands, yet I too have knowledge unexplored. The creatures you have just seen are, I believe, called birds and live in the air.'

'But that's impossible,' said Pelosus, 'how can they stay up there?'

'I don't profess to know the detail,' said Helzac, 'yet I am sure this is not the product of some sick mind.'

'How can you be sure?'

'Because I have three other such paintings in storage. I cannot display them for the birds are clearer to the eye and would be the cause of too many questions.'

'How do you know the name of these creatures?' asked Pelosus, resuming the examination of the picture through the lens.

'One of the other pictures names them on the reverse,' he said, 'and gives a close up of the creature in flight.'

'Can I see it?'

'To what purpose?' asked Helzac, 'I have known of these phenomena for many years, yet have kept it to myself. I cannot allow this information to become public.'

'But why not?'

'Pelosus, I have a role with great responsibility. This Citadel balances on a knife-edge of peace and prosperity. On either side lie hunger, war, anarchy and fear. The slightest doubt in the scriptures of the Saint could tip our existence off that edge and chaos would ensue. If the population thought even one second there may be another place, they would be demanding expeditions and exploration. Many men would be sent to their deaths on fruitless searches for a place that may not even exist. I cannot do that for the people would become impatient and challenge the structure that has served us well for so many generations.'

'But what if someone was successful?' asked Pelosus. 'What if even one person found this other place, surely it would make it all worthwhile?'

'And then what?' asked Helzac, 'how could we transport thousands of people to somewhere else without the means of doing so. The knowledge of any sort of alternative city or civilisation would be enough to end life as we know it here in Bastion. No, in this case, ignorance is bliss and that is why the council have kept such things to themselves over all these generations.'

'You know of other places?'

'Not as such,' said Helzac, 'these pictures hint at things I don't understand and I often wondered where these birds originated and where they land? Also, if they were as prevalent as they seem in the pictures, where are they now and why did they disappear?'

'Perhaps they do not land,' suggested Pelosus, 'perhaps they spend their life in the air.'

'I do not think so,' said Helzac. 'Look at the actual tower in the picture and focus on the far left castellation.'

Once again, Pelosus stared through the lens though this time directly at the tower. At first, he could see nothing but finally he could make out the tiny image of one of the birds, half hidden behind a stone and perched on the haft of a hunting spear.

'It's claws seem designed for grasping such things,' mused Pelosus.

'Yes, but where? Certainly not in the Citadel.'

'Fascinating,' agreed Pelosus.

'Such musings used to keep me awake at night,' continued Helzac, 'but now my dreams are of more spiritual things and I look forward to spending eternity with the Saint. That is, until you presented us with a change that is creeping upon us.'

'So all this time you knew there were possibilities, yet still you questioned me.'

'I had to keep up the pretence,' said Helzac, 'even the other council members are not aware of the situation although I am not sure about the Watchers. They keep themselves to themselves.'

'But why were these birds painted on this canvas?' asked Pelosus, 'why not just leave a note and instructions to keep the knowledge secret?'

'I do not know the answer to this,' said Helzac. 'It seems that open knowledge was not possible and these hints, for hints are what they are, were hidden amongst artwork that is easily accessible, yet hidden amongst the detail.'

'It doesn't make any sense,' said Pelosus, 'it's almost as if whoever painted the pictures were frightened of others knowing what they were doing.'

'And hence my initial instruction, Pelosus. Times are changing at a pace we cannot comprehend and the implications are yet unknown. I have kept this knowledge to myself for a long time and though it may not be of any use, I think we have to put everything on the table to try to make sense of it all. If indeed this other place does exist, then we have to explore all options.'

'Your Excellency, there is much to ponder here, so if you don't mind, I would like to return to my rooms and deliberate. Perhaps I can knit all this together and make some sense.'

'I agree,' said Helzac, 'though I have to reiterate that this conversation remains in this room for the moment. Is that clear?'

'Yes, Sire,' said Pelosus and with a deep bow, turned to leave the room.

Chapter 23

'I think the water's stopped rising,' gasped Amber breathlessly.

'I think you're right,' answered, Kenzo, 'try to find a handhold on the shaft wall to catch your breath.'

Amber's freezing fingers searched the slimy surface of the wall without success, her strength rapidly failing.

'It's no use,' she said, 'it's too smooth.'

'Same here,' gasped Kenzo, 'keep trying.'

'Over here,' said Flip unexpectedly, 'I've found something.' The two cousins swam over to Flip and found him clinging to a small horizontal bar set into the wall.

'Thank the Saints,' said Amber and for the first time in over ten minutes, she held on and relaxed her body.

Flip was clinging on to the bar and though he had moved sideways to make room, he seemed to be a bit higher in the water than the other two.

'How are you so high?' asked Kenzo between chattering teeth.

'There's another bar,' said Flip, 'under the water.'

Kenzo felt with his feet and banged his shin against a similar bar beneath the surface. He placed the sole of his foot on the submerged bar and stood upright, his extra height lifting him above Flip.

'Well done, Flip,' said Amber, 'I couldn't have lasted much longer.'

'Me neither,' said Flip, 'do you think the water will go away now?'

'I don't think so,' said Kenzo, 'if it is the tide, as I suspect it is, then the water will remain high for a few hours before dropping slightly, but it won't go away completely until next Moon-day.'

'We can't stay here that long,' said Flip, 'we're gonna die aren't we?'

'Not necessarily,' said Kenzo and reached upward with his free hand, searching for something in the dark. 'Yes,' he gasped, 'I thought so, another bar in the wall. I think these bars actually form a ladder.'

'A ladder?' exclaimed Amber, 'to where?'

'I don't know,' said Kenzo 'but I'm going to find out.' With an effort, he pushed up and reached further up the wall. 'Another one,' he said, 'I was right.' Within seconds, he was climbing up the ladder but before he had gone ten rungs his hand hit against something solid across the top of the shaft.

'There's some kind of wooden cover,' he shouted, 'I'll see if I can move it.'

Back down in the water, Amber and Flip gazed up toward Kenzo, praying that he would find a way out.

'*Ow!*' shouted Flip suddenly, 'what did you do that for?'

'Do what?' asked Amber.

'You kicked me.'

'No I didn't,' said Amber, 'I didn't touch you.'

'Yes you did,' said Flip and suddenly flinched again as something hit his leg.

'*Ow!*' he shouted even louder. 'Stop it.'

'I didn't do anything,' shouted Amber, 'I don't know...*Aaarrgh!*' She thrashed her legs violently. 'Flip,' she shouted, 'there's something in the water.'

Flip grabbed her by the arm with his free hand and forced her upwards on the ladder.

'Get out,' he shouted, 'quickly!'

Amber pulled herself up the ladder, crying out in pain as something took tiny bites from her legs.

Behind her, Flip was kicking violently and screaming in the dark, thrashing his legs as he tried to fight off the unseen horror.

'Flip,' shouted Amber as soon as she was clear of the water, 'come on.'

The boy reached up and grabbed a rail, tears flowing from his eyes.

'What's happening?' shouted Kenzo from above.

'There's something in the water,' shouted Amber, 'and its attacking Flip.'

'*Please, help me,*' screamed the boy hanging on to the rung with both hands.

'Amber get out of the way,' shouted Kenzo, climbing back down the ladder as quickly as he could, 'Flip, give me your hand.'

'*Help me,*' screamed Flip as something grabbed the back of his thigh with razor sharp teeth. Suddenly he let go of the rung and fell backwards into the water, his arms and legs thrashing violently as he tried to fight off the unseen attacker.

'*Flip,*' screamed Amber in terror. 'Oh my God, Kenzo, we have to help him.'

Kenzo grabbed Amber and held her tightly with one arm, the other curled around one of the iron rungs.

The surface was a boiling cauldron of thrashing water and even in the failing light of the plankton lamp, the two cousins could see the froth was a deep, blood red.

'It's too late,' shouted Kenzo, 'there's nothing we can do.'

Flip was drawn under for the last time and as Amber and Kenzo stared in horror, the waters calmed until they were still once again, the red surface broken only occasionally by the sail fins of whatever creatures had torn Flip apart. Amber sobbed in Kenzo's arms as the horror sank in.

'It's okay, it's okay,' said Kenzo gently, trying to calm her down.

'*No it's not!*' screamed Amber, prizing his arm from her, 'it's not okay. Flip is dead because of me.'

'Why because of you?' asked Kenzo, 'it's not your fault.'

'He helped me up the ladder, Kenzo, don't you see? He could have saved himself, but he pushed me up first. Flip saved my life, but it cost him his own.'

'There's nothing you can do now,' said Kenzo, 'what is done, is done. What we have to do is try to get out of here.'

'How?' sobbed Amber, 'I can't hold on much longer. We are going to die, Kenzo, can't you see? We are going to die!'

A sudden noise from above turned their heads upwards but their eyes closed quickly as a bright light flooded the shaft. Unseen hands slid the cover back, and a male voice called down the shaft

'Climb up,' called the voice.

Kenzo leaned to one side to allow Amber to lead the way and he followed close behind, making sure she didn't slip and fall into the waters below. Eager hands hauled them both over the lip of the shaft and they fell exhausted onto a slabbed floor, surrounded by men in black cloaks.

'Thank you,' said Amber, as someone placed a white sheet around her and she burst into tears again as the full horror of the recent events hit home.

Kenzo stood up and accepted his own sheet gratefully. Four men were in the room and he turned to face the one who seemed to be the leader, recognising the features, but not quite recalling where they had met before. Suddenly the memory came flooding back.

'Hello again,' said De-gill, 'welcome to the Watcher's-tower.'

Kenzo stared at the man who had offered him a fortune to kill Crispin months ago. Then he had wondered about the morality, but now it made total sense.

'De-gill,' said Kenzo, wiping the water from his face with the corner of the sheet, that boy, that thing, is down there, in the tunnels.'

'I know,' said De-gill. 'We are aware of the situation and are taking steps to deal with it.'

'What steps?'

'Suitable steps,' said De-gill, 'but that is for later. How did you come to be in the nursery?'

'The nursery,' gasped Kenzo, 'what on earth are you on about? One of our friends just got killed in there. Why do you call it a nursery?'

'Because that is what it is,' said De-gill. 'A place where the young of certain fish are born and grow in safety until they are big enough to take their place in the seas outside the Citadel.'

'What fish, Narwl?'

'No, not Narwl,' said De-gill, 'Ranah.'

'You have Ranah here?' gasped Kenzo, 'but that is crazy. Ranah are the biggest killers of the Hunters during the hunt. Why do you keep them here?'

'We do not keep anything,' said De-gill. 'They come and go as they please and have done so for centuries. It seems that many generations ago, our ancestors started feeding a few that had made their way into the tunnels and soon they associated this place with food. Since then, they congregate in the tunnels when the water is high; returning to the sea only when they are big enough to fend for themselves.'

'But they killed Flip,' said Amber, getting to her feet, 'that is unforgivable.'

'Nobody has ever accessed those tunnels,' said De-gill. 'It is only the fact that the waters are extremely low that enabled you to walk through them in the first place. Your timing was, shall we say, somewhat unfortunate and the Ranah did what the Ranah do best, they hunted.'

'But they killed him,' shouted Amber.

'Do not condemn a creature for doing what comes naturally,' said De-gill. 'This is the place where they get fed. The low waters meant they have not been fed for days, so, when they came across meat, they fed.'

'Meat,' said Kenzo in disgust, 'you refer to us as meat?'

'Is that not what we are?' asked De-gill, 'meat, flesh, bone. Are we not all the same? Ranah do not distinguish between potential prey, Kenzo, to them if it is not Ranah, then it is Ranah food. It is that simple.'

'This is unbelievable,' said Kenzo, 'adult Ranah are the scourge of our Hunters, yet you nurture their young under the Hunter's very noses.'

'It is the wheel of life,' said De-gill. 'Everything in balance in our tiny world. Everything has its place and everything has its role, even Ranah. But enough talk, we must get you warm and find you some fresh clothes. There will be time enough to discuss the ways of the world over the next few days. In the meantime, we must make you comfortable.'

'We have to get back to Pelosus,' said Kenzo, 'and warn him about that thing in the tunnels.'

'I am afraid it is too late for that,' said De-gill. 'As you are aware, the waters have risen once more and all links between the towers and the Citadel are cut off. The water will not fall again until next Moon-day, and until then, you are our guests.'

'But there must be a way,' said Amber, her anxiety rising, 'we have to warn the people of Bastion.'

'I am afraid not,' said De-gill, 'but fret not, despite our manner you will find us genial hosts. There are dangerous times before us and perhaps we can share our knowledge to mutual advantage. Please, come this way, we can talk more later.'

Kenzo and Amber followed the Watcher out of the room and made their way up a narrow stairway that followed the curvature of the outer wall.

Every twenty paces or so, they passed rooms leading off the stairway and within a few minutes, emerged into the courtyard at the centre of the Tower. They stopped for a moment and watched as several pairs of cloaked figures carried heavy white bundles from a row of carts and through another door.

'Oh my God,' whispered Amber, 'are they…?'

'They are the loved ones of the Citadel who have passed on,' said De-gill. 'Don't forget, this is our role in the wheel of life. Moon-day has ended for another month and now we will do what we are intended to do.'

'And what exactly is that?' asked Kenzo.

De-gill smiled, but did not answer the question.

'Come on,' he said, 'let's get you warm.' He led them into the smaller tower at the centre of the courtyard and the difference was immediate. The walls were painted white and decorated with glorious murals, ranging from market scenes to sea beasts. The floor was covered with a vibrantly coloured carpet the likes of which neither cousin had ever seen before, and its thick fibres were surprisingly warm to their uncovered feet.

'This is beautiful,' whispered Amber, looking around the entrance hall in wonder 'What is this place?'

De-gill had his back to them and took off his cloak before hanging it on a peg. Kenzo and Amber stared in astonishment. Under the dour black cloak, he was wearing a pure white tunic with matching trousers. His waist belt was of the deepest blue and a chain of ceremonial gemstones hung around his neck. He extended his arms and beamed a warm smile.

'Welcome to our home,' he said, 'please, come on up.'

They followed him up a small stairwell and into a hall where a huge fire roared its light and warmth around the busy room. Dozens of people lounged on luxurious couches; all dressed in a similar vein to De-gill, though the women wore white flowing dresses and were draped with coloured sashes rather than belts.

'Who are these people?' asked Amber in wonder.

'These are my fellow Guild members,' said De-gill.

'These are Watchers?' gasped Kenzo.

'Both Watchers and Midwives,' said De-gill. He turned around and clapped his hands.

'People,' he shouted, 'we have visitors. This is Kenzo and this is his cousin, Amber.'

Everyone in earshot called their welcomes and some came over to say hello in person. One older woman bustled over with a look of concern on her face.

'Oh, you poor thing,' she said to Amber. 'You must be frozen. Come with me. Let's see if we can find you something a bit more comfortable.'

Amber glanced at Kenzo in concern but when she received an encouraging nod, allowed herself to be led away. De-gill led Kenzo to the fire and another Watcher brought a tunic and trousers for him to put on. For a second, Kenzo hesitated and held the clothes awkwardly, still clutching the sheet around him.

'Is there a problem?' asked De-gill.

'Um, is there somewhere I could change?' asked Kenzo, self-consciously.

'Oh,' said De-gill, his eyes widening in understanding, 'I am sorry, privacy is not something we require here. Here, let me help.' He took the sheet edges and held it wide, allowing Kenzo to strip his wet underclothes and don the fresh clothing. When he was done, De-gill led him to an empty couch and arranged wine and food. The Narwl steaks were particularly delicious and complimented the bowls of various seafood harvested from the base of the tower where it met the sea. But his favourite were the perfectly shaped cubes of roasted Narwl meat interspersed with tiny fruits and strange vegetables, the strong flavours making his eyes water.

'These are wonderful,' said Kenzo, 'I have never tasted food so beautiful.'

'Our cooks are very talented,' said De-gill, 'and make up our own mix of spices unique to our trade.'

'Spices?' asked Kenzo.

'Tiny seed pods from plants we have managed to nurture over the years. Nothing on the scale of the farmers you understand, but sufficient to flavour our meals.'

'It is beautiful,' said Kenzo, 'may I have another?'

De-gill smiled and placed the platter before him.

'Help yourself,' he said, 'there is plenty more where that came from.'

He watched Kenzo eat in silence until the young man's hunger was satiated. Finally, Kenzo sat back and looked around the room in wonder.

'This is luxurious,' he said eventually, 'I had no idea.'

'Why would you?' asked De-gill, 'our trade demands sobriety and sombreness. The populace expects the image we portray in the Citadel. Here we can be ourselves and are no different to the rest of the people.'

'Still,' said Kenzo, looking around at the happy faces and sumptuous comfort, 'this is special.'

'We are very proud of our home,' said De-gill, 'but it is not so unusual. Each trade has its own ideas of comfort and express them in different ways. Our way is to display the opposite of our perceived persona. When you deal with death in all its guises, it is important to embrace life and all that it offers.' For the next hour, De-gill made small talk with Kenzo regarding life in the city. Finally, a murmur spread around the room and both men looked up to see Amber and the older woman re-entering the room.

'Wow,' said Kenzo, getting to his feet as Amber approached, 'you look amazing.'

135

Amber blushed furiously. Her gown was pure white like all the others but the sash that hung from her shoulder to the opposite hip was blood red, the only one in the room. Her hair was washed and brushed, and hanging softly around her shoulders.

'Quite the young lady,' said De-gill.

'Kenzo,' said Amber, 'they have a bath here, but it is bigger than ours, big enough for twenty people and not only was it filled with water, but it was hot!'

'Hot water?' said Kenzo in admiration, 'how can you heat so much water.'

'This fire,' said De-gill, indicating the flames. 'A series of channels lie beneath the hearth and a flow of water is constantly being warmed. As long as the fire burns, the water stays hot. One of our more special luxuries I suppose.'

'Amazing,' said Kenzo. He turned to speak to Amber but laughed out loud as he saw her leaning over a plate of food at the side of the room.

'Poor thing,' said De-gill, 'I forgot she hadn't eaten, she must be starving.'

'That's the cousin I remember,' laughed Kenzo, 'shall we join her?'

For the next few weeks, Kenzo and Amber enjoyed the Watcher's hospitality and even had their own rooms, a luxury unheard of in Bastion.

In the mornings, they slept late before sharing a sumptuous breakfast at their leisure and their days were spent talking to the Watchers or walking the courtyard to get some exercise. Every evening, they ascended the tiny stairwell to stand on the top of the tower and stare out over the seas toward Bastion. The waters had reached their previous level once again, but Kenzo knew, as everyone in Bastion now knew, the next time the waters fell, it would be to an unprecedented level and may not return.

One evening, the two cousins stood once again behind the castellated wall, though this time staring outward toward the horizon.

'What do you think is out there, Kenzo?' asked Amber.

'Who knows?' said Kenzo, 'other Citadels; perhaps other people.'

'The end of the world?' asked Amber

'Possibly, I suppose we will never know.'

'Do you think your father is okay?'

'I expect he is enjoying the peace and quiet,' laughed Kenzo. 'Probably taking the opportunity to do some entertaining.'

Amber nudged him in the ribs in mock disgust

'Uncle Tom doesn't do that sort of thing,' she laughed.

'Yeah, okay,' said Kenzo sarcastically.

Amber turned around and leaned her back against the wall to look over toward the Citadel as Kenzo continued to stare out at the horizon.

'Kenzo,' she said quietly.

'What?' he asked, over his shoulder.

'Everything is going to be all right, isn't it?'

'What do you mean?'

'Oh you know, all this business about Crispin; the water levels and the second city. It just seems that all around us, things that we have known all our lives are changing and I don't know if I like it.'

'I'd be lying if I said I was comfortable with it,' said Kenzo turning away from the open sea. 'I think there are things going on here that we don't understand, but I bet those in power probably know what's happening.'

'Who, the council?'

'Probably, but I think the Stargazer is the man who can shed some light on all this and as soon as we are back in the Citadel, I am going to ask him some straight questions. Flip was killed because of this Crispin thing and his family have a right to know what happened.'

'Well, we will be home tomorrow,' said Amber, 'and I for one, can't wait.'

'Why not? They are treating us well enough, aren't you comfortable?'

'I suppose so,' said Amber, 'they are very friendly, it just seems so, I don't know, contrived, I suppose.'

'I know what you mean,' said Kenzo, 'everyone is so friendly yet it seems we are being watched all the time.'

'Last night,' said Amber, warming to the subject, 'I was thirsty so I went to fill up my beaker from the pitcher in the Sanctum. Even though it was the middle of the night, one of the women appeared from nowhere to help me. It was as if she was already there and watching in case I left my room for any reason.'

'Oh come on,' said Kenzo, 'I don't think it's that bad, I would have noticed. There's certainly nobody in the corridors outside our rooms.'

'There wouldn't need to be,' said Amber. 'The only way out is through the Sanctum and all corridors lead there.'

'Yet there's nobody up here,' said Kenzo.

'There's no need,' said Amber. 'There's nothing up here to see and certainly no way out, but have you noticed, whenever we walk around the courtyard there always seems to be someone standing near the doorway to the lower levels? I bet if we tried to go back down there, we would be stopped.'

'Actually,' said Kenzo, 'come to think of it, on the night we were pulled from the shaft, they were very keen for us not to stay down there very long.'

'That's right,' said Amber, 'and if you remember, they also made sure we didn't see into any of the side rooms on the way up. Do you think they are hiding something?'

'Like what?'

'I don't know, but there is something going on here that they are keen to keep secret. Perhaps they just don't want the rest of Bastion to know they are actually quite nice people?'

'Oh yes, of course,' laughed Kenzo, 'I forgot that nobody else knows them like we do.'

'Anyway,' said Amber, 'I think it is worth taking a look around to see if there is anything else we can find out. What do you think?'

'I suppose it couldn't hurt,' said Kenzo, 'but somehow I think De-gill may have something to say about that.'

'Then we won't tell him,' said Amber.

'You mean sneak down there?'

'I do.'

'And how do we do that?'

'Easy,' said Amber, 'I have a plan.'

An hour later they joined De-gill and the rest of the Watchers in the Sanctum to have their evening meal and though they mingled freely and laughed along with the rest of them, underneath, they were both nervous about the plan they had made earlier. Finally, they both made their excuses and withdrew to their rooms, fully aware that the Watcher's socialising would go on long into the night.

Hours later, Amber woke from her sleep, roused by a gentle shake of her shoulder from her cousin.

'Amber,' he whispered, 'it's time.'

The young girl sat up and rubbed the sleep from her eyes.

'You ready?' she asked.

'Yes,' he said, holding up the plankton lamp, 'I reckon we've got approximately two hours before first light.'

'Right, I'd better get started,' said Amber and pulled the night robe around her. 'Good luck.' She stepped out of the room and walked along the corridor toward the Sanctum. Kenzo returned to his own room directly across the corridor and closed the door, leaving it ajar just enough for him to see out.

Amber reached the door of the Sanctum and took a deep breath before walking in. Sure enough, across the room, one of the older women was sitting on a couch, her legs folded up beneath her as she studied the scroll in her hands. As Amber approached, she looked up with concern on her face.

'Hello, Amber,' she said, 'are you okay?'

'Not really, Elora,' said Amber, 'I can't sleep.'

'Oh dear,' said Elora, sitting up, 'come and sit here, besides me.'

Amber did as she was told and Elora put her arm around her.

'What's the matter?' asked Elora, 'bad dreams?'

'I don't know,' said Amber, 'I just can't stop thinking of my mother back in Bastion.'

'Oh you poor thing,' said Elora, 'I keep forgetting you are still very young. Are you close to her?'

Amber played along, as though she had never known her mother, it was important that this woman believed her.

'Very close,' said Amber, 'and I'm sure she must be very worried about me.'

'Another few days and you will see her again,' said Elora comfortingly.

'I know,' said Amber, 'it's just that I miss her so much. Our rooms weren't very big but every night we used to spend the last hour together before she tucked me into my bed. It seemed that no matter what our trials and tribulations of the day, when she tucked me in, I used to feel so safe and slept soundly knowing she was around.'

Elora smiled and took Amber's hand.

'I tell you what,' she said, 'I know I'm no substitute for your mother, but what if I come to your room and tuck you in? Perhaps it may help you sleep.'

'That would be nice,' said Amber, secretly excited that her ruse had worked, 'are you sure you don't mind?'

'Not at all,' said Elora, 'come on let's see if we can sort this out.'

They both stood and walked back to Amber's room, Elora with her arm around Amber's shoulder to offer comfort. Amber climbed into her bed and Elora tucked in the cover tightly beneath the mattress.

'How does that feel?' asked Elora.

'Lovely,' said Amber, 'just like my mother used to do.'

'That's nice of you to say so,' said Elora, 'good night, Amber.'

'Good night,' replied the girl and closed her eyes in pretence of sleep, knowing fully that by now, Kenzo would have crept down the corridor, through the Sanctum and out into the courtyard. Part one of their plan had been successful and until first light, there was nothing more she could do. The rest was up to Kenzo.

139

Chapter 24

Pelosus woke from a deep sleep and reached out to light a candle, unsure what had awakened him. For a moment or so, he sat with his eyes shut, contemplating the previous day's activities before turning to reach for his gown.

As he turned, a tiny movement caught his eye and he called out in fright as he saw the silhouette of someone sitting in his chair across the room.

'Don't be afraid,' said a gentle voice, 'it's only me.'

Pelosus's heart was racing. Across the room less than a few feet away, the woman of his dreams sat quietly, waiting for him to wake.

'Petra,' he gasped, 'what are you doing here?'

'I came to see you,' she said.

The smell of Petra's scent was overwhelming and Pelosus realised it was this that had woken him up.

'I am honoured,' said Pelosus, 'but it is a strange time to be visiting, don't you think?'

'I accept that the time is unfortunate,' said Petra, 'but I have very busy schedules and this is the only time I am free at the moment.'

'Can I get you a warm brew?' asked Pelosus.

'No, I am fine,' said Petra, 'actually I should have woken you a while ago, but was enjoying your rhythmic breathing. I was tempted to join you but you looked so comfortable lying there, I did not want to disturb you.'

Pelosus gulped. Every word she uttered seemed laced with promise and despite him being fully aware that this was a trait of her trade, his mind was intoxicated with the hints of wonders to come.

'You should have,' he said before he had chance to stop himself. 'Sorry,' he added quickly, 'I didn't mean to…'

'It's okay, Pelosus,' she said, 'it is understandable and soon there will be all the time in the world to share our dreams. In the meantime we have an arrangement and I came here to see if there have been any developments.'

'Not much,' stuttered Pelosus, standing up to don his robe, 'I have managed to decipher the embroidery, but it doesn't make any sense.'

'You have found the message?' asked Petra, a hint of excitement to her voice, 'show me.'

'Allow me to light some candles,' said Pelosus and a few minutes later the room was alive with dancing candlelight. The Stargazer retrieved the handkerchief from a shelf and spread it out on the table top before pulling up a chair to explain what he had found.

'This embroidery hides letters within its thorns,' he said, 'they are very few and make out a simple sentence.'

'Which is?'

'Beware the Brotherhood.'

'And do you know what it means?' she asked.

'No, not yet, I have been busy on other assignments, but I should have time to research more today.'

'Pelosus,' said Petra, placing one of her gentle hands on his, 'I cannot lie, I am a little disappointed. I thought you would have more information than this for me.'

'I am sorry, Excellency,' he said, 'but with the command of the guard, the rationing of the food and the exploration of the second city, I have had no time to spend on this. I will try harder.'

Petra sat up straight, her hand leaving his abruptly.

'Exploration of the second city?' she asked, 'on whose command?'

'On the orders of Helzac himself,' he answered, 'but I thought you knew.'

'Of course,' said Petra quickly, 'he did mention it actually, how foolish of me to forget.' Her hand returned to his and a wonderful shiver ran up his spine as she rubbed it gently.

'Remind me,' she said, her tone now soft and gentle again, 'what exactly *were* you looking for?'

'Anything, really,' said Pelosus, 'especially any information about who lived down there and how they lived. It would seem obvious that whoever they were, they existed before the waters rose and if there are any clues as to why that happened, then there may be indications as to the cause and therefore, perhaps the cure.'

'And did you find anything?'

Pelosus thought quickly. This was a terrible position to be in. Two of the most powerful people in the Citadel were using him to their own ends and both had sworn him to secrecy. If either found out he had betrayed their confidence, then he would be dead within hours, the victim of an assassin's blade. He looked down at his lap, thinking furiously as to what to do when suddenly the most unexpected thing happened. Petra placed her hand under his chin and lifted his head. For a second she gazed into his eyes and before he could say anything, kissed him gently on the lips, lingering for a few seconds before breaking away. Pelosus's mind was spinning and all thoughts of secrecy had flown.

'Pelosus,' she said, gently caressing his cheek, 'I know this is difficult, but there is a chance that we both have a future together. Once the safety of our people is guaranteed, I will have more time to spend with you and we can plan how we are to spend the rest of our days together. But until then, we have to be completely open and honest with each other and hold no secrets. I understand that Helzac may have sworn you to silence, but this is more important than life itself. Now, why don't you tell me what you know?'

For the next half an hour, Pelosus relayed what he had found in the second city, withholding only the part about Helzac's paintings. Finally, he

141

sat back and they both stared at each other as the dawn light crept through the windows.

'So, does he believe you?' asked Petra.

'Hard to say,' said Pelosus, 'though he is certainly sceptical.'

'And did you find out anything about this Brotherhood?'

'No, sorry.'

'Not to worry,' she said, 'what you have told me is very interesting and may sway which way our decisions fall. Pelosus, there is one great secret of this Citadel that you need to know, yet I hesitate to share with you as should certain people find out, then we would all surely perish.'

'I thought you said no secrets?' said Pelosus.

'I did, and intend to keep that vow, but just give me a few more days, then I will tell you everything I know. Can you do that?' Once more, her hand sought his cheek and his eyes closed at the gentleness of the cool touch.

'Of course,' he said, 'no problem.'

'Good,' said Petra, 'now, could you bring me a glass of water, please, I am a bit thirsty.'

Pelosus rose and took a beaker to the side room where he kept the flasks of water.

When he returned there was no sign of Petra but a short note was left on the table where she had been sitting.

'Pelosus. Sorry I had to leave so suddenly, but I just remembered something important. I will see you soon. All my love, xxx'

The Stargazer picked up the letter and held it to his nose. It smelled of her perfume and his eyes closed once more at the memory of her presence.

For the best part of an hour, he sat at the table studying the handkerchief, often returning to his shelves of scrolls as ideas came to him, but always fruitless in his search for explanation. The one thing that came back to him over and over again, was the statement made by Petra that there was one great secret that she couldn't share with him yet. Perhaps if he had this secret, the message would become clear and it made no sense to hold on to it for a few more days. His life was already in danger, in fact, everyone's were, and a few more days may be the difference between life and death for hundreds of people. He needed to know what it was that Petra was hiding and if she felt anything toward him; then surely she would forgive him this indiscretion. He would follow her into the tunnels and ask her for the information.

He unlocked the double lock securing the frame to the wall and followed the Governess through the hidden panel.

The tiny tunnel spiralled downwards into the depths of the city, passing dozens of similar side tunnels on the way. Though he was intrigued about what was at the end of each one, he stayed on the main route, finally emerging into the seawater chamber Amber had discovered weeks earlier. He stared down into the depths, but unlike Amber, could see no water, just a seemingly bottomless dark pit.

Pelosus walked slowly around the ledge looking for any sign that would tell him which way Petra had gone. The answer came rather quickly as the beautiful smell of the Governess's unique perfume wafted out of one of the tunnels and he entered immediately, absolutely certain he was going in the right direction. Once again, he ignored dozens of side passages and within minutes, came across a solid wooden door blocking his way.

'Haven't come all this way to stop now,' he thought, and turning the iron ring, opened the door to step inside.

After the dark and damp tunnel, the light and warmth of the room was a welcome surprise. At its centre, a fire sent dancing light around the room and Pelosus stopped dead in his tracks as he absorbed the astonishing sight before him. All around the room, filling every inch of wall space, thousands upon thousands of scrolls sat snugly within their purpose-made alcoves.

'By the fingers of the Saint,' he whispered coarsely, 'I can't believe it.' He made his way over to the nearest wall and ran his hands over dozens of scrolls, talking to himself as he went. 'All this time, and this room was below my very feet.'

He heard a noise and spun around in fear. Across the room, a man was sitting at a table, his back toward him, yet obviously aware of his presence.

'Who is there?' asked the seated man without turning around.

'I am a friend,' said Pelosus nervously.

'You should not be here,' said the man, 'you are putting yourself in great danger.' He rose to his feet and turned slowly from the table to face him. Pelosus couldn't make out his features in the gloom, but could see that he was dressed in a long robe of dirty cloth, secured around the waist with a simple length of rope. His head was clean-shaven and he was obviously very advanced in years. For what seemed an age, nobody spoke as they stared across the flames at each other, but eventually the man spoke again, his voice, quiet and gentle.

'Who are you?' he asked.

'My name is Pelosus,' he replied, 'and I am...'

'The Stargazer,' said the man, 'I know of you. My name is Warden and I am the keeper of the scrolls. Please state your business, as this place is forbidden to citizens on pain of death. Quickly or I will call the guards.'

'I am sorry,' said Pelosus, 'I didn't know, but please don't call the guards, for I mean no harm. I only seek information.'

'About what?'

'About this whole situation.'

143

'You mean the disappearing sea?'

'Mainly that,' said Pelosus, 'though I am also interested about the Brotherhood of the Sark.'

The man gasped and caught his breath as he stumbled back against the wall. A coughing fit followed and his face grimaced in pain as he slid down the wall clutching his chest.

'Are you okay?' shouted Pelosus and without waiting for a reply, ran forward to help.

'Please,' gasped the man, 'my medicine.'

Pelosus turned to the table. In amongst the various scrolls there was a jug of water, a drinking beaker and a small bottle.

'Three drops,' said the man between coughs, 'in a beaker of water.'

Pelosus filled the beaker from the jug, and carefully allowed three drops of a thick green liquid to mix with the water. He handed it over to Warden who gulped it down as quickly as possible. Gradually his breathing slowed and he managed to sit upright.

'Thank you,' he said, 'I'm sorry about that. My heart isn't what it used to be and any shock can bring on the coughing.'

'What is this stuff?' asked Pelosus sniffing at the bottle, his nose wrinkling in disgust.

'Careful with that,' said Warden, 'in tiny doses it is a strong narcotic. It eases the muscles and stops the spasms, but any more than that can kill a man. Please help me up. When he was on his feet he turned to look directly at Pelosus who took a step backwards in shock as the fire light illuminated the old man's face.

Pelosus stared at the wound where the man's eyes should be. Not only was he obviously blind, but the angry horizontal scar straight across his face was evidence that they had been burnt out with a red hot bar.

'My god,' said Pelosus, 'what happened to you?'

'I'm sorry, I do not understand,' said the gentle voice, his head tilting slightly.

'Your eyes, what happened to them?'

'Oh, of course, forgive me. I am so used to the situation I forget that it is not the norm. My eyes were taken as a young boy as punishment.'

'Punishment for what?' asked Pelosus in disgust.

'For being curious,' said Warden.'

'What did you do?' asked the Stargazer.

The old man took a deep sigh as he remembered.

'I was caught spying on a Courtesan when she was being intimate with a client,' he said, 'and before you say anything, I know this is probably the favourite pastime of most young boys on Moon-day, but this lady was the Governess herself and her client was a well-known councillor with a family.'

'Who?' asked Pelosus.

'You wouldn't know him,' said Warden, 'it was a long time ago. Suffice to say I was lucky to escape with my life. If it wasn't for the kindness of the Governess, I would have been thrown from the city walls. As it was, she managed to calm him down and get him to agree to a commuted sentence. My eyes and a lifetime spent incarcerated in these rooms is the price I paid for my indiscretion.'

'That's awful,' said Pelosus. 'Have you been down here all this time?'

'It's not so bad,' said Warden, 'the first thirty years were the worst, but now I quite enjoy it. It's warm, safe and I have enough food to eat. I know every inch of this library and ensure the scrolls are kept in excellent condition.'

'How can you do that?' asked Pelosus, 'I mean, you can't see them, can you?'

'Trust me,' said Warden, 'when you have been here as long as I have, you get to know every scroll intimately. There are ten thousand, seven hundred and sixty three scrolls in this room. Each day I remove over a hundred, unroll them and check for signs of decay.'

'But how?' asked Pelosus.

'By feeling the texture,' said Warden, 'by smelling for damp, by tasting for mould, by listening to the way they unravel. When you have been without sight for as long as I have, your other senses compensate. I may not have eyes, Stargazer, but I have a far clearer picture of what this room contains than you do.'

'And what if you find damage?' asked Pelosus.

'Sometimes there is nothing I can do,' said Warden. 'Age catches up with everything so when the scrolls reach the end of their life, they give me a child who can't read, and they copy out the characters onto new parchment without understanding what they write.'

'Why would they do that?' asked Pelosus.

'So I can never learn their secrets, I suppose,' said Warden. 'If the children could read, they could pass on the information to me and information is power.'

'Do you know how old they are?' asked Pelosus,

'Not exactly, though there is one where the original scribe seems to have pressed too hard with his quill and the date can be made out by my fingers. It is dated over seven thousand years ago, but it is no way the oldest. In fact, it lies in this half of the room, all those behind you are much, much older.'

'This is tragic,' said Pelosus, 'to be surrounded by so much information yet not be able to read it. It must tear you apart.'

'It used to,' said Warden 'but time heals everything.'

'Who are they?' asked Pelosus.

'Sorry?' asked Warden.

'You said they give you an illiterate child. Who is it that controls these archives and subjects you to this lifetime of torture?'

'The Courtesans, of course,' said Warden, 'you are directly below the Pleasure tower, but surely you already know this.'

'No,' answered Pelosus, 'the tunnels are somewhat confusing.'

'Yes, I suppose they are at first, but you soon get used to them.'

'You have been there?'

'On a regular basis,' said Warden. 'In the beginning I felt my way only a few yards past the door, but over the years I explored further and further. At first, I kept my journeys secret, but my senses weren't what they are now and little did I know that for years, the Governess had me followed. When her spies finally reported I had no intention of fleeing these rooms, she allowed me full access and we now often discuss my trips into the catacombs.'

'And you know your way around them?'

'I do.'

'Then what are their purpose?' asked Pelosus, 'how many are there? Where do they go? I have so many questions; I do not know where to start.'

Warden fell silent for a few moments before speaking again.

'I will answer your questions,' said Warden, 'but before I do, I have questions of my own. Draw close.'

Pelosus stepped closer and Wardens hands sought the neckline of his robe. Before Pelosus could react, he tore the lapels apart, ripping his robe from waist to navel.

'What are you doing?' shouted Pelosus, but fell silent as the old man pushed him back against the wall and placed his right hand firmly over Pelosus's heart.

'Silence,' he whispered, 'I will ask you some questions and you will answer. Do not try to lie for if you do, I will know and will tell you nothing. Tell the truth and I will share everything I know. Understood?'

'Yes,' said Pelosus.

'Good,' said the strange man. 'Now, breathe deeply and answer truthfully, are you truly the Stargazer?'

'I am,' said Pelosus.

'And you have come here through the catacombs?'

'I have.'

'Are you alone?'

'I am.'

Pelosus could feel his heart beating through the tips of Warden's hands.

'Why have you come here?' continued the old man.

'To seek information,' said Pelosus.

'Do you intend me or any of the courtesans any harm?'

'No.'

146

'What would you do with this information?'

'Help the citizens of Bastion,' answered Pelosus.

'Final question,' said Warden, 'what are your feelings toward Petra, Governess of the Courtesans?'

Pelosus swallowed hard. He knew his heart was now racing and had no doubt that Warden could feel the thumping beneath his clawed fingers. He considered hiding his feelings but knew this man would detect any falsehoods. Finally he took a deep sigh and admitted his feelings aloud, not just to Warden, but to himself.

'I love her,' he said and flinched as Warden released his grip and stood back.

'I believe you,' Pelosus he said, 'your heart tells me you are an honest man. Ask your questions.'

Pelosus sat at the table while Warden brought a bottle of wine from an anteroom, his feet finding the route easily as they had done a million times before.

'It is a poor quality,' he said when he returned, 'but I seldom get visitors. So, Stargazer, how can I help you?'

'First of all,' said Pelosus, 'are we safe here?'

'Only the Governess comes here these days,' said Warden, 'but she is busy elsewhere and not due back for two days.'

'Busy elsewhere?' asked Pelosus.

'Entertaining?' said Warden.

'Oh,' said Pelosus, the disappointment obvious in his voice, 'I see.'

'Banish the thought, Pelosus,' said Warden, 'she affects all men thus.'

'Well, I suppose I have to wonder what it is you actually know,' said Pelosus. 'By your own admission, you are unable to read these scrolls, so perhaps I can help you. Perhaps I could withdraw the scrolls and read them myself, sharing the information you have guarded for so long.'

Warden laughed out loud.

'And how long do you think that would take?' asked Warden, 'there are over ten thousand scrolls here and we have but weeks before everyone in this city starves to death. You won't even have read the scrolls on one wall. I have been here over sixty years and I have not got through them all.'

'Wait a minute,' interrupted Pelosus, 'if I didn't know otherwise, that sounds like you have read many of them.'

'I have,' said Warden

'But how?' asked Pelosus. 'You have no eyes.'

'For many years I was lost in a world of ignorance,' said Warden. 'The Courtesans made sure that the boys they sent down couldn't read, so they were unable to pass on the secrets, but one day, one of the boys pressed

147

too hard with the quill and I found I could make out some of the script with my fingers.'

'What did it say?'

'Nothing of interest, but the point is, I realised this was a way for me to explore the scrolls. For an age I considered different ways of recording their writing, all to no avail, but eventually I came up with this.' He reached under the table and unclipped something attached on the underside.

Seeing Warden struggling with the weight, Pelosus crouched and helped the old man retrieve an oblong frame made from bone. The whole thing was approximately the same size as a standard unfurled scroll and the inside was filled with a smooth white substance.

'What is it?' asked Pelosus.

'This,' said Warden, 'is my copying tablet. With this I was able to copy anything that the boys wrote.

'But how?'

'The surface is a thin layer of wax, made from many melted candles. When the boys came to do the copying, I made sure that the blank parchment was sitting on the wax tablet. After that, all I had to do was ensure they pressed very hard with their scribe and when they had finished, lo and behold, I had an engraved copy in the wax.'

'Ingenious,' said Pelosus.

'All I had to do then,' said Warden, 'was run my fingers gently over the wax and the whole picture revealed itself before my missing eyes.'

'Hang on,' said Pelosus, 'that's all very well, but surely you couldn't do that with every scroll, where would you keep them all?'

'You are right,' said Warden. 'That was impossible, but don't forget, a lot of them were useless records. Nothing more than inventories, songs and prayers, that sort of thing, but in a world of darkness, these were beacons of burning light.'

'And have you read them all?'

'Alas no,' said Warden, 'don't forget I am governed by the frequencies of the scribes. Sometimes weeks go by before my wax tablet gets used.'

'That must be so frustrating,' said Pelosus.'

'It is, but even the few I have translated have made me gasp at the inaccuracies of our histories.'

'So did you write the translations down?'

'No.'

'But you can't remember them all, surely?'

'Like I said, when you have been without eyes for as long as I, your other senses make up. I may not be able to repeat the scrolls content exactly, but I certainly can recall the important ones.'

Chapter 25

Kenzo ran around the perimeter of the courtyard, keeping against the wall in the darkest of the shadows. Even though he was quite sure there would be nobody out here, there was no point in taking risks. Within a minute, he reached the door leading down to the lower levels and eased it open onto the stairway. He hesitated for a moment before taking the stair downwards, to the strange room where they had first entered the Watcher's Tower. A candle flickered in the darkness complimenting his ever-present Plankton orb and the contents of the room sprung into view before his eyes.

The first thing he saw was the covered shaft where he and Amber had been dragged clear of the seawater and he paused for a few seconds as the memory returned like a horrible hot wind.

Moving on, he walked around the room, taking in anything of interest. Several empty skin buckets sat neatly against the wall, each sitting neatly within each other and Kenzo recoiled sharply when he sniffed at one, containing a disgusting liquid in the bottom. In another corner, he found a pile of thin sheets, made of the similar type of cloth that made up his tunic. The sheets were stained badly and stuffed into baskets made of woven seaweed.

Finding nothing else of interest, Kenzo lifted the wooden cover from the shaft walls and held the lamp down into the darkness. At first, the sheer stillness of the water a few feet below reflected the image of the lamp and his own face perfectly, but the sudden appearance of a sail fin breaking the surface made him flinch as he recalled the horror of a few weeks earlier.

He turned to leave the room, but having an idea, he picked up the bucket containing the smelly liquid and poured it down the shaft. The result was instant and the water below thrashed into a cauldron of activity as the predators fought for the unexpected treat.

'Fish food,' he confirmed to himself and put the bucket back before replacing the cover over the shaft.

Kenzo checked the rest of the room for any hidden exits and finding none, made his way back up the curving stairway, this time, checking the side rooms as he went. In the first, he found piles of stained sheets similar to those he had seen back in the lower room. In addition, there were Narwl skin vats containing water where more sheets were being soaked. On shelves around the room were neat folded piles of clean and dry sheets, obviously having already been through the washing process and ready for being used again.

In the second room, the scene was more grisly and similar sized vats were full of Narwl entrails, obviously being stored ready for feeding the Ranah. Empty buckets were stacked in rows ready to transfer their grisly contents to the lower levels and the smell caused Kenzo to gag. He spotted another side room and walked in, holding his lit candle before him.

Immediately he saw a table draped with a sheet and though he was nervous as to what lay beneath, he pulled the sheet away, recoiling in horror at the shocking scene before him.

Under the sheet lay the naked body of a dead woman, the skin obviously a cold grey even in the limited light of the candle. Her eyes were staring sightlessly toward the ceiling and her lower jaw hung open in a silent scream. The sight of the dead woman was bad enough, but the state of the body filled him with revulsion. The whole of the upper body was gaping wide open from neck to navel and the innards had been completely removed. The cavity stared back at him like an enormous hungry mouth and for an age, Kenzo stared at the cadaver in horror. Finally, he came to his senses and turned away from the woman, his heart beating faster than it ever had before. As he did, he held up the candle and the revulsion deepened when he realised that there were at least five more tables in the room, all covered with the same sheets as the first. He felt no need to explore further and was quite certain that these sheets also covered similar atrocities.

He left the room of corpses and walked back through the room with the vats of Narwl entrails but suddenly stopped and spun around to face them, the full horror suddenly dawning upon him. The containers weren't full of fish innards, but human. The baby Ranah were fed on human entrails.

Kenzo's mind was spinning as the implications sank in. He knew the Watchers dealt with the dead, as the funeral pyres were constantly visible from the Citadel, but why disembowel them first? It made no sense and as for feeding the entrails to the fish, that was just wrong and he was sure that if the council found out they would put an immediate stop to it. He left the room, realising that the time must be getting on and he had to be back at the main tower before sunrise but as he climbed the stairs, he came across one more room.

'A few more minutes won't hurt,' he thought and entered the last room to investigate. This one was completely different. The walls were plastered smooth and were painted in a pristine white finish. The floor was spotlessly clean and slabs of smooth stone were used as work surfaces all around its edge. A slightly familiar smell hung in the air, a welcome relief from the pervading smell of raw meat that permeated the lower levels and rows of various knives and saws hung from hooks on the walls. He walked in, looking nervously around, before making his way to a solitary woven basket at the end of the room. He peered in, not sure what he would find, but once again recoiled in horror as he saw piles of bones, some still with strips of flesh attached to their bloody sides.

This was beyond comprehension. Why would the Watchers strip the flesh from the people's bones? Surely, they wouldn't feed the flesh to the Ranah as well, that would be unforgivable. The people of the Citadel thought when their family members died, the bodies were taken from the city, carried to the Watcher's tower and prepared for the final journey to the kingdom of the Saint. A ceremony that involved the anointment of oils and the saying of prayers for the dead before they were cremated in the holy fires. If they found out that their loved one's flesh was stripped from their bones before being cast to the predators of the deep, there would be riots in the streets.

Kenzo looked around the room in confusion.

'Why is this room so different?' he asked himself. 'Why is it so clean? Why did they go to so much trouble to keep it in such pristine condition if it was just used to butcher the cadavers, then?'

Kenzo had seen enough and turned to leave the room when he saw one more item that he had not noticed before, something that stood out from the crisp whiteness of the surrounding cell. In the furthest corner of the room, on one of the polished stone worktops, a much smaller sheet no larger than a tunic was draped over something much smaller than a body. The sheet was stained from whatever it was beneath, and though Kenzo guessed it was probably something horrific; his imagination wouldn't allow him to walk away without finding out for certain. He walked forward and without hesitation lifted the smaller sheet away, fully expecting to see a fleshless face staring up at him.

But it was no skull that revealed itself from beneath the sheet, but something a lot less threatening. A pile of neatly prepared meat chunks, each the same size and carefully prepared to match its neighbour. Now the sheet was off, the sweet smell was stronger and certainly not unpleasant. Suddenly Kenzo realised where he had smelled the aroma before, it was back in the Sanctum at meal times. Kenzo's mouth watered at the memory of the succulent meat and realised that not only were these cubes exactly the same size as those presented on the skewers, but were obviously smeared with the spices that gave them that wonderful taste.

Suddenly Kenzo stopped and his face dropped as the full implications hit home. The never-ending supply of bodies from the Citadel, the rooms where they were dismembered and the convenient way they disposed of the entrails. It all fitted together, yet the realisation was too horrific even to imagine. This room, that was so clean, was obviously a place of preparation and these cubes of meat the result of skilled hands.

'Oh no,' groaned Kenzo stepping backward, 'please no, not this.'

The meat cubes, the spices, the never ending supply of flesh, it was all so simple and made clear, horrifying and gut churning sense. The flesh of the dead didn't feed the Ranah of the sea, it fed the people of the Watcher's-tower.

Kenzo turned around and leaned his hands against the wall as he retched violently, spewing the remains of his supper over the spotless floor, mixing with the tears that fell freely from his horrified eyes.

Amber pulled her cloak tighter against the cold night air and glanced up at the sky. It was definitely getting lighter and she looked down into the courtyard for the signal she knew was due. She had been up on the top of the tower for an hour, anticipating the dawn and at last, the agreed time had come. She narrowed her eyes, staring at the doorway and right on cue, the sudden flash of a plankton orb being revealed from beneath a cape for the briefest of seconds. She answered the signal with one of her own before racing back down the stairs to her room.

Down below, Kenzo sprinted silently across the courtyard to the central tower, once again keeping to the darker shadows away from any prying eyes. But this time he was not so successful and deep inside the darkness of a room high in the outer wall, a pair of eyes narrowed as they followed his progress across the courtyard. De-gill knew that time was running out and he had to make a decision. The Watchers never allowed outsiders to come to their tower, they would never understand their ways and though circumstance had dictated these two had entered his world through no fault of their own, he knew there was no way they could be allowed to share the Watcher's secrets with the general population of Bastion. With a heavy heart, he picked up his black cape, and left his room to make the arrangements.

Across the courtyard, Amber reached her room, and picking up the water jug, smashed it on the floor. She bent down to pick up one of the shards and dragged it across her palm, gasping in pain as the ragged edge cut into her flesh. A few seconds later, she ran down the corridor and into the Sanctum, calling out as she ran.

'Elora,' she cried, 'I've cut myself.'

The Watcher sprang up from her doze and walked quickly toward the girl.

'Oh my God, Amber, what have you done?'

'I dropped the pitcher,' said Amber, 'and as I went to pick up the pieces, I cut myself.'

'You are having a bad night,' said Elora, 'here, let me see.'

Amber unfolded her fist and winced as the wound opened and the blood oozed between her fingers to drip onto the floor.

'Ooh, that's look sore,' said Elora, 'come on, let's get it sorted out,' and led Amber toward the ante room where they kept the medical aides. Amber followed, knowing full well that it would leave the way clear for Kenzo to re-enter the tower. Ten minutes later, the woman once more led Amber to her room.

'Thanks, Elora,' she said, 'I really appreciate it.'

'You've had quite a night,' said Elora, 'now why don't you try to get a few hours' sleep. Don't worry about breakfast, I'll put some aside for you, you sleep in as long as you like.'

'Thanks, Elora, I will,' said Amber.

As soon as the woman had left, Amber crossed the corridor and knocked gently on Kenzo's door. When there was no reply, she knocked again and eased the door open. At first her heart sunk when she couldn't see him in the gloom, but to her great relief, finally saw him sitting at the table with his head in his hands.

'Kenzo,' she whispered, 'thank God, I thought you weren't here, are you okay?'

Kenzo looked up at his cousin, wondering if he should tell her the awful truth. He quickly decided that though she had a right to know, now wasn't the time.

'I'm fine,' he said, 'just a bit tired, you okay?'

'My hand is a bit sore,' she answered, 'but apart from that I'm fine. Anyway, don't worry about me, tell me what you found.'

'Well, there's certainly no way out,' said Kenzo, 'not that I can see anyway, but I have concerns, Amber. There's something going on here that I don't understand.'

'Like what?' asked Amber sitting on his bed.

Kenzo proceeded to tell Amber about what he had found, though leaving out his suspicions about the source of the Watcher's meat.

'So you think they feed our dead to the fish?' asked Amber when he had finished.

'I do,' said Kenzo, 'and we need to tell the council as soon as possible.'

Before Amber could answer, the door creaked open, revealing Elora and De-gill, both draped in their traditional jet-black cloaks.

'De-gill,' stuttered Kenzo, 'what are you doing here? Why are you dressed like that?'

'I think you know why we are here,' said De-gill quietly, 'and I am so disappointed in you.'

'Disappointed, why?'

'Because I like you, Kenzo,' said De-gill, 'and have done so since I first saw you on that Moon-day months ago, when I asked for your help to locate Crispin.'

'But we haven't done anything wrong,' said Kenzo.

'On the contrary, you tricked us and left the Sanctum to explore those areas where our invitation did not extend, seen things not for your eyes and opened wounds long since healed.'

'I don't understand,' said Amber, 'all he did was try to find a way out. We didn't want to bother you.'

De-gill looked at Kenzo over Amber's head and when he saw the young man shake his head, realised that the soldier had not discussed the gory detail with his cousin.

'Still,' said De-gill, 'there are secrets here that should, and will remain our business and to that end, we have to withdraw our hospitality, at least until this business with Crispin is over.'

'What has Crispin got to do with this,' asked Amber, 'surely he is still in the Catacombs?'

'There is more to Crispin than you realise,' said De-gill. 'He represents a great danger to Bastion and unless we can stop him, then this great city and the lives of those who survive his wrath will never be the same again.'

'We know that he has changed,' said Amber, 'but despite this, he is still only one boy.'

'He was a boy,' said De-gill, 'but in the last month he has developed into something that bears no resemblance to the person you once knew.'

'What do you mean?' asked Kenzo.

'I will share no more details,' said De-gill, 'there is still a chance that this situation can be retrieved and no one need ever know anything different.'

'How?' asked Kenzo.

'With the death of Crispin,' said De-gill. 'Tomorrow is Moon-day and we can alert the council to the dangers. All the trades will combine forces and enter the Catacombs to find the creature - over four hundred men, armed with spears and swords. If we are lucky and he is still weak, we may triumph, but if he has matured to his full potential, then it is too late for all of us.'

'This is crazy,' said Amber, 'how can one boy be such a danger, it makes no sense?'

'It makes total sense,' said De-gill, 'and in time all will be revealed, however, due to your night time forays, we have no choice but to lock you in a secure place until this is over.'

'But why?' pleaded Amber. 'We can look after ourselves and we don't know anything about your precious secrets. Do we Kenzo?'

When there was no answer, she turned to her cousin.

'Kenzo?'

The young man and the Watcher were staring at each other in silence across the room.

'Kenzo, what is it?' asked Amber, 'what are you not telling me?'

'Nothing that can't wait,' said Kenzo. 'Do as he says, Amber, I promise you will be okay.'

'But...'

'Amber,' snapped Kenzo, 'go with Elora. I need to talk to De-gill.'

The two women left the room, leaving the men behind.

154

'You haven't told her?' asked De-gill.

'No, so there is no need for her to come to any harm.'

'What makes you think any of you are at risk of harm?'

'I am not a stupid man,' said Kenzo. 'There is no way you can allow me to carry the news of your atrocities to the council. The Citadel will turn against you and the other trade towers will storm this place. You will be cast from the walls of your own tower in disgust.'

'Really?' said De-gill quietly, 'and what makes you think that they will be surprised by the news?'

'There's no way they know about this,' said Kenzo, 'they can't. What self-respecting human would stand by and allow you to get away with cannibalism?'

'Cannibalism is a very strong word,' said De-gill, 'I like to think of it as economics.'

'What on earth are you on about, economics?'

'You have no idea, Kenzo,' said De-gill. 'Running a city as large as Bastion is a balancing act. The population is expanding and the Narwl harvest gets smaller each year. We are only one bad season away from starvation, and we need to nurture every source of protein we can, just to stay alive. When our loved ones die, their soul goes to heaven and what is left is no more than an empty shell made up of valuable resources that the city is desperate for. It would be collective suicide to discard such an ample and recurring source of protein to the sea.'

'What do you mean the city?' asked Kenzo. 'Nobody in Bastion eats your cursed meat.'

'Really? Tell me, Kenzo,' said De-gill, 'do you attend the Moon-day markets?'

'Of course I do,' said Kenzo, 'everyone does.'

'And do you ever partake of the Baker's wares. The gravy filled pies, the juicy pasties, and the savoury cakes. Which is your favourite, Kenzo? Which one makes your mouth water on the night before Moon-day?'

'No,' said Kenzo, 'you're lying.'

'And what about the meats from the Hunters, Kenzo? Yes there are Narwl steaks and Fish cakes and Crab sticks, but what about the sausages, the pates and the stews? What do you think is the main ingredient? Even you must have realised that they did not taste of that godforsaken fish that makes up the main diet of almost everyone in the Citadel.'

'You are lying,' shouted Kenzo, 'you would never get away with it.'

'Do you think so? Let me tell you, Kenzo, once, a long time ago, human meat was freely available in our markets. Our ancestors not only enjoyed it, but craved it. Tell me, what did you think of the skewers? Did you not enjoy them? Does your mouth not water even now at the thought? Don't

155

worry, Kenzo, this is not a failure on your part or anyone's part. You can no more control what makes up your cravings than you can count the stars in the sky. It is not your fault, Kenzo, it's nobody's fault. It's in your very make up. In every cell of every bone that makes up your body.'

'Now you're just talking rubbish.'

'Am I Kenzo? From the very first cell that duplicated to form the embryo you once were, this need is inbred. It's just that you have been ignorant of the facts, as have most people in Bastion. But not the council, Kenzo, we are aware of it and always have been. This is the secret of our race, Kenzo, a burden the ruling council carries with them and pass on to their successors.'

'I don't believe you,' said Kenzo, 'and even if it is true, why do you allow it to happen? Surely, there are other foods available; I would rather eat seaweed than human meat.'

'But therein lies the problem, Kenzo, you have no choice. The Bakers, Farmers and Hunters, don't supply the markets with the protein, as we prefer to call it, for profit, but necessity. We order them to do it.'

'But why?'

'Because the people need it.'

'I don't understand.'

'Hundreds of years ago, the Council at the time decided enough was enough and stopped harvesting the protein. Within weeks, the population was ill and people died in the thousands. At first they thought it was just an ague, but eventually realised, it was the lack of human meat. The guild of science at the time discovered that our physiology had come to depend on the supply of human flesh. They immediately reintroduced the practise and the death rate stopped. Over the years, we have carried out many experiments on inmates from the Prison-tower, and have been proved right on every occasion. Withdraw the protein, and we die. It is as simple as that.'

'But, if that is true, and the council knows this, why are you so keen to keep us here.'

'Because only the council knows. The population don't and if they did, then the reaction would be the same as yours. By the time we could explain, they would tear down this tower stone by stone without knowing the consequences. In effect, they would commit mass suicide.'

A long silence ensued eventually broken by Kenzo.

'So, where does that leave us?' he asked.

'That depends on you,' said De-gill. 'You are an intelligent man and I believe I can trust you to keep this information to yourself. However, tomorrow is Moon-day and if I am wrong, your words alone can bring down this entire city. I do not mean you harm, but I cannot allow you back into the Citadel, at least not yet. There are other pressing things that we must deal with first.'

'Crispin?'

'Exactly and let's not forget, if you had been successful in the task I gave you all those months ago, then neither of us would be here today. However, what is done is done and now we have to clean up the mess. You and your cousin will be held in one of our cells until it is over. Hopefully, by next Moon-day, everything will have calmed down and we can present you to the council to see for yourself that I am telling the truth. Don't worry, you will be well looked after, but it is the best I can offer. The moon has remained in the sky and the water is already dropping. The next twenty-four hours are essential to the very survival of our species, so I can't afford any interference from you. Now, if you don't mind, we have to go.'

De-gill stood to one side and allowed Kenzo to leave the room and make his way down into the Sanctum. Amber was sitting on one of the couches, flanked by two of the women. As they passed, Amber and the women stood and followed them out. They exited into the courtyard, but to Kenzo's surprise, turned left toward the external stairway leading up to the tower walls.

'Are we not being taken down to the rooms below?' he asked De-gill.

'No, the cells are built in along the castelades,' said De-gill. 'They are airy but we will provide you with fire for warmth. Don't worry, I'm sure that we can sort all this mess out and next Moon-day, you will be back with your families.'

Kenzo's mind was working furiously. There was no way they could escape the tower via the tunnels but he also knew that he couldn't stay here for another month. They made their way up onto the ramparts and toward the cell in the far wall. Suddenly, Kenzo had an idea, and called out to his cousin a few yards in front.

'Amber!'

'What?'

'Do you remember your twelfth birthday?'

'Sorry?'

'Your twelfth birthday, do you remember what we did that got us into so much trouble?'

'Yes but…'

'No buts, Amber, we need to do it again.'

'When?'

'Now!'

'But, Kenzo, it's too dangerous.'

'I know, but it's a chance we have to take,' he said, 'our lives depend on it.'

'Are you sure, Kenzo?' said Amber.

'I wouldn't be saying this if I wasn't,' said Kenzo, grabbing her arm. 'We can do this.'

'Okay,' she said, 'quickly though, before I change my mind.'

'Lose your cape,' he said, 'it will be too heavy.'

'What are you doing?' shouted De-gill, 'guards, take them to the cells.'

'Too late for that,' shouted Kenzo as he scrambled up onto the castellations, closely followed by Amber. 'Sorry De-gill, your explanations are just too convenient. There's no way you would ever let us leave here alive.'

'Don't be stupid,' shouted De-gill.

'Too late,' shouted Amber, 'time to go. Goodbye, Mr Watcher.' She turned to Kenzo, her heart racing with excitement. 'Ready?' she said, 'on three; one, two, three...'

In total unison, the cousins launched themselves from the tower wall, arms and legs flailing in an effort to stay upright as they plummeted to the waters far below.

Chapter 26

Warden and Pelosus sat across the table from each other, both caught in the awkward silence.

'So,' said Pelosus eventually, 'are you going to tell me about them?'

'About what?'

'The scrolls.'

'Oh those? No, I don't think I will,' said Warden.

'I don't understand; you have all this knowledge. Why can't you share it with me?'

'You didn't let me finish, Pelosus. What I was going to say was this. I won't share the knowledge of the Courtesan scrolls, for that would be futile. Trust me there is nothing there but hearsay, rumour and fairy tales.' He paused for a moment before continuing.

'You seem a good man, Pelosus. We are both men of learning and I detect honesty about you. I have not walked the streets of Bastion since I was a boy and have now grown so old that even the memory escapes me. However, I am aware that there are things afoot that are difficult to understand. I have a lot of knowledge within this aged brain but as my days pass, I find things more difficult to process. My mind becomes muddled and often I forget what it was I was supposed to be doing. My days are coming to a close, Pelosus and all of a sudden, I have realised that when I am gone, all the knowledge I have teased from this secretive room, will once again be lost forever. If I allow that to happen, then what would be the point? My life enduring all these years of darkness would have been in vain. I can't allow that to happen, Pelosus, my life has to be worth more than that. So no, I won't share the contents of the Courtesan scrolls, for they are but meaningless drivel.'

'However,' he continued eventually, 'I do have something else. Something so precious that no other person alive even knows it exists.' He stood up and retrieved a scroll from a nearby wall, his fingers having counted along the row until he found the right one.

'Open it,' he said, handing the scroll to Pelosus.

The Stargazer did as he was told and read the words to himself.

'It is the story of the Six-fingered Saint and the emergence of the Citadel from the waters,' said Pelosus. 'What is so different about this? Every child in Bastion knows the story.'

'Exactly, but look on the reverse and tell me what it says.'

Pelosus turned the parchment over.

'I can't,' he said, 'it is in a language I don't understand.'

'That's because it's in the language of our ancestors,' said Warden, 'all the scrolls in this side of the room are written the same and nobody, not even the Courtesans can read them.'

'So how is this one important?'

'At first, it confused me as it is the only scroll that has writing on both sides, then as I realised the implications, it was as if my sight was being returned. What if it was the same story?'

'So what?'

'Don't you see? If that was indeed the case, then I had a direct translation, two sets of scripts saying exactly the same thing, and if I had that, I could directly compare some of the words of the ancients with those in our tongue. After that, it was relatively straightforward to replace the letters on the older scrolls with ones I could understand, and by the time I had finished, I could read the language of our ancestors.'

'That is amazing,' said Pelosus in awe, 'it must have taken you a long time.'

'Almost ten years,' said Warden, 'but worth every second, for as I got more expert in the translation, all these became available to me.' He swung his arm in an arc indicating the scrolls on the older side of the room, 'and let me tell you, Pelosus, the contents of these are not like the others within these walls, oh no. No fantasy or religious claptrap in these documents, these tell an entirely different story altogether.'

Pelosus let out a gasp of excitement. For most of his life he had suspected there was more to the histories than what they were taught and at last he was about to find out the truth.

'First of all,' said Warden, 'you need to clear your mind of everything you know and everything you think you know. What I am about to say will be like nothing you have imagined and certainly nothing that any living eyes have ever seen. I want you to imagine a place where the sea is a mere fraction of its present size, there are no Citadels and there is land as far as the eye can see.'

'I am familiar with the concept,' said Pelosus.

'Now imagine this land folded like the ripples of a thrown garment. Land that rises to enormous heights and dramatic low places, interspersed with endless plains and forests of growth. A place where plants the likes of which we can never imagine, grow in such abundance, that no amount of harvesting could ever deplete their numbers. Rivers of water run freely at the bottom of these valleys and creatures of untold diversity scurry amongst the undergrowth, making their way of life in a place of plenty.'

'You seem to be describing the heavens of the Six-fingered Saint,' said Pelosus. 'To consider such a place exists in the physical world is considered blasphemous within the city.'

'I have no doubt that it does,' said Warden, 'but I have no time for such idiocy, for if people encouraged dialogue instead of banning it, the Citadel would be a far more harmonious place. Please bear with me and eventually my ramblings will make sense. Anyway,' he continued, 'in this place, larger creatures feed on smaller ones. As we feed on the crabs and fish of the sea, the strong land animals feed on the weak. Over time, the strongest survive and over a length of time that we cannot even begin to imagine, a predator evolves with cunning and a capacity to adapt to its environment. Over countless millennia, this animal becomes the dominant creature of its surroundings and evolves to become one of the most intelligent and feared species on the planet.'

Pelosus was enthralled. As a man of science, he often harboured thoughts of the origins of man, but seldom had the chance to express them in case he ended up in the Prison-tower.

'I know what you mean,' he said with excitement. 'Years ago, I had a colleague who expressed similar sentiments. He theorised that as the Ranah dominates the Narwl, such was surely the way of the world. Nobody of any sense believes the Citadel just rose from the water, that's preposterous. You only have to examine the causeways to the towers, the way these Catacombs are hewn from solid rock or even look at a simple stairway to see the hand of mankind, and the way that you describe their evolution makes total sense. But if what you say is true,' he continued, 'then this place is not a gift of some unseen deity, but one built by the hands of men, the dominant predator on the planet.'

Pelosus stopped talking and stared across at Warden who had fallen strangely quiet.

'Are you okay?' he asked.

'I'm fine,' sighed Warden, 'just waiting for you to stop spouting that semi-religious Narwl crap.'

'But, you said…'

'What did I say, Pelosus?'

'That man had evolved to become the dominant predator.'

'I think that you will find that I said, "A dominant predator emerged." At no time did I say it was man.'

Pelosus's jaw dropped open, taking in the implications of what Warden was suggesting.

'You mean we are not the dominant species?' he asked.

'The answer to that is complicated,' said Warden. 'If I was to answer either yes or no, I would still be correct. For you to understand, I have to tell you a story as if to a child. Suspend your scepticism for a while longer, Pelosus, and prepare yourself for a truth almost too horrible to comprehend.'

'What you have to remember,' said Warden, 'is that the things I am about to describe, took place over a time you cannot even begin to imagine. At first, man, or should I say the ancestors of man, did indeed take their place amongst the higher echelons of the food chain. So successful were they that they came to dominate the world and the population grew to unimaginable numbers, eventually using up all the resources of the planet. Ultimately, their way of life was unsustainable and eventually imploded. Food was almost

161

impossible to find and though some managed to scrape an existence in isolated pockets, starvation, disease and war took its toll, resulting in a relatively tiny amount of humanity surviving. Mankind had taken the planet to the tipping point and though nature has a way of healing itself, it takes time. For ages, this world must have been a barren wasteland with tiny pockets of people scraping a living wherever and however it could. But even those who managed to survive must have found life unimaginably hard and when the food ran out, some would have turned to the only place left where they could find sustenance.'

'What do you mean?'

'When someone is starving, they will do anything to survive and as people died, meat became available.'

'You mean…'

'Cannibalism,' confirmed Warden.

'But that's appalling,' said Pelosus.

'Is it? What would you or I do in the same circumstances, I wonder?'

'I don't know,' said Pelosus, 'but I would like to think that I have enough moral fibre not to lower myself to those depths.'

'Spoken like a man who has never hungered,' said Warden. 'But I digress, the point is, at first it was probably just the odd bit here and there and only in certain areas, but as time went on, it became a habit and eventually, as time progressed and generations passed, it became a way of life. I know it's hard to take, but imagine a people who not only ate their own dead, but actually encouraged a high birth rate to ensure an adequate supply of meat.'

'But that's not sustainable,' said Pelosus. 'Once you start killing, the death rate would exceed the birth rate and the numbers would plummet.'

'Possibly,' said Warden, 'but don't underestimate the numbers involved here. We are talking about millions of people all scratching a living from a struggling planet. It was a dire time of horror and desperation, but throughout all this was one constant, the survival of the fittest. Those who were strong took advantage of the weak and harvested them to suit themselves. Over thousands of years, some isolated groups preyed on the poor until it became the norm and eventually there was a divergence of paths in the way each group evolved.'

'That is unbelievable,' said Pelosus.

'But true, nevertheless,' countered Warden, 'but cannibalism comes at a price. Like inbreeding, it has a fundamental effect on the very cells of the human body. After a while, it makes you ill, the structure of the cells change and develops in different directions. Random abnormalities appear and left unchecked, run in directions abhorrent to the normal human form.'

'What are you saying?'

'Those who survived predominantly on human meat would have evolved differently to the main human bloodline. Over time, their bodies would have changed. Little by little, each surviving generation would be slightly different to the one that went before. Weak mutations would die out naturally, but where one enhanced the survival rate of their own bloodline, then that change would remain and the process starts all over again. Finally, given time, it is highly likely that they would evolve into a form unrecognisable to what we are today.'

'What sort of abnormalities are we talking, here?'

'Who knows? Every birth would be unique, every new-born creature different to the one before. Cell abnormality would be rampant and many would die within hours of their birth. Organs would be incomplete or missing and the death rate would be huge. However, occasionally, a successful birth would occur, complete with all the parts necessary to live. They may have been in an order unfamiliar to us, but successful all the same. Imagine these creatures then successfully breeding, their deformed bodies the norm, yet developing even more as they continued along their own evolutionary path. Over thousands of years, the abnormalities would settle and a standard form emerge, one so different that they would be difficult to recognise as a cousin of man.'

'And this really happened?'

'It did, or so says the parchments.'

'They could be wrong?'

'They could, but there is so much more in the scrolls, all equally as fascinating but easily proved.'

'Hang on, what were they called?'

'Who?'

'These creatures.'

'I think you know what they were called.'

'The Sark?' ventured Pelosus.

'The Sark,' confirmed Warden, 'and until today, I thought I was the only person alive to know of them. That was why I was so shocked when you first came in and said their name.'

'Okay, if what you say is true, then where are they now?'

'Well that's where it becomes interesting. As the human population fell, the planet returned to some semblance of normality and life became sustainable once again. However, now there were two major species, one a predator and the other its prey. Over time, the Sark not only preyed on humans, but also enslaved them to build their cities. Places of safety and strength placed high on the tops of mountains where they were safe against any attack.'

'Attack from whom? I thought they were the top predator.'

'They were, but they were also in the minority. Mankind had survived the dark times and though billions died, there were still huge amounts alive around the world. To them, the existence of the Sark would be as normal as night follows day and I think we can safely assume that there

163

would be constant conflict between them. As the humans grew in strength once more, they became such a threat that the Sark had to build huge cities, impregnable to any human assault. Behind those walls they carried out their own obscene existence, leaving the safety of their cities only to hunt random individuals such as travellers or anyone out wandering on their own.'

'Travellers?'

'Don't forget the overall picture, Pelosus, we are talking about a place where a man could walk on land for all his life and never see the same place twice. Centres of civilisation would sprout up everywhere and though it could take many months to travel between them, people certainly did so.'

'So what did these Sark look like?'

'Now that's a question I can't answer,' said Warden. 'The scrolls refer to them everywhere, yet so far, I have found no description. There are many scrolls yet un-deciphered and it is my dream that one day I will uncover a description, but alas, I have had no success as yet.'

'And what of their cities?' asked Pelosus. 'Do you have any description of those?'

Warden laughed out loud.

'Pelosus, for an intelligent man you can be a bit stupid. Have you not realised yet? I thought I was the one who cannot see, yet you have spent all your life walking around with your eyes closed.'

'Bastion is a Sark city?' gasped Pelosus as understanding finally dawned.

'It is. Designed by the Sark and built by enslaved human hands.'

'This is incredible,' said Pelosus. 'All this time seeking knowledge and the evidence was all around me.'

'There are none so blind as those who will not see,' said Warden.

'But you said they built their cities on top of mountains, not on islands. Why build a city here where they would be at the whims of the Moon-day tides.'

'Because, my dear Pelosus, at the time this city was built, there was no sea. This city was indeed built on top of a mountain, in fact, one of the highest mountains on this side of the planet. The water came much later.'

'Wait a minute,' said Pelosus, 'I understand the theory of the waters being drawn along by the moon's gravity each month, but it always returns when the Moon continues the journey around the planet. The only difference is that now, it evaporates completely into the atmosphere and that is why it is disappearing.'

'Only partly right,' said Warden. 'Yes the moon is responsible for moving the water, but we lose none to the atmosphere. It just remains in vapour form for far longer due to the gravitational pull and deposits it somewhere else from whence it cannot return.'

'Where?'

'I don't know, perhaps beyond a range of mountains that holds in this sea. Wherever it is, it is this which is responsible for the loss of the seawater.'

'But if what you say is true and this place dominated a mountain top, then that means that there were once lands all around it, probably inhabited by our ancestors.'

'I believe so.'

'Then where did the sea come from in the first place?'

'A simple reversal of the process that I just explained,' said Warden, 'I believe that this planet's surface has always been at least half covered with water. Eons ago, it was the other half of the planet and the horizons that encircle us now were fertile lands were populated by humans yet over lorded by Sark. One day, or even over the space of thousands of years, something happened in the heavens that I do not even pretend to understand and the Moon's orbit changed. This effected the monthly movement of water and it started being deposited on this side of the world. Somehow it stayed here, perhaps by encircling mountain ranges, and again, over a period of time the water levels rose.'

'That would have affected the humans in the valleys.'

'You are correct and once again mankind was at risk as millions died. Some would have escaped to the new lands being formed beyond the ranges, but many more would have been trapped in isolated pockets and sought safety on higher ground.'

'On other mountains such as these?' suggested Pelosus.

'Probably, but when the waters continued to rise even those refuges were denied them until, finally, there was only one place left to go.'

'Here,' said Pelosus.

'Exactly.'

'You think they assaulted this city and took it from the Sark?'

'No, not at all. The Sark cities were built especially to repel such attacks, but as the humans became more desperate, the stronger the Sark's position became. Don't forget, they relied on humans for their food, so it made no sense to allow them to die out. No, I think they struck a bargain, safety from the waters in return for meat, human meat.'

'That's preposterous,' said Pelosus, 'who would sacrifice themselves for just a few days extra life? I would rather drown.'

'Oh at first,' said Warden, 'I'm sure it would just be the dead that were bartered. Those who died of old age or disease would be a small price to pay for the life of the young, but over time, I believe the Sark exploited the situation and the life of the surviving humans descended into a hell that is almost too horrible to contemplate.'

'Which is?'

'They were farmed!'

Chapter 27

Kenzo surfaced, coughing and spluttering. He had hit the water awkwardly and had the breath knocked out of him. He looked around, seeking Amber and was relieved to see her surface alongside him.

'You okay?' gasped Amber when he stopped coughing.

'I think I swallowed half the bloody sea,' said Kenzo.

'That was higher than I thought,' said Amber, treading water furiously.

'It was,' said Kenzo, 'are you ready?'

'It looks a long way,' said Amber.

'We've swum further than this on Moon-day,' said Kenzo, referring to the annual swimming races that occurred every year between the youngsters of the city. 'The distance between causeways is much further.'

'You sure?' asked Amber, 'it doesn't seem like it.'

'Positive,' lied Kenzo, 'don't worry, we'll take our time and take plenty of rests. We'll be there in no time.'

'Yeah, but the gates are locked.'

'It's Moon-day, remember,' said Kenzo, 'the water is already falling. In an hour or so, the water will be lower than the causeways and the gates of the city will open.'

'If I can stay afloat that long,' gasped Amber, 'okay, let's go.' Once again, they struck out with occasional rest periods where they flipped over onto their backs to catch their breath. Finally, they reached a small slope leading up to the gate the Bakers used to enter the city. They dragged themselves out onto the stony surface and lay on their backs, gasping for breath.

'That must be some sort of record,' gasped Amber to the sky.

'It was a long way,' agreed Kenzo, 'perhaps I should ask the Hunters if there are any vacancies?'

'I don't think so,' laughed Amber, 'between this and the shaft in the Watcher's-tower, I've had enough of the sea to last me a lifetime.'

'Yeah, me too,' said Kenzo sitting up, 'come on, let's go.' He approached the gate and banged as hard as he could to attract the attention of anybody on the other side.

'Hello,' he shouted, 'anyone there?'

Braille was glad of the change from keep duty. It was boring and the other squads took every opportunity to tease him about what he was missing in the city, so when Fatman had asked for volunteers to man the gates on Moon-day, he had jumped at the chance.

'Why are you doing that?' asked Ufox, shocked that the giant man had actually volunteered for an extra duty.

'Because, my little fart-breath friend, I know the shift is only for eight hours. That means I will be knocking off just in time to join in with the celebrations tonight. You, on the other hand, will be up for selection when Fatman selects the night guard, so, while you are dragging sorry arses to the cells all night, I will be spending this on the best whore I can afford.' He tossed the Star-stone over to Ufox who stared at it in amazement.

'Where did you get this?' he asked in envy.

'Now that would be telling,' said Braille, 'but I reckon that little sparkler may get me a bash at the Governess herself. What do you think?'

'Or four of the prettiest at the same time,' said Ufox. 'Why don't you take some leave and book yourself in over at their tower for a week.'

'Can't wait that long,' said Braille, 'and besides, with all this crap going on with the rationing and everything, we don't know what's coming next. Nah, I'll have my fun tonight, though your idea of four Courtesans is a good one.'

So it was that with half a mind on his anticipated evening of lust and debauchery, Braille had found himself on gate duty when someone banged on the gate from the outside.

'What the...? Who's out there?' he shouted.

'Open the gate?' shouted Kenzo, 'please, we need help.'

Braille slid a vision panel to one side and peered through.

'Kenzo,' he shouted in surprise, 'what the shit are you doing out there? Don't you know Moon-day doesn't start for another hour?'

'Braille,' said Kenzo, not sure if he was happy or not to see his old friend, 'we are not out here from choice; let us through, we need to see the council.'

'You got someone else out there?' asked Braille with interest.

'Yes, Amber,' said Kenzo, 'open the gate.'

'That's your pretty cousin isn't it?'

'Yes.'

'Where are your clothes?'

'We had to get rid of them in order to swim, now open the gate.'

'Is Amber half naked too?' asked Braille hopefully.

'Braille,' shouted Kenzo, but before he could finish he was pushed aside by Amber, stretching up on tiptoe to meet Braille's eyes through the hole in the door.

'Yes I'm half naked, you dumb oaf,' she snarled, 'and freezing my bloody arse off. Now, if you don't open this gate, I swear I will tear it down with my bare hands and use your balls for earrings, now, open this damn gate.'

'Whoa, girly,' said Braille, 'no need to be so rude to your uncle Braille now, is there?'

'You're not my bloody uncle,' shouted Amber, but before she could say anymore, she was pulled aside by Kenzo.

167

'Don't argue with him, Amber, you'll get nowhere.'

Behind them, the creak of one of the giant gates being eased open told them that Braille had come to his senses and they turned to enter the safety of the city.

Kenzo and Amber squeezed through the gap and stood shivering in their wet undergarments. Kenzo realised there was unexpected silence and looked up to see Braille and his comrade leering at Amber in ill-disguised lust. He turned to Amber and realised her own undergarments were clinging to her body and leaving nothing to the imagination.

'Give me your cape, Braille,' he said.

'What?' asked Braille.

'Your cape, take it off and give it to Amber.'

'Why?'

'To cover her up, for Saint's sake,' said Kenzo, 'can't you see she is freezing?'

'I can see she's not a little girl anymore,' said Braille. 'Seems like your snotty nosed cousin turned into a fine young woman.'

'Come anywhere near me,' said Amber, 'and I'll show you how feisty this young woman can be.'

'Ooh, touchy too,' said Braille with a smirk, but despite this, he gave his cape to the girl, much to the disappointment of the gathering crowd.

'Right,' said Kenzo, 'we need to get to the keep as quickly as we can.'

'I'll take you,' said Braille.

'I do know the way,' said Kenzo, 'we will be fine.'

'Dressed like that?' asked Braille. 'You will probably be arrested for flashing and she will get raped by the first arsehole who takes a fancy. Mind you,' he whispered, 'I don't suppose there's a chance of me and her…you know, seeing as we are such good mates and all.'

'Braille!' shouted Kenzo. 'For Saint's sake, this is serious.'

'Okay, okay,' said Braille, putting both his hands up in mock defence, 'I was only asking.'

Without further ado, they made their way through the city avoiding the crowds accumulating for the Moon-day celebrations wherever possible. Within fifteen minutes they were walking across the courtyard of the keep and approached the inner tower. Kenzo rapped on the door and an official looking man answered, looking down his nose at them in disdain.

'We need to see Pelosus,' said Kenzo.

'He is not here,' said the man.

'Then where is he?' asked Kenzo, 'this is urgent.'

'I don't know where he is,' sighed the man. 'Now, if you don't mind, I have work to do.'

'Wait,' shouted Kenzo, putting his foot in the door to stop it closing, 'what about Petit the clerk, is he here?'

'Do you have an appointment?' asked the man.

Before Kenzo could vent his frustration, a voice called out from within.

'It's okay, Bennett,' said the voice, 'I will speak to them.'

The man called Bennett opened the door to reveal Petit standing behind him.

'You have returned,' he said.

'Yes and I have news,' said Kenzo, 'but these are things we should not speak of in public.'

'Then you had better come in,' said Petit and stood aside to allow them into the Tower of the Saint.

'Not you,' said Petit, looking up at Braille.

'I'm with them,' said Braille. 'We come as a package.'

'Is this correct?' asked Petit, looking at Kenzo.

Kenzo looked at Braille and the comical look of pleading in his eyes.

'Yes,' he sighed, 'I suppose so. I will take responsibility for him.'

'Yes, you will,' murmured Petit, 'follow me.'

Kenzo, Amber and Braille followed Petit up the stairs to his chambers and took seats at his table. Bennett brought warm brew and they waited patiently until everything had calmed down. Finally, Petit joined them at the table and looked around expectantly.

'Right,' he sighed, 'what is all this about?'

Kenzo glanced over toward Bennett, standing in the corner.

'It's okay,' said Petit, 'Bennett holds my full trust, so you can speak freely.'

'Well,' said Kenzo, 'since we last spoke, we managed to locate the missing boy.'

'You returned to the Catacombs?'

'We did.'

'Is he alive?'

With a deep breath, Kenzo told the clerk about everything that had happened over the course of the last month, including the perceived threat from Crispin and the revelations of the Watchers. The clerk let him talk without interruption, clinging on to every word until finally, Kenzo sat back and waited for Petit to speak.

'That is some tale,' said Petit eventually, 'and you are sure about this Crispin thing?'

All three nodded.

'I saw it with my own eyes,' Braille lied, 'it were *orrible*.'

'Okay,' said Petit, 'I have to think about this. Pelosus is away at the moment but he may have more knowledge about this phenomenon. I would like to take his counsel before we overreact.'

'But the longer we wait, the more danger we may be in.'

'Nevertheless, we will wait,' said Petit. 'The last thing we need is to start a panic in the streets before we actually know what this thing is, so, first things first, have you eaten?'

Amber realised she had not eaten all day, and hid a smile when Braille shook his head so vigorously that she thought it was actually in danger of falling off.

'Right,' said Petit, 'I will arrange for you to be fed and to get some rest. When Pelosus is back, you will tell your story to him and together we will deal with this situation to the satisfaction of everyone.'

'Will there be steak?' asked Braille, his mouth watering.

'I'm sure cook can find some,' sighed, Petit. 'After all, if there are no steaks in the Tower of the Saint, then what is the world coming to? I will arrange someone to take you to the kitchens and prepare a place for you to rest. You have done well, Kenzo and I am sure Pelosus will look kindly on a promotion.'

Kenzo gulped. A promotion already? Fatman would be livid.

'Thank you, sir,' he said.

'Good,' said Petit, 'you stay here while Bennett and I make the arrangements.'

He turned and walked out of the room leaving the two cousins and the soldier behind him. Within half an hour, Amber, Kenzo and Braille were in the tower basement and sitting around another table. However, this time it was an enormous kitchen table made from planks of Narwl bone polished to a gleaming finish. All down the centre lay a row of dishes containing the sort of food the commoners of the city could normally only dream of.

'I have never seen so much food,' said Amber in awe, wondering where to start.

'Me neither,' mumbled Braille through the mouthful of crab meat he had already grabbed before sitting down, 'I don't know what you are involved in, but whatever it is, keep doing it.'

'Judging by the size of the cook, this is probably just her lunch,' whispered Kenzo, glancing at the enormous woman busying herself at the far end of the kitchen.

'Kenzo,' hissed Amber, shoving an elbow into his ribs, 'stop it, you are being unkind.'

'But I have never seen such a fat woman,' said Kenzo, 'look at her, she is huge.'

They all stared at the back of the woman who was now berating a kitchen servant about the standard of cleanliness in her area.

'She is big,' agreed Braille, 'but I'd have a crack at it.'

'Braille, shut up,' hissed Amber, glaring at him, 'she's coming over.'

'Everyone all right?' she shouted as she approached, her breath wheezing from her overworked lungs.

170

'Fine, thank you,' said Amber. 'It all looks so good, we don't know where to start.'

'Well,' said the cook, 'You take your time and help yourselves but don't forget, leave room for afters. I have a lovely Apple and Sugar-shell pie in the oven and nobody makes Apple and Sugar-shell pie like Daisy.'

'Daisy?' queried Kenzo.

'Yup, that's my name, Daisy. My mother named me after the tiny flowers that grow out of the Citadel walls each spring.'

'Oh,' said Kenzo slowly, wondering how on earth someone as big as this woman could seriously be called Daisy.

'What's Sugar-shell pie?' asked Braille suddenly.

'You've never tasted pie?' asked Daisy in mock horror and seeing the blank faces on the other two, burst out in laughter.

'Well, my dears,' she said, 'you three are in for one of the best treats of your life. Get some meat and biscuits down you and I will bring you the best thing you have ever tasted. By the time I have finished with you, you will think you have died and gone to heaven.' She turned away to return to the inner kitchen, laughing to herself as she went.

'Never had pie,' she laughed, 'how absurd.'

An hour later all three lay on soft couches in one of the Tower ante rooms. Braille was groaning and holding his stomach.

'My guts hurt,' he said, seeking sympathy from the other two.

'I'm not surprised,' said Kenzo, 'you had four portions of that pie, let alone all the meat you ate.'

'Three and a half,' said Braille, 'I left some.'

'You have to admit,' said Amber, 'it was delicious.'

'It was,' said Kenzo, 'but I think we all overdid it a bit.'

'Does everyone in the Tower of the Saint eat that well?' asked Amber.

'Apparently so,' answered Kenzo, 'it pays to be somebody of importance in Bastion.'

Slowly the chatter died down as the heat of the fire had an effect on the two tired cousins and eventually, all that could be heard was their heavy breathing as they slept the sleep of the exhausted.

Though tempted to take an afternoon nap himself, Braille was painfully aware that he had a busy night ahead of him and if he raised the ire of Fatman, he could well end up on night duty, so with a hint of jealousy, he left them sleeping and made his way out of the keep and back to the gate.

Back in the Tower of the Saint, a tapestry hanging on one of the walls moved slightly and two people stepped out of the hidden doorway to stare at the sleeping youths.

'How long will they be asleep?' asked Bennett.

'Several hours,' said Daisy, 'I laced the pie with Socaine, the Sugar-shell masked the taste.'

'Good,' said Bennett. 'Call the others and move them into more suitable accommodation.'

As Daisy waddled away, Bennett approached Amber and leaned over to brush her hair gently.

'Sleep well, pretty one,' he said, 'you are going to need all your strength, very, very soon.'

Chapter 28

Pelosus and Warden talked for hours until the older man tired.

'Is there anything else?' asked Pelosus.

'Not much really?' sighed Warden, 'I have no doubt that the scrolls contain all the answers you require but alas, I have only scratched the surface. The knowledge in these alcoves is indeed huge but at best, I can translate no more than one or two a month. It deserves better attention, Pelosus, from someone who can devote their full attention to unveiling their secrets, someone like you.'

'And I can imagine no better way to spend the rest of my days, Warden, but there are events afoot that I fear will snatch this privilege from me.'

'The disappearing seas?'

'Exactly, and after listening to you, I fear it is a problem that is not going to go away. I suspect that once more the heavens conspire to alter the balance of this world and the seas are undertaking the process of relocating to the other side of the planet.'

'I think you are right,' said Warden, 'and you should make the suitable arrangements for your people to leave the Citadel.'

'I will, and you will come with us, along with all your scrolls. That way, your work can continue and you can be part of it.'

'I fear not, Pelosus, my bones are tired and I feel myself failing inside. I am not long for this world but at least I can go to my maker knowing the little knowledge I have gleaned through my life has been passed on.'

'There is one more question I need to ask, Warden,' said Pelosus. 'If all you say is true and the Sark ended up farming our ancestors, where are they now? How come there is no sign of them, or of their way of life?'

'I'm afraid I can't help you with that one, Pelosus,' he said, 'you will have to work that one out for yourself.' He stood up and held out his hand. 'Good luck.'

'Thank you, Warden,' said Pelosus, 'I will never forget what you have done for us and when all this is over, I promise we will continue where you left off. Who knows? We may even name a library after you.'

'That would be nice,' said Warden. 'Now, you should go, you have a lot to do.'

Pelosus took the man's hand and pulled him in to hug him tightly before leaving the chamber of scrolls and making his way back through the Catacombs.

Fifteen minutes later, he entered his own room and closed the panel doorway behind him. On the table, he saw a bowl of fried seaweed with Narwl strips in a Sugar-shell sauce and half a bottle of wine. He smiled, Petit had obviously been in the night before and left him his favourite supper, and though it was almost dawn, the food was still edible and he sat at the table, surprised at how hungry he actually was.

As he ate, Pelosus considered everything he had been told by Warden, his mind spinning at the astonishing revelations. As strange as it all seemed, it was all entirely feasible and somehow felt very true. The strange way the moon was affecting the sea, the origin of the Citadel, the artefacts from the lower city, it all made complete sense.

Today was Moon-day, and if he were correct, the water would be lower than it had been for three months, ever since that first meeting in the council chamber. If it was, it would more or less prove the theories correct and they would have to make plans to leave the Citadel. Not immediately, as they could probably sustain the population for a few more weeks, but as the sea receded, their food sources would be harder to reach and the drinking water could dry up at any moment. He sat on the bed, knowing full well that he should go straight to the council, but desperate to sleep.

'Just a few minutes,' he thought, 'an hour at the most.' He lay down and within seconds, was fast asleep.

Outside the Citadel, the waters were falling rapidly, far faster than they had ever done before. In the towers, the tradesmen fussed over their carts, making sure their wares were ready for the short journey across the causeways to the Moon-day market. Weavers packed clothes, capes and blankets, knowing full well that winter was coming and these were the items that would sell more readily, while the Bakers piled their mouth-watering treats into baskets, the source of the meat still a secret to all but those in the higher echelons of the order.

All were ready. The Courtesans were preened to perfection, Hunters dressed in their finest parade gear, even the Farmers had made a special effort, their carts of fruit, and vegetables swathed in flowers that had just come into season.

Finally, the bells tolled and the age old tradition of Moon-day started again as it had for thousands of years. The tradition had been handed down from generation to generation and though everyone in the Citadel looked forward to it with great excitement and expectation, there were some individuals who knew that today was the last Moon-day this Citadel would ever see.

Kenzo opened his eyes and looked around the room in confusion. As his memory returned, he realised that this wasn't the room in which he had fallen asleep. The room was sparsely furnished with two basic beds and a table with a jug of water and two bone cups. Amber was fast asleep on one of the beds and despite his repeated attempts, he could not wake her. He stood up and staggered to the door to try the handle, but found it locked.

'Hello!' he shouted, 'anyone there?'

174

When there was no answer, he returned to the bed and sat back down. Though he fought it, the feeling of exhaustion was overwhelming and he lay back down, the effects of the Socaine still strong in his system. Within seconds, he had fallen asleep again.

Marek the Brewer was strangely silent. Gone was the brash character that so many people loved and just as many hated. He had no time for banter, for this was the day he had dreamt of for most of his adult life, the day he became unbelievably rich and powerful. All the Brewers were hung over, having partaken of too much of their own wares the night before. Ordinarily they would have been busy loading their carts but surprisingly, Marek and his family had offered to load all the carts on their behalf, a surprising yet welcome offer that they took full advantage of, not guessing the ulterior motive of their trusted colleague.

In the streets of the city, the day-to-day worries were forgotten in the excitement of the market. The council had given the go ahead for the night celebrations and rumours were rife that Arial would return to deliver them from rationing and the threat of the disappearing seas. Not only that but it was also rumoured that in celebration of the Saint, there would be cheap alcohol available to encourage a celebration the like of which had never been seen before. The more optimistic of the men even talked about the Courtesans offering their skills free of charge, though that was probably wishful thinking. The more sceptical dismissed the rumours as nonsense but despite this, there were a hard core of religious zealots peddling out their prophesies to anyone who would listen.

In the barracks, even Fatman seemed to have chilled out and he stood most of the men down for the evening celebrations with only an unlucky few chosen to man the gates. The rest changed into their casual clothes and started on the extra alcohol rations, issued to all those not on duty. In the barrack room, Ufox was perplexed at the absence of Braille so close to the celebrations, but despite asking around, nobody knew where he was.

Chapter 29

Pelosus finally woke up and after peering through the window, realised that he had slept most of the day. He washed the sweat from his body and donned a new tunic. There was a council meeting due in a few minutes and he had to provide an update, summarising what he had learned so far. Grabbing some Narwl biscuits to eat on the way he made his way to the council chambers, knowing that the last time he had gone he had little to report, but this time was different and he would blow them away with his news.

Inside the council chamber, all the heads of the various trades were present and already sitting in their seats as they awaited the arrival of Helzac. When he finally took his seat, all eyes turned to the Clerk.

'Well,' said Helzac, 'shall we begin?'

'Yes, Sire,' said Petit, and left the room for a moment before returning with Pelosus.

The Stargazer stood at the end of the table and looked around at the great and the good before him, nervous about how they were going to react about the truth of their ancestry and the fate that awaited them.

'Hello, Pelosus,' said Petra with a smile, 'welcome back, I trust you have some welcome news for us?'

'I have news, your Excellency, whether it is welcome or otherwise, is your judgement.'

'Sounds intriguing,' said Petra. 'Please, sit down and begin.'

'If it is all right with you, Excellency, I would rather stand.'

'Of course,' said Petra, 'whatever makes you comfortable.'

'Oh for Saint's sake, cut the pleasantries and get on with it,' snapped Razor.

With a deep breath, Pelosus started his story, telling the council everything he had learned both from the exploration of the second city and his night spent in the chamber of the scrolls. Throughout the tale each of the councillors, all fascinated by the story, questioned him yet needing clarification of some of the more astonishing claims. Finally, he stopped talking and the run of questions dried up. Razor broke the silence with his typical direct opinion.

'I have never heard such a complete load of Narwl shit in my entire life,' he said.

'I am sorry you think that, Sire, but it is true, nevertheless.'

'Prove it,' said Helzac.

'Sorry?'

'Simple,' said Helzac, 'where is your proof? We have nothing but your words and a few wooden plates with dreamt up beasts carved upon them. I see nothing and have heard nothing that proves this story has one scrap of truth about it.'

'There is other evidence available,' said, Pelosus, 'evidence in the possession of people within this very room that will add credence to my story.'

'What evidence?'

Pelosus stayed tight-lipped, hoping that Helzac would reveal the story about his paintings, or Petra would reveal the story of the lace handkerchief, but nothing was forthcoming.

'Pelosus,' said Razor, 'what other evidence do you speak of?'

'I cannot say, Sire,' said Pelosus, 'I have said too much already.'

Razor turned to the rest of the council.

'Does anyone here know what this fool is talking about?'

Silence ensued and Razor turned to Pelosus, his tone even more scathing.

'Stargazer,' he said, 'you have just placed yourself in an incredibly dangerous position. First, you come in here preaching blasphemy, then you implicate unknown councillors in your lies and refuse to name them. Do you realise what this means? A life in the prison tower at the very least.'

'You can speak to the Warden yourself,' said Pelosus, 'the room of scrolls exists in the Catacombs. I can take you there.'

'I have no doubt you can,' said Razor, 'for we all know of this room, and indeed the role of the Warden. There is nothing new in that but the scrolls we are familiar with tell the story of the Six-fingered Saint and his divine role in the formation of our city.'

'But the other scrolls,' said Pelosus, 'the ones written in the tongue of our ancestors, they are all there for you to see.'

'Admittedly there are scrolls there that we cannot understand, but therein lays the flaw in your story. Nobody can understand them.'

'I know but the Warden can back up what I have told you.'

'An old man whom you have confirmed is starting to lose his mind,' said Razor. 'His ramblings are the product of a lifetime of incarceration by the beautiful Governess.'

Petra threw him a sarcastic smile before speaking up.

'Pelosus,' she said, 'Warden has been down there for almost eighty years and his mind is not what it used to be. How can you be sure what he says is true?'

'I can't,' said Pelosus, 'but he was so…convincing.'

'Then you have fallen for the words of a liar,' said Razor, 'I accept that there are things happening to the sea that we don't understand, but I cannot accept that it is in the process of being carted across the world. As for our ancestors being food for some unknown type of monster, answer me this, where are they know, Pelosus? Where are these super beings you speak of?'

Before Pelosus could answer, the door burst open and eight armed men ran into the room, each taking up position behind a councillor. Pelosus turned around and saw the clerk calmly locking the door from the inside before turning around to face the confused faces of the council.

'I think I can answer that question,' said Petit quietly, 'they are here, in this very room!'

'Petit, what are you doing?' asked Pelosus

'Be quiet, Stargazer,' said the clerk, 'and sit down. You have been unlucky enough to have become embroiled in something above your station.'

'What on Earth are you on about?' shouted Razor. 'Who do you think you are?'

'Shut up, Fisherman,' said Petit, 'before you say something you may regret.'

'I'm not putting up with this shit,' started Razor, and stood up to confront the small man. Before he could take a single step, he felt the sharp edge of a knife being held against his throat from behind and he was forced back into his chair.

'Do as he says, Fisherman,' said the man holding the knife, 'or this blade will sever your jugular quicker than you have ever despatched a Narwl.'

'I don't know what this is all about Petit,' said Helzac from the head of the table, 'but there had better be a bloody good explanation.'

'Oh, there is,' said Petit, 'now, I suggest you all listen very carefully to what I have to say, for depending on the outcome of these next few minutes, some of you may have seen your last Moon-day.'

'Okay, Petit,' said Helzac, 'you have our attention. What is this all about?'

'First of all,' said Petit, 'let me introduce myself properly, my name is Petit and I am the Grand Master of the Brotherhood of the Sark.'

'And what exactly is that supposed to be?' asked Razor.

'All in good time, Fisherman,' said Petit.

'I am a Hunter,' snarled Razor, 'and if you refer to me as Fisherman one more time...'

'You will what?' asked Petit, 'attack me? I don't think so, Fisherman, you will be dead before you get out of the chair, now listen, all of you. The balance of power has changed in Bastion and you are no longer in charge here.'

'Then who is?' asked Helzac.

'The Brotherhood,' said Petit, 'so until you are told different, that means me.'

'That's absurd,' snapped Razor, 'as soon as the word gets out about this pathetic little coup, the guard will throw your bodies from the city walls.'

'Razor, shut up,' said a quiet voice, 'there are things going on here that you don't understand, so let's hear what the man has to say.'

178

Razor glared at De-gill but shut his mouth. It wasn't often the Watcher spoke, but when he did, others listened.

'Very sensible,' said Petit and started to pace around the room. 'What I have to say to you will be disturbing, frightening and go against everything you ever believed. However, saying that, my good friend Pelosus here has made my task much easier by preparing the ground for me. And, may I add, quite succinctly.'

'You believe me?' ventured Pelosus.

'Believe you?' laughed Petit, 'considering that a few weeks ago you were nothing more than a humble Stargazer at the beck and call of these so-called leaders of men, I think you have worked wonders. Not only have you managed the city in a time of extreme crisis but while you were at it, uncovered most of the true history of Bastion. During this time, as our city stumbled blindly toward the worst crisis it has ever seen, these people around you drank and fornicated their nights away, ignoring what has been staring them in the face all this time, the return of the Sark.'

'Wait a minute?' said Helzac, 'that makes no sense; you said the Sark are already here, in this room, yet Pelosus has regaled us with some absurd story about fantastical creatures who fed on the flesh of men. Which is it to be, Petit, make up your mind?'

'You are right,' said Petit, 'there are two completely different claims here, yet both are correct. You see, Pelosus did indeed tell you the truth. Everything he explained happened more or less, as he said. Yes, there are some inaccuracies but in essence, the history of Bastion according to Pelosus is correct, but what happened next is just as important and it is essential you take it on board to understand the magnitude of what is about to unfold before your very eyes.'

'As Pelosus has already stated, the Sark pursued their own branch along the evolutionary tree and became the most feared predator this planet has ever seen. But even feared Hunters can be brought down by sheer numbers and that is why they built these Citadels, for security. Everything was fine, and the world was in balance, the humans holding their place in the lowlands, while the Sark dominated the high places, descending only to feed. However, when the world flooded, everything changed and faced with extinction, the humans struck their deadly deal with the Sark. What was left of the human race moved into the Sark cities and a life of servitude. First, they bartered the dead and the dying in return for food from the sea, but eventually, as the waters finally took over completely, the Sark had them exactly where they wanted, totally reliant on their charity. The Sark took full advantage of the situation and their tastes soon demanded the fresh and healthy meat of the human young. At first, our ancestors resisted, but a few realised there was no choice and colluded with the Sark, making agreements that they would provide the flesh they craved, in return for immunity from

179

the cull. The Sark realised the benefit of a hierarchy between them and their prey, so agreed to give these people dominance over their fellows in return for complete devotion. Thus, was born the Brotherhood of the Sark.'

'The agreement was sealed and the city developed into four areas. The outer towers were tasked with growing food for the human population, the forerunners of the trades we see today. The lower city, the one that has been uncovered by the water, was used to hold the majority of the people, while the Brotherhood lived in the Citadel itself. The Sark dwelt within this very keep, able to look out from on high at everything around them.'

'Our own ancestors sold each other as food?' gasped Pelosus, 'that's unbelievable.'

'An unfortunate state of affairs, but entirely necessary,' said Petit, 'survival of the fittest. At least this way, the human race would survive.'

'But surely they didn't go to their deaths voluntarily,' said Helzac, 'didn't they fight back?'

'On the contrary,' said Petit, 'after a while and with some very careful indoctrination by the Brotherhood, the population came to welcome the chance to be selected. Every Moon-day, the favoured few would attend a great religious ceremony down in the second city and the whole population would gather to sing their praises as they ascended to the Citadel above.'

'The temple,' said Pelosus, 'of course.'

'You know of this place?' asked Petra.

'Yes, while I was in the lower city, I found a temple carved into the very bedrock beneath Bastion. At its centre, a wide shaft disappeared into the rock above and when I was in the Catacombs, I came upon it again as it ascended to the upper city. I assumed it would have come up somewhere in the keep.'

'It does; in fact, it ends in this very room. Strip out the table around which you all sit and the shaft descends straight down from here to the temple, a direct route via which the Sark could descend to attend the rituals.'

'But this table is built of stone,' said Helzac, 'and has been here for thousands of years.'

'Built for a purpose,' said Petit, 'to hide the truth. Anyway, over generations it became a ritual embedded in the very psyche of the population and although they did not know their ultimate fate, the role of chosen one was a position coveted by everyone in the lower city.'

'Yet all this time the Brotherhood would have known the truth?' asked Helzac.

'Yes, my predecessors knew but again, human memory is very short and after a while, they saw no shame in farming the people of the lower city. To them, they were an inferior race, fit for nothing else except feeding their masters.'

'So where are the Sark now?' asked Petra.

'Well, despite their dominance, there was a problem. They were relatively few in number, probably no more than a few dozen or so and relied on fresh Sark bloodline from other groups across the world. As the waters kept rising, they became more isolated and started to breed amongst themselves.'

'There were other groups?' gasped Pelosus

'Undoubtedly, though they were probably wiped out as their own Citadels were swamped by the seas. Anyway, without other groups of Sark to breed with, they started to inbreed and as we know, inbreeding leads to extinction.'

'They died out?' asked Helzac.

'No, on the contrary, they simply adapted and brought in a new blood line to carry their seed.'

'I don't understand,' said Pelosus, 'you said there were no other groups.'

'The women,' said Petra quietly, realising the only possible option, 'they used the human women.'

'Surely not,' said Helzac, 'how would that work?'

'Perfectly well, actually,' said Petit, 'don't forget that we shared a common ancestor, so our basic cells and bloodlines were entirely compatible. The male Sark used the human women as carriers of their spawn to continue the species.'

'But surely the cells of the Sark would not necessarily dominate the human cells,' said Pelosus, 'I would have thought that as the older of the two bloodlines, the human cells would be stronger.'

'And often they were,' said Petit, 'usually, a union between Sark and human resulted in a human child, but occasionally, it resulted with the offspring they desired. A lethal occurrence for the mother, it has to be said, for Sark offspring have the habit of tearing through the mother's womb with tooth and claw.'

'Oh my God,' said Petra.

'Yes, an unfortunate state of affairs, but nature has a way of balancing these things. Anyway, once again, generations passed and eventually the bloodlines became entirely mixed and every one of the humans within the Citadel could boast an ancestor of pure blood Sark. A claim that was something to be proud of, may I add.'

'Your ancestors were Sark?' asked Razor in disgust.

'Indeed they were,' said Petit, 'as were yours.'

'That's impossible,' said Helzac. 'We all have human ancestors and can trace them back hundreds of years.'

'A mere speck of time in the greater scheme of things,' said Petit, 'I can assure you, that inside your veins, Sark blood flows alongside human blood.'

'Even if what you say is true,' said Helzac, 'you still haven't answered my question. What happened to the true-blood Sark?'

'Simple,' said Petit, 'they simply died out. We are not sure why, but the stories passed down in the Brotherhood, tell of a day when they were all found dead. We believe it was something to do with the effects of the moon as it changed trajectory, but we can't be sure. Now you can imagine the problem this gave the Brotherhood, their masters were gone and they had no source of food, so they did the unthinkable, they continued the pretence.'

'They kept taking the sacrifices?'

'They did at first, though they knew it couldn't last. By now they were used to the taste of human flesh, but it was not enough, so once again they adapted, focussing on other sources of food. They started to harvest the sea plants around the base of the outer walls, experimented with catching Narwl and even devoted areas to nurturing the few plants that managed to survive amongst the nooks and crannies of the city. That went on for a few years, but then came the final blow, after a period of stability the waters rose for the last time, breaching the outer walls and flooding the lower city.'

'But what about the people down there?' asked Pelosus.

'There was nothing they could do,' said Petit, 'it happened overnight. Several hundred were pulled from the water, but thousands died. The survivors were absorbed into the Citadel and though at first there was a certain level of conflict, the Brotherhood managed to keep their sordid secrets hidden. Once again, time was a great healer and though there were undoubtedly many more trials to overcome, they eventually achieved a sustainable level of existence. The Brotherhood became a hidden society and the council of the trades emerged to manage the day to day life of the Citadel. That is where your histories begin, Helzac, when the Sark died out. Then and only then did Bastion settle down into the metropolis it is now.'

'If what you say is true, Petit, how come nobody in the city remembers, how come there is nothing in the histories.'

'Oh there are, but humans are a very strange race, Helzac, people remember the things they want to remember and when there are things best forgotten, they get rid of the evidence. The first council arranged the removal of anything around the city that referred to the Sark. Scrolls were burned, pictures hidden, statues torn down and carvings defaced. Wherever there was any indication of the previous way of life, it was removed.'

'But why?' asked Petra, 'why keep the truth from everyone?'

'To keep the population's expectations low,' said Petit. 'This is a very small city with a very large population. It was necessary to keep the peace in a very stressful environment.'

'So here we are,' said Razor, 'right up to modern day. Even if what you say is true, surely all that is in the past and has nothing whatsoever to do with what is happening now?'

'Not quite,' said Petit, 'for there is an on-going legacy, one that we live with every day of our lives, isn't that right, De-gill?'

All heads turned to face the Watcher who had remained silent throughout most of the meeting. For a few seconds, De-gill stared at a mark on the table as if expecting it to say something. Finally, he looked up and took a deep breath.

'Everything he said is true,' he said.

The collective gasp around the table turned into murmurs of disbelief.

'And you knew about this all this time?' asked Helzac.

'I did.'

'Who else knows?'

'The elders of my trade and the midwives.'

'The midwives?' said Petra in confusion, 'what have they got to do with this?'

'Tell them, De-gill,' sneered Petit, 'tell them all about the murderous role your trades play in all this.'

De-gill stared at the Clerk, with a clear warning in his eyes.

'Don't do this, Petit,' he said, 'it's not too late to sort this out.'

'Tell them,' snapped Petit.

Silence fell again before Razor spoke up once again.

'Well,' he said, 'what are you waiting for De-gill? What could possibly be so horrific that even the Governor of the Watchers hesitates to share it?'

Chapter 30

Down in the courtyard of the keep, something was wrong. The music had stopped and everyone was milling around in confusion. One group made a circle around a young girl who lay in a bloody crumpled heap on the floor, her shattered body the centre of an ever-expanding pool of blood. The screaming had stopped, but in its place, people were sobbing after witnessing the poor girl plummet from her trapeze far above the celebrations. An artist ripped his facemask off and stood over the body in shock.

'What happened?' he asked in disbelief.

'I don't know,' said a red haired woman alongside him, 'she must have lost her grip.'

'Never,' said the artist. 'She was the best performer we have ever had, been doing it since before she could walk.' He took off his multi-coloured jacket and knelt down to cover the girls shattered head. As he did, he was suddenly shoved forward by the woman with red hair as she fell right across the body.

'What the...?' started the artist and pushed himself back up to his feet in surprise. No sooner had he stood up, when his legs collapsed beneath him and he fell to his knees again.

'What's happening?' he asked, looking around in confusion.

All around him, people were collapsing to the floor and even as his eyes started to blur, he saw four more girls fall to their deaths from their trapezes far above. The crowd started to panic and as people collapsed in their dozens, those not affected started to rush for the gates. Some at the front fell to the floor and were trampled underfoot by the stampede, but those who did manage to reach the giant gates found them locked and many were crushed to death by the throng behind them.

Despite the unexplainable sight of hundreds of people collapsing all around them, some individuals remained unmoved, standing quietly to one side as the drama unfolded. Within ten minutes, the courtyard was in relative silence and the bodies covered the paving stones like a thick carpet of flesh. Finally, a soldier emerged from the shadows and approached one of the few remaining men standing.

'No going back now,' said Fatman.

'Nope,' said Marek, 'I just hope that Petit is right and the sightings can be verified.'

'Think you got enough men to shift all these?' asked Marek, sweeping his arm over the mass of bodies.

'Well, including those of us in the Guard,' said Fatman, 'there are about two hundred of us in here and another thousand or so out in the city, ready to round up those who spurned your poisoned ale.'

'I wonder how Petit is getting on with the council?' said Marek.

'I don't know and don't really care,' said Fatman. 'We can do this without those interfering spongers. As far as I am concerned, they should be fed to the Ranah.'

'I suppose you're right,' said Marek, 'come on then, let's get started.'

Groups of men and women banded together and stacked the bodies into piles, interspersed with bundles of dried weed soaked with Narwl oil. Any who were simply unconscious were despatched with skinning knives, before being added to the piles while those who had not drunk the ale at all, were rounded up at spear point and tied back to back against the wall, their fates yet to be decided. Within a couple of hours, over a dozen funeral pyres lit up the night sky, a clear statement of intent from the Brotherhood.

Kenzo woke for the second time and stood up from the bed. He tried the door once again, but it was still locked. A moan from behind him alerted him to the fact that Amber was waking up and he sat by her side, his head pounding with pain.

'Ohh,' moaned Amber, her eyes still shut, 'what happened?'

'I think we were drugged,' said Kenzo, 'I don't know why but somebody has moved us into a cell and locked the door. Here take this, it may help.' He gave her a glass of water from the table and waited patiently as she gulped greedily to appease her dry mouth. Finally, she sat up alongside him and looked around the room.

'Where are we?' she asked.

'I don't know, somewhere in the keep, I guess,' he said. 'It looks like we were moved when we were unconscious.'

'But why?'

'I have no idea,' said Kenzo, 'but this whole thing is getting weirder and weirder. Come on, we have to get out of here and let the council know what's going on over at the Watcher's Tower. Give me a hand.'

They tried forcing the door together with little effect, and finally sat down once again, realising it was hopeless. They sat in silence, waiting for someone to come and finally heard a noise in the distance.

'What was that?' asked Amber sitting up.

'I think it was a door slamming,' said Kenzo, 'perhaps someone is coming at last.'

The noise level increased and Kenzo was about to call out when he heard a woman's voice in the next cell.

''Hello, who is there?' said the unknown woman, 'I need to see somebody, there seems to have been a mistake.'

The sound of a door being unlocked gave Kenzo hope, and he was about to call out when the woman spoke again.

'Oh, thank you,' she said, her voice exhibiting the gratitude she obviously felt, 'can you tell me what is happening, please? Why am I here?'

Suddenly her tone changed as the sound of a scuffle broke out.

'Stop it, what do you think you're doing? Get your hands off me.'

The sounds of a struggle got stronger, interspersed with the woman's curses as she was overpowered. Kenzo estimated that there were at least three men involved, one of whom was obviously in charge.

'Let me go,' screamed the woman as she was dragged up the corridor, 'what's going on? Please, what are you going to do to me?'

Then a voice that Kenzo recognised came and his blood turned cold. It was Fatman.

'Stop the whining, sweetheart,' said Fatman, 'me and the boys just want some entertainment. Play along and you won't get hurt. Who knows? You may even enjoy yourself.' The woman's screams drowned out the laughter of the three men, until the sound of a door slamming, plunged the cell into silence once more. Kenzo turned to Amber and saw her face was grey with fear.

'Oh my God,' she whispered, 'that poor woman. Are they going to do what I think they are?'

'I don't know, Amber,' said Kenzo, 'this whole situation is crazy.'

The sound of the viewing panel being slid across from the outside made them spin around, and they saw the face of Bennett peering back at them.

'Bennett,' shouted Kenzo, 'what is going on? Why are we here?'

'Oh, we've got something special lined up for you,' sneered Bennett. 'That pretty little thing there is going to be Crispin's girlfriend, after he finishes with the last one of course but that shouldn't take long, he seems to be getting through them at quite a pace it would seem.'

'What are you on about?' asked Kenzo.

'Oh, don't you know, Kenzo? After all these years of the Brotherhood keeping the true histories to themselves, at last the prophesies have come true. The true lords of Bastion will once more take their place in the seats of power above the Citadel.'

'You're not making any sense,' said Kenzo.

'No, perhaps not, but I can't be bothered to explain. Let's just say that in the very near future, your little cousin over there will be the proud parent of a very interesting baby. That is, if she survives the birth of course, apparently it tends to get a bit, shall we say, messy?'

'Over my dead body,' said Kenzo threateningly, 'nobody will come anywhere near her while I'm alive.'

'Totally understandable,' said Bennett flippantly, 'but, fortunately you won't be. Very soon, Crispin will have finished with the latest batch of young girls we provided, and then he'll probably come and get you himself.'

'Me?' said Kenzo, 'what does he want with me?'

'You still don't get it do you, Kenzo? Crispin is like nothing you can ever imagine. His needs are completely different from ours and there is a clear distinction between the uses of human men and human women. The ladies are mates, as simple as that, whilst the men, or should I say some of the men, and you in particular, serve a very different purpose altogether.'

'Which is?'

'Lunch,' said Bennett, and stepped back from the door, laughing at his own joke.

Kenzo was about to say something, but the man's laugh was cut brutally short, replaced by the sound of a body hitting the door. A key rattled in the lock and the door eased open.

Amber stepped back against the wall, and Kenzo stepped in front of her, picking up the water jug as a weapon. Finally, the door reached its limit and the huge figure of Braille stepped over the unconscious Bennett to join them in the cell.

'Braille,' squealed Amber and ran past Kenzo to throw her arms around the giant soldier, giving him a massive kiss on the cheek. Kenzo lowered his water jug and smiled at his friend.

'Are we glad to see you?' he said.

'Been looking for you for a while,' said Braille, 'woke up with the mother of all hangovers and as I hadn't drank anything, guessed somebody was up to no good. Looks like I was right too, there's gangs of thugs running riot in the city.'

'Why?'

'Not sure, but it seems anyone who resists is being killed outright. There's even a load of our mates amongst them, except from those who were killed as they slept. If I hadn't fallen asleep in the latrine, I would be dead as well.'

'Well, whatever the reason, I'm glad you're here; now, let's get out of this place.'

Kenzo ducked passed Braille and out into the corridor. Amber went to join him, but was stopped by Braille, grabbing her arm.

'Amber,' he said.

'Yes Braille.'

'That kiss just now.'

'What about it?'

'Does that mean we're engaged?'

'Braille,' gasped Amber, 'you are unbelievable, now come on, let's go.'

'Worth a try,' mumbled Braille, as he followed the cousins into the corridor.

'Well, De-gill,' said Helzac, in the council chamber, 'we're waiting.'

De-gill looked around at the expectant faces and realised it was time to share what he knew.

187

'Petit is correct,' he said eventually. 'The Sark did indeed die out, but not before leaving an awful legacy. Though they did indeed mate with human women, only some of the children born developed the Sark form, however, the others were just as dangerous. Not consciously, because outwardly, they looked the same as you or I. No, the danger was within, unreachable yet just as deadly. You see, they had Sark blood, crawling around their veins like an incurable virus and as they grew older and had children themselves, the virus passed from father to child. Eventually, every person alive was a carrier, and still is. Ordinarily, this wasn't a problem, but occasionally, the virus manifested itself in the birth of a different sort of child, one who, as a single cell in the mother's womb, had succumbed to a Sark cell and developed certain features common with those monsters.'

'I thought the young of a Sark tore through the womb of a human mother,' said Petra.

'When fathered by a true blood Sark, they did,' said De-gill, 'but these were weaker. Sometimes it would be just the skin colour, or the shape of the head, pointed claws instead of fingers, that sort of thing, but left alone they could develop into something more sinister and even the repopulation of the Sark was a possibility. Whatever council was sitting at the time, decided they would not allow that to happen and issued an edict that a midwife must attend every birth. My trade was tasked with supplying the midwives and since then, there has always been a guild based here in the city.'

'What was it they did?' asked Petra, already guessing at the horrible answer.

'When any baby was born with any features of a Sark, they were terminated,' said De-gill.

'You killed them?'

'We did, but you have to realise, if they had been allowed to live, God knows what they may have turned out to be.'

'You murdered our babies?' said Petra again, a disbelieving tone in her voice.

'Only the tainted ones,' answered De-gill.

'Tainted, what gave you the right to decide who was tainted?'

'The council gave us the right,' said De-gill, 'and the safety of our people gave us the right.'

'Don't patronise me, De-gill,' snapped Petra, 'you are condoning infanticide.'

'For heaven's sake, Petra, we are talking about the survival of the human race,' snapped Helzac, 'give the man a break. If it wasn't for the actions of the Watchers, heaven knows what we would be facing now. But I still don't know how what all this is to do with your presence here, Petit, and this so-called Brotherhood of the Sark.'

'Tell him,' said Petit quietly, 'tell him of your failure, De-gill.' Once again, De gill paused, but finally he took a deep breath and finished the story.

'Yes we killed the children,' he said, 'but always in the interests of the people, however, occasionally, we kept one and took them back to our tower.'

'What for?'

'You have to understand,' said De-gill, 'it was important we understood how these creatures lived and if necessary, how to kill them. We had to study their physiology, to understand them and in essence, to know our enemy.'

'You kept them alive?'

'For a short time, yes, but as soon as they showed any sign of growing strong, they were terminated immediately, at least until the arrival of Crispin.'

'And who is he, exactly?'

'Crispin was born a few years ago and was brought to my attention by one of the midwives.'

'Why, was he deformed?'

'No, on the contrary, he was perfectly formed. The only thing different was the manner of his birth.'

'What was so different?'

'He was born in some sort of cocoon.'

'A cocoon?'

'Yes, some sort of mucous sac that was almost impenetrable. We had never seen anything like this before, so we moved it to our tower for scrutiny.'

'And what happened?'

'A few weeks later, he emerged as a normal human boy in every way we could see. We were fascinated and kept him locked safely away as he developed, and let me tell you, that was quicker than anything we had ever witnessed before. By the time he was five years old, he had the appearance of a boy twice his age and the strength of a full grown man.'

'What happened to him?' asked Petra.

'He escaped a few weeks ago,' said De-gill, 'and I suspect with the help of that man there.'

'He escaped?' asked Helzac, 'where is he now?'

'I have no idea,' said De-gill, 'I suggest you ask the Clerk.'

They all turned to Petit.

'Oh, I know where he is' said Petit with a smirk, 'and may I say, you wouldn't recognise him. In fact, you could say the boy is all grown up.'

'What do you mean?' asked Helzac.

'I mean, he is on the verge of emerging into the city to reclaim his rightful place as ruler of Bastion, Helzac. No longer is he a scared little boy tortured at the hands of the Watchers. Oh no, he has attained the full form denied to others of his kind over all these years, and may I say, a form that is as majestic as it is terrifying.'

189

'What are you talking about, Petit?' snarled Razor, 'what form does this creature take?'

'A form that you cannot even imagine,' said Petit, 'yet it is one that has been visible to you all your life. Open your eyes councillors and look again at your true ruler.' He held out both arms toward the far end of the room.

Everyone spun around to stare, but nothing happened. For several seconds nobody spoke, but the silence was finally broken by Petra.

'Where?' she asked.

'In front of you,' said Petit, 'carved into the very walls that have housed the council all these years.'

'But that's Arial, the Six-fingered Saint,' said Petra, 'not some flesh eating monster.'

'Is it, Petra?' asked Petit, 'and how do you know that?'

'Because we have always known so,' said Petra, 'the histories are clear. The Six-fingered Saint founded our city.' As she finished the sentence, her voice lowered, realising her words also described the alternative history recently outlined by De-gill.

'I see you are beginning to accept the possibility, Petra,' said Petit, 'but perhaps you still have doubts. Trust me Governess, this, the most famous carving of Arial in the whole Citadel is based on the form of the Sark. More like him will be born soon. The mighty Sark will once again dominate this world, and of mankind will tremble in fear.'

'But you people in this room have a chance offered to no other man, a chance to be part of it. To keep the powers you currently enjoy and more. All you need to do is kneel and call him master, to swear allegiance to his race and do his bidding without question.'

'But even if this is true,' said Helzac, 'I don't understand what he wants from us?'

'He wants nothing,' said Petit. 'It is I who saw the sense in this meeting. Over the next few days, there will be massive upheaval in Bastion. The population will be confused and frightened, and they will need leadership from those whom they trust. Who better to do that than those who have led them all their lives? Even as we speak, members of the Brotherhood are going door to door, rounding up the unworthy with those who resist, facing violence and possible death. Hundreds if not thousands may die, but you have the power to avoid this. You can make them realise that resistance is futile and there is only one logical outcome.'

'You want us to deny the existence of the Six-fingered Saint and worship some monstrosity in his place?' said Razor, 'are you mad? There is only one saviour and that is Arial. I will never deny him, even if it costs my life.'

At first, there was a shocked silence in the room, but then a chuckle escaped Petit's lips. Another followed and soon, all the Brotherhood present were laughing out loud, much to the consternation of the Hunter.

'What's so funny?' he said as the laughter died down.

'Oh, Razor,' sighed Petit, wiping tears of mirth from his face, 'are you really that blind? All your life the truth has surrounded you, yet you decide not to see. Look around you, even within the walls the signs are as plain as day.'

'No that's rubbish,' said Razor, 'throughout the city there are countless statues of Arial and their features look as normal as you or me. From the description given by De-gill, they bear no resemblance to this Crispin you speak of.'

'Features simply formed in the sculptor's own likeness,' interrupted Petit.

The colour drained from the Hunter's face as the full horrific truth sunk in. Throughout known history, the people had worshipped the Saint as a saviour, yet all this time they had actually been revering the memory of the Sark.

'I don't believe it,' he said, 'it can't be true.'

'But it is,' said Petit, 'and quite ironic, really. All this time, whilst actively putting down the true history of your ancestry, you have kept alive the memory of the one true Saint.'

'No,' said Razor, 'I don't believe it, I won't believe it.'

'Believe what you will,' said Petit, 'but if you don't believe your own eyes, I fail to see what it is you will believe.'

'What choice do we have?' asked Helzac.

'Oh you have a choice, Helzac, submit to the Sark's will or die; it is as simple as that.'

'I suppose you and your henchmen are going to murder us in cold blood?' asked Helzac.

'Oh no, these men are here for my safety only. You are free to leave as soon as you like.'

'I don't understand, why would you leave us go?'

'I am not a violent man, Governor, but I don't need to be. Crispin is nearing his physical maturity and when he does, there is no one alive who can stand against him. But you don't have to die; you can live out your lives in luxury.'

'All of us?'

'Not all, admittedly,' said Petit, 'unfortunately, there are some who have a debt to pay.' He glanced over toward De-gill.

'You disgust me,' said Helzac.

'I care not how you feel, Helzac, you no longer have any importance here.'

'And where is this so-called beast?' asked Razor. 'How do we know he even exists?'

'Oh, he exists all right,' said Petit, 'and you will see him soon enough.'

'You'll never get away with this, Petit,' said Helzac, 'the guard will overthrow these few deserters as soon as they find out and put down this pathetic rebellion of yours.'

'The guard?' asked Petit in mock surprise, 'you mean those soldiers who are staunch Brotherhood supporters and are taking over the city as we speak? Or do you mean those who are still lying on their blood soaked mattresses with their throats cut? Either way, I feel they won't be putting anyone down, do you?'

'The people then,' said Helzac, 'they will never allow this to happen.'

'Oh, I am sure they will be upset,' said Petit, 'but nothing we can't handle.'

'And if we say no and decide to fight?'

'It doesn't matter,' said Petit. 'In fact, I think Crispin will quite enjoy the hunt, after all, it's not as if you can run far is it? Now, if you don't mind, I have things to do. I suggest you go back to your families and consider what has gone on here today very carefully. I will expect your answers by last light tomorrow.'

Chapter 31

Kenzo, Amber and Braille made their way down to the exit and peered out into the courtyard.

'Oh my God,' whispered Amber, 'what's that smell?'

'Burning bodies,' said Braille, 'there're piles of them all around the Keep.'

'What happened to them?' asked Kenzo.

'Poisoned, I think,' said Braille, 'just like my mates in the barracks, though some were killed by a professional hand.'

'How do you know?' asked Amber.

'The way the throats are cut,' said, Kenzo, 'in the guard, we are trained to avoid the front of the throat and go straight for the artery to save time. It's located at the side of the neck and some of these bodies have been killed in that manner.'

'We need to get out of here,' said Kenzo. 'Do you think it is safe to try and get to the city?'

Braille pulled his knife from its sheath and spun it in his hand.

'One way to find out,' he said, 'follow me.' Without waiting for an answer, he stepped out into the deathly quiet courtyard.

'Oh, those poor people,' whimpered Amber, as they passed one of the funeral pyres, 'who would do such a thing?'

'I have no idea,' said Braille, 'but I intend to find out. Come on, let's get out of here.'

They continued toward the main gates and as they neared, Amber slipped on a pool of blood and fell crashing to the floor. Kenzo turned to help her up.

'You okay?' he asked as he extended his hand.

'I think so,' said Amber sitting up and rubbing her ankle, 'it's just twisted, I think.'

She looked up at the two men's horrified faces as they gazed over her head, back toward the way they had come.

'What's the matter?' she asked, afraid to turn around, 'what's there?'

'Stand up, Amber,' said Kenzo gently, 'and whatever you do, don't turn around.'

'What is it, Kenzo?' she said, getting to her feet, 'you're scaring me.'

'Walk toward me, Amber,' he said, 'nice and slow. No sudden movements and do not turn around.'

Alongside Kenzo, Braille stared in the same direction, beads of sweat running down his face.

'Kenzo, I'm scared,' said Amber, her voice shaking.

'It's okay,' said Kenzo, 'keep walking toward me.' He slowly lifted one hand and she reached out to take it, grabbing his fingers tightly as she made contact.

'It's seen us, Kenzo,' said Braille, 'we have to get out of here.'

'Okay,' said Kenzo. 'Walk with me, Amber,' and he started to walk backwards toward the gate, his gaze never leaving whatever it was that had caused both soldiers to look so scared. Within thirty seconds, they reached the gate and Braille stood to one side, allowing the two cousins to exit before following them out and closing the gate.

'Do you think he will follow us?' asked Kenzo.

'I don't think so,' said Braille, 'he was too preoccupied.'

'Who was it?' asked Amber.

'Are you okay?' asked Braille to Kenzo, effectively ignoring the girl.

'I think so,' he answered.

'Kenzo, who was it you saw?' she asked, 'why wouldn't you let me look?'

'Don't worry, Amber,' said Kenzo, 'I'll tell you another time.'

Amber pulled her arm from his grip in anger.

'Kenzo,' she said, 'I don't know who or what you saw in there, but I swear if you don't tell me right now, I will go back in there to see for myself. Now, what is it that was so horrendous?'

Kenzo looked toward Braille, seeking his support.

'Don't expect me to back you up,' said Braille, 'I wouldn't mind some answers myself. What was that thing?'

Kenzo looked back at Amber.

'I think it was Crispin,' he said, 'and he looked like something out of your worst nightmares.'

The councillors filed out of the chamber, closely followed by the Stargazer.

'Pelosus, wait,' said the clerk.

The Stargazer paused before turning back.

'You haven't said much,' said Petit, 'what are your thoughts?'

'My thoughts,' sighed Pelosus, 'I would say, troubled.'

'Why?'

'Where should I start? The fact that the waters are falling and will soon disappear completely or the fact that despite a lifetime of being told differently, I have now found out that there is probably a land mass somewhere over the horizon. Or maybe, it is the fact that someone who I considered a friend is part of a secret society harbouring a previously unknown species, predatory in nature. Perhaps, it may be the realization that this creature is part of our own bloodline that concerns me. For heaven's sake, Petit, it is no wonder I am troubled; the possibilities are endless. Aren't you at all worried about all of this?'

194

'Worried? Why should I be worried? My ancestors have prayed for this day for millennia and I consider myself honoured that the opportunity has come during my lifetime. This is not a threat, Pelosus, but an opportunity.'

'An opportunity for what?' gasped Pelosus, 'to be ruled by creatures who see us as a food source. What sort of existence is that?'

'An existence of security and stability,' said Petit. 'Aren't you fed up with the same old routine, subsistence rationing with nothing but the walls of this city as the limit of your ambition? Can't you see that for someone like you, this is an opportunity to explore your theories? You could have unlimited power, Pelosus, the chance to do whatever you want and who knows, when the waters recede far enough, the chance to travel further afield, safe in the knowledge you have the protection of the Sark.'

'Why would I need their protection?'

'Wasn't it you who said that the loss of the sea will initially result in thirst and hunger? Submit to their service and that will never be an issue. They have ways of providing, Pelosus. Food, water, riches, all are benefits that they bestow on the Brotherhood in return for our services.'

'And what services are they, Petit, the herding and murdering of your fellow man?'

'Yes that's a part of it,' said Petit, 'but just a small part. The rest is building and overseeing the labour as they develop their cities. Recording the histories and accompanying them as they travel further afield.'

'Travel further afield?'

'Listen, Pelosus, the waters are dropping rapidly and before too long, the tops of other mountains will start to appear, some perhaps even in sight of this Citadel.'

'Barren islands full of nothing but rotting seaweed and sugar shell crabs,' said Pelosus, 'what benefit could be possibly gleaned from them?'

'Don't think of them as destinations, Pelosus, but as stepping stones to other places. Within months, Crispin and his fellows will set out to redress the imbalance of this world and reassert their rightful place, not only in the Citadel, but also the world around us. You could be part of this, Pelosus, to reap the opportunity to do what you have always desired and to explore beyond the horizon. Don't get bogged down by sentiment, this is just natural selection. Think carefully Pelosus, make the right decision and you can rule the human population beside me, answering only to the Sark.'

'I need no time to think, Petit,' said Pelosus eventually, 'I have already made my decision. The fact that Sark blood runs in my veins is burden enough. I will not strengthen the existence of their species by betraying my own. I will not join you, Petit, the answer is no.'

'So be it, Pelosus,' said Petit. 'At least I tried. Goodbye old friend, the next time we meet, I fear it will be as adversaries.'

'Then make this the last time you use the word friend, Petit, for you do not merit that title.' With that, Pelosus turned and followed the councillors down the corridor, slamming the door behind him.

Braille and the two cousins ran away from the keep toward the city.

'Where are we going?' shouted Amber as Kenzo dragged her down the slope.

'Away from there,' he said, 'at least, you are.'

'What do you mean?' asked Amber, as they reached the first row of buildings. 'Where are you going?'

Kenzo turned around and took both of her hands.

'Look, Amber, I don't know what's going on here, but a lot of people have died back there. This creature, whatever it is, seems to have a fundamental part in all this. A few months ago, I was asked to find and kill him. I failed to do that, so in some way, I feel responsible.'

'That is absurd,' said Amber, 'nobody could have known how he was going to turn out.'

'That may be true,' said Kenzo, 'but nevertheless, I have to go back.'

'No, Kenzo,' said Amber, 'there's no knowing what he will do to you.'

'I have to, Amber,' said Kenzo, 'I haven't seen Leona since we last went into the Catacombs. I need to know if she is okay.'

'But she could already be out here,' said Amber.

'I know, but she could also be back there and in terrible danger. Until I know otherwise, I will not be able to think straight.'

'What about me?' asked Amber. 'What am I supposed to do?'

'Go home and barricade yourself inside. Wait for me there. I'll go back to the keep, and check her quarters. If she's not there, I'll come straight back, I promise.'

'I'll come with you,' said Braille.

'No, you go with Amber, she may need protection. With half the guard dead and the other half working for Petit, who knows what characters are wandering around taking advantage of the situation? Don't worry, I'll be fine.' He walked backwards a few steps before turning around and running back up the slope.

'Be careful,' shouted Amber, but received no answer except for a wave of the hand.

Braille and Amber watched Kenzo approach the gate, and, after opening it slightly to peer around the edge, disappear inside. They waited a few more seconds before Braille broke the silence.

'Just you and me now, Babe,' he said, 'don't worry, I'll look after you.'

'Oh for heaven's sake,' mumbled Amber, before turning around and making her way back toward her home quarter. Braille followed close behind and though he irritated her with his constant babbling, Amber was glad he was with her.

Kenzo closed the gate slowly behind him and stared around the courtyard, but there was no sign of the creature. His heart was racing as he made his way around the perimeter wall, but when he was opposite the doorway, he didn't hesitate and ran across the space and into the dark corridor beyond.

Voices could be heard in the distance and he ducked inside a side room as a group of guards dragged a beaten and bedraggled old man between them to an unknown fate. When they had passed, he made his way along the corridors to where he knew Leona had her rooms. Her door was slightly open and he eased it further inward before peering into the gloom.

'Leona,' he whispered, 'are you there?' When he received no answer, he quickly checked the linked rooms before turning to leave. Once again, he heard someone approaching and hid behind the door as the unseen man greeted someone coming in the opposite direction. Kenzo strained to hear the conversation.

'Petit,' said the first man, 'how did it go?'

'As well as could be expected,' said Petit, 'what happened to you?' Bennett rubbed a large bruise on the side of his head.'

'Jumped from behind by some idiot soldier,' he said, 'don't worry, I'll catch up with him and get payback.'

'There'll be time enough for that,' said Petit,

'Do you think the councillors fell for the invitation?' asked Bennett.

'We will soon see. Make sure the men are armed with Narwl spears and keep themselves hidden in the servant's quarters. When their people are all in the keep, let the men loose. Spare no one. Without the controlling influence of the trades, the rest of the city will soon crumble.'

'What about the Stargazer?'

'No luck there,' said Petit, 'he was the one person I genuinely wanted alongside me. He alone had the courage to stand up to me, the only man amongst the bloody lot of them.'

'Where is he now?'

'Packing his things in his room,' said Petit.

'Are you going to let him go?'

'I can't,' said Petit, 'he has spent the last few months organising the population and gained a lot of admirers. He could easily gather a following and we can't risk that, we have come too far.'

'Do you want me to deal with him?'

'That would be good, do you want some help?'

'No, he is an old man, I will go immediately.'

'Bennett,' said Petit, 'make it quick, he has been a good friend.'

Kenzo heard the sound of a knife being unsheathed.

197

'I understand,' said Bennett, and the two men went on their own way.

Kenzo stood behind the door, knowing that the Stargazer was about to be killed. Though he owed the Stargazer nothing, there was no way he could stand back and allow an old man to be murdered in cold blood. He looked down the corridor to make sure Petit had left and with a deep breath, walked in the opposite direction, following Bennett up to the Stargazer's chambers.

Pelosus had a woven bag open on the bed and was busy putting his most valuable possessions inside. He heard steps coming along the corridor and turned to see Bennett entering the room.

'Bennet,' he said, looking at the knife in the man's hand, 'don't tell me you are part of this as well.'

'Sorry, Pelosus,' said Bennett, 'this thing is bigger than any of us. The very future is about to change, and unfortunately that means some will fall by the wayside.'

'You've come to kill me?'

Bennett nodded.

'We can't afford to let you organise any sort of resistance.'

'I thought this Crispin creature was all powerful?'

'His name is Arial, and indeed he will be, but don't forget he is still relatively young and all this is new to him. He needs the guidance of the Brotherhood until he reaches his prime, then he will decide his own future.'

'But what if that future doesn't include you and your friends?' asked Pelosus, 'have you thought about that?'

'Then it is a fate that I will accept with all my heart,' said Bennett.

'By all that is holy, you really are fanatics,' said Pelosus.

'Your words, Pelosus. Now, this is unpleasant enough as it is, I suggest you turn around and kneel down. I will make this as painless as possible.'

Pelosus stared at him for a while longer, before doing as he was ordered.

'Cut deep, Bennett,' he said, holding his head back to reveal his wrinkled throat, 'the world you desire so much holds no attraction for me. I would rather explore the next world, than remain with you in this.'

'So be it, old man,' said Bennett and stepped forward, his eyes focussed on the outline of Pelosus's prominent jugular vein on the right side of his neck.

Pelosus closed his eyes and despite being a man of science, muttered a prayer under his breath, waiting for the exquisite pain that would signal the end of his life. A few seconds later, he heard what sounded like a grunt and opened his eyes again.

'What are you waiting for?' he asked, 'get on with it.'

When there was no answer, he looked over his shoulder and scrambled along the floor away from the horrific scene behind him. Bennett was still standing where he had been a few seconds earlier, but the smug look had been replaced with one of pain and horror, as a clawed hand squeezed tightly around his throat. Pelosus stared above Bennett's head at the beast that had curtailed his imminent death and realized with mind numbing horror that all the incredible stories he had heard in the past few days were all true. This was undoubtedly Arial and mankind's legacy had at last come back to haunt them. The Sark had returned to Bastion.

Kenzo ran up the familiar stairs he and Leona had trodden all those weeks ago. He hoped it was not too late to save Pelosus, as he had stupidly taken a wrong turn, but had now regained his bearings. With no time for caution, he ran as fast as he could, calling out the Stargazer's name.

'Pelosus,' he screamed, 'don't trust him, Bennett's going to kill you.'

He burst through the door of the Stargazer's chambers and stopped in horror at the scene before him. Pelosus was sprawled in a crumpled heap at the far end of the room, his face pouring with blood as a result of a severe blow. Bennett's body lay on the floor but the most horrific thing of all was the creature standing in the centre of the room.

Arial stood upright, his naked skin shining black in the dim light of the Plankton lamp. He was almost half as tall again as Kenzo, but with wiry legs and arms. His chest was broad, and his shoulder blades rose higher than his head. His face was definitely human, but much narrower with an elongated chin and his prominent eye ridges slanted sharply upwards, away from the black eyes with white pupils. He had no hair on his head or indeed any part of his body, and the pointed ears swept backwards alongside the wrinkled skull. Despite all this, Kenzo was transfixed by one thing and one thing only, the sight of Bennett's severed head dangling from one of Arial's clawed hands.

'*Get out*,' screamed Pelosus from the corner, 'it's too late, save yourself.'

The creature looked up and stared at Kenzo, his jagged predatory teeth laced with torn flesh and dripping with blood. He opened his jaws to their full extent and let out a soul-searing scream, forcing the man back in fear as the stench of death swept over him like a wave.

'Run!' screamed Pelosus from behind the creature, 'save yourself.'

Kenzo knew it was too late for the old man. There was no way he could tackle the monstrosity, so with the primeval scream still ringing in his ears, he turned around and ran from the room as fast as he could and down through the gloomy corridors, closely followed by the pursuing figure of Arial. Just as he thought he was going to be caught, he saw an opportunity and after running through an open doorway, slammed it shut behind him and wedged a chair beneath the handle. Immediately, the creature crashed into the door and Kenzo put all his weight against it to ensure it stayed shut. After a few attempts, the creature gave up and Kenzo heard him walking back the way he had come. After a few minutes Kenzo turned and run out of the building. As he burst out of the door, he smashed into a group of people and fell sprawling to the floor. Immediately he jumped up, but was grabbed by an enormous man who pinned him against the wall.

'Steady on, son,' said the big man, 'what's the rush?'

'Who are you?' asked Kenzo.

'My name is Helzac.'

'The Governor?'

'Yes,' said Helzac, 'and these good people are the council. Now why don't you tell me who you are?'

'I am Kenzo,' said the young man, 'and I serve in the Citadel Guard.'

'Shouldn't you be on duty?'

'Looks like a deserter to me,' said Razor.

'No, I'm not,' said Kenzo, 'I was given leave by Pelosus to seek a boy called Crispin and got isolated in one of the towers. I have only just returned and was looking for Pelosus when we were drugged by the cook and locked up in the keep.'

'Why would anyone do that?' asked Razor, 'and how did you get into one of the trade towers in the first place? You know they are off limits.'

'We got lost in the Catacombs,' said Kenzo, 'and ended up in the Watcher's-tower. Look, if you don't believe me, ask him.' He pointed toward De-gill

'Do you know this man?' asked Helzac.

De-gill stared at Kenzo for a while wondering whether to support his story or dismiss him as a liar.

'I do not know if he tells the truth over the keep,' said De-gill, 'but he was indeed a guest of ours for a month.'

'Still doesn't mean he wasn't involved in all this,' said Razor, indicating the scene around him, 'we already know that Petit has most of the Guard working for him.'

'I know nothing of this,' said Kenzo, 'only that we are wasting time and if we don't get out of here pretty quickly, we may not get another chance.'

'Explain,' demanded Helzac.

'There is some sort of creature back there,' said Kenzo, 'up in the Stargazer's rooms.'

'Describe him,' snapped De-gill.

'I didn't hang about too long,' said Kenzo, 'but he is roughly human in form, but much taller with clawed hands and a horrifying face. When I left, he had just killed someone called Bennet.'

'And what of Pelosus?' asked Petra.

'I don't know, but he was trapped in there so is probably dead by now. There is no way anybody could overcome that thing.'

'It must be Arial,' said Helzac, 'he must have been in the central tower all this time.'

'It certainly sounds like it,' said Razor, 'we should go back in there now, while he is cornered and stop this charade once and for all.'

'Are you crazy?' gasped Kenzo, 'have you seen this thing?'

'Boy, I have killed two Ranah in my time and more Narwl than I care to think of, each ten times his size. This thing holds no fear for me.'

'Then you are mad,' said Kenzo, 'he will rip you apart in a blink of an eye.'

'Perhaps we can reason with him,' said Petra.

'Reason with him?' Kenzo sneered, 'that thing is like nothing you can imagine. I don't even know if it can talk.'

'This is an opportunity too good to miss,' said Razor, 'kill the beast and we hamstring Petit, there will be no need to bring our people into the city.'

'You can't bring your people here,' said Kenzo, 'I overheard Petit plotting against you.'

'But he invited us to join him,' said Petra.

'Governess, as we speak, his followers are getting ready to surprise you and cut down your trades without mercy. You need to get out of here and rally your people. Group together and fight this man, otherwise, who knows what will happen?'

'How do we know you are telling the truth?' asked Razor.

'I don't know any way of convincing you,' said Kenzo, 'but I give you my word, everything I have just said is true. If you don't believe me, go in and see for yourself.'

The group of Governors looked between each other, all looking for answers. Finally, it was Razor, who once again broke the silence.

'I have heard enough,' he said, 'I am going back in there to deal with this thing once and for all. Who else is with me?'

'We will need weapons,' said Kelly the Brewer.

'There are weapons aplenty in the barrack rooms,' said Kenzo, 'I can show you where.'

'I will come too,' said De-gill.

'As will I,' added Rimmer of the Weavers.

The two other Governors confirmed their involvement before they all turned to Helzac.

'You are the best of all of us, Helzac,' said Razor, 'our chances would be enhanced with you there.'

The Governor looked at Petra for a long time and squeezed her hand before turning to the men.

'I too will come,' he said.

'Helzac, no,' shouted Petra, 'who will lead the city if you fall?'

'Petra,' answered Helzac quietly, 'everyone here has led privileged lives, enjoying the best this great city can offer. We have accepted the riches and the accolades in return for spouting out edicts as we see fit. Bastion is on the verge of collapse and we alone now have the chance to avoid catastrophe. How could we ever face them again knowing that when we were needed most, we turned and ran?'

'Then I will come too,' she said.

'No, you won't,' said Helzac, 'I need you to provide a figurehead to the trades. If we all fall, act quickly and nominate successors to each of us. You will have to assume the Governorship and lead them forward. They will need strong leadership and will have to gel quickly if they are to have any chance of putting down this uprising. If worse comes to worse, at least the towers can be defended while you negotiate a peaceful outcome.'

'But Helzac…?'

'But nothing,' said Helzac, 'this is now no longer a request, it is an instruction. Do as you are told.'

Petra shut her mouth, knowing fully that arguing with the giant man was futile. Helzac turned to Kenzo.

'As for you, young man, I appreciate the offer of help but I have a far more important job for you. I am placing the safety of the Governess in your hands. You grew up on these streets and know how the city works, take her into your care and see her safely back to her tower. Our normal routes are denied us and over the years, we have lost sight of the ways of the people. I suspect that on her own, she would not last more than an hour.'

'And my own family?'

'Take them with you. They will be far safer with the trades than out on the streets at the mercy of Petit's thugs. Right, tell us where to find these weapons you speak of and be on your way.'

Five minutes later, Kenzo had left the keep and was leading Petra through the narrow streets of the city. All around them, they could hear shouting interspersed with the occasional scream. The air was thick with smoke from unseen fires and people ran everywhere, trying to escape the madness. Kenzo grabbed a small boy as he ran past.

'You,' he shouted, 'come here.'

The boy looked petrified and rivulets of blood ran from a wound above his eye.

'Please, Sir, don't hurt me,' he cried, 'I haven't done anything, honest.'

'Whoa, slow down,' said Kenzo, 'what makes you think I am going to hurt you?'

'You're one of them, Sir,' said the boy, 'the soldiers who are killing everyone.'

'Did they do this to you?' asked Petra, wiping the blood from his face with a handkerchief.

'Yes, lady,' he said, 'when my dad wouldn't let them in, they broke down the door and beat me up.'

'Where is your dad now?'

'They killed him, miss,' sobbed the boy, 'stuck a knife right into him.'

'What about your mother?'

'They dragged her and my sister into another room and I heard the soldiers laughing even though my sister was crying. I tried to help them, miss, honest I did, but they beat me up and threw me into the street. I was going to get my uncle to help but I can't find him.'

'Okay,' said Petra, crouching down so she was the same height as the boy, 'first of all, what is your name?'

'Lenny, miss.'

'Right, Lenny, I promise you this man is not one of those soldiers, his name is Kenzo and he is on our side. My name is Petra and I want you to come with us and show us where you live. Perhaps we can help, okay?'

'Yes, miss,' said the boy, grabbing her hand, 'it's this way.' Within minutes, they were at the end of a street that had obviously seen the efforts of the Brotherhood's soldiers. Furniture was burning in the streets and smoke billowed from windows. Bodies lay everywhere and at the far end, Kenzo could see the retreating figures of at least ten men as they sought new victims.

'Which house is yours?' asked Petra.

'That one, miss.'

'You stay here,' said Kenzo, 'I'll check it out.' Within a few minutes, he returned and Petra knew by the look in his eyes, that the news wasn't good.

'Where are they?' asked the boy.

'They are…um…not there,' said Kenzo, 'they must have escaped.'

'Then, I have to find them,' said the boy and tried to get past the two adults.

'No,' said Kenzo, grabbing his arm, 'I think you should come with us, you will be safer.'

'But I have to find them,' said the boy, 'if my dad is dead, how will they live? I am the man of the house now.'

'Oh, sweetheart,' said Petra, embracing him in her arms, 'I'm sure they will be fine for a while. You come with us and when this is over, we will try to find them together. How about that?'

'Promise?' asked the boy.

'Promise,' said Petra.

'Okay,' said the boy and took her hand once again. They made their way out of the street and toward Kenzo's own quarter.

'That's one promise you will not be able to keep,' whispered Kenzo.

'Why not?' answered Petra in similar tones.

'Because they are both dead.'

'Are you sure?'

'Both had their throats cut, though not before they were raped.'

'Oh my God,' said Petra, 'what is happening to this city?'

'I don't know, Governess,' said Kenzo, 'but it is not looking good.'

The members of the council followed Kenzo's directions and entered the temporary barrack rooms. The first reaction was horror when they saw the blood sodden mattresses.

'Drugged and murdered,' said Razor, 'these must have been the ones loyal to the council.'

'Nothing we can do now,' said Helzac, 'look for knives or swords.'

'Forget knives,' said De-gill, 'you need Narwl spears.'

'We can't go back to my tower now,' said Razor, 'there is no time.'

'We don't have to,' said De-gill, 'these soldiers carried out guard duty, so they had access to ceremonial spears. They should be here somewhere.' Within a few minutes they found the armoury and each armed themselves with one of the highly polished spears, engraved with scenes from city life all along the shaft.

'These wouldn't last one strike on a Narwl,' said Razor, 'far too thin.'

'We don't need them to last,' said Helzac, 'as long as one finds its mark I will be happy. De-gill, you said you studied their physiology, is there anything you can tell us about the best place to strike?'

'As far as I know, he had the same basic structure as us,' said De-gill, 'though I cannot comment on his internal organs. We can only assume, they are in the same place but if in doubt, pierce the head.'

'Right,' said Helzac, 'no point in putting it off any longer, let's go.' Without further ado, the men left the barracks and made their way toward the main stairway leading to the top of the tower.

Kenzo ran back to his own house as quickly as possible, though it took longer than expected due to the amount of detours needed to avoid the trouble. Fires had been set everywhere and more than once they had to use their enveloping blanket of smoke to shake off some of Petit's henchmen. All around people were screaming and groups of armed men herded families at sword point toward the city perimeter. Finally, he saw the street with the familiar red doors and seeing no intruders, he ran as fast as he could to burst into his home. All around, the furniture was smashed and everything of value was gone.

'Amber,' he shouted, 'where are you?' He heard a noise in the back room and tried the door without success. 'Amber, are you in there?'

204

The sound of furniture being dragged out of the way preceded the door being opened and Amber ran into Kenzo's arms.

'Where have you been?' asked Amber, 'you were ages.'

'I'll tell you later,' said Kenzo. 'Gather your things, we have to go. Where's Braille?'

'Oh, Kenzo, it was awful,' said Amber. 'When we got here, they were already in our house. Braille called them some names and there was a terrible fight. He managed to kill two of them, but one had a lance and they stabbed him through the side.'

'Is he dead?' asked Kenzo.

'I don't think so, they all jumped on him and tied him up. I was hiding over there in the alley and when they took him away, I came in here and barricaded the door. Do you think he is all right?'

'Braille is as tough as they come,' said Kenzo, 'it'll take more than a mere scratch to take him down. This is Petra and this young man is Lenny. Petra is the Governess of the Courtesans and she is taking us to her tower while all this mess gets sorted out.'

'What about Leona? Was there any sign of her?'

'Nothing,' sighed Kenzo, 'but to be honest, she could be anywhere. Anyway, throw some stuff in a bag, I'll see if there is any food left in the box but be quick, those men could come back any minute. '

'Come on,' said Petra, 'I'll help you pack.'

A few minutes later, they were making their way toward one of the main gates of the city. As they neared the perimeter the crowds grew and soon they were part of a much bigger crowd, all fleeing the attention of the Brotherhood's thugs. In the distance, they could hear the sound of beating drums over the screams of individuals, as the approaching gangs forced them from the centre of the city. The four fugitives ran with the crowd until they finally shuffled under the archway and out onto the causeway leading to the Pleasure-tower.

'There are hundreds of people here,' said Petra, 'there's no way we can take them all in the tower. There's hardly any room as it is.'

The sound of the drums got closer and the crowd packed further along the causeway, distraught that they had nowhere else to go. In the distance, similar crowds were appearing on the other causeways as indeed they were at the far end of the city. Through the gates, the crowd could see a large squad of armed men holding lances before them with a line of drummers behind, all advancing toward the gate, driving the stragglers before them.

'Oh my God,' said Amber, 'what are they doing? Surely they don't mean to kill us all?' Before Kenzo could answer, the soldiers came to a halt just inside the gate and the drumming stopped, but rather than advance onto the causeway, they did something completely unexpected. They slammed the gate. A murmur crept around the crowd, everyone unsure as to what was happening.

'What are they doing?' asked Amber again. 'They can't just leave us out here, surely?'

'I don't know,' said Kenzo, 'not even Petit is that sick.'

Gradually the pressure from the crowd eased, as they spread throughout the available space on the causeway, with some going back up to the locked gate in confusion, while others took the opportunity to stare at the uncovered city below them. Kenzo and Amber followed Petra as she made her way to the gates of her own tower, but all three stayed back as they watched people banging on the gates without effect.

'I don't understand,' said Petra, 'there's always someone on gate duty.'

'Petra,' said Kenzo, 'how many of your people were in the Citadel for the celebrations.'

'Most, if not all of them,' said Petra, and her eyes widened as she realised the implications. 'Oh, my God, Kenzo, you don't think...?'

'I don't think anything,' said Kenzo, 'it's pointless panicking. For all we know, they could be spread out all around the city on any of the other causeways.'

'But all those poor people murdered in the keep,' she said, 'how do I know my girls are not amongst them?'

'I suspect we will find out soon enough,' said Kenzo, 'but in the meantime, we have a bigger problem on our hands.'

'Which is?'

'How do we get in there?' said Kenzo, indicating the tower looming above him. Suddenly, a familiar voice rang out in the crowd.

'Kenzo!'

The young man spun to face the familiar voice and his face lit up when he saw his old friend barging his way through the crowd toward him.

'Braille,' shouted Kenzo, 'where have you been?'

'Had myself a bit of an argument with some of our old mates,' said Braille.

'An argument?' said Kenzo, staring at the bruises, 'by the look of your face, it was a bit more than an argument.'

'Yeah, but you should've seen the other guys.'

'I can well believe it,' said Kenzo, 'how did you get away?'

'Had to buy my way out,' said Braille, 'cost me a bleeding fortune.'

'How much?'

'A bloody star stone,' said Braille.

'You have got to be kidding me.'

'Nope, it was either that, or end up as fish food, mind you, I did manage to negotiate somebody else's release as well.'

'Who?'

Before Braille could answer, another voice rang out along the causeway, this time female.

'Kenzo!'

'Leona,' gasped Kenzo in astonishment and the couple ran into each other's arms.

'I have missed you so much,' said Kenzo. 'How are you? Where have you been?'

'Oh, Kenzo,' she said, tears flowing down her face, 'when you didn't come back, I thought you were dead. I tried to tell Pelosus but there was so much going on in the city, he decided he couldn't help. I tried coming myself, Kenzo, honest I did, but I couldn't get myself to go into the sewers. Oh, Kenzo, I am so sorry.' She broke down into floods of tears and Kenzo held her once more.

'It's okay,' he said, 'we're here now and I'll never leave you again.'

'Kenzo, look,' interrupted Amber, and pointed up to the Citadel walls.

All along the castelades, soldiers were leaning over and lowering bundled tarpaulins into the city far below the causeways. The crowds were fascinated and all sorts of theories were bandied around about the contents of the giant parcels. The questions aimed up at the soldiers went unanswered, but eventually they finished their task and the people once again returned to quiet confusion. Finally, the gates opened and a cordon of guards advanced onto the causeway, their spears levelled to drive the people back from the gate. Behind them, another group of men dragged a large box out of the gate and retreated quickly, closely followed by the soldiers. Up above the gates, another figure appeared high on the castelades and Kenzo recognised Petit, obviously waiting for the noise to die down so he could address the people below.

'Citizens of Bastion,' shouted Petit, 'I am a representative of the Brotherhood of the Sark and I am here to offer you a choice. What you have witnessed these past two days is unfortunate, but necessary in the greater scheme of things. However, it is time we bring the killings and the destruction to a close. You have just seen my men lowering parcels into the city below. These parcels contain food, water and clothing. Over the next few days, there will be many more such parcels and this will continue everyday going forward. We don't want anyone else to die, but I have done everything I can and your lives are now in your hands. Before you, is a box containing everything you need to continue living with your families.'

'Open the gates,' shouted a man, 'let us back in to the city.'

'The gates will not be opened,' said Petit, 'and you will no longer be allowed back within these walls. You can stay there if you want to and though tonight will be very cold, I have no doubt you will survive. But ask yourselves this, how many nights will you survive without food and water? I have done everything I can, the rest is up to you.'

Petit disappeared from view and group of people surrounded the box, prying open the lid. Kenzo forced his way to the front and waited in anticipation.

'What is it?' asked a man near him.

'I have no idea,' said another. 'It looks like a box of plaited weed.'

'It's a ladder,' said Kenzo, having seen similar training aids in the barracks, 'I think he expects us all to move into the city below.'

Chapter 32

Helzac and the rest of the council stood in Pelosus's room, staring at the carnage. The furniture was trashed and all around, flesh and bone had been strewn everywhere in what was obviously a frenzied attack.

'Oh my God,' said Helzac, 'what happened here?'

'I think that is obvious,' said Razor and brushed past him to enter the room. Within minutes, he confirmed that the rest of the chambers were empty and they returned to the corridor.

'What now?' asked Kelly.

'He is still in this building somewhere,' said Razor, 'and we are not going to waste this opportunity, come on, he can't be far.'

'Look,' said Rimmer, pointing to a row of bloody claw prints on the floor.

'Come on,' said Razor, 'it's pointless waiting any longer, we have a job to do.' They returned to the stairwell and after a few moments, found the faintest bloodstain on the stairs leading upwards.

'He must have gone up to the castelades,' said Helzac, 'and if he has, there's no way out.'

'Then what are we waiting for?' said Razor, 'we've got him cornered, let's get this done.' He led the way up the stairs, and slung the door outwards into the open air, spear held low before him.

The crowd on the causeway was a throng of opinion and argument. Half of the people were for descending into the lower city, whilst the other half were adamant they should be let back in to Bastion. Many tried banging on the sealed gates of both towers to no avail and finally a strong willed man called for order.

'Listen,' he shouted, 'enough of this argument. Nobody here can tell his neighbour what should and shouldn't be done, but let me say this. Night falls in a few hours and we could all be stuck up here to face the elements. I am all for fighting but we can't get near our enemy and our hands are tied. I have my family with me and they are cold and hungry but below us, there are empty houses, bags of food and bundles of fireweed. I know it is not ideal but perhaps it is better to take this opportunity for tonight at least and re-evaluate our strategies in the morning. Look to the other causeways either side of us, for they have obviously been given the same choices as us and have already deployed their ladders.'

Sure enough, the people could see that below the other causeways, some people had already reached the city floor, and were spreading out to retrieve the food bundles.

'If we continue to argue,' said the man, 'we will be at risk of not only losing the food parcels below, but also the choice of the better accommodation. I for one will wait no longer and will take my family down to the city. Argue as much as you want, but without me.'

He jumped down from the wall and started to pull out the ladder. A few seconds passed before other men stepped forward to help him. Within ten minutes, the ladder had been secured and a group of men had already started down, their aim to secure the parcels before any of the other groups reached them. Up above, the remainder busied themselves with organising how the women and babies in particular were going to descend.

'Looks like they anticipated this,' said a voice and withdrew a woven basket and a single length of rope from the box, 'all we need to do is secure the children in the basket and lower them down.'

Within the hour, there were people swarming throughout the city below and queues of people above patiently waiting their turn.

'Are we going down?' asked Amber, looking up at Kenzo.

'I don't see any other option,' said Kenzo. 'We can't stay up here forever. I suppose there's no difference living down there as living in the Citadel.'

'Kenzo, can I speak to you alone?' interjected Petra.

Kenzo nodded and walked a few yards away, out of earshot.

'What is it?' he asked.

'Kenzo, there is something you should know, something that was only revealed to the council this morning. Those people have been forced down there for a reason.'

'Which is?'

'There is no way out of that city, Kenzo. They will be secured for the rest of their lives within those walls, relying on those above for food and water.'

'Like a prison?'

'I suppose so, yes, but it is worse than that. Apparently, they will be expected to provide these Sark, or whatever they are called, with human sacrifices as payment.'

'What,' gasped Kenzo, 'surely you are mistaken?'

'I'm afraid not, Kenzo, I know it is hard to believe but apparently it used to be the accepted way of life many generations ago, right up until the seas rose and breached the outer walls.'

'Are you sure?'

'As sure as I can be,' said Petra.

'That's horrible,' said Kenzo, 'we need to tell them.'

'Wait,' said Petra, grabbing his arm, 'to what end? All that would do is create fear and panic. They have suffered enough these past few days.'

'But they have to know,' said Kenzo.

'They will find out soon enough, I suspect,' said Petra, 'at least allow them this brief respite.'

Kenzo looked around at Leona, Amber and Lenny. All three were smiling as they watched Braille trying to entice an obviously uninterested lady.

'What about us?' said Kenzo, eventually.

'I see no other option,' said Petra, 'we will have to join them sooner or later but the queue moves very slowly. It would seem we will be spending at least one night on this bridge, so let's see what tomorrow brings.'

Kenzo nodded grimly.

'Don't tell the others yet,' he said, 'it will be hard enough to sleep tonight without the extra worry.'

'Okay,' said Petra and returned to the rest of the group.

Up on the central tower of the keep, the creature heard the door open behind him and turned to face the men emerging from the stairwell. A low rumbling noise from the depths of his throat vibrated through the very masonry of the tower, clearly audible to the frightened men opposite. All seven trade Governors lined up side by side, each with a hunting spear held parallel to the floor and each silent in awe, as the full horror of the beast finally became evident before their eyes.

'Keep your nerve,' said a sweating Razor, 'and spread out.' All the men moved forward, forming a semi-circle around the beast.

Arial's mouth opened in a vicious snarl, the uneven teeth still bloody with bits of flesh, and tried to advance toward them before being forced back by the points of the men's weapons. His clawed hands swung uselessly at the spears and slowly he was forced back across the tower floor before being forced up onto the castelades.

'That's it,' shouted Helzac, 'we have him, keep going, force him over.'

With renewed confidence, they surged forward but before they could drive him over the edge, he did something completely unexpected, he turned and jumped.

For a second, the councillors were amazed but then all ran forward to witness the creature plummet to his death.

'I don't believe it,' said Helzac and they all stared uncomprehendingly as the creature extended his arms and stretched out two flaps of skin before gliding across the courtyard to land against one of the opposite walls. As he reached the surface, he extended his clawed hands and feet to grip onto the masonry, before turning to face the floor and scurrying down the vertical stonework to the courtyard below.

'Oh my God,' whispered Kelly, 'what on earth is it?'

Before anyone could answer, the door behind them burst open again and two dozen men ran onto the tower, each brandishing their own spears. Fatman followed them out and addressed the councillors.

'Throw down your weapons,' he said, 'or you will die where you stand.'

After a few moments of hesitation, the cornered men threw down the useless ceremonial spears and Helzac stepped forward.

'I am Helzac,' he said, 'and I am the Governor of the Citadel, I demand to speak to Petit.'

'You gave up your right to demand anything the minute you decided to return here to kill Arial,' spat Fatman.

'Nevertheless, I want to speak to the person in charge.'

'You are speaking to him,' said Fatman, 'now, hurry up for I am getting bored.'

'Right,' said Helzac, 'in that case, I demand… no, *request* that you take us out of here and release us into the Citadel.'

'Release you? Oh, I don't think so, Helzac, far too late for that. No, you are more trouble than it's worth. Now get down on your knees.'

'Why?' sneered Razor, 'not even you will spear a man in cold blood.'

'Who said anything about spears?' asked Fatman, 'we are also educated men, Helzac, and as such, have a far more civilised method of punishment.' He looked over his shoulder and beckoned another man forward to throw a pile of rope on the floor. Helzac focussed in on the noose at the end of one of the ropes and swallowed in fear.

'No, you wouldn't,' he said, 'on what premise could you possibly condemn us to hang?'

'Treachery,' said Fatman, 'despite being allowed to leave, you deliberately returned to kill the saviour.'

'There is no such crime written in the statute,' said Helzac.

'Then I will add it tonight,' said Fatman.

'But,' cried Kelly with panic beginning to rise in his voice, 'you can't do that. What about a fair trial?'

'Fair trial?' sneered Fat man, 'you've just had it. Guilty as charged.'

With that, the armed men rushed forward and overpowered the council, tying their hands behind their backs.

'Any last words, Governor?' asked Fatman.

'Yes,' said Helzac, 'damn you to hell,' and spat squarely in the soldier's face.

Slowly the sun rose over the outer walls of Bastion, sending tendrils of creeping warmth onto the few huddled bodies still on the bridge. Kenzo stood up and peered over the edge, instantly jealous of the glimmer of fires through the windows far below.

'Good morning,' said Petra as she joined him, 'it looks as if it is almost time.'

Kenzo watched Braille as he helped the last of the population climb over the edge to descend the ladder.

'I suppose so,' he said, 'better wake them up. At least there is food and warmth down there.'

'Okay,' she said and returned to the three youngsters, still huddled together for warmth against the Pleasure-tower door.

'Amber,' she said quietly, shaking her by the shoulder, 'wake up, sweetheart, it's time to go. You too, Leona.' The girls woke, though remained still as they came around.

'Are we going down to the houses now?' asked Lenny, as soon as he woke up.

'Yes we are,' said Petra, smoothing his hair.

'Are my mother and sister down there?'

'They may be,' Petra lied, 'so I need you to be brave and climb down the ladder with me. Can you do that?'

Lenny nodded.

'I'm not afraid,' he said, 'I am good at climbing.'

'Good,' said Petra. 'Right then, if we're all ready, let's go.'

They stood up, but before they could go anywhere, a sudden clang from behind the door rang out and they all stepped back in shock.

'What's that?' asked Amber.

'It's the sound of the bolts being withdrawn,' said Petra, 'oh my God, there's someone in there.'

The door slowly opened and a familiar face peered around the edge. Everyone stared in surprise but the look on the face of Kenzo was one of total confusion.

'Pelosus,' he said eventually, 'I thought you were dead.'

Fifteen minutes later, Kenzo and the rest of his group sat in a luxurious room of soft furnishings and bright colours, listening to Pelosus tell his horrifying tale of how he faced the creature. Leona was tending his cut face with a bowl of water and a soft cloth.

'Anyway,' concluded the Stargazer, 'the thing is, by the time the creature returned from chasing you, I had escaped through the hidden doorway in the panelling and came here via the Catacombs and the chamber of scrolls.'

'Chamber of scrolls?' queried Kenzo.

'Yes,' he said, but before he could expand, Petra and Amber returned to the room with platters of food.

'I'm afraid it's not hot,' said Petra, 'as the fires have been left unattended, but at least it is cooked.'

Kenzo looked at the plates of Narwl steaks and Weed-bread, his mouth watering before noticing the skewered chunks of spiced meat.

'I'll just have some Narwl,' he said smiling up at Petra.

213

'You sure?' she asked, 'the spiced steak is particularly delicious.'

'No, I'm fine,' he said, and watched silently as everyone else dug in, their appetites ravenous after so much time without food. Finally, they sat back and discussed their predicament.

'So,' said Petra eventually, 'what is the situation?'

'I'm not quite sure,' said Pelosus, 'if what you say is correct, the rest of the Council members have made a stand against Petit and his cronies but at the moment, there is no way of knowing whether they have been successful or not.'

'Even if they manage to kill this thing,' said Kenzo, 'I can't see how Petit will stand back and relinquish everything he has gained over the past two days. The city is more or less in his hands and anyone who dared to stand against him is either dead, or starting a new life down in the other city.'

'We could stay here,' suggested Amber.

'We can't,' said Petra, 'at least, not for long. There's not much food and no fire-weed.'

'How much food have we got?' asked Kenzo.

'Enough to last a couple of days,' said Petra, 'a week at the most.'

'Then there is no other option,' said Kenzo, 'we have to join the others in the lower city and take our chances.'

'There is one more option we haven't considered,' said Pelosus, 'one that I hesitate to suggest.'

'Speak your mind, Pelosus,' said Kenzo, 'we are in a desperate situation here and all ideas need to be aired.'

'We could leave the Citadel altogether and go somewhere else.'

'Where?' asked Leona, 'there is nowhere else.'

'On the contrary, child,' said Pelosus, 'the one good thing that has come out of these last few days is agreement that we are not as isolated as we have always thought. There are other places in this world and I now believe there may be landfall not too far from here, even perhaps, just beyond the horizon.'

'Near the smoke,' said Kenzo suddenly.

They all turned and looked at him quizzically.

'What do you mean, Kenzo?' asked Amber.

'The smoke,' he repeated. 'When I was a little boy, I saw smoke just over the horizon. At first, others laughed at me, but I know what I saw. It was only when I was threatened with the Prison-tower as a madman that I decided to shut my mouth. Now that threat is gone, I can tell you with certainty, I saw smoke over the horizon and as we all know, water doesn't burn.'

'With what I learned from the Warden, combined with what we heard in the council chamber from Petit and De-gill, I think we can safely say there are other places in this watery world of ours and not too far away.'

'And how do you suggest we get there?' asked Petra.

'I've thought about that,' said Pelosus, 'we can use the Hunter's boats. They don't need them anymore and if we can just get to them, we can strike out across the sea and get away from this place.'

At first, the group were silent but Petra finally spoke up.

'I'm not sure, Pelosus,' she said, 'how would we know which way to go?'

'With this, Excellency,' he said, producing the handkerchief she had given him many weeks earlier.

'You have decoded it?' she asked in amazement.

'I didn't have to,' said Pelosus, 'it wasn't in code. All those hours I spent trying to decipher what it meant, when all the time, it was as obvious as the stars in the sky.'

'But what does it show?' asked Kenzo, as Pelosus spread the handkerchief out on the table.

'That part there on the edge,' said Pelosus, 'at first, I thought it was a stain of sorts but when I studied it under a magnifying glass, I saw that the edge of the stain is too defined, as if it has been deliberately dyed. That leads me to believe that it represents an area of land.'

'Why?'

'The rest of the cloth is blue, except for the embroidery around the edges of course but that small part there is brown. Why would anyone dye a small part of one edge brown without a reason?'

'I have no idea,' said Petra.

'Neither did I,' said Pelosus, 'and I was also intrigued as to why there was embroidery only along three sides, so once again, I examined it under the glass and I noted that the three with the embroidery are very neatly finished with fine stitching. The fourth, though cut very carefully, is not sewn and leads me to believe this piece of silk, as you call it, is only half the size of the original and if we had the other half, we would probably see this brown stain expanded into something much, much bigger.'

'Like a land mass?'

'Exactly!'

'Fascinating,' said Kenzo, 'so, assuming you are right, where is this land?'

'Well that posed another problem,' said Pelosus, 'as the Citadel is not represented on this map and there is no other reference, there is no way of knowing in which direction it lies. It could be anywhere.'

'So it is useless, then,' said Kenzo.

'It was,' said Pelosus, 'but as I said, when you know what you're looking for it becomes as plain as the stars in the sky.'

'How?'

'Because those dots are indeed the stars in the sky, it is a star map.'

'I don't understand,' said Petra, 'you of all people would have seen that, you are a Stargazer for Saint's sake, how did you not see it before?'

'Because it bears no resemblance to any known star map,' said Pelosus, 'for weeks, I searched for meanings that weren't there and then one day it hit me. You said it was from the days of the temptress Sallette when she went over to the Watchers.'

'It is,' said Petra, 'though temptress is a very strong word.'

'Whatever,' said Pelosus, 'but I searched the histories for reference to Sallette and I had to go right back to almost the beginning of the records for any reference.'

'And?'

'It was thousands of years ago,' said Pelosus, 'and the night sky at that time bore no resemblance to the one we see now.'

'It doesn't?'

'No, since the time of Sallette, the stars we know have moved, or should we say, the orientation of this planet has changed and we no longer see the same sky. The stars on this material probably shine down on the other side of the earth.'

'But how does that help us?' asked Kenzo.

'Because there are three stars represented on the map that are still visible in the sky,' said Pelosus, 'the three in Arial's belt.' He pointed out three dots on the edge of the silk. 'Though the rest are unfamiliar, those three are still visible just before dawn. They are the same stars and with that information, we can orient the map to suit the night sky as it is now.'

'But how do you know they are in the same place,' said Petra, 'you said the Earth has moved its position.'

'And indeed it has,' said Pelosus, 'but that is the easy part. I have studied the skies almost all my life and my observations, as well as those of my predecessors, have evidenced the miniscule movement of the stars over the generations. Miniscule but enough to establish a pattern and all I have to do is apply that calculation backwards to establish where those three stars were at the time of Sallette.'

'I can't say that I follow this,' said Kenzo, 'but I think you are saying that you know where this land lies.'

'I do,' said Pelosus, 'by my calculations, the belt of Arial currently lies seventeen increments west of where it did all those years ago. I have marked these two lines on the silk,' he said, indicating the marks, 'by aligning this first line with the centre star of Arial's belt, this second line indicates the way we have to go.'

Everyone fell silent until Kenzo spoke once more.

'And you are sure of this?'

'I am willing to bet my life on it,' said Pelosus.

'How far away do you think this land is?'

'I don't know but the fact that you say you once saw smoke is very encouraging. I estimate a few weeks away in one of the rowing boats.'

'Weeks?' said Kenzo, 'what would we do for water and food?'

'We could load a second boat with provisions,' said Pelosus, 'and catch fish as we go. If we ration the water and catch the rain, we could last for months if necessary.'

'It would be very uncomfortable,' said Kenzo.

'But feasible,' countered Pelosus.

'Assuming we run with this,' said Kenzo, 'how do we get to the Hunter's boats?'

'As the water drops, the boats are left high and dry on the exposed rocks at the base of their tower,' said Pelosus. 'It is a long way down and I could see no way of reaching them, but Petit has unwittingly given us the means to solve that problem.'

'He has?'

'The ladder, all we have to do is retrieve it from the causeway and drop it over the seaward side of the tower. Once we climb down there we can walk along the rocks to the boats and drag them to the water.'

Kenzo turned to Petra.

'What do you think?' he asked.

'Compared to the alternative,' said Petra, 'I think it is an excellent idea.'

'Anybody object?' asked Kenzo looking around the room.

'That's it, then,' he said, 'everyone, get some rest. This afternoon, we will pack everything we need and do as Pelosus suggests.'

Everyone rose to find a place to sleep but before they left the room, Lenny came running up the corridor.

'Lady,' he shouted, 'the soldiers are coming, the soldiers are coming.'

'What do you mean?' asked Petra, dropping to her knees.

'I went up onto the tower,' said Lenny gasping for breath, 'and I saw the soldiers coming across the bridge.'

'Are you sure?' asked Petra.

'Yes, miss, and I think they are building a bonfire.'

'Everyone, wait here,' said Kenzo, 'I'll see what's happening.'

Out on the Tower, Kenzo and Braille could see Petit's soldiers had left the Citadel and had made their way out onto the causeway. The first thing they did, much to Kenzo's despair was cut the top of the rope ladder, causing it to fall to the city below, but more worryingly, he could see that they were stacking piles of fire-weed against the door below his feet. Within minutes, a soldier set light to the bonfire and stood back as the flames roared upward to burn down the locked gates.

'Shit,' said Kenzo and the two men ran back down into the tower.

'Grab your things,' shouted Kenzo, 'they're trying to burn down the gate. We have to get out of here.'

'But the ladder,' shouted Pelosus, 'we need the ladder.'

217

'Too late,' said Braille, 'they've cut it loose. We have to find another way out.

'There is no other way,' said Petra.

'There has to be somewhere,' said Kenzo, 'think Petra.'

'We could go along the outer causeway,' she said, 'over to the Watcher's tower. I have a key to the side gate, given to me by De-gill.'

'What's the point?' asked Pelosus, 'they will simply follow us.'

'At least it will buy us some time,' said Kenzo, 'come on let's go. Petra, you lead the way, Braille and I will barricade some doors to slow them down.'

Everyone jumped into action and they ran along the outer causeway between the towers with the sea on the right and the lower city on the left. As promised, Petra produced a large iron key and opened the side gate.

'Why did De-gill give you that?' asked Pelosus.

Petra's withering look suggested he wouldn't want to know the answer.

'Never mind,' said Pelosus.

'What now?' asked Petra as Kenzo and Braille followed them in.

'I don't know,' said Kenzo, 'but at least we've got some time.'

'Perhaps, we can find something to make a ladder,' suggested Braille.

'Not enough time,' said Kenzo.

'Then that's it,' said Petra, 'we just wait here until they burn this down as well.'

'I'm not being taken down into the lower city,' said Braille, 'I would rather die at the end of a spear than at the hands of that thing.'

'Kenzo?' interrupted Amber quietly.

'If we can just find some weapons, we can take a few of them with us,' said Braille.

'Kenzo,' said Amber again, with more forcefulness.

'What?'

'Ranah,' she said.

'What about them?'

'I heard somewhere that they live in the depths of the sea and seldom came to the surface.'

'That's right,' said Kenzo, 'but what has that got to do with anything?'

'Tell me more,' said Amber urgently, 'it's important.'

'Allow me,' said Pelosus. 'The Ranah, Amber, unlike the Narwl, prefer to live in the deeper waters and coming to the surface only to hunt Narwl. We don't know why, but think it is something to do with aversion to the light.'

'Amber, why is this important?' asked Kenzo.

218

'Think back, Kenzo,' said Amber with a hint of excitement in her voice, 'when we first came here.'

'What about it?'

'Do you remember how we entered the tower?'

'Yes, we climbed up the shaft where Flip was killed.'

'Exactly and what killed him?'

'Ranah,' said Kenzo, beginning to see where she was leading.

'That's right and De-gill said they fed them every day through the month except Moon-days, when they disappeared with the tide, only to return a few days later.'

'What are you saying?' said Pelosus.

'If you are right,' said Amber, 'and the Ranah only live in the depths of the ocean, there must be a breach in the wall. How else could they keep coming back for their disgusting food?'

'I think she's right,' said Kenzo, 'there must be a hole in the wall or a tunnel leading out below the normal water level.'

'You don't know that,' said Petra, 'and even if you are right, it could be a very small hole.'

'No,' said Amber, 'some of those fish were as big as me. It must be big enough for us to squeeze through.'

'Then we have to try,' said Pelosus, 'Amber, can you show us this shaft?'

'Follow me,' she said, 'but, grab some plankton lamps from the tunnels as we go. It's going to be very dark.'

'Then what are we waiting for?' asked Kenzo, 'everybody collect as much food and water as you can and let's get out of here.'

Within ten minutes, Amber was leading them down toward the shaft that would hopefully take them away from Bastion forever.

219

Chapter 33

The sun was sinking toward the sea as Kenzo dragged himself out of a small natural hole in the rocks, closely followed by the rest of the group. Fingers and knees were bleeding and everyone was stinking of seaweed and covered with slime. The three women and the child sat together sharing tears of relief, as they sat outside the Citadel wall and stared over the endless sea.

'I can't believe it,' said Pelosus as he joined Kenzo and Braille, 'I thought those tunnels would never end.'

'We are here now,' said Kenzo, 'and there's no going back. I just hope you are right about that map.'

'Me too,' said Pelosus, 'but, we'll never know until we try. Now, all we need are the boats.'

Braille looked around at the women.

'They can't go on any further,' he said, 'I'll go on and bring the boats back here.'

'I'll come with you,' said Pelosus.

Braille stared at the Stargazer.

'You're pretty tough for an old man, aren't you doc?' he said.

'I'm just as knackered,' said Pelosus, 'but there's no other option, now come on, let's go before Petit's cronies realise what we are up to.'

Two hours later, Pelosus, Kenzo and Braille were in one boat, rowing hard away from the city. Close behind them and tethered to the first by a length of rope, the second boat contained Leona, Petra, Amber and the sleeping boy along with the parcels of stores. Frightened of pursuit and the possibility of spears raining down on them, the men pulled as hard as they could until they were out of range. Finally, they stopped and looked back at the Citadel, still looming high above them in the gathering gloom.

'Well we've done it,' said Kenzo, staring back at the Citadel. 'We've escaped the city. I just hope we've made the right decisions.'

Though it was getting dark, the whole of the inner city walls were lit up by countless fires as the Brotherhood cleansed the Citadel of any remains of the incumbent population. Walls glowed yellow in the flames and the central tower of the keep stood out above all the others.

'Oh my God, what's that?' asked Amber, pointing at the illuminated keep walls.

They followed her pointing hand and as their eyes made out the detail, they could see the bodies of seven men hanging by the neck from the battlements.

'Oh no,' cried Petra, 'not that, please, they didn't deserve that.'

'Let's get out of here,' said Kenzo and Braille joined him to row the boat hard in the opposite direction. In the boat behind, Leona comforted

Petra the best she could, realising that nothing she could say or do could ease the pain the older woman felt, after seeing seven of her colleagues murdered.

Pelosus still stood in the lead boat, staring back at the Citadel a little longer than anyone else did, his heart aching as he saw the only place he had ever known in his life go up in flames.

But despite this, the overall emotion was one of horror. Horror at the destruction of the city, horror at the waste of human life, but most of all, horror at the sight of a sinister black figure crawling up the vertical walls toward the corpses of the murdered councillors.

Pelosus resumed his place in the boat and grabbed at the oars.

'Are you all right?' asked Kenzo.

'Yes,' snapped Pelosus, 'let's just get out of here.'

He looked up one last time and watched Arial, the six fingered Saint, the last of the Sark, symbolically regaining his rightful place as ruler of Bastion. As the spidery form reached the first of the hanging corpses, Pelosus, Stargazer of Bastion, shut his eyes tightly and rowed as if he was rowing for his life, the salty tears running down his face, matching the salt of the rapidly receding sea.

The End

More books by K M Ashman

The India Sommers Mysteries
The Dead Virgins
The Treasures of Suleiman
The Mummies of the Reich
The Tomb Builders

The Roman Chronicles
The Fall of Britannia
The Rise of Caratacus
The Wrath of Boudicca

The Medieval Sagas
Blood of the Cross
In Shadows of Kings
Sword of Liberty
Ring of Steel

The Blood of Kings
A Land Divided
A Wounded Realm

Novels
Savage Eden
The Last Citadel
Vampire

Audio Books
Blood of the Cross
The Last Citadel
A Land Divided
A Wounded Realm

Printed by Amazon Italia Logistica S.r.l.
Torrazza Piemonte (TO), Italy

13207848R00130